DANGEROUS GAMES

FROM NOWHERE THE big man produced his own knife, and flicked open the blade with a practiced snap of his thick wrist. Without pause he jabbed it down at my eye.

Screaming again, I twisted my head to the right and felt fire burn down the left side of my face as the blade flayed my cheek open. The point of the knife stuck up from the earth below where my head had been.

Pain abruptly coalesced the rampant fear inside me into an old friend I thought I'd left behind me on the soccer fields. Like a striking snake, I snapped my head back and clamped my teeth into the big man's index finger, which was along the blade of the knife. I bit down into I felt bone.

The big man's screaming echoed my own . . .

Tor books by Paul Bishop

Citadel Run
Sand Against the Tide

Other books by Paul Bishop

Shroud of Vengeance

PAUL BISHOP

CHAPEL OF THE RAVENS

TOR

A TOM DOHERTY ASSOCIATES BOOK
NEW YORK

This is a work of fiction. All the characters and events portrayed in this book are fictitious, and any resemblance to real people or events is purely coincidental.

CHAPEL OF THE RAVENS

Copyright © 1991 by Paul Bishop

All rights reserved, including the right to reproduce this book, or portions thereof, in any form.

Cover art by Paul Stinson

A Tor Book
Published by Tom Doherty Associates, Inc.
175 Fifth Avenue
New York, N.Y. 10010

Tor ® is a registered trademark of Tom Doherty Associates, Inc.

ISBN: 0-812-50583-2
Library of Congress Catalog Card Number: 90-28455

First edition: August 1991
First mass market printing: October 1992

Printed in the United States of America

0 9 8 7 6 5 4 3 2 1

For Dell
who matched intensity with intensity,
passion with passion,
and brought light to the heart of the
dark beast

PROLOGUE

"COME ON, ENGLAND! Get off your dead legs and run! The idea of the game is to score goals!"

It was a typically miserable English crowd and a typically miserable English afternoon. The rain had turned the usually immaculate Wembley Stadium football pitch into a muddy quagmire. Almost all traces of the field's chalked markings had been obliterated, and the players' uniforms were so mud encrusted it was nearly impossible to tell one side from the other.

With my weight balanced forward on the balls of my feet, I waited to defend England's goal against the onslaught of the West German offense. Hardy Kruger, the West German center forward, had neatly sidestepped Robby Hunt's ill-timed sliding tackle and was cutting through the mud toward me. His stoic determination to score was obvious to the partisan crowd which was already roaring in dismay.

The second half of the game was aging rapidly. The score was still a goose-egg apiece, but that wasn't from lack of trying on the part of the West Germans. They had dominated the play since the opening whistle and had kept me diving for shots all afternoon. I was wet, tired, and freezing cold, and my legs were beginning to tremble with the defensive effort. If the pressure continued, it was only a matter of time until a shot slipped past me. But not this time. I could turn the bastards back one more time. I was not going to let them score. Not this time.

As Kruger continued his run, the crowd noise rose higher and higher in anticipation. The game was an international match, part of the tournament process which would culminate at the World Cup in Italy a year down the road. Because of the importance of the game, even the rotten weather had not stopped the English fans from turning out in force. Cheering and jeering, they ate fish and chips and prayed some soccer hooligan didn't decide to blindly chuck a five-pound sledgehammer into the crowd just for the fun of it.

To cut down Kruger's shooting angle, I moved toward the right goalpost. My feet were numb from being immersed in a muddy puddle, and all my limbs felt limp and lethargic. Instinct told me I should be moving out to challenge Kruger, but I held my position when the wide periphery of my vision picked up Kurt Wagstaff, the West German left winger, flying across the field to give Kruger support.

There is a soccer tradition that goalkeepers and left wingers are insane. It is a popular myth with some basis in fact. But while I might have one or two screws loose, Wagstaff had a complete Erector Set shaking free in his head. In my book, he was positively certifiable. His determination to score often overrode all physical impossibilities, and although modern playing tactics have made the left wing position almost extinct, Wagstaff has kept the breed alive with his hard-driving finesse and style. He was easily the most dangerous scoring threat on the West German team, and was possessed by a frightening, demented frustration when he failed to put the ball in the back of the net. The longer a game went on without him scoring, the harder he pushed. Today, he was pushing harder than ever.

I continued to hold my ground, unwilling to commit between Kruger and Wagstaff. Finally, Lampy Norbert, our center half, came to my rescue. He belted over on the long stilts he calls legs and forced Kruger down into the corner of the penalty area.

"Stay on him!" I screamed at Lampy.

The play had drawn me all the way over to the right goalpost, so I received a nasty shock when Lampy slipped in the mud and Kruger deftly lobbed the ball in a high arc across the goal mouth. I scrambled backwards and came out of the net to try and punch the ball away. But even as I jumped, I knew I wasn't going to be in time. Without looking, I knew Wagstaff would be behind me, his head rising like a ground-to-air missile aimed at the ball. A split second later there was the solid thud of forehead meeting ball leather and Wagstaff sent a head shot streaking for the lower left corner of the net.

Inexplicably, I knew the ball could be stopped. Physically I was exhausted, but my mind refused to accept defeat. Reactions, honed by years of practice, took control of my body and snapped it backwards across the face of the goal like a rubber band. My arms and legs were fully extended, fingers straining for the touch of rounded leather, and in that moment I knew the true joy of my chosen profession. It was an exhilaration beyond the highest level of consciousness. I was perfectly performing something for which I had been destined since the spark of my conception. I watched the ball as it bounced once in front of the goal line, and then my fists reached it and punched it around the outside of the goalpost for the save.

My body slammed to the ground, blasting all the air out of my lungs, and I thought for a split second I was dead. There was no noise. No feeling. Nothing except a fulfilled oblivion.

Eternity only lasted, however, until the stunned crowd erupted into an almost tangible force of cheers and screams. I was trying hard to start breathing again when Lampy Norbert's orangutan arms wrapped around my chest and pulled me to my feet. The muddy field gave up my six-foot-one-inch, one-hundred-and-ninety-pound frame with a reluctant sucking noise, like water disappearing down a drain.

"Good on you, Ian!" Lampy yelled in my ear as he pounded me on the back.

I forced air into my lungs, sneaking it past Lampy's iron embrace, and grinned sheepishly as I was swamped and congratulated by the rest of the team.

"Chapel! Chapel! Chapel!" The crowd was chanting my name before breaking into the slow traditional chorus of "ENG-LAND, ENG-LAND, ENG-LAND," as they waved banners, scarves, and flags, and went berserk tooting horns and twirling gigantic noise-ratchets.

Hardy Kruger stood in shock on the spot from where he'd crossed the ball over my head. On the other side of the goal, Wagstaff was slumped on his knees in the mud. His hands were curled into tight fists, the knuckles showing white even through the covering grime. Maniacal hatred burned from eyes set deep in his Germanic features. The stare singed my own retinas before he turned his face away from me. I ignored him and returned my attention to the field.

Rain continued to pour as play resumed, but the momentum of the game had been reversed. Our offense had discovered new life, and the West German goalie found himself being kept busy for a change. Instead of feeling relieved, though, I was unreasonably agitated. Adrenaline tingled like a live wire across my fingertips, and I envied Wagstaff who was all over the field, playing like a demon.

He was a one-man team, intercepting passes and stealing the ball away from opposing players with reckless sliding tackles. I lusted after his freedom. I was confined to the boundaries of the penalty area, waiting for the game to come to me, while Wagstaff was making or chasing the play at his own instigation. He had the ability to electrify the crowd, and every time he touched the ball he brought them to their feet.

I continued to shout encouragement and directions at my

fullbacks, but each time they turned one of Wagstaff's attacks away I felt a vague disappointment. It was as if a challenge were not being met—Wagstaff's unstoppable desire to score matched against my immovable determination to keep a virgin net. After the last miraculous save, the confrontation was inevitable. Wagstaff and I both knew it. The other players were aware of it. And the crowd was demanding it.

Tension continued to coil until Wagstaff beat an offside trap and sprinted toward a long pass with an open field in front of him. Robby Hunt was chasing him down, but had no chance to stop him fairly. In desperation, Robby threw a vicious sliding tackle which brought Wagstaff down from behind in the penalty area.

It had been a "professional" foul, one purposely done to avoid a sure scoring situation. It drew an immediate whistle from the referee as Wagstaff sprawled across the muddy turf. The West Germans were awarded a penalty kick. Robby was red carded for dangerous play and ejected from the game for the few remaining minutes. As he walked dejectedly off the field, I smiled and gave him a thumbs-up. There could be no blame placed on his shoulders for what fate had planned.

The whole game was finally down to just Wagstaff and me. The referee moved all the other players out of the penalty box, and then paced twelve yards out from the center of the goal line and plopped the ball down in the muck.

I set myself and tried to clear my mind. Wagstaff walked forward and slightly adjusted the position of the ball. He then moved back and positioned himself for his approach. I couldn't move my feet until Wagstaff made contact with the ball, a rule which made stopping the shot almost impossible. Anticipation was the only chance I had against a player of Wagstaff's caliber.

I knew the West German wouldn't try anything fancy; the time for flash had come and gone. I was in the way of the ball reaching the back of the net. Wagstaff was determined to put it there. I was determined to stop him.

The referee blew his whistle, and Wagstaff began his approach. As he moved toward the ball, he didn't even attempt to throw me off with a body sway or any other form of misdirection. Instead, he came straight at the ball, full speed ahead with every ounce of strength he had within him.

I stood waiting in the middle of the goal, realizing, only a split second before it happened, exactly what Wagstaff had in mind. The shot came at me like a bullet train, punching the ball into my chest with such force I felt it must have smashed a hole right through me. If it hadn't been for the tick of precognition which braced me forward, I would have been knocked over backwards into the goal.

Twice in past history, the power of Wagstaff's shots had sent balls tearing through the nylon nets at the back of goals. Once, he'd even exploded a ball against a goalpost. This time the shock waves from his shot devastated my chest cavity. I felt several ribs snap, and watched helplessly as the ball rebounded away from me and back into play.

Immediately, I realized Wagstaff was depending on the rebound to give him the scoring opportunity he craved. The penalty shot itself had not been an attempt to make a goal, but a personal punishment for me. If the ball had driven me far enough back into the goal to score, the humiliation would have been icing on the cake. It would have been nice, but not necessary.

I forced myself to move, but it was like wading through a mountain of spun sugar. A red haze filled my eyes and the roar of the crowd was reduced to a muted throb at the back of my brain. Everything seemed to be moving at half speed as I watched Wagstaff jump toward the ball. He was sure of his victory, as if it were a move he had practiced over and over until it was second nature.

From somewhere beyond reason, I was again flooded with the knowledge that I could stop the ball. I dove blindly toward it even as Wagstaff's foot slashed forward with terrifying power. The tips of my gnarled fingers touched the rough surface of the ball, but my arms refused to respond and gather it into me.

Sliding through the mud on a collision course, I could only watch in horror as Wagstaff's shooting foot changed targets with an infinitesimal movement and collided with my face.

ONE

MY BROTHER GERALD stuck his head around my office door and spotted me rubbing my fingers under the black eye-patch covering the socket where my right eye had once been.

"Caught you," he said with a grin.

"Damn it, Gerald! I can still feel the eye there. It's like I only need to raise the eyelid to see with it again."

"Come on, Ian. The doctors say it isn't possible to feel that way about an eye. It's not like you lost a leg or an arm and can suffer from ghost limb syndrome."

"Sod the doctors," I said plaintively.

Gerald shook his head and stepped all the way into the office. "Have you seen this?" he asked, tossing the morning copy of London's *Daily Mirror* onto my desk. It was folded to the sports page.

With my good eye, I glanced down at the three-paragraph filler Gerald had circled with a red pen. I often wondered why I thought of my remaining eye as "good," as if the other one had been plucked out for being bad.

"Bloody hell," I said in surprise.

The small headline to the article read: RAVENS GOAL-KEEPER PASQUAL MADDOX FOUND MURDERED IN LOS ANGELES.

"This is the first I've heard of it." I picked up the paper to scan the article. "I didn't even know Pasqual was playing again. And who in the world are the Ravens?"

Six years ago, Pasqual Maddox had been one of the best goalkeepers in Italy, if not the world, but he'd been caught up in a match-fixing scandal which rocked the entire structure of soccer in Italy. Two Italian goalkeepers had received full lifetime bans. Pasqual had been lucky to get away with only a five-year ban, but in a profession where you are old at thirty, those five years added up to a "professional life" ban.

Gerald lifted up his glasses and rubbed his own eyes. It was contagious, like yawning.

"After your injury, while you were refusing to read the sports news," he said in a mock sarcastic voice, "Maddox's playing ban was lifted. He was apparently living in Los Angeles at the time and signed on to play with the Ravens, an expansion team in the American Indoor Soccer League."

"Indoor soccer? I'm surprised Pasqual would even agree to play in America. Soccer has always been treated like a redheaded stepchild over there." I paused, musing. "Italy wouldn't take him back I suppose?"

"Not a chance."

I tapped the article with my finger. "He was probably too slow, anyway, after a five-year layoff. Still you figure his murder would rate more than three paragraphs. I wonder if the LA papers carried a bigger splash?"

"Surely you jest. To rate a splash in Los Angeles, you have to be a major athletic star, say a professional wrestler or a roller derby prima donna."

"Anybody ever tell you you're a cynic, Gerald?"

The article in the *Mirror* was too short to do credit to Pasqual's colorful history. Instead, it confined itself to the facts of his demise. His body had been discovered in an alcove behind the Acropolis sports arena by two street people looking for shelter. He'd been horribly beaten and his wallet was missing. The street people had called an ambulance, but Maddox had died on the way to the hospital without recovering consciousness. The investigation was continuing, but the police believed the murder to be part of a string of vicious muggings plaguing the area. The coroner's verdict determined that Pasqual had been kicked to death by two or more assailants. No arrests had been made. The article was cut and dried news reporting at its worst.

"Did you know Maddox?" Gerald asked, and I looked up at him in distraction.

"Ummm, yes. But only in passing. We weren't friends, only acquaintances." Both instances when I'd spent time of any consequence with Pascal, I'd found him to be a conceited prig. The fact that I didn't speak Italian, and that his English was almost indecipherable, could have had a lot to do with my impression.

Gerald pulled a pipe out of his sweater pocket and began to fiddle with filling it. "Do you think any of the Italian sports magazines will pick this up?"

"In time," I replied. "But they won't play it up. The entire country still holds a grudge against Maddox and the others involved in the match fixing. The Italian press isn't going to go out of their way to herald the man. It would be too much like putting their dirty laundry back out on the clothesline."

Gerald was hovering, not saying anything. It was his way of letting me know he was expecting some kind of response from me.

I tried to anticipate him. "You want us to run something on Pasqual?"

"I'm just the publisher of *Sporting Press*." His reaction was only slightly overdone. "You're the editor, you decide if you want to cover it. I've heard you're thinking about doing an issue focusing on the American soccer scene as a companion to the special issues we did on Germany and Brazil." He was being evasive.

"What's this all about, Gerald?"

"About?"

"Come on. What's going on in the labyrinth you call a mind?"

Gerald ignored me and changed the subject. "How have you been feeling lately?" He put his tobacco mixture away and took a seat in one of the two easy chairs on the visitor's side of my desk. I could see trouble coming.

"I'm fine."

"Physically and mentally?"

More than a year had passed since I'd left my right oculus and my playing career on the muddy turf at Wembley. England had continued playing in the World Cup tournament rounds and had even made it through to the final four before being eliminated. I hadn't watched.

The year had been a harsh passage of time for me, filled with operations and plastic surgery and the constant mental anguish of knowing I would never play between the sticks again. The image of Wagstaff's boot exploding into my face was etched across my memory like a never-changing mural. If someone had asked, I would have said I'd rather be dead.

After three operations, the doctors stated the trauma to my face was too great to make an inconspicuous glass eye feasible. In a way the news came as a relief. I was more comfortable with the empty socket hidden behind an eye patch. With the decision made, the nightmares of my real eye being crowded out of my head by a glass orb declined.

I fixed Gerald with a cold, one-eyed stare. "Physically the doctors tell me I'm in great shape. I still manage to put five miles under my feet before gracing you with my presence each morning."

"And otherwise?"

"You know how it is, Gerald," I said with some anger seeping into my voice because of the grilling. "I'd gouge your eye out if it could be put into my head and I could get between the goalposts again. Look, where is this leading?"

"Nowhere. Nowhere," Gerald spluttered, and looked shocked. "I'm just concerned about you."

Gerald is only two years my senior, but he gives the appearance of portly comfortableness usually associated with the latter years of middle age. While I was playing for international crowds, he was making his own mark in the world by establishing a modest magazine empire. His company published two popular general interest titles, a woman's monthly, a hobby digest, and a children's activity periodical.

He'd also been the one steady rock in the eternity which followed my injury.

A strange phenomenon occurred when it became clear I would never be able to play world-class soccer again. Instead of having time to wonder what the hell to do with my life, I was deluged with alternative job offers. In a way, this situation made recovery more difficult, as I was in no shape emotionally to make decisions.

Money was not much of a consideration. I'd made more than my share during my brief career, and Gerald had increased it a hundredfold with solid business investments. Still, choices needed to be made, so I started out by turning down a lucrative request from a men's shirt maker who wanted to splatter my eye-patched mug across their advertising campaign. I didn't feel comfortable exploiting my handicap in that manner. This decision did not sit well with Gerald for business reasons, and he was further incensed when I continued to turn down other endorsements of the same nature.

I was pleased and flattered when Wolverhampton, my league team, offered me a coaching position, but I couldn't bring myself to face it. Similarly, the offered opportunity to become the color commentator for television's ''Match of the Week'' was attractive. However, making soccer ''small talk'' was beyond me while my heart was breaking because I wasn't out on the field myself. If I couldn't play soccer, I felt that I wanted to run as far away from the game as possible.

The whole decision-making situation was further complicated by the Fleet Street leeches who had laid siege to the hospital and, later, to my home. For weeks they tried everything their devious minds could think up to get an interview with me, or a candid photograph of my injuries. During my career, I'd been generally treated well by the press, but after the accident, I had not been emotionally capable of confronting them.

Gerald finally convinced me to organize a bedside press conference where I tried to answer all questions. The reporters still weren't happy, though, because I refused to remove the bandages which partially covered my face. They continued their harrassment, and the stress of the situation continued until I became old news, replaced by bigger and juicier scandals.

Eventually, the tangent my life followed came from an unexpected source. A therapist, who was trying to help me deal with the traumatic emotional problems of losing my eye, suggested I try to explore my feelings by writing them down. It was meant as a form of self-catharsis, and it worked wonders for me. I wrote reams and reams of rambling prose; sometimes vehemently venting my anger over never playing in goal again; other times eloquently exploring the meaning of soccer in my life, or writing pages which ran the gamut from playing advice to game/life philosophy.

One evening, in a random moment, Gerald picked up my scribblings and seemed to find something in them of great interest. With a ferocious single-mindedness, he badgered me until I consented to let him work them into a series of columns to be published in one of his general interest magazines. I regretted the decision almost immediately and tried to renege, but Gerald would have none of it.

When the magazine containing the first column hit the newsstands, I felt emotionally naked and hid in my house for a week without answering the phone. However, the following weekend, Gerald turned up on my doorstep carting a sack full of reader mail generated by my column. He was full of enthusiasm for other articles he wanted me to write, and the more he talked, the more he made me come around to his way of thinking. Looking back, I can see my brother was being his usual crafty self—I'd been wallowing in self-pity for too long, and Gerald figured he'd found a way to drag me out of it.

Before long, we'd hammered out the structure for a new addition to Gerald's magazine line. Within six months *Sporting Press* was on the newsstands with a two-hundred-thousand print run and a sixty-two percent sales rate. The figures, my new boss assured me, were a success by any standard.

I didn't mind the job. It couldn't replace what I had lost, but it kept me busy and broke the brooding moods I fell into when I had time on my hands. The magazine also allowed me a lifeline to the world I'd left behind. Even though I had originally shunned similar situations, *Sporting Press* allowed me to deal with the soccer world on my own terms. If my emotions got away from me, I was able to turn to issues involving any of the other major sports the magazine covered or throw myself into the never-ending editorial tasks which this new position constantly dumped across my transom.

I tried to keep the magazine's tone fair and impartial when dealing with volatile or scandalous issues. This factor, coupled with the strength of my past athletic performance, helped me to consistently come up with new angles and insights not exposed by other publications covering the same scene. The players trusted me, and I valued that trust. I was mostly happy with my new life, but somehow I felt Gerald was about to drop a spanner in the works.

"Do you remember Da taking us to the football matches when we were wee 'uns?" he asked as he sat across from me now. The question seemed to come out of the blue.

"Like it was yesterday," I replied.

Our father was a retired policeman. He was a caring and loving man, and when I was in the hospital, he took it upon himself to answer all of the thousands of letters and cards sent to me by well-wishers. I was overwhelmed by the outpouring of public affection and regretted I couldn't answer each correspondent myself, but the job was far too enormous for the shape I was in.

When Gerald and I were kids, Da would often stretch his minimal policeman's pay to take us to the local football team's Saturday games. The cheap, standing-room terraces behind the goal nets became our stomping grounds, and I retain a vivid memory of Da standing tall, singing chants with the rest of the crowd, while holding me on his shoulders with one hand and cuddling Gerald next to his side with the other. Somehow the noise and the crush of the terraces held a special kind of magic and became like a second home. Even when Gerald and I became old enough to go to the games by ourselves, we still made straight for the terraces at the home end of the field.

It was from the terraces that I first found myself fascinated by goalkeeping. I don't think anyone consciously sets out to be a goalkeeper. It is a skill and an occupation which chooses you—not the other way around. Directly in front of the terraces, the huge rugged men who tended the nets loomed against the sky like mythical giants. To Gerald and I, our tousled heads barely able to poke over the guardrail, they appeared to be as awesome as gods.

Over time, we came to know each goalie's individual traits; how they warmed up, who wore gloves or hats, and who jumped up before each game to touch the crossbar for luck. We knew which keepers added extra flash and flourishes to their saves, and which ones worked extra hard to make everything look easy. And should, by chance, a goalie turn to acknowledge the crowd, we felt he was talking directly to us. Standing out as they did from the inaccessibility of the other field players, these men quickly became our heroes.

At school, Gerald's health had turned him to the pursuit of academic excellence. I, on the other hand, had inherited the hardy constitution and build of some long-forgotten Saxon ancestor. As I grew inches in height and girth beyond my brother, Da was given to humorous pauses of wonder about the possible involvement of the milkman or the post-man in our conceptions.

Because of my size, I relished the physical challenges of the playing field. I was also thrust into the role of protector when the local toughs tried to take liberties with Gerald or someone we counted as a friend. Since Gerald was always willing to help me catch up academically, it seemed only natural for me to use my talents to protect him and the others. From these confrontations, however, I began to re-alize that I did not conceptualize fear in the same way as my peers.

For me fear wasn't an emotion to run from. It was an emotion to be embraced, conquered, and then cherished with an ever-challenging compulsion. The same trait might lead others to become boxers, policemen, or explorers—men for whom fear holds no significance. The stronger the trait in an individual, the better the chance of excelling in a chosen field.

One afternoon, while I was still in the junior form at school, Gerald and I joined the crowd waiting to watch the seniors play a crosstown match with Links Road School. However, before we were able to get settled, Hollingsworth, the physical training master, approached and asked if I would fill in for the senior goalie, who'd sprained an ankle that morning.

"I've never played in goal," I told him, inwardly excited at the prospect.

This fact didn't seem to bother him. "You're the right size, son," he told me seriously. "Let's see if you've got the cut for it." He tossed me the senior goalie's solid black jersey and put a hand on my shoulder. "Goalies are a dif-ferent breed. We'll soon know if you're one of them. Just do your best."

Gerald told me later that my grin wrapped around my neck, but all I remember was trying to keep my teeth clenched so my heart couldn't jump out of my throat.

The position instantly came alive for me. In one too-short game, I realized I was embarking on a fanatical crusade to constantly defend an eight-foot-high by eight-yard-wide, invisible, vertical plane, from being penetrated by a spherical leather intruder. From that day on, I never wanted to do anything else.

As my goalkeeping skills became apparent, several scouts from Third Division teams recommended me to their organizations. I was eventually signed as a schoolboy amateur and then, at sixteen, as a professional. My gigantic salary was ten pounds a week. I did double duty with the youth team, and had the first big thrill of my life when we won the Football Association Youth Cup as a dark-horse team battling against all odds.

I took two years out of my professional footballer's life for National Service, the last year of which I did with the SAS in Ireland. I could have spent the entire time in soft jobs, playing football for the army, but I chose a harsher route which provided me with a sense of confidence and self-worth I've never lost. Even in the dark days after my eye was sucked from its socket, there was still at the bottom of my soul a case-hardened mantle of self-esteem which constantly fought back against my despair.

After the army, I returned to my Third Division team as a full-time professional, only to be sold at the end of the season to Chelsea. My new team was being relegated from the First to the Second Division, and needed new blood for their goal. Though Chelsea was taking a step down, it was a step up the professional ladder for me.

I set out to learn everything about the geometry and skills of goalkeeping, but my time with Chelsea was, unfortunately, undistinguished. After two seasons they put me up for sale and were as surprised as I was when the First Division Wolverhampton Wanderers offered to pick up my contract. Both Chelsea and I jumped at the chance.

The Wolverhampton goalkeeping coach was a wizened old man called Sticks. He looked like he could be blown over by the mildest breeze, but he taught me more about goalkeeping and life than anyone I have ever known.

Under Sticks's guidance, fortune began to flow my way.

His judgement of my potential was quickly justified when I started in goal for the season which saw Wolverhampton win both the FA and the European championships. Five seasons later, I was called as an alternate for England's national team behind Peter Shilton.

Shilton looked like he would be starting for England forever. However, just prior to the West German game, he came down with the flu and I had my first start. And then Wagstaff's boot exploded my life.

If I'd never reached the pinnacle, I might have found it easier to accept leaving the game behind. Easier to dream of what might have been than to be tormented by what could never be again. I tried to tell myself I was lucky, but it didn't do much good.

Bringing my mind back to the present, I put the sports page with the news of Pasqual Maddox's death on my blotter and stood up.

"You're making me nervous, Gerald," I said, trying to put some good nature in my voice to hide my anxiety. "If you have something to say, then spit it out."

"Ian, really, I . . ."

"Don't deny it," I told him. "I know you."

I walked around the desk with a smile, put my hand on Gerald's elbow, raised him gently from his seat, and escorted him to my office door. "If you're going to be shy about whatever it is you've got up your sleeve, Mr. Publisher, I must tell you I don't have time to drag it out of you. My feature editors are in a full-blown flap with the legal department over the current issue, so I can't even begin to think about any special American soccer issues." When he hesitated, I fluttered my hands and shooed him on his way. "Come on. Get out of here. I'm terribly busy, and you know how cranky you get if we miss deadline." Gerald left the office reluctantly, but without complaint, and I returned to battling journalistic windmills.

The first of many crises was resolved by contacting a staff writer and promising to marry his ex-wife if he would machine-gun me a reworking of a lead article. He said he wouldn't wish his ex-wife on anybody, and settled instead for a bonus large enough to pay her alimony for the next few months.

The solving of one problem, however, quickly made way for others, and I spent the better part of my day chasing lost photographs, dealing with inferior artwork, remasking botched layouts, and settling squabbles among my usually efficient staff. By four-thirty I was knackered and my empty eye socket throbbed monotonously. *Sporting Press*, however, was back on track.

The chair behind my desk looked inviting, so I plopped down in it with a cup of tea and a soggy tomato sandwich. As I ate, I flipped idly through the personal mail I'd brought from home. Most of it was routine, but at the bottom of the pile was a crisp white envelope covered with barely decipherable chicken scratches where the address should be.

I recognized the chicken scratches immediately. I'd spent a year reading them in the SAS when their perpetrator, now Sir Adam Qwale, was my section leader. I hadn't, however, seen the likes of them since my discharge.

I tore open the envelope and found an invitation to spend the coming weekend at Sir Adam's country estate. The hair on the back of my neck prickled. Between Gerald's strange behavior and this bolt from the blue directed by Sir Adam, I had a feeling the wheels of my fate were being manipulated and I was helpless to stop them.

TWO

ATHER THAN FIGHT the Friday evening traffic jams, I relied on British Rail to get me within striking distance of Sir Adam's estate. Ever since a *Sporting Press* reporter had crashed his car on the way to covering an event in Scotland, causing me to dash off on the spur of the moment to fill in for him, I've kept an overnight bag in the office. This precaution saved me from having to race home for a change of socks and a toothbrush.

When the train arrived, fifteen minutes late, I took the bag down from the net shelf over the padded seat and stepped down onto the platform. I was in unaccountably good spirits. Feelings of foreboding still rambled around in my subconscious, but since there was nothing I could do about them, I'd decided to enjoy the prospects of the pleasant weekend promised by Sir Adam's invitation.

"Mr. Chapel?"

I turned at the sound of the lilting feminine voice and was confronted by a young woman of striking features and mature composure. She was wearing a knee-length brown suede skirt with a modest slit up the left side. A pair of brown leather boots caressed her trim legs, and an expensive, umber-colored silk blouse hugged her smallish breasts. The whole outfit was topped off with a short suede jacket that matched her skirt.

"I'm Paula Qwale, Sir Adam's daughter," she said, extending her hand. "Daddy sent me to meet you since he wanted to do evening stables with Hocker before you arrived."

"Hocker?" I asked, releasing her hand.

"Yes. John Hock—Hocker. He's Daddy's trainer. They have two runners tomorrow, Penny Dreadful and Thief-taker. Daddy wants to make sure they're well turned out."

"I'm sure he does."

"This way," she directed, turning on her heels and taking long strides towards the station exit. "My car is parked in the lot."

Outside the station, soft sunlight was fighting a losing battle against the arrival of dusk. Paula's step on the parking lot gravel was graceful and assured. Following behind her, I felt like an awkward puppy. I'm not terribly good around women, especially young and attractive ones. It isn't that I feel inferior, only that I never had much of a chance to develop any social skills at school. By the time every other boy in my form was discovering girls, I was far too busy pursuing playing-field glory to notice. My hormones finally caught up with me, but I wasn't attracted overmuch by the easy accessibility of soccer groupies, and I was never in one place long enough to establish a lasting relationship.

Her car turned out to be a beautiful red '68 Alfa Romeo Spyder. Its convertible roof was secured down, and the black glove-leather interior beckoned an invitation. On the open road, Paula surprised me by driving with concentration and skill. There was none of the devil-may-care abandon I'd expected from a rich Daddy's girl. She wasn't trying to impress me, just transport me from one point to another in comfortable style. I was appreciative enough to compliment her.

"Thank you," she said with grace. "I drive in rally races quite a bit, and it teaches you about being safe. You take risks when necessary. Not just for the hell of it."

Another point in her favor. Her words, however, were the same I'd heard from her father before numerous patrols in Northern Ireland. In profile she had the pale complexion, high cheekbones, Roman nose, and prominent chin which the English associate with good breeding. The whole was complemented by a long neck, wrapped in an umber silk scarf, and a profusion of thick auburn hair piled at the back of her head. Several wisps had escaped to flutter across her forehead in the wind flow, and she continually tried to secure them behind her ears. While we drove she kept up a torrent of chatter about her father's horses and her university activities. I put her age at eighteen or nineteen. A sophisticated and charming package. Tenacious too, if I was any judge. Without a doubt her father's daughter.

"I saw you play once against Scotland," she said, suddenly changing subjects. "You were super."

"Thank you, but I'm surprised. You don't strike me as the type to spend your afternoons mixing it up with soccer hooligans."

"Not everyone who attends a football match is a hooligan."

"Sometimes I wonder," I told her. Vivid memories flashed through my head of standing in goal with a rain of coins and rubbish pelting me in the back. If we were losing, the barrage was often thrown by our own fans.

"Daddy took me. He followed your career closely, said you were the greatest goalie England ever produced."

I laughed, making her look at me with a trace of anger, as if I had no right to challenge her father's words. "I'm sorry," I told her, "but I didn't get to play the game long enough for anyone to pass such a judgment. I respect your father and appreciate his sentiments, but there are many goalkeepers whose careers surpass mine. I was lucky enough to play for England. If I'd played longer . . ." I let the thought dribble off.

She was silent for a moment and returned her concentration to her driving. She seemed to be digesting my words, chewing them over and then spitting them out again to see how they compared with whatever other impressions her father had given her of me.

"Does it still bother you? Not playing, I mean."

I looked at her, ready to take umbrage, but her countenance suggested interest, not malice.

"Every moment of every day, asleep or awake."

"I'm sorry."

"Don't be. It's my burden."

The countryside was still whipping by when Paula turned the steering wheel deftly to the left and darted into an unmarked side road hidden between hedgerows. "We'll go in the through the back," she said. "It's faster, and you don't strike me as someone who cares about impressive approaches."

The old cart track we had turned onto was bordered on both sides by tall hedgerows tangled with wild roses, sleeping morning glories, and bramble bushes. The shrubbery gave way suddenly to the immaculately kept grounds, surrounding the Wren's Haven Farm manor house. Even the gravel driveway betrayed no sign of the last vehicle to arrive or depart.

There were several cars already parked along the row of garages where Paula pulled the Spyder to a halt. She hopped quickly out of the car with an intriguing flash of leg, and I had to move fast to keep up with her as she entered the rear door of the manor. Inside, she acknowledged two women busy cooking in the kitchen. From their cheerful return greetings it was obvious she was well liked.

As we moved through into the manor lobby, a voice called out from one of the side rooms. "Oh, Paula! You didn't bring Mr. Chapel in through the kitchen did you?"

"Don't be a snob, Mother," Paula said, leading me into the room and giving a severe-looking woman a peck on the cheek.

I smiled and shook Lady Qwale's extended hand. She was

a handsome woman who managed to maintain a regal bearing without being tall.

"I'm glad you could come, Mr. Chapel. I know Adam has been thoroughly looking forward to your visit."

"Please call me Ian," I told her.

"All right, Ian, then we should dispense with all pretenses and you should call me Amanda."

"Thank you."

"Why don't you let Paula show you your room? You can freshen up and join Adam at the stables. Paula will take you. She loves those silly horses as much as her father does."

"They're not silly, Mother."

Lady Qwale looked at me and rolled her eyes with amusement. I liked her immediately and knew she was gently teasing her daughter on purpose.

Ten minutes later, after I'd unpacked my small case in a comfortable guest room, Paula led me out onto the grounds again. The stables were situated about a quarter of a mile behind the main house, giving perspective to the full range of the land owned by Sir Adam. I knew large estates like Wren's Haven were few and far between in England these days. Especially ones that weren't open to the paying public on weekends in order to make financial ends meet.

When Paula and I entered the stables, Sir Adam had his back to us. He was standing with another man at the entrance to one of the stalls, stroking the nose of a pitch-black thoroughbred. The horse seemed to be enjoying the attention as much as Sir Adam appeared to enjoy giving it.

"You've done a fine job, Hocker," he told the man with him. "I'm sure we'll do well tomorrow." I recognized the deep rasp of Sir Adam's voice even though it had mellowed some with time.

"It'll be an enjoyable run, any road," said Hocker. "I'll be putting my money on our chances." He too gave the horse a pat and then turned away from the stall. He nudged Sir Adam when he saw us.

Sir Adam looked around. "Well, well, hello, hello," he

said, taking my hand and shaking it for all he was worth. "It's very good of you to come, Ian. You're looking fit." Even in grubby jeans, tattered gray crew-neck sweater, and Wellington boots, Sir Adam couldn't disguise his breeding. He looked exactly what he was—a gentleman. He introduced John Hock, and handshakes were exchanged again.

"She's a beautiful horse," I said, referring to the black animal who cocked an eye in my direction.

"Watch it or Thieftaker will take a nip out of your shoulder for calling him a she," Sir Adam said with gentle amusement. I blushed slightly, which made Paula laugh.

"I'm sorry. Horses obviously aren't my strong suit."

"If you want to see a real lady, come on and have a look at this ill-tempered filly." Sir Adam led the way over to another stall occupied by a mangy-looking animal of indefinable color.

"Penny Dreadful," Hocker announced.

"And she certainly is," contributed Paula with affection in her voice. "Don't let her looks fool you, she's the best steeplechaser in the stable, won more prize money than all our other horses put together."

"That either speaks highly of Penny Dreadful, or poorly of the stable," I said and regretted the quip the moment it was out.

Sir Adam found it amusing, though, and laughed even harder when he saw the hurt expression on Hocker's face. "You'll have to excuse Hocker," he told me. "Very sensitive about his gee-gees."

"It's all right," I told Hocker. "I once played on a football team who all looked like they were something a cat would reject in the rubbish, but we took the FA cup anyway."

Hocker returned my smile, joining in the offered truce.

"Let's get back to the house," Sir Adam suggested. "Dinner will be on soon, and we can talk afterwards." It was a subtle way of telling me not to ask questions about my invite until the right time. I accepted it in stride as I was enjoying myself and the surroundings. We're all a bit snobbish at heart.

Back at the house, though, my feelings of foreboding returned in force when I was introduced to the other week-end guest.

Sir Adam did the honors. "Ian, I'd like you to meet Nina Brisbane. She's here visiting us from America."

There was an awkward pause, as I'm sure there always would be whenever this woman was introduced. She was tall, with beautiful long legs shown off to their best advantage under a knee-length teal dress. The silky material of the frock highlighted the femininity of curves which would make male heads turn wherever she went. As spectacular as it was, though, it was not her body which riveted your attention—that honor was reserved for the full black veil which completely obscured her facial features.

"Hello," I said finally. "Are you enjoying your stay?"

"Very much," she said, politely ignoring my awkward pause. "Although, I was hoping for a little more rain." Her voice was thick and smoky, her tone unself-conscious. She seemed at ease with the reactions the veil drew.

"More rain?" I said. It was an uncommon sentiment.

"Yes. I live in Los Angeles, where winter lasts for about four hours one afternoon in January. The rest of the time the sun doesn't know when to shut up. I enjoy changes in the weather. They break the monotony"

Once you were past the shock of the veil, Nina Brisbane appeared to exude urbane professionalism and charm. Her manner suggested you should take the fact of her veil as no more than a trapping of fashion. Still, it was impossible not to stare intently at the folds of heavy black lace. Impossible not to guess at what unspeakable horrors the veil might cover.

"Are you here on business or a holiday?" I asked to keep the conversation flowing.

"I have business with Sir Adam, but I also hope to do some shopping in London."

"What kind of business are you in?"

"My family owns several sports franchises. . . ."

"Quite," Sir Adam interjected suddenly. "Shall we sit and eat," he said, taking Nina's arm and leading her away.

Dinner was served in the formal dining room, with two kitchen maids keeping the dishes moving with silent precision. At first it was difficult not to watch Nina gracefully maneuver her food under her veil, but she handled the operation so well it soon became mundane. Sir Adam, playing the genteel host, led the conversation through various subjects and reminiscences. Everything was as it should be, but my appetite had died and I could only pick at my food.

Gerald might be the genius in my family, but I've never been accused of being stupid. Both Gerald and Sir Adam are devious bastards. It was a one-horse race that one of the sports franchises owned by Nina Brisbane's family would turn out to be the Los Angeles Ravens. A team that just happened to have a dead goalkeeper. I felt sick to my stomach.

The other shoe dropped after dinner while Sir Adam and I were alone in his study for brandy and cigars.

Sir Adam started in with the authority I remembered well. "I can tell by your pallor and the beads of sweat on your forehead that you've already figured out part of the reason for your weekend visit. I told your brother you wouldn't fall for the subtle approach."

"Only part of the reason?" I asked. It was a major effort to force words past the constriction in my throat. I felt as taut as a violin string.

"Oh, relax, Ian," Sir Adam said, waving his arms in frustration. "Sit down. You're acting like I'm going to ask you to chop off your arm or something. I'm going to offer you a job of work, that's all. I'm half owner, with Nina, of the Los Angeles Ravens indoor soccer team. We need a new goalkeeper. I want it to be you."

Even though I'd anticipated what was coming, I was shaken by the shock of it. The armchair behind my knees accepted my bulk without complaint. "How could you even ask . . . ?" I was stunned and stuttered over the question.

Sir Adam took the chair across from mine and leaned forward in concentration. "You were one of the best goal-keepers in the world. You were also the best soldier I ever had the pleasure to command. In Ireland you proved your savvy and street smarts. You couldn't have survived the operations we did there without it. I need both your talents."

"What the hell are you talking about?"

"Pasqual Maddox wasn't accidentally killed in some late-night mugging as the police want us to believe. He was murdered by some bastard with much more at stake than a watch and a wallet with a few dollars in it."

I felt anger bursting inside me. "I've only got one bloody eye!" I screamed. "Are you so blind you didn't notice? How do you expect me to get between the sticks again?" I stood up, quivering like an epileptic. The brandy in my glass sloshed onto my hand. I looked down at it and then hurled the entire snifter at Sir Adam. It smashed against his chest, but the sod didn't even flinch.

I took a step toward him, my fists clenching. Anger and pent-up frustration were boiling over inside me. I was going to pulverize him. Before I could take a second step, though, the door to the study unexpectedly burst open and John Hock ran in. He was out of breath and black smears covered his face and hands.

"Sir Adam," he gasped. "The bloody stables, sir! They're on fire!"

THREE

THE STABLES CERTAINLY were on fire. Even from the main house we could see red-orange flames dancing across the stable roof, and black columns of acrid smoke clouding the air.

"What happened to the sprinkler system?" Sir Adam yelled at Hocker. Everyone was now running, feet pounding heavily on the gravel path.

"Some effin' bastard pulled the bloody wires out from the main control box." Hocker's voice held an unhealthy rasp, his lungs already filled with smoke.

A sudden blur sprinted past us and then transformed into Paula Qwale. Her father stuck out a hand to restrain her, but she eluded him easily and ran into the burning stall rows.

The enclosed stables consisted of two rows of eight stalls on either side of a wide walkway. A large roof covered the whole structure in order to keep the area drier in the unpredictable Downs weather. Entrance was gained through huge sliding doors at either end.

I tried to follow Paula, but was forced to make way for a groom who stumbled out through the open double doors leading a terrified horse by a makeshift rope halter. The groom's water-soaked shirt was tied roughly across the horse's eyes. Several other grooms with horses followed in quick succession before Paula emerged from the smoke with both Penny Dreadful and Thieftaker in tow. Tendrils of her hair were singed and a gash on her left arm was bleeding profusely.

Hocker hurriedly organized a bucket brigade while Paula and Sir Adam took charge of moving the horses away to a clearing. Amanda Qwale, the house servants, and Nina Brisbane all arrived in a rush to pitch in. Faintly, the sound of a fire truck siren could be heard over the cackle of the flames.

I grabbed a young groom who was rushing around in a panic and accomplishing nothing.

"Where's the sprinkler box?" I asked loudly, receiving a blank look in exchange. I shook the boy harshly. "Pull yourself together, man. Where's the sprinkler box?" His eyes finally focused on me, but when he made an effort to speak, his mouth only opened and closed like that of a fish. He tried to gesture with the arm I didn't have a grip on.

"If you can't tell me, show me," I said, pushing him roughly in the direction his flailing appendage indicated.

The groom scampered off around the outside of the stable building. I loped after him, stopping once to haul the groom to his feet again after he tripped over them, and once to avoid being trampled by a terror-stricken horse who broke through the fire-weakened stable wall to save himself.

Through the horse's escape hole I could see into the stables. The fire was getting the upper hand, but there was still a chance. Urged on by the horrible sounds of still-trapped animals, I skidded to a stop at the building's rear, where the groom pointed a shaking hand at the sprinkler power box. The hard plastic which formed the box casing was bashed in and splintered. Wires protruded out of the damage in every direction, looking like angry snakes.

Above the sprinkler controls there was a large metal fuse box with a main switch which provided power not only for the sprinklers, but also for the more frequently used equipment, such as the automatic trough watering system and the stable floodlights. I threw the switch, plunging the area into darkness, and tore my fingers up ripping open the outer shell of the vandalized sprinkler box to further expose the inner wiring.

The first house I'd ever bought had needed to be entirely rewired, and I'd taken great pleasure in learning how to do it myself with help from an electrician uncle. I only hoped I'd retained some of what he had taught me.

Working by the light of the flames, I fumbled quickly to reconnect the sprinkler control wires, and then threw the main power switch. The stable floodlights came back on, indicating the fire hadn't damaged the electrical system yet, but nothing happened with the sprinklers. I turned off the main again and delved back into the wires.

Two quick sessions of trial and error later and the sweet sound of water pouring out of sprinkler heads burst into reality. There was a cheer from the bucket brigade at the front of the stable, but it could just as well have been for the arrival of the fire crew.

I turned to the young groom, who was enthusiastically jumping from one Wellington-booted foot to the other.

"That was super, mister," he told me excitedly. "How'd you do that having only one eye and all? Umm . . . I mean . . ." A scared look came into his eyes as he realized he might have unwittingly insulted one of his master's guests.

I put my hand on the boy's shoulder and shook him gently. "I know what you mean, son. But just because I've lost an eye doesn't mean I've lost half my brains as well."

The groom started to stammer. "I . . . I . . . I know. I'm sorry. I . . ."

"Didn't think?" I finished for him.

"Yeah."

"It's okay. You were a big help. Don't worry about having your feet so far down your throat you'll need a cesarean to tie your shoelaces from now on.''

I received a blank look in return for my attempted humor. I could tell the boy was now convinced that some of my brain cells had fallen out through the hole in my head. The situation amused me and my lips twitched into a grin. Perhaps I was growing up. Or, perhaps, I was just getting used to small-thinking people who couldn't help believing handicaps of any kind turned you into something less than a whole person.

The young groom headed back towards the activity centered at the front of the stables. When he moved away, I saw a figure standing by a tree in the distance. The figure realized I'd seen him and began to walk rapidly away. It confused me. Why would anybody connected with the stables or the estate leave the area when he might be needed? Instinct made me call after the figure, who responded by breaking into a jog.

It was clear, because of the damage done to the sprinkler controls, that the stable fire had been deliberately set. I also knew that people who deliberately set fires get a thrill from staying around to watch the destruction. Before I'd even made a conscious connection between the two facts, though, my feet were running in the direction of the fleeing man.

Further away from the stables the luminescence of the floodlights and the fire dropped drastically. Struggling to see through the dim moonlight, I thought I'd lost sight of my quarry until a shadow moved suddenly into the entrance of the estate's hedge maze. If the figure had remained still, I wouldn't have seen him in the darkness, but his lack of patience gave him away.

I sprinted to the maze and slipped quickly inside the seven-foot-high, tightly leafed walls before stopping to listen. Ahead of me and, I estimated, one pathway over, I could hear harsh breathing and set off in pursuit. The maze was beautifully constructed and maintained. Twice I ran into dead ends and was forced to retrace my steps to a pathway I thought I recognized. My only consolation was that the person I was chasing seemed to be encountering the same problems. Every time I thought he'd lost me, or I'd lost myself, I caught another earful of laboring lungs or shuffling feet which pushed me on.

A small park, at the heart of the maze, unexpectedly opened before me. At its center, reflecting in the moonlight, was a lily pond with a silent fountain. The pond was surrounded by an aesthetically pleasing array of trees and flower beds. My quarry was casually sitting on a white-slatted park bench, making exaggerated breathing noises. He was short and slightly built, with uncombed lanks of hair spilling down his forehead and across his eyes. He smiled at me, revealing a mouth overfilled with crooked, protruding teeth.

I took a step towards him, my attention fully on any furtive moves he might make. Suddenly, though, a heavy blow caught me across the backs of my knees and dropped me face-first onto the manicured turf. I started to roll to one side, but the sole of a huge boot planted itself with vicious force on my spine and drove the air out of my lungs.

Screaming panic messages shot through my nervous system to the already jammed reception center in my brain. A hand, which felt large enough to be the mate to the boot in my back, reached down and grabbed the jacket I was wearing and tugged it down until my arms were pinned to my sides. I struggled to escape, but could find no leverage. A smaller hand nestled in my hair and jerked my head up and back until I was looking into the face of the slim man I'd been chasing.

"Not so tough now are you, you Limey bastard?" His accent was a thick Dublin brogue. He emphasized his question by spitting in my face. The thick slime of mucus stung horribly in my good eye. Reaching out with a filthy hand, he pulled off my eye patch and laughed when he saw the puckered skin beneath it.

Rage and shame surged through me and I felt like a wild animal caught in a vicious trap. If I could have chewed off a leg to get at my tormentor, I would have done so gladly.

Violently, I rolled over onto my back and kicked out with both feet. There was a gratifying grunt from the huge shape behind me, but my elation died when the smaller man kicked me in the head with the steel toes of his Doc Martin's. Reality spun away into a foggy haze which became worse when the weight of the big man dropped heavily onto my chest. He leaned forward and kneeled painfully on my biceps. The fetid smell of the man filled my nostrils.

"Get it over with, Liam," he said to his smaller companion.

Liam crouched down again and leaned over me. His upside-down face leered at me with a sickly grin.

"This will teach you to keep your British nose out of Irish business," he said. I had no idea what he was talking about.

He snickered open a large switch knife, its professionally burnished blade refusing to reflect light. He moved it toward the bulging stare of my left eye and I screamed so hard I felt the effort in my groin.

Liam feinted with the knife and then held it steady above the center of my retina. I watched with morbid fascination as the droplet of sweat slid off his fingers and slithered down the knife blade to hang in quivering anticipation from the point.

"Tables turned now, eh boyo? No bloody SAS to back you up. Just us, the Sons of Erin, keeping an eye out for you."

His laughter tore through my brain. *Not my eye! Not my eye!* The words chased after each other at hyper speed. My entire body felt like wet pulp, and fear had taken on a new mask. I screamed again as Liam moved the knife. Again he pulled it back with a maniacal laugh.

"Stop mucking about, you stupid git," said the big man on my chest. He reached out with one of his huge paws and cuffed Liam's head hard enough to knock him over.

"Corr! Whatchya' do that for? I'm just having me bit o' fun." Liam sounded like a disgruntled child. With one hand he massaged the impact point on his ear.

"Belt up."

From nowhere the big man produced his own knife, and flicked open the blade with a practiced snap of his thick wrist. Without pause he jabbed it down at my eye.

Screaming again, I twisted my head to the right and felt fire burn down the left side of my face as the blade flayed my cheek open. The point of the knife stuck up from the earth below where my head had been.

Pain abruptly coalesced the rampant fear inside me into the old friend I thought I'd left behind on the football fields. Like a striking snake, I snapped my head back and clamped my teeth into the big man's index finger, which was along the blade of the knife. I bit down until I felt bone.

The big man's screaming echoed my own and he jumped away from me, the force of his movement stripping the skin from his finger as he pulled clear.

"Sean!" Liam yelled in astonishment.

I spat bloody flesh from my mouth and rolled to my feet. Sean stood in shock, watching blood pulse from his shredded digit. Shrugging clear of the jacket which pinned my arms, I slammed a fist squarely into the center of his face and rocked him back on his heels. I hit him again, this time dropping him to the grass, and turned to face the smaller Liam.

Smaller, though, did not mean less dangerous, as attested to by the automatic pistol in the Irishman's tiny fist. Reacting immediately to the threat, I threw myself sideways and rolled back into the maze corridor. Bullets penetrated the hedge walls preceded by the high-pitched, popping sounds of their percussion.

I kept moving.

There were no odds in going back to play hero. My face stung like hell and the vision of the knife above my eye still blocked out all other thought.

I realized Liam was yelling at me. "Stay away from Los Angeles, you bastard, or next time the Sons of Erin will be after more than your eye!"

The whole situation made no sense to me. All I wanted to do was get out of the maze and back to some form of understandable reality.

* * *

"What the bloody hell is going on, sir?" Even though my voice was harsh, I couldn't break the old habit of respect for command.

We were back in Sir Adam's study where we'd been before the evening's fiasco had started. Slumped in a red leather wing chair, Sir Adam looked far worse for the wear. Dirt and grime liberally covered his usually immaculate countenance, and dark bags drooped from beneath his eyes. He sighed heavily and refilled his brandy glass from a decanter placed strategically on a butler table to the right of his chair.

"I wish I knew, Ian. I truly do." He waved the bottle at me and then set it down again when I gave him a negative shake of my head. "Tell me," he continued, "why didn't you inform the police about the attack on you in the maze?"

I shrugged. "You know very well that having been one of your SAS bullyboys in the past, I'm still bound by the Official Secrets Act. You make lots of noises indicating you've put your cloak and dagger away. Yet within hours of arriving here, I'm involved in a nightmare I thought I'd left behind years ago in Ireland. I did my duty, but I didn't understand the battle then, and I understand it even less now."

When I'd finally found my way back to the maze entrance, I had seen that the fire brigade had the stable fire under control, but the air had still been thick with smoke which aggravated my throat. The horses had all been saved, but I could still hear them whinnying uncertainly. Shock had made me feel light-headed, and an ambulance attendant had grabbed me by the arm and made me sit through his efficient, but painful cleansing of the deep cut sliced in my cheek by Sean's knife.

Sir Adam's personal doctor had arrived a short time later and sutured the gash closed, after first attending to the similar wound on Paula's arm. The doctor had reasonably assumed I received my injury the same way Paula had—from the flashing hooves of a terrified horse. I had done nothing to change his thinking. Nor had I added my tuppenceworth to the inevitable police investigation. It was only later that I cornered Sir Adam and filled him in, using rather impolite terms.

"This Liam character . . . He told you to stay away from Los Angeles? You're sure?"

"I'm half-blind, not half-deaf. And I wasn't about to go back and ask him to explain himself. Who knew you were going to ask me to go to Los Angeles?"

Sir Adam was thoughtful. "Just about everyone in the Ravens organization, including all the players, knew we were considering you as a replacement for Maddox. However, only Nina Brisbane knew my ulterior motive for pushing your name to the forefront. There is something going on in the team which resulted in Maddox's murder, I'm sure of it. The police want to stick with the easy explanation, but I don't buy it.

"I still can't believe you would even consider me after everything I've been through." I couldn't keep the indignation from seeping into my voice.

"Self-pity doesn't suit you, Ian," Sir Adam said. He glared at me like a commander dealing with an out-of-line subordinate.

"It suits me just fine. And I don't give a damn if it suits you or not!" I let a pause fall over the conversation before asking: "Who are the Sons of Erin anyway? And what do they have to do with your activities in Los Angeles?"

"I'm not really sure. I have put my cloak and dagger, as you call it, away. But I still have my sources. . . ."

"Like consultant to MI8, the Prime Minister's special fanatics task force?"

Sir Adam looked shocked. "How do you know about that?"

I laughed. "My God, sir. The government might be able to put a gag order on what the press prints in this country, but it can't stop juicy tid-bits of gossip from flashing through Fleet Street like a lightning storm. Special Branch and MI5 could learn a hell of a lot from the intelligence-gathering skills of hungry journalists."

"But you're the editor of a sports magazine."

"That doesn't mean my ears are closed in the Fleet Street wine bars and pubs. You never know when you might pick up a lead on a great story."

"You never cease to amaze me." Sir Adam refilled his glass.

"Yeah, well. What about the bastard Sons of Erin?"

"They're a splinter faction of the Irish Republican Army, as you could figure out for yourself. Far more violent in their doctrine, but up till now they haven't been known to do anything more than talk a good game. We hadn't paid much attention until they were linked with recent rumors of revitalized interest in IRA funding from American shores. In the last ten years funding from America has almost disappeared. The Irish 'troubles' are being seen for what they are—no longer a religious, political, or sovereignty struggle, but terrorism for terrorism's sake. Part of the whole movement to bring anarchy to all stable governments.

"IRA funding now comes basically from Soviet sources via Lebanon and Libya—the goal being to establish a type of British Cuba. But suddenly a new American funding source has reared its head."

"What does all this have to do with the Ravens indoor soccer team and the murder of Maddox?" I asked.

Sir Adam shrugged his shoulders. "I have no idea. I don't even know if there is any connection past what happened here tonight. And even that could be some kind of a red herring."

Both of us were quiet for a period of time. I finished my brandy and set the glass down on a small side table.

"Well?" Sir Adam asked eventually.

"Well what?"

"Will you go to Los Angeles?"

I waited a beat. "Absolutely not."

"But . . ."

"Damn it!" I was suddenly angry all over again. "None of this changes the fact that I have only one eye . . . . that I'll never be able to play in goal again. You want an investigator? Send one of your current whiz-kids."

"You're the only one with the soccer skills to enter the team without drawing attention."

"I've already drawn more attention tonight than I need for the rest of my life. I got out of the 'troubles' once with my skin intact, and I'm out of soccer for good. Get somebody else." I walked over to the study door and opened it.

"Ian!" Sir Adam called after me.

I turned to face him, my hand still on the doorknob.

"I wouldn't care if you were fully blind. Or if you had no arms or legs. This is football we're talking about, soccer if you like. Countries have stopped wars for the game. It is bigger than any one person. Bigger than any one team. I love the game. You love the game. No matter what you say, it's in your blood. You suckled it in with your mother's milk. If something threatens the game, we have to do whatever we can to save it." He paused and I just stared at him.

"Look, Ian," he said in desperation, "the Ravens can't survive a major scandal. America is the only country in the world where the game isn't a national institution. A new team like the Ravens is facing destructive forces from every angle. Even though they've established a good enough record to reach the play-offs this season, the fan support isn't there yet.

"Facility expenses are skyrocketing even though Nina Brisbane's father owns the complex. The players themselves are nervous about the team's future and it's affecting their play at a time when they need to be at the top of their form. If Maddox's murder is tied in to something larger which relates to the team or the league, we have to clear it up quickly and with a minimum of fuss, or the Ravens will become the next casualty of the American pro game. It could be years before Los Angeles gets another team. Soccer needs you back, Ian, and it needs you back now."

I glanced at my watch. If I hurried I could still catch the late train back to London. Keeping silent, I walked through the door and closed it behind me without hesitation.

FOUR

BY THE TIME I arrived at the train station, I'd changed
my plans. I wasn't quite sure what to do with the car
I'd "borrowed" from Sir Adam's garage, and eventually decided to park and lock it in the station's lot with
the keys inside under the floor mat. Next, I woke up a sleepy
minicab driver by wafting a five pound note under his nose,
and convinced him to deposit me on the doorstep of a small
country hotel where an equally sleepy reservations clerk
checked me in.

The change in plans was due to several factors. If Sir
Adam wanted to continue his efforts to convince me to go
to California the first place he would start looking for me
would be back in London. More importantly, if Sean and
his mate Liam—the Benny Hill of the IRA—decided to have
a second go at me, they would also try London first. If their
information sources were good enough to pinpoint me at
Wren's Haven, they would have little difficulty finding my
permanent place of abode. I wasn't up to dealing with either
scenario, hence the small hotel.

I asked for a room with a private bath, and to my surprise and delight it contained a huge ball-and-claw tub instead of just a shower stall. I stripped off and gave my aches a long hot soak. To complete my overhaul, I bribed the reluctant clerk to fix a brew-up and some bacon sandwiches for a midnight nosh.

I kept my mind blank, refusing to think about anything other than creature comforts. Perhaps when the sun appeared and chased away the demons of the dark night, I would be able to place the evening's events in perspective. With a feather mattress wrapped around me like a comforting womb, sleep came with surprising ease.

Six blissful, oblivious hours later I opened my eyes as the light of the false dawn began to tremble on the windowsill. I felt fully rested, even invigorated, and quickly swung my legs out of the bed before the feeling could fade. I doused my face with cold water and donned workout gear.

Fifty fingertip push-ups started things off, followed by two hundred stomach crunches with legs hooked over the top of the bed. I did another fifty push-ups, the last twenty with fingers in agony, and four more sets of various abdominal crunches. I believe physical power and health emanate from the center of the body. Without the stomach and abdomen being in the best possible shape, the rest of the body will never achieve peak performance. I ran through all the crunches again, took a two-minute break, then did them a third time. Perspiration soaked my sweatshirt.

Finally, I laced on running shoes and took off into the early morning mist. I ran for miles and miles through the countryside, blazing trails up soft-surfaced hillsides and down through meadows of wild flowers and lush, knee-high grass. I felt I could go on forever. Taking solace in the mind-numbing routine of exercise, my brain was consumed with the efforts of physical action. My aesthetic mind was a universe away—unreachable by the problems of a reality I didn't want to face. I had been offered a chance to play soccer again. Not the same variation of the game I was accustomed to, nor even the same level, but still a chance to return to "the game." My face was too wet with sweat for me to notice the tears streaming from my good eye. I fought the thoughts from my mind and ran and ran.

The oblivion couldn't last forever. Back in London on Monday morning the demons came out to play again. I hadn't outrun them.

"Not you too, Gerald?"

"Yes, me too. And Da. And Zoe and the twins." Gerald loved to throw in the opinions of his wife and children if he thought it would prove a point. "It's time for you to get back to doing what you do best. No more acting like a spoiled child forced to go to piano lessons. You belong on a soccer field. And I don't give a fig if it is a different type of soccer field. It's still soccer, and there's still goalposts for you to excel between."

I was sitting up in the bed of my London flat. Gerald had stormed in unannounced, using a key I'd once given him for emergencies. He'd awakened me so roughly, I'd thought Sean and Liam were back. It was obvious Gerald knew all about the excitement at Wren's Haven, and he was bound and determined to have his say about the affair.

"Why didn't you come to work this morning?" he asked. "Do you think hiding here is a practical solution to your problems?" Gerald's pudgy hands were on his hips and there was battle blood in his eyes.

"I didn't have any problems until you and Sir Adam decided to stick your fingers in," I said.

"Of course you had problems!" Gerald's voice rose an octave in anger. "Only you refused to recognize them. People have to constantly be aware of saying the wrong things around you or they send you into a mood it takes you days to recover from. You think life has been bloody hard on you, and you wear your resentment like a suit of paper armor."

"You're not happy with my work at the magazine?" I felt my face flush. This tirade was not like my brother at all.

"Don't be stupid. You wouldn't still be working for me if I didn't believe you were the best editor going."

"Then why tip over the applecart?"

"Because the apples are all rotten. You'll never truly be yourself again until you either face up to your limitations or overcome them. If you go to Los Angeles you'll have the chance to do so. Then, if you want to come back, I'll welcome you with open arms and we'll set the journalism world on its ear."

"Gerald, I'm half . . ."

"Don't say it," he shouted. "Half-blind! Half-blind! It's your excuse for everything. And it's just not true!"

"What do you mean?" I said in outrage.

"You've lost an eye, but you're not half-blind. I've talked to your doctor. . . ."

"You bastard," I said throwing the covers off and standing up.

Gerald stepped forward and shoved me down. I bounced on the bed in shock.

"Shut up and listen to me." His voice held an unaccustomed menace. "I've talked to your doctor. He told me some interesting facts; like losing an eye only cuts down your vision by ten to fifteen percent. He also told me you've been doing a series of eye exercises which have reduced the lack of vision in your case to about five percent. A hell of a lot different than half-bloody-blind, mate!"

I felt cold all over.

"I've lost far more than just part of my peripheral vision," I said. Bile rose up in my throat, but I swallowed it down. "With only one eye my depth perception is almost nonexistant. I'd never be able to judge the distance or speed of an oncoming ball."

"Why the bloody hell not? Don't think I haven't noticed the way you make those slight double-take movements with your head. I asked your doctor about them, and he said he'd taught you how to do them to triangulate distances. You know how to cope with the depth perception problem. It might not be perfect, but it isn't an acceptable excuse."

I was silent. I was embarrassed at times by the almost
birdlike head movements I had to make in order to judge
distances. I thought I had done a pretty good job of hiding
the affliction, but obviously not.

Gerald misinterpreted my silence as weakening resolve
and charged on with his argument. "Come on, Ian. It's not
like you would be the first one-eyed goalkeeper to ever grace
the field. Gordon Banks went to America and played in the
outdoor leagues after he lost his eye in a traffic accident."
Gerald was pulling out every dirty trick in his bag. Gordon
Banks had been one of England's greatest goalkeepers and
a personal hero of mine. "If he can do it . . ."

"Gerald, please leave," I interrupted quietly.

"What?"

"Get the hell out!" I yelled, standing up again.

"No," Gerald said firmly, but at the other end of the
audible scale.

"Well, if you won't leave, I will," I said. I moved across
the room and stepped into a pair of well-worn Levis before
dragging a sweatshirt over my head. A pair of heavy motorcycle boots completed the not-so-dashing ensemble. Gerald was silent during the dressing process, standing on the
far side of the bed with his arms crossed. His anger and my
deliberate movements spoke loudly enough for both of us.
I moved past him, and grabbed a leather jacket and a scarf
from a hook on my way out the door.

On the street outside the flat, Gerald's voice taunted me
through an open window.

"You can't run away any longer, old son," he said.

I gave him a two-fingered salute over my shoulder and
didn't look back.

Well, I'd made a right cock-up of that. Overnight my life
had converted into a soap opera.

I was getting very good at making dramatic exists, but I
was losing friends fast. I was angry. A deep, down-to-the-
bone kind of angry. But not at Sir Adam or Gerald. At
myself. Self-pity is a narcotic with an addiction as strong

as any tangible drug, and I'd wallowed down to the rock bottom.

Entering the detached garage in back of the flat, I zipped a pair of leather pants over my jeans and put on a full-face crash helmet. The BMW Rally Sport turned over eagerly on the first attempt and I moved it outside to let it idle on the center stand while I closed and locked the garage.

The BMW was a two-year-old RS-90 model with the traditional opposing cylinders which you could use as foot pegs to warm your feet in cold weather. The most recent BMW, the K-1, has the innovative four cylinder in-line engine. "Innovative" in this case means a high-tech rework of the four-in-line Indian bikes manufactured in America in the thirties and forties. There was no doubting the power of the K-1. It would get you up to a ton in nothing flat and keep you there all day, but the need to do a hundred plus miles an hour on a motorcycle was not real high on my list of priorities. Upgrading, therefore, didn't strike my fancy. With the peripheral vision and depth perception problems caused by having only one eye, I had enough trouble staying upright on two wheels without all the extra power. Bloody hell, self-pity was overshadowing my whole outlook on life. It was more than addictive. It was totally destructive. God help me.

The weather was overcast. Thunder rumbled in the distance with the promise of rain. I tried to kid myself that I was driving aimlessly, but all along I knew exactly where I was going. Heavy London traffic held me up for a while, but once I broke through to the outskirts of the city it was clear sailing to my old home football grounds in Wolverhampton.

My stomach was making audible noises to remind me it was lunchtime, but instead of finding a nosh bar, I parked in the team lot and pounded on the player's entrance until Harry Gordon, the equipment manager, angrily opened the door.

" 'Ere, wot's all this racket about, eh?" He was built like a huge ball, almost as wide as he was tall, with shiny black eyes, and a drinker's broken blood vessels in his cheeks and nose. His fearsome expression changed to one of surprised pleasure when he recognized me. We'd always got on well.

"Ian! Wot a surprise,' he said, and grabbed my hand in a two-fisted grip. "Prodigal son returning 'ome, eh?'' He was pumping my arm like he expected water to spurt from my mouth.

"Not really, Harry. I just need to wander around and have a bit of a think.''

"Like you used to on the day before a game, eh? Be like old times, eh? Come on in.'' He stepped aside to let me through.

"Many of the lads about?'' I asked.

"Ooh no, man. Always take Sunday and Monday off. Any road, this time of year, being off-season, there's only a morning practice. You remember, I'm sure, eh?''

I nodded my head.

"Some of the younger lads from the youth team are having a kick about on the pitch, though, if you're interested, eh?'' he continued to chatter. "And a couple of the regulars will be in for therapy later, eh?'' His habit of ending most sentences with a questioning "eh'' hadn't diminished since I'd last seen him.

"Thanks, Harry. But I really don't want anyone to know I've been around. You know how it is?''

"Ooh, say no more. Say no more. I haven't seen you, although it really is good to, eh?''

I laughed. Harry probably didn't have any idea "how it is,'' but he was too much of a gentleman to press the matter. If I didn't want anyone to know I was around, it was good enough for him.

"Let yourself out, then, when you're ready, eh?'' he asked.

"Absolutely. No worries, eh?'' I replied. It was catching.

"I'll get back to it then, eh? Thankless task keeping up with this lot, I'll tell you. Don't let your smiling mug be a stranger, my son. Hear?'' He gave me a wink and a nudge before waddling off down the hallway. Salt of the earth was Harry.

When he was out of sight, I sighed for old times and sniffed in a huge breath of air. The scent was everything I remembered. A witch's brew of sweat, liniment, anticipation, expectation, and something indefinable. A scent which stayed with you, and could sneak up on you when you least expected it from some hidden part of your memory. I was warm and safe. I was home.

At the end of the long hallway which led off to the right was the locker room. I walked slowly down to it and entered. Thin wooden benches, supported at intervals by metal posts, ran the length of each aisle serving the lockers on both sides. My old locker was two rows in on the aisle. A new nameplaque now adorned the front of it, and for a moment I had the feeling none of my past history existed.

"It's about time you got here," a voice said quietly from behind me. "I'm an old man, you know. I don't have time to waste standing around waiting for some youngster to make up his mind about where his best interests lay."

I hung my head down without looking around.

"How did you know I'd come here, Sticks?"

"Do you have to ask? You're like my own son, Ian. And when you're hurting, and nobody else wants to hear about it, you come home because there is always a place set for you at the table."

I turned around with tears in my eyes and hugged the man who'd been the most influential figure in my life. My own father always loved me and looked out for me, but I'd been playing soccer for almost my entire formative years, and it was this man who had nurtured my career and helped me achieve the level of greatness of which I was capable. His given name was Moses Johns, but I'd always known him as Sticks.

We broke the embrace and stood looking awkwardly at each other as I got my emotions under control.

"Come on," Sticks said eventually. "I've a new batch of Juniors on the field and I want you to take a look and tell me what you think. They're mostly tripe, but there are one or two good-uns."

We walked out of the locker room, down the familiar player's tunnel, and onto the field. A light rain was falling as two teams of fifteen- and sixteen-year-olds, one wearing red shirts, the other wearing blue, raced around the field with incredible energy. Sticks and I stood under large black umbrellas and watched the back and forth.

"Who's the young lad making all the going for the blues?" I asked. "He looks familiar."

"He should. He's Geoff Hunt. Robby Hunt's oldest son."

"He can't be. Robby isn't old enough."

Sticks laughed. "It's a cruel world when we first begin to doubt our immortality. You're old enough for the boy to be your son."

"Never," I said in mock outrage. "He definitely inherited his father's skills, and he's a natural leader to boot. Unfortunately he also inherited his father's temper."

On the field Geoff was giving one of the other lads a bollocking over a rough tackle until the Junior's coach, who was refereeing the action, intervened.

"Makes friends fast, doesn't he?" I sad.

"He'll learn," Sticks commented.

Tall and thin, Sticks always appeared to dress like a rag-and-bones man. The team paid him well to scout for them and train their goalkeepers as only he knew how, but you'd never guess he had a penny to his name from his clothes. His face was all long lines and angles, hollow cheeks, and thin lips. He had a pair of miser's eyes, the kind that could spot a coin in the gutter at a hundred yards. Those eyes didn't miss much else either, and were in constant movement, like hyperactive children.

Until someone pointed out that the event occurred in 1890, Sticks often had young lads believing he was single-handedly responsible for the introduction of goal nets. To hear him tell it, Sticks had been playing soccer since before goalkeepers were first mentioned in the Football Association laws in 1871. He could tell great stories of the days when goal areas were no more than two posts stuck in the ground with a tape across the top. His actual age was impossible to tell, somewhere between his late sixties and early eighties.

The man's entire life had revolved around soccer. In his prime, he was a cut above any other goalkeeper until arthritis ate into his knees. Since then he'd trained others to become the best they could between the sticks on the playing field, and also between the sticks of their personal lives. He was an orphan who never married, but his family was the largest I'd ever known.

Play on the field had resumed and Geoff Hunt made a spectacular run on goal. Another blue player broke into the clear and called for the ball. Hunt ignored him and instead sent off a rocket shot which was beautifully saved by the red goalie.

"What do you think?" Sticks asked.

"It was a hell of a shot, but he'd have been better to pass off and not hog the play." I replied.

Sticks stamped his foot. "Don't be a daft bugger. I wasn't talking about the Hunt boy. The goalie. You think I'm wasting my remaining years by changing over to training center forwards all of a sudden?"

"I'm sorry." I laughed. "What's the lad's name?"

"Sid Doyle."

As we spoke, Doyle came out of his goal to jump up and pull in a particularly dangerous right cross. In doing so, he took a nasty blindside clip in the ribs. He absorbed the punishment, however, and held on to the ball. The foul was hidden from the referee by a cluster of bodies and went unpunished. A few minutes later, though, the blindsiding offender received a bloody nose during another goalmouth confrontation. I had to hand it to Doyle. He was crafty. Even I didn't see the elbow he threw, and I was looking for it.

He'd proved he could look out for himself, and the more I watched the easier it was to see that Doyle's goalkeeping skills were full of raw potential. Best of all, he had good balance and his moves were intuitive rather than planned. He also looked like he was enjoying every second of the game.

"He has heart," I told Sticks. "And he's certainly fast. What's his history like?"

"Last year playing for his school team, he only allowed six goals. Two of those were penalties. He saved our other penalties during the course of the year and was named to the England School Boy team. His first cap."

"Impressive accomplishment."

"He's going to be one of the great ones. I can feel it in here, like I did with you." Sticks tapped the center of his chest with two bony fingers. "He's got talent, and heart, and a single-minded dedication to being the best he can be. He's just like you were at his age, but he's going to be better because he's already learned to overcome his limitations."

Before I could ask Sticks what he meant by that last comment, the referee blew the whistle on the field and sent the two teams to shower.

"Do you want to meet him?" Sticks asked suddenly, and walked off toward the locker room without waiting for my reply.

"Sure," I said lamely, and followed in his wake.

We walked back into the locker room where the boys were now indulging in various stages of undressing, showering, and horseplay.

"Hey, you're Ian Chapel," said one of the lads who spotted our entrance.

"Am I?" I said, pleased to be recognized.

"Yeah," said the boy. "I used to watch you all the time on the telly through the bars of my crib."

"Cheeky bugger," I said, and laughed.

Sticks dragged me away to where Doyle was standing in shorts and socks. His build was thick and powerful, with large leg muscles and an abdomen an alligator would have envied.

"Sid, I think you recognize Ian Chapel," Sticks said, introducing me.

"Not 'arf," Doyle enthused. He shook my outstretched hand. "You've been my hero ever since I was a young nipper."

"What is this? I'm not in a wheelchair, you know."

Doyle blanched at my tone of voice. "Oh, no, sir. I only meant . . ."

"Don't worry about him," Sticks told the young man. "Age makes people testy."

I smiled at the boy and told him I'd enjoyed his play. "I especially liked the way you handled the chap who blindsided you," I told him. "You can't let them get away with that nonsense or they'll just try it on again."

"He'd been asking for it all game," Doyle said. "I don't like coming on like the heavy mob, but I had to put a stop to it. I didn't think anyone noticed."

"Part of the game, unfortunately," I said sympathetically. "Still, the feeling you get when you stop a sure goal makes it all worthwhile."

"Nothing like it in the world," Doyle agreed with a wide, sincere smile of his own.

"Better get showered now," Sticks interrupted. "I want you in the sand pit early tomorrow. We need to sharpen your reaction time some more."

Doyle shook my hand, and I turned to walk away. When Sticks didn't follow, though, I turned back.

Doyle was sitting down on one of the thin wooden benches and was talking with one of the other boys. He'd removed his shorts and his left sock. As I watched he rolled down his right sock and revealed a prosthesis which started about six inches below his knee and ran down to a flesh-colored lump of plastic where his foot should have been.

I looked at Sticks who was studying me intently with his beady little eyes.

"You set me up," I said without heat. "You're a bigger bloody bastard than all the others put together."

FIVE

PAIN THROBBED THROUGH my thighs, and I was finding it impossible to drag enough air into my lungs. On the opposite side of the sand pit from me, young Sid Doyle was jumping around with seemingly endless energy. I hated him.

Doyle kept his body in a half crouch, his legs pumping up and down in the heavy sand as he ran in place.

Sticks sat looking down at us from the top of the pit, a grim expression on his face. He suddenly barked the word, ''Left!'' and both Doyle and I launched ourselves in full dives to our left sides.

The sand was damp and unforgivingly hard. Doyle, however, bounced like a rubber ball and with catlike quickness he was back on his feet an instant after landing, his legs again pumping away like pistons in a perpetual motion machine. My weary old bones weren't anywhere near as fast to recover.

''Too slow, Ian! Too slow! Get your knees up,'' Sticks berated me.

I forced my legs to move faster, feeling the pain in muscles which threatened to turn to taffy under me.

My effort was ignored and several agonizing seconds passed before Sticks shouted, "Right!"

Doyle launched himself effortlessly to the right. I had tried to anticipate the call and dove left again, hitting the ground hard. I tried to convince myself to jump up, but I knew the effort wasn't worth it. Instead, I laid there in blissful agony and prayed the apocalypse would come.

"My God, man. What have you been doing with yourself in the last year? I thought you told me you were still in shape." Sticks glared down at us from the grassy knoll on which he was sitting. With his jaunty red hat cocked at a rakish angle he looked like a garden gnome. "Okay, take a break," he said, more to Doyle than to me. After all, I was already taking one.

"Sod it," I said under my breath.

"What was that?" Sticks demanded.

"Nothing."

Sticks stood up and shook a finger at me. "Don't whine. You know I hate whining. The object of this routine is to quicken your reaction time. If you react to the commands, you won't dive in the wrong direction. If you try to anticipate, you will inevitably make a wrong choice."

"Sod it," I said again, louder this time.

"Okay," said Sticks, overriding me. "Let's have the pair of you out of the pit."

I scrambled out after Doyle, and stood trying to catch my breath. Walking over us, Sticks took my hands in his. He held the backs of them up to his eyes and scrutinized them.

"What a mess," he commented. "How bad is the pain?"

His clear assumption of pain was a telling point.

"Most days the pain is marginal, except when the weather is making drastic changes," I told him. "Aspirin works wonders. Sometimes, though, I have to take so many they make my ears ring."

Sticks made an odd noise—somewhere between a grunt and a snort—which I knew indicated his understanding of the situation. "Take a good look at these, Doyle," he said, holding up my paws for the younger man's examination. "This is what you have to look forward to."

My hands are not a pretty sight. At some time or another, I've broken every finger except for my left pinky. There was never time to allow the breaks to heal properly, and as a result the bones had set themselves into a serpentine nightmare. The fingernails of three digits are permanently black, and two more are missing altogether. The second knuckles of the ring and index fingers on my right hand are also nonexistent; all injuries resulting from sliding, slashing, or stomping cleats attached to the boots of attacking forwards.

Doyle made no comment. I couldn't blame him, as there wasn't much to say. Maimed hands are by no means unusual for a professional goalkeeper, and I was willing to wager Doyle already had a few scars of his own.

Sticks dropped my hands in favor of picking up a battered bicycle. "Come on," he called over his shoulder, and set off pedaling for all he was worth. "I've got a surprise for you."

Doyle started to sprint after Sticks's departing figure. His gait was slightly odd, but he could move. Perhaps if I could pull off his prosthesis and hide it, I'd stand a chance of beating him to wherever we were headed.

The night after I'd been hit with the stinging revelation of Doyle's physical condition, Sticks took me on an old-fashioned pub crawl. We'd talked a lot about my missing eye and my chances of ever playing in goal again.

"You can't go on blaming soccer for the loss of your eye," he'd stated quietly after the third or fourth pint of John Courage.

"You don't know what you're talking about," I said, knowing he was nearer to the truth than I wanted to admit.

Drawing down an enormous swallow of beer, he came at his point from another angle. "When your father retired from the Met did he stop being a policeman?"

"I'm not sure I follow you."

He waved his free hand in the air in a gesture of frustration. "When your da was handed the gold watch, or the brass baton, or whatever it is they give policemen when they retire from service, did he suddenly stop believing all the things his job taught him over the years? Wasn't being a policeman more than a job to him? Wasn't it a way of life? Something he believed in?"

I shrugged my shoulders noncommittally. "He told me once he couldn't and wouldn't be anything else. Da never worried about questioning the reason for his existence. He believed he was put here to protect our family and those around us by putting villains in jail."

"That's right," Sticks said as he leaned intensely toward me across the small pub table. "Your da was an exceptional copper. Police work ran through every fiber of his being. It gave him an image of himself and allowed him to become an artist of criminal investigation. He would never have been happy delivering milk, programming computers, or building houses. He could have done any of those things, but being a policeman was what he did best."

"So?" I asked pointedly.

"Don't act thick. You know what the point is. Soccer is your version of police work. It defines who you are. Soccer didn't ruin your life by gouging out your eye. It gave you your life. Without soccer you might still have your eye, but you wouldn't have known the joy, the completeness, of your reason for existence. Yes, the game demands total commitment. And yes, she can be a harsh mistress. But she is also the most seductive and fulfilling of lovers. She is calling you back, and you can't say no."

I knew he was right. Somehow I'd known I would play again from the second Gerald threw down the story of Pasqual Maddox's death in front of me. I'd been fighting it like mad, but Sticks was definitely right. And because he was, I decided we should both get drunk.

Somewhere around the fifth public house, the enormity of the events at Wren's Haven began to sink in. Two bastards had tried to throw me into a world of living darkness from which there was no return. The attack was not randomly directed at anyone from Sir Adam's estate, it was specifically targeted to blind me—to stop me from going to Los Angeles—to stop me from even trying to play in goal again. It was clear someone believed I was a threat of some kind and was determined to neutralize me in the worst possible way. I would have felt better if they had tried to kill me outright.

By the eighth pub it became a foregone conclusion I would be going to Los Angeles. Vaguely, I remember drunkenly calling Sir Adam to tell him I'd changed my mind. I made one stipulation though; Sticks was to come with me. I received no argument. Sir Adam said he'd be in touch the following afternoon.

However, if I'd known I would be running halfway across the city during the morning, I would have given the whole project a pass. Even Doyle was beginning to show signs of fatigue by the time we stopped at an old, disused ice skating rink. He was definitely favoring the leg with his prosthesis, but it wasn't in him to verbalize the pain.

We were both walking in circles to cool down when he surprised me. "Does it ever feel like your eye is still there?" he asked quietly, almost like he was afraid I'd bite his head off.

"Sometimes. Mostly at night in light sleep, when I have the good eye closed too. I feel all I have to do is wake up and I'll see with both eyes again." It felt strangely right to be admitting things that I even had trouble talking to my own brother about to this relative stranger. "How about you?" I asked in return.

Thick knuckles reached down and rapped slowly on the plastic appendage. "Yeah. In my dreams, like you. Or sometimes, when I'm thinking completely about something else, I suddenly feel the toes wriggling."

"How did it happen?" I asked.

"Playing silly buggers as a kid. I was dodging across the tracks in front of a train on a dare and tripped. The train sliced it off and sealed it flat all in a split second. Amazingly, I didn't bleed to death. I've always been lucky, though—the train tracks were right behind a hospital.'' Doyle's head had been down as he related his story, his voice an echo of a hopeless dream of physical completion, but suddenly he looked up at me with a huge grin on his face. "I'll tell you what," he said. "Some night, when you're not planning to use it, let me borrow your leg for the evening and I'll lend you my eye."

"Sure," I agreed. "Easy as swapping car keys."

He laughed and so did I. Gradually, I started to laugh harder and it became contagious as we both began to giggle uncontrollably. Tears started to stream down both our faces, and I felt a huge outpouring of tension.

I was astonished with myself. With everyone I'd previously talked to about my injury, I'd been defensive. They were whole and I wasn't—they could never fully understand. Doyle was the first person I'd talked with since the injury who instinctively knew, really knew, what I felt like inside. We put our arms around each other's shoulders, our heads side by side, and laughed, and cried, and gasped for breath.

'' 'Ere, what are you two on about?'' A voice interrupted us, and we both looked up to see Stick's head poking around the door of the skating arena. Still holding on to one another, Doyle and I exploded into another fit of giggles.

"God preserve us from fools and idiots," Sticks said, rolling his eyes. "Whenever you're through, you can come inside and we'll work off the rest of your excess energy." For some reason his attitude made us laugh all the harder, unable to stop. Sticks scowled and disappeared from view, leaving the door open behind him.

When we'd calmed down slightly and were wiping the tears of laughter from our eyes with the bottoms of our shirts, I asked Doyle another direct question. "How far do you hope to go in this game?"

"I don't know, really," he told me seriously. "I take it a day at a time and see what happens. It's tied in to this theory I have about competition."

"Oh?"

"Yeah. I figure there are two types of competition. The first is one where you're competing to be the best. It's a competition you can never win because there will always be someone better than you eventually.

"The other type of competition is where you compete with yourself. You push yourself every day to go further than you did the day before. Every time you do so, you win. I like being a winner. So I strap on this damn hunk of plastic every day and push myself to be the best I can. And every day I come home a winner. I couldn't live my life any other way."

I looked at this young boy and felt a deep sense of shame. I told him so, and he had the good grace to look slightly embarrassed and grin shyly.

I also felt a huge metaphoric weight lifting from my shoulders, like somehow I'd been through a catharsis, and my spirits began to soar.

"Come on," I said to Doyle, roughly putting my arm around his shoulders and dragging him along. "Let's see what Sticks has cooked up."

Inside the skating rink, we were surprised to find several of the other boys who'd been playing in Doyle's game the previous day. They were milling around in the center of the iceless rink, kicking balls back and forth across a ratty expanse of artificial grass. At each end of the rink, small goalposts had been installed flush with the rink boards.

"What do you think?" Sticks asked, waving his arm around the set-up like a proud father.

I looked at Doyle and then back at Sticks. "I'm impressed. How did you get this together on such short notice?"

"Indoor soccer isn't unknown in this country. A lot of teams are using five-a-side tournaments during the off-season to keep players in shape and to work on ball skills. This old place is used for practice sessions." Sticks shrugged. "Of course, in America you'll be playing six-a-side, and the playing surface will be in far better shape, but this will serve our purpose.''

"Which is?'' I asked.

"Isn't it apparent? We're here to give you your first taste of being back in goal. I also want to try and get you acclimated to playing in a much smaller goal area. You need to get a feel for the ball rebounding off the boards, something you've never had to deal with before.''

I felt the blood drain from my face. My resolve of minutes before was weakening in a rush of apprehension. If Sticks noticed, he made no comment. I took a step backwards, or tried to at any rate. Doyle, sensing my anxiety, had moved up directly behind me to cut off my escape. He put his hand firmly in the small of my back and guided me gently out onto the playing area.

"Come on,'' he said. "It'll be a good lark.''

My heart was in my mouth and I couldn't return comment.

"Okay, this is the way it will work,'' Sticks told us. He indicated two of the six lads who'd been kicking the balls around. Both wore black jerseys. "Barry and Dick will always be playing offense no matter which team has the ball.'' He motioned in turn to two other players wearing red jerseys. "Philip and Peter will be on your team, Ian. Noddy and Geoff will be for Doyle.'' The last two boys were wearing blue jerseys. "This way there will always be a four-on-two attacking situation and more shots on goal. As long as Philip and Peter have the ball, Barry and Dick will help them attack Doyle's goal. When Noddy or Geoff take the ball away, or Doyle makes a save, Barry and Dick will then attack the other way. Clear?''

"If you say so,'' I said, shaking my head and moving down the playing surface to take up a position in the far goal.

The goal itself was approximately twelve feet wide and six feet six inches high. The dasher boards ran away from either side of the goal and were topped with Plexiglas. I felt like a pro golfer on a miniature golf course.

A few minutes into the game, though, I felt like an idiot.

As play started, Barry and Dick came down the field toward me, passing the ball easily between them. They were still a distance away when Dick suddenly fired a shot on goal. I knew instinctively that it was going wide to the left and that there was no one there to receive it. My sluggish reflexes, though, failed to respond when the ball bounced off the unfamiliar boards, whizzed past me in front of the goal, and was easily tapped in for a point by Noddy, who had run through on my blind side. I stood flat-footed, feeling silly.

I struggled through the next few minutes in a frustrating effort to adjust my depth perception under game circumstances. I felt clumsy and unsure. Where once I had dominated, I now felt intimidated.

If I was going to succeed, I had to face my fear of allowing others to see how I coped with my handicap. I couldn't just walk off the field, now that I had come so far. Somehow, I had to acknowledge my handicap and overcome it. Swallowing my pride, I began to use the quick back-and-forth movements of my head to gain perspective on the speed and distance of the ball.

A minute or so later the attackers were rushing me again. This time I came out of the goal to grab the ball, and ended up in a rough-and-tumble tussle with Geoff, who was running through with the ball. Sticks blew his whistle, and I thought rightfully so. Didn't Geoff realize he was roughing the keeper? Who did he think he was?

"Hand ball." Sticks called out the foul.

"What?" I said confused. "What are you talking about? He was all over me." I was outraged.

"And so he should be," said Sticks. "You're half a mile out of the penalty area."

I looked down and realized I was way outside of the marked square where I could legally use my hands. I was still playing the game by outside field dimensions. I would have to learn to make allowances for more than just my missing eye.

Ten minutes, and three hand balls later, Sticks blew his whistle again sharply and walked over to me. My only compensation was that Doyle was experiencing the same problems of adjustment and had two hand ball penalties of his own.

"I thought this might happen," Sticks told me. He then reached over one of the dasher boards and retrieved two odd looking contraptions. "Put that round your waist," he said, handing one of the jerry-rigged objects to me and the other to Doyle.

I examined this new addition to my wardrobe with a skeptical eye. Basically it was a weight lifter's belt with a long, thick elastic cord attached to a ring at the back. When Doyle and I put the belts on, the cords trailed behind us like long black tails. The other players were enjoying themselves immensely at the sight of us. Sticks grabbed the length of cord from behind me, and tugged steadily on it. It stretched out like a rubber band and began to pull me backwards.

"What in the world are you doing?" I asked in exasperation, although it was clear what was coming.

Sticks continued to pull me backwards until he was able to attach the free end of the cord to an O-ring set in the floor behind the goal.

"This should help you solve your adjustment problem. As long as you stay in the area where you're supposed to be, the cord won't have any effect. Should you stray past your limit, though, I think the effect will be a good learning experience."

"Personally, I think you're stretching things a bit," I commented, but nobody laughed.

Once Doyle was similarly encumbered, play resumed. For a while everything went fine. If I felt inclined to move out past my area, the cord tightened to keep me in check. Soon I actually began to feel comfortable and was able to start concentrating more on the movement and rebounding of the ball. I'd lost my initial reluctance and was really beginning to enjoy myself. My good eye moved constantly from side to side, taking in as wide a view as possible. The hours of eye exercises I'd done to improve my peripheral vision were starting to pay dividends.

I watched Doyle make a nice save at his end of the field and throw the ball in an outlet pass to Noddy on the right side of the field. Noddy moved the ball down easily as Philip and Peter moved back to defend. Barry and Dick came into the picture to give support, but Noddy gave the ball away on a high pass to Geoff who was streaking down the left wing. I had anticipated the play, knowing Philip and Peter would be out of position, and raced over to cut down the threat.

Geoff gathered the ball in with a nice soft touch and moved toward me. I crouched down as he approached and used my body to cut down his shooting angle. He moved to dribble the ball around me and I began a dive for the ball at his feet. As I did so, the cord behind me stretched to its fullest limit and snapped back to dump me on my backside in a pathetic, out of control, heap of arms and legs. Everyone, even Geoff and I, burst into hysterical laughter.

I knew right then it was going to be a long season.

SIX

SIR ADAM AND I sat alone in the conference room which *Sporting Press* shared with the other magazines under Gerald's domain. Actually, Sir Adam was the only one sitting. My backside was still sore from repeatedly being slammed onto the floor of the ice rink. I stood with my back resting against one of the grass cloth-covered walls. I'd eventually become comfortable with the right distances and angles for playing on Sticks's makeshift indoor soccer field, but I'd paid a high price. I might never be able to sit down again.

Gerald's conference room had at one time been a row of three unattractive boxlike offices. Seeing their potential, though, Gerald had contracted for the three rooms to be knocked together to form one long, slender rectangle. Large double-glazed windows had been fitted in the outside walls, and a decorator had been hired to fill the finished product with thick, honey-colored carpet and matching drapes.

Two A.J. Kellers, showing pre-1900 golfing scenes, adorned the walls, and a huge, highly polished mahogany table squatted in the center of the room with matching ball-and-claw chairs. Gerald thought he'd scored a set of genuine Victorian antiques when he'd found the table and chairs going cheap in the Portobello Road. I'd never had the heart to tell him I'd found a ''Made in Taiwan'' sticker under the seat of one of the chairs.

Sir Adam took a water decanter off a silver tray situated near him on the conference table. With a practiced hand, he splashed its contents lightly across the healthy measure of whiskey already reposing in his glass. Sartorially splendid in a dark blue blazer, gray slacks, Italian loafers, crisp white shirt, and the inevitable regimental tie, he made a toasting gesture in my general direction and tore off a manly mouthful in the way characteristic to the British upper class.

''Not drinking, Ian?'' he asked me.

''I'm in training.''

''Glad to hear it.'' He settled himself more comfortably in his chair and cleared his throat before starting in. ''I hear you were pretty good on the practice field today.''

I smiled. ''Let's not lie to each other. Sticks probably told you I'm a broken-down ex-ballplayer with arthritic hands, limited peripheral vision, slow reflexes, and delusions of grandeur. I spent more time on my ass today than I did on my feet, and a bunch of recently weaned youngsters seemed to score on me at will. I've told you I'll go to Los Angeles for you, and I appreciate what you are trying to do for me, but I want you to know what you're getting.''

A look of steel came into Sir Adam's eyes and the flesh of his face suddenly took on the hard gauntness which had commanded so much respect in the army. ''Get this straight, mister.'' His voice matched the seriousness of his features. ''This is no mercy mission to help you rebuild your self-confidence. I have a lot of money invested in a team which is about to enter the play-offs for the first time in its short existence. It's a team which has the lowest crowd gate in the league. If the fans don't turn out for these last remaining games, there is a strong possibility the franchise will fold.

''My starting goalkeeper has just been murdered, there

are rumors circulating that he was throwing goals, although only God knows why, since the betting on soccer in America is next to nothing, and nobody seems to be able to do sod-all to help the situation.'' He paused to take another bite from his whiskey.

He continued in a more normal tone. ''I want you in LA because I think your name value will attract potential fans. If your name doesn't do it, then maybe they'll come out to see if the highly touted one-eyed wonder will fall flat on his face. Everyone loves a winner, but they love a loser who makes a fool of himself even more.''

I felt my face flush. ''So, you're dragging me to LA so I can destroy myself in public this time?'' I felt myself about to lose control again.

''Don't be stupid. I believe in you, and I believe you still have the skill to help the Ravens win it all. If I didn't, I'd be asking someone else to do the job. You want me to know what I'm getting into. Well, I want you to know what you're getting into.''

I pushed off the wall and poured myself a glass of water. Unsteady depth perception reared its head again. To combat it, I put a finger on the rim of the glass and used it to guide the lip of the water pitcher to the rim. Until I'd learn this little trick, I'd chipped more glasses and teacups than a ham-handed dishwasher. When I wasn't destroying crockery, I was pouring tea and every other liquid over the furniture. When my little performance was over, I drank the water down without pause and went through the whole routine again. I felt a little better.

''You want me to be more than a goalkeeper, though, don't you?'' I asked.

''Yes. That's why I need you, Ian, and nobody else. I love soccer, always have. It's more than a game. More than two teams kicking a silly ball around. It's an art, a magnificent blending of color, movement, power, and emotion played out across a living canvas. Like so much in art, the whole equals far more than the sum of the parts. My god, man, I don't need to tell you this. You love the game as much as I do.

"The problem is, there is something happening to soccer in America. The death of Pasqual Maddox is only one of the visible symptoms of the illness, but it's one which can perhaps be traced back to the source. If the Ravens fail as a team, then next year more teams may fold, and the year after that perhaps the whole league. It's already happened in the American professional outdoor leagues. They've been forced out of existence and it will be a long time before they spring to life again. If indoor soccer fails, it will be even longer before soccer can make a comeback. Perhaps never." Sir Adam paused and knocked the remainder of his drink back in a defiant manner, as if daring me to challenge his somewhat melodramatic assessment.

"Are you saying there is some kind of central cancer which is threatening to destroy the league for some reason?" I asked.

Sir Adam waited for a beat or two before answering, searching my inquiry for any glint of mockery. "No," he finally answered. "I'm not as paranoid as you appear to think. What I do believe, though, is that there are a lot of different cancers eating at the American game, some worse than others. If we can cut out the really bad ones, then perhaps we can work on curing the rest. I need you to act like a scalpel. You understand soccer, you know the people involved, and you are in the unique position to come at the problem from the inside. If Maddox's death is connected to the team, I need you to find out how and then do something about it."

"Bit of a tall order, isn't it? Especially given the time frame we're talking about."

"I didn't say it was going to be easy. But it still has to be done."

Each of us glared directly at the other as if involved in some juvenile stare-down contest. Inside me, self-doubt battled with the loyalty and friendship I felt toward a man I'd always respected. Loyalty and friendship won. Easily.

There was a time, before the "Sir" became part of his name, that I would have laid down my life for Adam Qwale, and I had no doubt he still wouldn't hesitate to give his for me. The respect and experiences which create such feelings are hard won, and once established, are even harder to put aside. My explosion during the weekend before, when I'd thrown my brandy at him, was an exception, understandable only because my emotions had been on a raw edge.

I took a deep breath. "Tell me about the Ravens."

All the muscles in Sir Adam's face seemed to relax at once, as if a puppeteer had suddenly released their strings. "Great! I knew you'd come around." Enthusiasm seemed to gush forth from him in electric waves. "The Ravens are part of the Brisbane family of sports franchises."

"Nina Brisbane's family?"

"Yes. Her father is Terrance Brisbane. Multimillionaire several times over. Irish to the core of his soul, though he's never set foot on the sacred soil. His great-grandfather emigrated to America and began to amass a fortune in the construction business. Grandfather Brisbane moved the fortune into distilleries and speakeasies, running booze and flappers during Prohibition like a low-profile Al Capone. Daddy Brisbane took the fortune out of the illegal rackets and into hotels, restaurants, laundries, and fast-food chains.

"When Terrance stepped into the family money, he too was blessed with the golden touch. His fortune has quadrupled in the last thirty years as he poured it back into real estate and construction. For fun he owns sports franchises. When he found he couldn't buy any of the teams in his Los Angeles home base, he built his own sports complex—the Acropolis—and brought new franchises to the area."

I broke into the spiel with a question. "How did he manage to get the established leagues to let him form new teams? I thought there was a long list of potential owners waiting for opportunity to knock."

"Money is all in La-La Land."

"Yes. But don't all of the other potential owners have money?"

"True for the most part. But none of them have a ready-built sports complex waiting to be filled. Brisbane earned a lot of favors while building the complex, and all of them were called due when he approached the leagues. He now has an ABA basketball team, an NHL hockey team, an indoor tennis franchise, a professional volleyball team, and the Ravens."

I shook my head in wonder. "Money and power—it's amazing what that combination can accomplish. How did you get a chunk of the action?"

"Terrance might be a financial whiz, but his family relationships have never been smooth. Terrance has two daughters: Nina, whom you've met, and Caitlin. The girls have never really gotten along, especially since Nina's horror." I raised my eyebrows at that, but Sir Adam stayed with his original subject. "Terrance refuses to play favorites. So, to test which of the girls should inherit controlling interest in his business dealings, he has given each of them two sports franchises to run. Caitlin has hockey and volleyball. Nina, tennis and soccer. Their track records in the business of running the teams will determine who takes over as chairman of the board when Terrance retires. The Ravens have proven to be a tough fiscal entity. When Nina ran into some financial problems with the team, I was able to help her out."

"Does that put her in a difficult position with her father?" I asked.

"Not necessarily. It was a smart financial move, and Caitlin is having problems of her own with the hockey franchise. Needless to say, the sisters don't get along. Either of them would go to great lengths to see the other one fail."

"So, as go the Ravens, so goes the Brisbane fortune—at least as far as Nina's concerned," I said.

Sir Adam nodded and refilled his glass from the whiskey decanter.

"What happened to Nina's face?" I asked directly. "Why does she wear a veil?"

"Ahh . . ." said Sir Adam. "There lies a tragic and, I'm afraid, a truly Irish tale."

I looked confused and Sir Adam lowered the level of his whiskey again, as if seeking fortification.

"I told you Terrance Brisbane was a staunch Irish supporter, although he's never been closer to Ireland than Finnian's Bar and Grill in New York."

"What you're telling me," I interjected, "is he financially supports the IRA, having no idea what the 'troubles' are about, and thinks it makes him a big man in the eyes of the Irish community."

"You've got it, but then it's a typical story," said Sir Adam. "The sorry part of the situation, though, is that unlike most other American IRA money sources, who have now decided it's unfashionable to be seen supporting a terrorist cause, Terrance Brisbane is still known to be knocking huge amounts of financial resources into the IRA coffers. He doesn't use legitimate funding mediums any longer, but money is flowing from somewhere in the Brisbane business empire. As you have assumed, I'm still in a position to know such things."

I tried to look wise. "And, should you come across the source of said income while involved in a business arrangement with Brisbane's daughter, you could again prove yourself of service to Queen and country."

"You sound as if you disapprove."

"Corr! Not me. Anyone who supports the bloody IRA rabble deserves to be taken down. But what does this have to do with Nina?"

"Well, while Terrance Brisbane hasn't been to Ireland, his daughters have been welcomed there on several occasions. Six years ago, Nina was staying with a family whose patriarch, Auggie McBride, was a member of high regard within the IRA hierarchy. McBride, however, was also an army informer of long standing whose luck finally ran out. When he was exposed, he was murdered and dismembered at an IRA Council meeting. His body was mailed in pieces to Army HQ, and his entire family marked for execution as an example to others.

"It was Nina's misfortune to answer the door when the executioner came calling. She took a twelve-gauge shotgun blast in the face through the glass of the entryway. The rest of the family was murdered outright . . . McBride's wife, two daughters, one son, and the mother-in-law. Somehow, though, Nina was still alive and conscious when the police arrived.

"They rushed her to the hospital, but most of the right side of her face and the inside of her mouth was caved in from the impact of the shot. She could barely breathe. She could not swallow, talk, or see, and she was bleeding to death. The doctors performed a dubious miracle—a sixteen-hour operation which not only kept Nina alive, but also made life possible outside of a hospital environment. Various parts of her body were used to recreate her upper jaw, eye socket, and cheekbone, the rest was reformed like a huge human jigsaw puzzle. One eye was saved, as was her tongue. Somewhere, through all of this, Nina was able to identify the shooter, Duncan Finlas, a known IRA gunman, who was captured trying to escape the country three days after the shooting.

"Finlas was put behind bars for life, and Nina survived the seventeen operations which followed to give her face some type of human form. Unfortunately, the success of the facial rebuild, though brilliant in medical expertise, fell far short in the . . . Well, you can imagine why the veil is necessary. Nina was a beautiful young woman whose face was changed into a grotesque mask."

"And her family still supports the IRA cause after something like that happened to his daughter? I can't believe it!" I felt outraged.

"That doesn't make it any less true. Nina is an amazing person. She's fought back from the dead and has forged ahead with her life with amazing zeal. When she refused to play the martyr for the IRA cause, Terrance decided to take up the curtain call. He has all the power and money he could ever need, but the IRA gives him a purpose for living. Somehow he's managed to turn Nina's tragedy into the British army's fault, a position he refuses to back down from. He's become a fanatic, a convert to the cause—and there is nothing more dangerous.''

I pulled out a chair and gingerly perched my sore posterior on the center of the cushion. ''Do you think the murder of Maddox has IRA connections?''

''Impossible to tell. Maddox had no known IRA connections, but he did have known criminal ones as evidenced by his involvement in the Italian betting scandal.''

''What about the rumors he was letting goals be scored on purpose?'' I asked.

''Unsubstantiated. I've not been able to chase down the source of the rumor. As it stands, it's locker room gossip only.''

''Someone with Maddox's past indiscretions is always going to be faced with someone else spreading rumors about his current activities.'' I was thoughtful. ''The police think the murder was a mugging gone wrong?''

''Yes.'' Sir Adam stretched his legs out in front of him and crossed them at the ankles. He ran a scraggly claw of a hand over his face, and for the first time I noticed that he looked old. ''From what they tell me, Los Angeles is quickly earning the nickname 'Murder City' that once belonged to Detroit and Miami. The police are looking for the easiest route to get the murder off the books or into the inactive file so they can get onto the next case. The local group of soccer hooligans, one English import I'm sure the rest of the world could do without, seems to be the easiest target for the blame.''

''Are the police doing any further follow-up?''

''You'll have to check with them, but I shouldn't think they'll be doing anything more unless further evidence comes to light. The detectives in charge are Briggs and Gill. They were polite in their supercilious way. . . .''

''The same the world over,'' I said putting in my tuppence-worth.

Sir Adam nodded his head in agreement. "They seem like good men, but they don't have much to go on, and numerous other cases are making demands on their attention."

"What if they're right and it is this bunch of kids?"

"Then find the buggers and let justice run its course."

With a touch of formality, Sir Adam brought several envelopes out of his blazer and passed them over to me.

"I think you'll find everything you need in there—airline tickets, a visa and work permit for the States, health insurance card, etcetera. Your plane will be met at the other end, and I've taken care of all your accommodations. There won't be anything to worry about in that regard. I know Gerald acts as your agent and business manager, so I have worked out all the contract negotiations and other paperwork with him."

"Was he happy with it all?"

"Your brother is a shrewd man. I'd hate to be up against him in a corporate battle. He's satisfied I'm treating you squarely, but he drives a hard bargain."

"Now you know why he's my business manager. Is there anything else we need to cover or are you just going to wish me good luck?" I stood up and so did Sir Adam. My backside was relieved.

"There is one other small item you might be interested in before you go."

"Yes . . ." I said expectantly.

"How would you like a crack at the two bastards who burned down my stables?"

SEVEN

THE FOUR MEN gathered around the hood of a black
sedan looked up as Sir Adam and I exited the taxi
which had delivered us to the Limehouse side street.
In the falling evening dusk, I could see the group were a
tough-looking bunch, but I reserved further judgement for
the moment. Some of the toughest characters I'd ever run
across in the SAS would make Lord Peter Wimsey look like
Charles Bronson. You could never tell.

Because of the presence of the taxi driver, the only thing
Sir Adam had told me in the cab was that we were on the
way to meet an operations team. The men by the sedan
appeared to fit that category. The tallest of the group stepped
forward and nodded to Sir Adam. A smile broke out on his
face when he looked at me.

"How have you been keeping, Ian? I was sorry to hear
about your troubles."

I took a closer look at the man, mentally subtracted several years of hard living from his face and added a thatch
of thick black hair to his bald pate.

"Denny Malcolm? Is that you, old son?" I laughed, recognizing him as another mate from my army days. Sir Adam seemed to have remained in touch with more than one of us.

"It's now Inspector Malcolm, Special Branch, but you can still call me Den." He gripped my arm and we pounded each other on the shoulder.

"Who's your crew?" I asked, looking past him at the three other men still standing in the background.

"A few hand-picked lads who enjoy a punch-up. These little sorties of Sir Adam's usually end up with fists flying."

I looked at Sir Adam. "You really haven't let your cloak and dagger gather much dust."

"Not true. Not true. Occasionally, I have to call in the heavy mob to help keep them on their toes, but it's nothing like the old days."

"Thank God," Den and I said in unison and then laughed.

Den turned and pointed toward his companions. In physical appearance they were as alike as peas in a pod—same height, weight, and general impression of command presence and fitness.

"The ugly bugger on the left is Reggie Leggit," Den said by way of introduction. "He's on special attachment to MI8 from the SAS. He saw quite a bit of action in the Falklands, and from all accounts he'd rather fight than screw."

"Hope he fights better than he screws," said the bloke standing next to Leggit with a comical grin plastered across his face.

"How would you know how I screw?"

"Your dear old mum told me. . . ."

Leggit responded by cuffing his compatriot roughly around the ears.

Den snorted and the two men settled down. "The comedian is Derek Watford. Up through the ranks to Special Branch and, God help me, my partner. If he caught his winkie in the loo door he'd have something funny to say about it."

Watford scrunched up his rubberlike face to the point where his lower lip almost touched his nose. It made him look like he was swallowing his face. You couldn't help but laugh. "At least my whatsit's long enough to catch it in the loo door," he said, returning his face to what passed for normal. "Not like some folks I know."

Den ignored him and moved on to the last introduction.

"Harry Martin is another one of Sir Adam's MI8 goons. Came over from the Middle East spook squad didn't you, Harry?"

"That's right," Harry said in a rolling Scot's accent. He stepped forward to shake my hand. "It's a right pleasure to meet you, Ian. Too bad you weren't born north of the border. Then you could have played with a real soccer team."

"As I recall England beat Scotland only last week in an international."

"Ahh . . . How can you consider that game a win? The referee had his whistle caught in his throat, was blind in one eye, and couldn't see out of the other?" He looked at my eye patch and hurriedly added, "No offense."

"I've always said that about Scottish teams," I replied drolly.

"If you gents are through?" Den spoke up in a stern voice and guided me away to the front of the sedan. There he waved at three items scattered across the hood. "I think you'll find these interesting. We came up with the photos through the descriptions and first names you gave us of the blokes who attacked you at Wren's Haven."

The photos Den was referring to were a couple of eight-by-ten, black-and-white glossies of the monsters who'd tried to gouge my eye out. I felt my heart suddenly kick into a higher gear and jump up from my chest to block my throat. My response must have been visible because Den reacted to it with a tight-lipped grimace. "Yeah," he said. "That's the way I feel about them, too."

"You know them?" I asked.

"Sean Brody and Liam Donovan. Bloody murdering Sons of Erin. Offspring of the devil. Been chasing them for three years, ever since they pulled a bank job in the Fullam Road and killed two of my best men in the process.''

I silently picked up the photo of Sean Brody and studied it. His face looked like a cross between a bulldog and a mastiff, all jowls and knotted muscle.

''The IRA christened him 'The Slab,' '' said Den. ''The tag came about when Brody got tired of drilling the kneecaps of IRA informants and began dropping slabs of concrete on them. He made a major gaff one day, though, and broke the back of an IRA chieftain's favorite nephew. Brody had mistaken the nephew for a British informer whom he physically resembled.

''The chieftain went berserk and put out a contract on Brody. However, it cost the IRA three valuable men to find out Brody was too tough to kill. The contract was cancelled. Instead, Brody was simply excommunicated from the movement—too much of a loose cannon, even for those bastards. The edict didn't cramp his style, though, since he soon found his talents in demand by the Sons of Erin.''

Den stuck out a bony finger and poked at the photo of Liam Donovan.

''This one is even worse,'' he said. ''Donovan is a sadist of the first mark. Loves to kill with a knife and has lost count of the number of men he's sent to hell. He has no political commitment past whatever group will support the satisfaction of his violent desires. The IRA originally sent him to Libya where he was trained to become a specialist with explosives.

''He was a loner until he hooked up with Brody. They've been inseparable ever since, and it's a partnership blessed by the devil's luck. Using Donovan's skills and Brody's brute force, they've taken down banks, armored cars, and betting shops—never hesitating to kill, never leaving behind any witnesses willing to testify. As far as our informants are concerned, the pair have been in hiding in Ireland since the Fullam Road blag brought so much heat down on them. Even the IRA has put a price on their heads, but they aren't actively pursuing the contract after their last experiences with Brody. This is the first we've known of them being back in England, and I want them before they get away again."

I wanted a piece of them too. "How did you find out where they were holed up?"

Den scratched his head before replying. "Strange, that. A woman called up the Special Branch office and asked to speak to me. It was obvious she knew I'd been in charge of the Fullam Road investigation. Her voice was muffled, like she had her hanky over the phone mouthpiece. No discernible accent, no background noises, and of course she refused to identify herself. She just flat out stated that if we wanted Brody and Donovan, we'd find them tonight at The Squire and Pipe, second floor, last room at the rear."

"Have you considered the possibility of a set-up?" Sir Adam asked.

"Oh, I've considered it," said Den. "But I don't give a tinker's damn, if there's the slightest chance of catching up with these two sorry bastards. I figure the informant is probably a jilted girlfriend, or something of the sort. That's usually the way this type of thing happens."

Picking up the third item from the hood of the vehicle, Den turned it toward me. It was a hand-drawn floor plan of The Squire and Pipe.

"The pub is two streets over, facing the docks," he explained. "It has a long history of being a safe house for scum, especially those sympathetic to the Irish cause." He stuck out another of his skeleton-like fingers and traced a route along the floor plan. "The stairs are off to the side of the front door, which gives us a slight advantage. In a short while a squad of uniformed rozzers are going to raid the pub and cause a ruckus in the main room. We'll be going through the door right behind them and heading straight up the stairs. With any luck we'll reach the back room before Brody and Donovan even know anything is amiss."

"And if we're not lucky, we'll give 'em a belly full of this," Watford stated blandly, and swung out a sawed-off shotgun from under his overcoat. It was suspended from a lanyard looped over his right shoulder.

Den stared hard at his partner. "I hope we're not lucky," he said under his breath.

The silence seemed to stretch out after Den's statement until the radio unit on the lapel of Leggit's coat crackled.

"The uniforms are standing by." Leggit interpreted the barely audible static for us.

"Let's do it, then," said Den. He picked up the items from the sedan hood and stuffed them into an inside coat pocket.

"What about armament for Sir Adam and me?" I asked.

Sir Adam looked slightly startled. "I won't be needing anything. I'm too old for this sort of tommyrot. I'll just be standing by to pick up the pieces."

"All right," I said. 'But that still leaves me."

"I'm sorry, Ian.' Den spoke quietly. "I'm letting you come along on the raid as a favor to Sir Adam, and because I know your form, but I draw the line at issuing shooters to civilians. If you want to come, you'll have to rely on your size and your hand-to-hand skills if it comes down to it. Are you still in?"

I flexed my shoulders to ease the tension in them. "Last one to the top of the stairs buys the beer."

There were two lookouts outside the pub. One, a young-ish looking boy with thinning hair, a pockmarked face, and wire-rim glasses, lounged in the front entranceway. Every few minutes he would walk out into the street and casually look up and down the main road which fronted the dock causeway.

The second lookout was slightly less obvious. He was hidden in the shadows of the rise and fall of the roofing, in a position that commanded a view of the entire dock area. His presence was given away by the laziness of an ill-hidden cigarette glow. Den, Sir Adam, Harry Martin, and I watched from the cover of a large freight container. Behind us, a huge deserted ship creaked at its docking like it was possessed.

Suddenly, the glow of the roof lookout's cigarette arched out into the night and his body completely disappeared into the shadows. Within seconds the dark silhouette belonging to Reggie Leggit appeared in his place. He raised a hand slightly in our direction.

"One down," said Den, and we turned our attention to street level where Watford was initiating a drunken gait toward the pub entrance. The lookout in the entry chose that moment to step out into the street for a glance around. He looked directly at Watford, whose features were scrunched up in the face-swallowing contortion he'd shown off earlier. Watford stuck out a palm and said something to the lookout which none of us could hear.

The lookout responded with harsh noises, and Watford began to grope at the man's jacket lapels in his appeal for charity. When the lookout pushed him away, Watford sat down hard in the street. A more pitiful heap of humanity I'd never seen, but he didn't seem to faze the lookout who walked toward him and kicked an unfriendly foot into Watford's midriff.

Like a phoenix rising from drunken ashes, Watford grabbed the offending foot and pushed it into a far higher arc than its owner initially intended. Off balance, the lookout slammed to the roadway on his back, the air driven from his lungs—cutting off any chance of a warning cry. Watford rolled onto his feet with the grace of flowing water and smashed the back of his fist, hammerlike, into the face of his adversary. The man slumped like a rag doll with no stuffing, and was dragged into a dark corner of the night by his belt and trouser cuff. The entire incident had taken less than ten seconds.

Den nodded at Harry Martin, who spoke into the radio pinned to his lapel.

"Charlie ten to Zebra one—it's a go. I repeat—it's a go."

With Sir Adam hanging back, the rest of us moved out from behind the large shipping container and scrambled to meet Watford at the pub entrance. Before we could get there, though, a half dozen panda cars roared onto the dockfront roadway. Lights and sirens were ominously absent.

The small police cars pulled up in front of The Squire and Pipe, and each disgorged four bobbies of such gargantuan size it was a miracle of modern policing that they all fit into the tiny vehicles. Without hesitation, and with obvious glee and determination, the uniformed mob charged up the three steps leading to the entrance and barged into the pub with drawn truncheons.

Hot on their heels, Den pushed by me and took the stairs to the second floor two at a time. Behind me, Martin and Watford each had a hand on my back pushing upwards. We passed Reggie Leggit in the top hallway as he was dropping down through an overhead skylight.

Watford had his shotgun unsheathed and was covering our back for any activity from the doors we were passing in our quest for the back room. Dispensing with any legal technicalities, Den hit the last door on the landing with the surprising force of his meatless shoulders and blasted it off its hinges. The sight which was revealed staggered all of us into momentary nonaction.

The scene in the room looked like something out of an X-rated film. Brody and Donovan were each on separate, sheet-worn, sagging beds. Both of them were naked and coupling athletically with thin angular women.

The montage was stunning in its surprise, it was the last thing we'd expected to find behind the locked door, and our hesitation was deadly. Brody was the first to recover, throwing himself off the bed and toward us with all the power of an enraged bull. The revolver in Den's hand cracked twice and blossoms of red spurted through the hair on the big man's chest. The trauma didn't even slow him a little. The women began screaming hysterically.

Still in the saddle, Liam bent sideways to grab a stiletto from the bedside table. Quick as a ferret, he threw it with incredible accuracy into the throat of Harry Martin, who was trying to bring a shotgun to bear on the action. Martin dropped the gun, which discharged into the floor, and grabbed at his neck as he tumbled to the ground.

Liam reached for another knife, but I had no chance to see what he did with it because Brody, his legs pushing him forward like pile drivers, wrapped his arms crushingly around Den, and drove him backward into me and through the door.

I heard Den cry out in pain as Brody tried to punch his head through Den's body. Behind the pair of them, I was hopelessly pinned against the far wall of the hallway. A fourth body piled into our scrum as Watford entered the fray. He scraped Den and Brody off of me with a driving tackle which took the three of them to the floor. When I looked up, I saw Liam framed in the doorway, a look of hatred on his face as his arm pulled back to let fly with the other knife.

This time there was no hesitation on my part as I dove to the floor. The knife thudded into the wall where I'd been standing a millisecond before. Rolling to my feet, I charged toward Liam's naked figure.

I wasn't fast enough, however. Liam moved with startling speed. Seemingly in one movement, he turned back into the room, bounced off the bed, and crashed out through the pane window on the far side of the room.

I ran to the shattered window and looked down. Liam's woman began hitting me with tiny, hard fists. I grabbed both of her hands and shoved her away from me. Outside the window, it was a fifteen-foot drop to the roadway, but Liam had survived it and was staggering upright on shaky legs. A couple of old dock goats, who had been making their way to the pub, stood staring in fascination at the naked apparition which had crash-landed at their feet. I couldn't believe Donovan's luck.

It was funny how my world had changed. A week earlier, I'd merely been going through the motions of living—not happy, not sad, just existing. And it was okay by me. I didn't care anymore. I had cut off my nose to spite my face. If I couldn't be what I wanted to be, or do what I wanted

to do, then fine, I'd continue to go through the motions—
no more, no less—until it was over.

Since then, though, I'd been beaten, pushed, provoked,
and forced to confront the evilness of my self-pity. The
dying embers of the man I once was had been fanned to
life again. I'd started on the road back, and now all the old
fighting reactions within me screamed for me not to let Liam
escape.

With a pillow from the bed, I knocked out the worst of
the remaining glass shards from the window and climbed
through. I maneuvered quickly but carefully until I hung
down from the sill facing the outside pub wall. Tiny splin-
ters of glass cut into my fingers, but I pushed out from the
wall with my feet, released my grip, and dropped into space.

I landed on the balls of my feet, cushioned the shock
with my knees and rolled forward on my shoulder, which
brought me up sharply against the pub wall again. The
gravel of the roadway had abraded my hands and torn
through my trouser knees and jacket shoulder, but I didn't
have time to worry about the damage. I scrambled upright
and took off at a fast jog in the direction I'd last seen Liam
heading.

The trail was easy enough to follow. The glow from the
streetlights eerily illuminated splashes of fresh blood from
Liam's wounds. It would be amazing if the man didn't bleed
to death before I could catch up with him.

As I rounded the bulk of a freight container, a slight
sound made me duck instinctively. A two-by-four stud whis-
tled over my head and smashed into the corner of the container right over a "Fragile" sticker. Liam pulled the board
back for a second swing, but I stepped inside and hit him
twice in the face as hard as I could.

The blows staggered him, but he didn't go down. Instead,
he jabbed out with the board and caught me in the side
under the ribs. I dropped to the ground and lashed out, my
foot striking his knee. That got him, and he went over backwards, his head striking hard on the edge of the dock. Another two feet further and he would have been in the water.

"You!" he said as we both regained our feet and forced air down our lungs in preparation for a second bout. "You one-eyed git. We should have done for you upon that bloody farm."

"Why didn't you?" I asked.

"Made the mistake of trying to follow orders instead of instinct."

"Whose orders?"

"Get stuffed." Liam feinted toward me with his right fist and then followed up with a left jab which caught my cheek as I rolled away from the punch.

The blow opened up the gash originally made by Sean's knife. Blood ran down into my mouth. The taste was . . . invigorating. The pain . . . ecstatic. Yes, ecstatic. I was living now. Living again.

Even in the dim light, Liam must have seen the change of intensity in my features. I'm sure he did because suddenly I became aware of the fear in him. We circled each other warily.

"Wot you grinning at?" he asked unsurely.

I hadn't realized I was. Then I felt the tension at the corners of my mouth.

"I'm enjoying this," I said.

"You're crazy. There's no difference between you and me. You know that, don't you?"

"There's a world of difference."

"Hardly. You love pain. I can see it in your face."

"I love your pain," I corrected him. We were both standing still now, Liam with his back to the water, both panting like rabid dogs. "How does it feel?"

"How does what feel?"

"To see your mate killed before your very eyes. Sean was your best mate, wasn't he? You'd finally found a kindred spirit, and now he's gone. He's lying up there right now, a hulking pile of flesh and bones festering in his own excrement. Think about how you feel. And then think about the feelings of all those left behind by the victims you've murdered."

"I'll get you, you bastard. I'll come back and get you. And then I'll kill everyone in your entire family." Liam took a fake step forward and then turned to run for the side of the dock. A heartbeat later, he was diving into the murky waters of the harbor.

I was right behind him, but I still wasn't fast enough. The shock of the cold water exhilarated my entire body, but my groping fingers failed to connect with anything even remotely human. I thrashed around and around, dove under the surface again and again until my lungs screamed for mercy. I searched the waterline of every ship within swimming distance. Liam was gone. But I knew he wasn't dead. He'd be back. He'd promised.

"What the hell happened to you?" Sir Adam asked as I dripped back into the pub.

"Had an urge to go fishing."

"Catch anything?"

"Nothing but a cold. You should have seen the one that got away, though."

Sir Adam nodded his understanding. "We'll get the river police out."

"Won't accomplish anything. If he's alive, he'll be long gone by now."

"Still, we have to go through the motions. If they can drag up a body we'll be able to fill in another integer in the equation."

"Aye, you're right. But you know as well as I do that, like Brody, Liam is not the sort to die easy." I paused as a uniformed constable came up and whispered something in Sir Adam's ear and was then waved away. "How are things here?" I asked.

"A bit of a bloody mess."

The uniformed bobbies had herded everyone over into the public bar to keep better control. The private snug where we were was empty except for official presence. I walked to the bar and helped myself to a brandy. I knocked it straight back and poured another which I took over to the table where Sir Adam sat.

"Den is upstairs filling in the locals." Sir Adam indicated the direction with a shrug of one shoulder. "There are two dead."

"Harry Martin?" I asked.

"Yes. And Sean Brody. He died hard. He took three blasts from a shotgun, but he still kept coming forward like something out of a nightmare. A fourth blast finally took him down."

"Did he live long enough to tell anyone anything."

"Only long enough to tell us to sod off. That was it."

"Damn."

"How about Donovan?"

I thought about our conversation, to try and remember anything pertinent. "He said something about acting under orders at Wren's Haven."

"Interesting, but we figured as much. He tell you who?"

"Fat chance."

"Hmmm . . ." Sir Adam made a noise in acknowledgement. "What now?"

I looked at him. "There's too many coincidences for all of this not to be tied together somehow. The death of Maddox, the problems with the Ravens, and Sean Brody, Liam Donovan, and their mysterious orders." The taste of blood reasserted itself in my mouth. "They're all pieces of a puzzle which fit tightly together. I can feel it, and I won't stop until I've found out how. I'm not going to sit around waiting for Liam to pop up out of the blue to wreak his vengeance."

The second brandy burned down my throat, and when I spoke again my voice was coarse. "When does my plane leave for America?"

EIGHT

THE RAVENS POPPED for first class seats on British Airways. During the twelve hour trip from London to Los Angeles, Sticks and I considered the gesture nothing short of a blessing. Wallowing in the luxury, Sticks kept up a steady patter with the stewardess and imbibed vast quantities of free champagne and beer. I stayed confined to mineral water in hopes of getting the upper hand on jet lag—which is often aggravated by alcohol.

I had eaten the fairly decent food, watched the fairly indecent movie, and napped on and off while constantly trying to find a comfortable position for my legs. Sitting in the first row behind the bulkhead helped, but flying has never been my favorite mode of transportation. I don't have a fear of flying; it's just that, even in first class, it's so uncomfortable.

"I was in the States with Wolverhampton back in 1967," Sticks said suddenly.

"In Los Angeles?"

"That's right. Well before your time."

"Was it some kind of tour?" I asked.

Sticks settled himself back in his seat with another can of beer. "We played a whole summer season here. Back then there was a huge effort to get soccer off the ground in America. There were three business groups interested in starting a professional league, but only one, led by an entrepreneur mannie by the name of Jack Kent Cooke, was able to obtain official sanction from the United States Soccer Federation."

I nodded my head to show Sticks I was listening. It didn't take much more to keep him going once he got started on the history of the team he'd been with since year one.

I already knew the USSF was the national controlling body for soccer in America. They had been both a blessing and a curse for the game in the States, but anyone connected to a professional soccer league not sanctioned by FIFA, the world governing body of soccer, or a FIFA-ordained national controlling organization—such as the USSF—would be branded as outlaws and banned from playing anywhere else in the world.

FIFA had recognized the USSF in the early 1900s when soccer in America was little more than pick-up games between colleges and occasional ethnic leagues started by immigrants homesick for their national sport. It was this ethnic factor, however, which played hell with soccer gaining a footing among traditional American sports. Teams with names like Clan McKenzie, New York Hungarians, Anglo-Saxon F.C., Spanish-American F.C., and Over-Seas F.C. tell the story. Each team was composed of immigrants, each jealously guarding the honor of the old country, which did little to spread or endear soccer to the American mainstream fan.

Sticks was continuing with his monologue. "The Cooke mannie had a two year plan to start importing players for his league from around the world and from the American colleges. However, the two business groups who didn't receive the nod from USSF got together and decided to get in a year ahead of Cooke by starting a 'pirate' league."

"They actually tried to buck the FIFA sanction?" I was shocked. Right or wrong, FIFA had a worldwide monopoly where soccer was concerned. Going up against them was like David taking on Goliath and forgetting to bring his sling.

"These were American businessmen looking to make a profit, and they weren't going to let an organization of amateurs stand between them and their money. They didn't believe FIFA was influential enough to stop them."

"They must have had a rude awakening when they started trying to recruit."

"Oh, aye. They were only able to attract fourth-rate, over-the-hill, or broken-down players who had nothing to lose if FIFA banned them from playing anywhere else in the world. Still, somehow they got enough personnel together to start a league."

"How did Jack Kent Cooke respond?"

"Cooke didn't want this pirate league stealing his thunder. So, instead of waiting his time and recruiting individual players to make up the teams in his new United Soccer Association league, he imported complete foreign teams to represent the cities that had been assigned franchises. Good old Wolverhampton was brought over to represent Los Angeles. When the invitation was extended, we had just fought our way back into the First Division, after our two year relegation to the Second Division, and it seemed like a good way to celebrate."

The stewardess came by with another beer for Sticks and another mineral water for me.

"Wait a minute. I vaguely remember hearing something about this American trip when I first joined the Wolverhampton Junior team. Didn't we win the championship or something?" I asked.

"Spot on. The final game was one to remember. We were matched up against the Washington Whips. They were represented by the Aberdeen Dons of Scotland. We'd split games with them during the regular season, and there was certainly no love to be lost in any England-Scotland outing, as you well know.''

I nodded my head. International matches between England and Scotland were among the fiercest rivalries in the world.

''It was an aggressive, high-scoring game,'' Sticks reminisced. ''The score finished up five-five at full time. Six-six at the end of the first overtime. Eight-eight at the end of the second overtime. And finally, Derek Dougan put the winner in during the sudden death overtime to make it the Los Angeles Wolves nine and the Washington Whips eight. It was a blood and thunder match.''

''Sounds like quite a spectacular one. What happened to the league afterwards?''

''The same thing which has always happened to American soccer. Both the pirate league and Cooke's league eventually folded due to infighting within the USSF, bad gate receipts, and a lack of effort to bring American players into the game.''

''Is that the bottom line? Or is there some other reason why the most popular sport across the rest of the world can't generate enough interest to support a professional league in North America? I mean, people have killed themselves and each other over the game elsewhere.''

''Bah!'' Sticks snorted. ''There's a whole list of reasons for soccer's troubles in America. Everything from American fans not being satisfied with a low-scoring sport to the lack of ability to develop a distinctive American style of play. As far as I'm concerned though, the biggest reason is that American kids aren't weaned on the sport like they are elsewhere. There isn't a crib in Europe or South America that doesn't have a soccer ball in it before it has a baby to cradle. In America the cribs have footballs, baseballs, or basketballs in them. Soccer is an afterthought.''

''You paint a grim picture.''

''But not an unrealistic one. There is a bright side, however.''

''Oh, yeah.''

"Interest is picking up. Look how well the U.S. team performed in the last World Cup."

I gave Sticks a dirty look.

"Don't start with me," he retorted, reading my mind from my expression. "I'm not going to tiptoe around you like everyone else does. You didn't get to play in the bloody tournament yourself. Well, that's just too bloody bad. Find a way to live with it, or go cry in someone else's beer."

I grunted. Changing the attitudes which I'd worn like a cloak of armor since my accident was not going to be an overnight job. But I'd have to keep trying.

"As I was saying," Sticks resumed, "the U.S. team did better than ever before in the last World Cup tournament, and that has helped to generate interest in the fact that the next World Cup, in 1994, will be played in America. If the USSF plays their cards right, they might even be on the brink of bringing soccer to the forefront of the American consciousness.

"The youth movement in the country is strong and getting stronger everyday. In fact there are more kids involved in youth soccer leagues than in all the youth football and baseball leagues combined. The college game is getting stronger and is even producing a few players of a high enough caliber that they are able to find positions on teams in Europe or South America. The spark is ready to be struck, and this time, perhaps, it will be enough to set off the prairie fire which will sweep the soccer revolution across the nation."

"Fancy talk," I said, impressed.

"Beer talk," said Sticks. He crushed the can in his hand, put it on the floor beneath his seat, burped gently, and closed his eyes to sleep.

As we thundered on toward our destination, I thought about what Sir Adam had said about the Ravens not being able to survive a major scandal. I thought about American soccer on the brink, and I wondered about fate and my part in the scheme of things to come. My stomach began to fill with butterflies. I was actually going to play in goal again.

A few days earlier that concept had been absolutely beyond me. I was scared, but I kept thinking about what Sid Doyle had told me—every day you go out and compete against yourself. If you always do the best you can do, you always come back a winner. I was tired of being a loser. I was going to have to go out and do my one-eyed best. I fell asleep and dreamt I was in the land of the blind where the one-eyed man is king.

As we stepped out of customs into the reception lounge at Los Angeles International Airport, a rapier-thin black man stepped forward. He was wearing a sharp-fitting black suit, wraparound sunglasses of the thin band style currently in vogue, and a peaked chauffeur's cap.

"Mr. Chapel and Mr. Johns." He gave out our names in a posh English accent, making them a statement instead of a question. "Ms. Brisbane sends her apologies for not being here to greet you. Unfortunately she had to attend a business meeting with her father. My name is Reeves. I'm to install you in your digs and then deliver you to the Acropolis."

Without further ceremony, he loaded himself up with our gear in a display of strength and coordination that belied his build. I wasted a second wondering how he picked us out of the crowd and then realized I was the only patch-eyed man in the terminal. As Reeves took off with our luggage, I gave Sticks a querying frown. Falling into step, we followed the young man to where a royal blue limousine was waiting silently in a red zone.

Our luggage was packed in the vehicle's voluminous boot, and Reeves installed us within the cocoon of the car's plush interior. He slid himself into the drivers seat and turned to talk to us over the backseat. "How was my English accent and manners?" he asked.

I laughed. His accent now was broad Texas.

"I'm serious," he said, switching to the nasal tones of Brooklyn. "I have an audition coming up for a role as an

English butler in a new sitcom. You guys have been my first chance to do my act for the real thing."

Sticks glanced at me. "Sitcom? Audition? Real thing?" His expression suggested we'd landed on Mars.

I put a reassuring hand on his arm. "You were letter-perfect," I said to Reeves. "Had us fooled all the way."

"All right!" the young man said with excitement and clapped his hands. "You gents just relax while I get this elephant to the space station." He now oozed ghetto jive. I was sure it was as put on as the rest of his repertoire.

I sat back with a laugh.

"Did you understand a word he said?" Sticks asked in bewilderment.

"Welcome to LA, pardner."

"Thank goodness Reeves's English accent is better than your Texas twang."

Sticks poured champagne and twiddled with the television dials. I looked through the tinted windows and had my first up-close look at an LA freeway traffic jam.

"I could get very used to these creature comforts," Sticks said. He twisted open a bottle of ice cold mineral water which had been nestled next to the champagne and handed it to me. "No wonder the Ravens are operating at a loss. First class flights, limousines . . ."

"I think you can attribute the VIP treatment to personal, out-of-pocket expense by Sir Adam," I interjected. "I certainly don't see this type of treatment as the norm even if this is the land of plenty."

"Guilt coming home to roost on the big man's shoulders?" Sticks asked.

"Sir Adam Qwale has never experienced the emotion of guilt in his life. Underneath his amiable, country gentleman exterior is a heart as cold and hard as the balls on a brass monkey. When we were operating in Ireland, he was an absolutely ruthless bastard. He demands value for money. We're going to pay the price for his largess."

The limousine swiftly took us from the airport's downtown location, across the natural dividing boundary of Mulholland Drive which ran across the crest of the Hollywood foothills, and into the diverse communities of the San Fernando Valley. Using his many accents, Reeves provided us with a nonstop travelogue which helped to begin my orientation to the city. Eventually, using a rich Irish brogue, he informed us we were switching from the northbound 405 freeway to the westbound 101. A few seconds later, he was pointing off to the right side of the vehicle to indicate the Greek-flavored architecture of the Acropolis sports complex. We traveled past it and exited the freeway a few miles further at the Topanga Canyon off-ramp.

Everything around us seemed spread out and yet jammed together at the same time. The stores and car sales lots appeared huge by English standards, but they appeared one after another in an almost seamless puzzle picture of concrete and steel. The only patch of green anywhere was the small park which circled the Marriott Hotel to which Reeves delivered us.

"If you gents will check in at the reservations desk, I'll make sure your cases are brought right up. Once you're installed to your satisfaction, I'll be waiting down here to take you to the Acropolis." Reeves had reverted to his English butler's toffee-nosed mode of speech. He opened the door for us, and we stepped into the climate-controlled environment of the hotel's lobby.

Within ten minutes, we were treated to more evidence of Sir Adam's excess. The reservations clerk was a competent young woman who seemed to have been briefed to expect our arrival. She had a sparkling, toothpaste-ad smile and she turned the wattage up as she handed a key to the bell captain and told us to "Have a nice day."

A silent elevator took us up to a two-bedroom penthouse suite with a large common room and kitchen. It was lavish beyond anything either Sticks or I had ever experienced. There was a discreet knock at the suite door which opened to reveal another bell man with our luggage on a large trolly. The bell captain, seeing me struggling to sort out some American money, assured me that was not necessary as everything had already been taken care of in advance. I glanced at Sticks, who looked as if he had dropped through Alice's rabbit hole.

Our cases were brought in and stored away, lights were turned on, towels fluffed, cabinets and refrigerators opened to reveal stores of drinks and snacks. A large basket of fruit wrapped in brightly colored cellophane, and the inevitable bottle of champagne were trotted out for admiration. Finally, the bell captain bowed his way out the door, also telling us to "Have a nice day."

The whole set-up was overwhelming and unnecessary, but if Sir Adam had set it up, then who were we to complain?

I took a quick shower while Sticks bounced on both beds to decide which bedroom he wanted, and within thirty minutes we had rejoined Reeves in the limo. With consummate skill, he negotiated his way through traffic and sped us back to the environs of the Acropolis.

The sports complex itself was a huge circular building set in the middle of a gigantic empty parking lot. The surrounding territory was obviously designed as a recreation area within the city. Reeves informed us that we were in the Sepulveda Basin, which encompassed the Acropolis, Balboa Park, a golf course, running paths, bike paths, roller skating paths, model airplane flight sights, a reservoir and dam, barbecue pits, picnic tables, and tennis courts. Like most things in America, it was done on a large scale.

The exterior of the Acropolis was festooned with huge columns carved into effigies of Greek gods. Zeus and Poseidon did battle with thunderbolts and tridents across two opposing columns, Athena strummed a zither on another, and Aphrodite graced a fourth. Over the main entrance, Apollo rode his sun chariot in a curve above six-foot Greek style lettering which spelled out: ACROPOLIS.

"Impressive?" Reeves asked.

"In a gaudy sort of way," I replied. "Do you know what the seating capacity is?"

"Seventeen thousand."

"How often is it filled?"

"You're getting into questions which are out of my area. I just drive for Ms. Nina."

"It's a little late in the game to start playing hard to get. The role of the closed-mouthed confidential employee is far from your best. The gossipy know-it-all is a far more interesting character anyway."

It was Reeves's turn to laugh. "You want to hire on as my drama coach or something?" He hesitated for a moment, as if marshalling his thoughts.

"Listen," Sticks whispered during the pause. "You've managed to silence the mouth that moves at the speed of light."

I elbowed him, not wanting Reeves to hear him and take umbrage, although that was highly unlikely. I'd dealt with characters like Reeves before, and knew that, once you got them to start dishing the dirt, almost nothing would stop them. Nina Brisbane's driver could be a good source of information.

"Most of the Corinthians' basketball games are filled to capacity. Mr. Brisbane didn't mess around when it came to laying out money to attract talent to the team. They've made the play-offs the last four years straight—and for a five-year-old expansion team that feat is almost unbelievable. The local fans have really shown their support and appreciation."

"What else draws?"

"The rock concerts do big business, and the special boxing and wrestling events pack in the crowds."

"What about the soccer and hockey teams?"

"LA's other hockey team steals most of the thunder from our own Blade Runners, and the Ravens crowds rarely run over five thousand. The tennis and volleyball teams are gaining in popularity, but that isn't saying much. Neither operation has developed much of a following as a team sport."

If that were true then it looked like Nina and Caitlin Brisbane were both fighting uphill battles to keep their team franchises solvent. It didn't sound like either one had the inside track to Daddy's fortunes.

Reeves pulled the limo up at the player's entrance and ushered Sticks and me out of the vehicle and through a set of large double doors. We passed through a very modern locker room and weight room and on into a long corridor. The sound of soccer balls bouncing off boards could be heard coming from the far end.

"The Ravens are having a practice session," Reeves informed us. "Ms. Nina and the others you need to meet should be waiting for you. I phoned ahead. When you're finished, I'll be available to take you back to the hotel."

We left the dark of the corridor and stepped out onto the pathway surrounding the playing surface. Twelve oddly clad bodies were engaged in a scrimmage, racing up and down the artificial turf with genuine intensity.

The play was coming toward our end of the building and the ball suddenly ricochetted off the Plexiglas directly in front of my face. I was startled and looked out onto the field with irrational anger to see who had kicked the ball.

Time seemed nonexistent. I couldn't breathe. My heart ceased beating. I went deaf. All play had suddenly stopped. Staring at me with a mocking glare was my worst nightmare.

Kurt Wagstaff.

NINE

"SO! THE ENGLISH primadonna has decided to come out of hiding."

The sarcasm in Wagstaff's voice wrapped around me like a suffocating shroud. My heart started beating again, slamming around in my chest as if it were a wild animal. I felt dizzy and disoriented and put a hand on Sticks' shoulder to steady myself.

"Stay tough, son," Sticks said quietly.

"Did you know about this?" I asked back in the same tone.

"I never would have let them break it to you this way if I did."

I felt hot all over and I knew the expression on my face must have made me look like an idiot. I fought for control.

Somewhere I found my voice. "Look at this. Kurt Wagstaff. How the mighty have fallen." It all came out a little squeaky, but it hit home. Wagstaff's face clouded over as if a freak storm was passing across it. Dark images moved in the pupils of his eyes like sharks beneath a deep sea.

The two of us stood, as if rooted to the ground, engaging in some kind of juvenile stare-down contest, until another voice broke across the scene.

"Well, somebody sure knows how to make an entrance." The tone was sensuous and smoky—familiar. I broke eye contact with Wagstaff and looked toward the speaker. Because of the voice, I was expecting to see the veiled visage of Nina Brisbane. Instead, I was confronted by the beautiful face of a woman who in every other physical attribute could have been Nina's twin. I was instantly sure this was Caitlin Brisbane.

She laughed gently when she saw my expression. It wasn't a pleasant sound. It was as if she luxuriated in possessing the surface beauties which had been torn away from her sister. This was not the first time she'd played this trick.

"I'm Caitlin Brisbane," she said, and extended a slim hand. "From what I understand, my sister is pinning some very high hopes on you, Mr. Chapel." She held on to my hand for several seconds longer than was necessary.

"I hope her faith won't be misplaced."

"I'm sure it won't." The tone of double entendre in her voice was heavy-handed, filled with greedy sexual promise.

By this time the rest of the team had gathered around to see what all the commotion was about. Sticks and I walked forward and stepped through an entrance door in the wooden, waist-high barrier which surrounded the playing area. The Plexiglas, which Wagstaff had smashed the ball against, only augmented the wooden barrier behind each goal.

The players made a pathway as we approached them, and Nina Brisbane walked through them from the other end to greet us. She wore tight-fitting jeans over black high-heels, and a eggshell-blue silk blouse topped with a single strand of pearls. The black veil was held securely in place by a matching pearl headband. It was a simple outfit, yet she wore it—as she did the veil—like the height of fashion.

"Good to see you, Ian," she said in the voice which was so like her sister's. "I see you've met Caitlin." I sensed she was looking over my shoulder to where I knew her sister was standing. "And this is my father, Terrance Brisbane." She turned to introduce a man large in both girth and height and possessed of the fullest head of white hair I'd ever seen. "He, of course, owns the Acropolis and all its various enterprises." He had penetrating eyes above a veined drinker's nose, and the full pouting lips which he'd passed on to Caitlin. They looked better on her.

He said hello in a thick and obviously phony Irish brogue, and shaking hands with him was like arm wrestling a polar bear. He gripped my hand before it was fully pressed against his palm, and then ground down on my knuckles. I smiled at him as I brought my other hand forward as if to make an oversincere two-handed grip. Surreptitiously, I pressed a knuckle into a pressure point on the back of his hand. Pain flickered briefly in his eyes and he released my hand quickly. He smiled—a polar bear discovering a penguin who fights back. I think he was actually amused.

Other introductions followed quickly. Dressed in ill-fitting sweats of black and green—the Ravens' team colors, Stavoros Kronos, the Ravens' coach, was a fireplug-sized man with a bald head and a fierce disposition. The names of the team members, Hank Decker, Chico Juarez, Pat Devlin, Pepe Brazos, Jackson Bopha, Alan Hardacre, and others, rolled by so fast I knew I would have trouble remembering them all. Other than Wagstaff, who was milling around on the perimeter of the group, I knew none of the players personally. I was, however, familiar with the reputations of a couple.

There were two final introductions. Nick Kronos, the coach's son, was introduced as one of the team's backup goalies. He shook my hand, but gave me the evil eye to let me know he wasn't pleased with my presence. I'd probalby put him out of a starting job, so I could understand his feelings.

The Ravens' other goalie gave me a warmer welcome and also another shock. Bekka Ducatte was tall, with the build of a dancer except for perhaps a bit too much breadth of shoulder. Her muscles were long and lithe and possessed a definition which only comes from years of hard workouts. She was wearing shorts and an old Ravens uniform shirt which had been cut off at the midriff. Below the shirt, the muscles of her abdomen rippled easily and displayed a navel which would have done any female genie proud. A long rug burn, caused by sliding on the artificial turf of the indoor soccer surface, ran down the length of her thigh. It looked painful.

Her strawberry-blond hair was bobbed short in front and was drawn into a shoulder-length ponytail in back. A minimum of makeup covered the scattering of freckles across her high cheekbones, and ice-blue eyes looked out from under long lashes. On first impression, she was just another of the vaunted California golden girls, but a second look immediately told you she was far more. I had a sense that she was something special and my breath caught in my throat.

"It's a pleasure to finally meet you," she said as she shook my hand. Her mouth was a little wide, the lips naturally red and bee stung. As a feature, though, it gave the warmth back to her face which the ice of her eyes detracted. "Your timing in goal is incredible. The best I've ever seen. I've studied films of your games over and over." In the background, I heard Wagstaff snort in disgust at this statement.

My tongue was so thick that, "Thank you," was the best reply I could come up with. My heart was slamming around in my chest again, but for a totally different reason than before. I'd never in my life experienced such a strong initial reaction to a woman. Things were happening too fast for me. Between being ambushed by Wagstaff and having Bekka set off my emotional fireworks, I felt out of control.

It was ridiculous. I'd never been afraid of anything in my life. Anger, frustration, self-pity, and bitterness were old friends, but fear was a stranger I was not yet prepared to meet. I shook myself mentally. Wagstaff be damned, the bastard owed me and I was not going to hide any longer.

I turned to Stavoros Kronos, the coach, "Where can I kit up?" I asked.

"Aren't you jet-lagged?" Nina asked in surprise when she overheard my request.

"Working up a sweat is the best way to catch up and get the kinks out," I told her. I turned away to follow Kronos back to the locker room.

Sticks shot me a concerned look, but I knew what I was doing. I was taking charge of my life again and letting the chips fall where they may.

The practice game was charged with electricity. I'd started out a little tenuously, but as I warmed up I could feel my old game concentration coming back along with my confidence. At first there were few shots on goal and those I deflected or scooped up with little problem. None of the shots came from Wagstaff, however. He was always there, playing on the opposing team, working for an open shot, but I was able to keep short-circuiting his opportunities.

Bekka was playing in goal at the other end of the field for the black team while I was playing for the green. It was only a practice session, but as it was a warm-up for the play-offs, Stavoros drove everyone relentlessly. His Greek accent was heavy, but his voice was loud and intrusive and everyone got the message. His combination of English and Greek expletives was as colorful as it was imaginative.

As the practice wore on, I was able to see the distinct differences between the Ravens' two playing lineups. The front line for the green side had a distinctly Latin flavor, led by Pepe Brazos, Chico Juarez, and Danny Castalano. Brazos and Juarez were both Mexican. Short and fast, their style of play blended well with the flamboyant personality and incredible footwork of the Brazilian Castalano—who was rapidly becoming the local fan favorite.

The short, quick passing techniques of the Latin type of game leant themselves well to the indoor soccer environment and provided the high-scoring games which the American crowds expected. The style also appealed to the heavy

Latin populations in Los Angeles who made up the bulk of the soccer fans in the area.

Backing up the Hot Tamales, as the Brazos, Juarez, Castalano front line was called, were two American players, defenders Hank Decker and Mitch Dakota. I learned later that both young men had come up through the ranks of the collegiate system; Decker from Yale, and Dakota from the University of Southern California. Both were solid, if unimaginative, players. Like many American players, their previous experience had failed to give them a vision of the game which is second nature in other parts of the world—a vision which puts the game on a metaphysical level where every pass and every move is part of a larger, some would say, cosmic, game plan. This is not to say that Americans can't become good players—both Decker and Dakota were very good—only that they won't become great or inspired players until they recognize and reach for the same mystic magic in soccer that they apply to their other national sports.

By contrast, the black team's front line of Wagstaff, the diminutive Irishman Pat Devlin, and the tall South African Jackson Bopha, took their brand of soccer directly out of the relentless, deliberate, long passing attacks of the European playbooks. They had made the Ravens the first team to successfully bring the air game—involving head shots and passing—to indoor soccer which, because of the confines of the field and goals, is usually played most successfully with the ball below waist level.

The defense for the black line also carried on the European tradition with Alan Hardacre, once a top sweeper for England's Spurs, and the Hungarian, Birch Bloodworth. The Hungarian had been nicknamed "Blockhead" because his massive square head appeared to be directly attached to his muscular shoulders without the aid of a neck. Bloodworth was the team's enforcer and had spent more time in the penalty box—a device American indoor soccer had stolen from hockey to spice up the game—than any other Ravens player.

It seemed to me that it would have been more logical to

have me playing with the black team's European-style lineup. However, in a real game the goalkeeper is very rarely substituted, while the other players are frequently alternated en masse to keep fresh legs on the field—another innovation American indoor soccer has borrowed from hockey. Thinking about it, though, I figured that after my initial confrontation with Wagstaff, Kronos wanted to match us against each other to see if sparks would fly. If there were going to be fireworks, it was for sure that the coach wanted them out of the way before the play-off games started.

He didn't have long to wait before his worst fears became a reality.

Pepe Brazos had taken a wall pass from Castalano and with a quick touch had pushed it underneath the leaping body of Bekka Ducatte for a goal. While he and the other Hot Tamales held a subdued celebration, I watched Nick Kronos behind the player's bench arguing quietly, but vehemently, with his father. It was clear he thought he should be in goal on the playing field instead of Bekka, but Brazos's shot had been neatly placed and I doubted if Nick could have stopped it either.

On the ensuing kickoff, Wagstaff pushed the ball to Jackson Bopha who started a dribbling run up the field with the considerable skill. He passed off eventually, but got the ball back on a give-and-go from Devlin to beat Alan Hardacre on the right side and then let loose with a power shot on goal.

I jumped up a little to catch the ball between my arms and my stomach. This helped to absorb the power which might have caused a rebound had I caught the ball against the harder surface of my chest. As I touched down again, I took a terrible whack between my shoulder blades which drove me to my knees. The blow had been delivered with consummate finesse, hiding the jolt and making my fall look like uncoordination on my part. I held on to the ball, though. When I regained my feet, I turned quickly to confront

Wagstaff. He stood casually with a familiar, insolent grin plastered across his dark Germanic features.

I restricted my anger to hissing the word, "Bastard."

"No more than you," he hissed back through his goading smile. "And there's much more where that came from," he said before jogging slowly away and deliberately bumping shoulders with me as he passed.

I stared after him.

"Get the damn ball in play, Chapel!" The shout from Stavoros broke the spell and I threw the ball accurately downfield to the feet of Chico Juarez.

Bloodworth, who had been badly out of position when Brazos had scored, moved quickly this time to break up the Hot Tamales' play. Ruthlessly, he cut down Chico Juarez with a vicious sliding tackle which should have been reserved for game play instead of practice. Chico ended up in a heap after tumbling arse over tea kettle.

I waited for an explosion from Stavoros, but it never came. Instead, Bloodworth moved down the field like an out-of-control locomotive. In indoor soccer, the fullback defenders play more like outdoor soccer midfielders and often take the ball through on offense. Jackson Bopha dropped back to cover the hole left by Bloodworth, while Wagstaff and Devlin raced to assist him.

Watching the play develop, I felt a cold chill slide up my spine. For a split second, I caught Wagstaff's eye and realized I was being set up. With deliberation, depending on shock value to throw the play slightly off, I did something which I never would have considered a day or two earlier. I grabbed the bottom of my black cotton eye patch and ripped it from my head before throwing it like a gauntlet onto the playing field. Uncovered, the puckered pink scarring of my empty eye socket glared out defiantly at the world.

The action caused Bloodworth to hesitate for half a step, but Wagstaff took much of the sting out of the gesture by intentionally trampling over the discarded patch. The black front line continued their approach.

Bloodworth sent a high cross, from left to right, to the head of Devlin. In a neat display of skill, the young Irishman nodded the ball down to his feet and volleyed a pass low across the goal mouth. The ball ran across the top of the penalty box, putting it at the farthest point of my control. I dove for it, stretching full out before I saw the error of my action.

Wagstaff was running in, his leg muscles unleashing for a deadly shot. I saw his foot twitch as if changing targets again, as it had done over and over, ad nauseam, in my nightmares. If Wagstaff was testing my nerves, he was in for a shock. I slid across the artificial turf toward him, ignoring the burning pain in my forearms. At the last second, instead of going for the ball, I pushed up with my hands and pumped hard with my legs. My body propelled forward and I drove my head into Wagstaff's unprotected midsection.

Crashing to the floor, he grabbed at me with his hands and pulled me down with him in a tangle of arms and legs. We rolled around like kids fighting on a schoolyard, the other players jumped out of our way to avoid the melee.

I heard Bekka Ducatte's voice rising over the rushing in my ears. "Stop them! Stop them before they hurt themselves!" she yelled.

I felt a hand reach out to pull me away from Wagstaff, which resulted in the German managing to get in a head butt.

Another voice broke in with an order. "No, let them fight it out." It was Stavoros. "If they're stupid enough to carry grudges let them get it out of their systems now."

Blood was pouring out of my nose and it tasted coppery in my mouth. I broke free of the hand restraining me and drove my thumbs into Wagstaff's side. He howled in pain and rolled away from me. I let him go. If it was a fight he wanted, I wasn't going to wrestle with him. I wanted to be on my feet.

The combat was going to be tricky. I'd been trained in some very deadly arts in the SAS, but as much as I hated

the man I didn't want to cripple him. The short-term satisfaction of such an action would quickly be offset by the
remorse of sinking to his level. However, I was damn well
going to make sure he knew he'd been in a room with a
tiger.

Both of us were on our feet, surrounded by a circle of
yelling players and staff. Caitlin Brisbane's cheeks were
flushed with excitement, her eyes dancing with blood lust.
Nina Brisbane, however, was conspicuous by her absence.

I waited for Wagstaff to make the first move, and he came
in fast and low like a charging bull. I did a fast double take
with my head to judge my distance, and stepped to one side
like a toreador. Caught off balance, Wagstaff blundered past
me. I hit him with a hard, open-handed blow over his left
ear. He returned the favor with a stiff-handed jab to my ribs.
We disengaged and began to circle.

Wagstaff was wary now, curbing the fire of his anger in
favor of a calculatingly cold brutality. He had a reputation
as a hard man and he was giving me no indication to the
contrary. I could feel him sense my reluctance to commit
him grievous bodily injury, and I knew he harbored no such
worry.

He moved in now, like a cat pouncing at its prey. He
threw a barrage of punches and tried to tie me up in a clinch
in which he could beat me at his leisure, but I was more
than ready to meet him and far more than willing. I parried
his punches on my forearms, slipping them easily, but I let
him have a couple of free body-shots to think he'd hurt me.

When he made his move to clinch me, I slipped inside
his reach, grabbed his shirt with one hand and his extended
right wrist with the other. I turned my hip into him and
threw him with a movement I'd practice over and over in
the SAS until it was second nature. I held on to his wrist
and as he sailed through the air I twisted his arm so that it
popped out of the socket. Wagstaff screamed with pain as
he slammed to the ground.

I have to give the man credit for guts. With the sweat of
excruciating agony beading on his forehead, he picked him-

self up off the floor, turned away to face the playing area's retaining wall, set himself in position, and then slammed his shoulder into the boards to pop it back into place. It was obviously an injury he'd experienced before, and he knew instant relief would come once the appendage was back in joint. It would swell up and be sore later, but the immediate pain was over.

Like a wounded lion, he suddenly charged at me with a terrifying rush which caught me off guard. He collided with me and we crashed to the artificial turf in a flurry of driving elbows and gouging fingers. I went back to using the tips of my thumbs, a routine taught to me by a tough Sergeant Major, and drove them unmercifully into Wagstaff's ribs, groin, and kidneys, but he seemed beyond pain. However, when he started raking his stiffened fingers again and again toward my good eye, I decided to put an end to the festivities.

I chopped down hard with my forearms and broke the armlock which held me to Wagstaff's chest, and rolled away. As we came to our feet, I attacked with a series of hard-hitting, open-handed blows to Wagstaff's head, and then followed up with jabs to his iron-hard midsection. When he moved to retaliate, I used my leg to sweep him off his feet.

He landed hard on the ground, his head bouncing off the surface like a rubber ball. I gave him a second to allow his vision to clear and then cocked back my leg to kick him in the face.

I watched his expression change. An eye for an eye: I saw it run clearly through his brain. It was the vengeance he would have sought, and he could easily conceive of some-one else taking the same line.

"No!" he screamed and rolled away with his arms covering his face and head.

I made to follow him, but I felt the light touch of Sticks's hand gently land on me from behind.

"It's finished," he said softly.

Adrenaline raced through me looking for an outlet, and I turned toward a loose soccer ball and unleashed my kick.

The ball shot like a rocket across the playing area and into the stands.

There was a general hubbub as all the onlookers began to talk at once. Sticks put his arm around my shoulders as I stood staring at the ground and breathing heavily. I could still taste blood in my mouth and I was beginning to shake.

"Would you have done it?" Sticks asked, knowing I was asking myself the same question.

"I wanted to."

"That's not the same thing."

"I know, but it's as close as I ever want to come."

Bloodworth and Devlin had helped Wagstaff to his feet. He staggered slightly, but pushed them away and walked unsteadily toward me. Everyone fell quiet. I couldn't believe he was coming back for more.

He stopped in front of me and stared hard into my one eye. "You fight like a German," he said.

I figured that was supposed to be a compliment.

"And you've got the guts of an Englishman," I told him.

He nodded and extended his hand. I shook it. He held on to my hand for a second and then spoke, "Between us we'll teach the rest of the bastards in the play-offs what soccer is all about."

The ball shot like a rocket across the playing area and into the stands.

There was a general hubbub as the onlookers began

TEN

"**W**HAT KIND OF display of macho belligerence was that supposed to be out there?" Nina Brisbane was spitting mad and I couldn't say I blamed her.

We were alone in her Acropolis office where she had demanded, via Stavoros, that I present myself after showering. The office itself was not large, but it was still intimidating because of its stark decor.

Behind a white antique desk, a picture window displayed a solid green expanse of golf course. On the opposite wall, a low white love seat sat beneath a huge Angus Myrtle original. The scarlet and black slashes of paint which screamed across the canvas gave credence to the painting's attached title—*The Heart Of Chaos*. I wondered if Nina had chosen it for its aesthetic value, its monetary value, or because it pertained to something more poignant in her personal life.

Between the desk and the couch, two ornate visitor's chairs stood patiently on the antique white carpet. I sat in one of the chairs while Nina Brisbane wound down.

"Sir Adam assured me you were going to be an asset to this team. I think the statement he made was, 'He'll be the difference between winning the play-offs and abandoning the franchise.' This team is on the edge and from what I saw out there this afternoon, I may as well put my head in the noose and kick the chair out from under me. I'd rather do it myself than wait for Caitlin to do it."

I saw my chance to interject and perhaps get something useful out of this conversation. "Just how bad is the relationship between you and your sister?"

"What relationship?"

"Like that, is it?" I took the cold compress away from the scratches around my good eye. The blood seemed to have stopped oozing, but I wasn't going to win any beauty contests for a while. A fresh black cotton patch was respectfully back in place over my puckered socket, and I had to keep twisting around in my chair to relieve the aching residuals of the fight.

"My sister and I hate each other as only people who are related can. I don't give a damn about my father's money or the control of his business interests—I'm good enough to make it on my own in any other business I choose—but I'll be damned if I'm going to let Caitlin walk away with everything just because she's currently Daddy's little favorite. She's got about as much business sense as a fence post and has an IQ to match." Quivering with anger, she stood up from the chair behind her desk. "But all of that is beside the point. We were talking about your behavior."

I was rightfully chastised, but I was aching too much physically to put up with any more haranguing. "You're right," I told her sincerely. "Both Wagstaff and I were out of line, but we're now at a point where we can concentrate on playing soccer instead of trying to score points off each other. The fight was stupid and juvenile, I'll grant you, but perhaps it was the best way to stop further trouble between us. I could rant and rave about being ambushed with Wagstaff's presence. . . ."

"I didn't know . . ." Nina tried to interject, but I overrode her verbally.

"It doesn't matter. Let's put both the ambush and the fight behind us and get on with saving the Ravens and winning the play-offs."

Nina still stood behind her desk, leaning forward now, with her fists on the polished tabletop. She didn't say anything for a bit, and I could feel the heat of her glare burning through her veil.

"Do you really think we can win the play-offs?" she asked finally. The emotion in her voice was almost pleading. Perhaps, as she'd said, she could make her mark in any other business she chose, but making it in her father's world was far more important to her than she was willing to let on. I sensed her desperation had much more to do with gaining her father's approval than getting the upper hand over her sister.

"I'm in no position to give you any guarantees," I told her. "I believe Sir Adam has an overinflated view of my talents both on the playing field and in the investigative sense. However, I agreed to give you my best effort, and I will."

"I'm not interested in any investigation." She had taken on a haughty tone. "The police are handling the Maddox murder, and I don't see how it affects the Ravens except as a publicity tool. My only concern is seeing this team win the play-offs and keeping this franchise afloat."

"Quite the ice queen, aren't you?"

"How dare you."

"I dare because it's true. A man is dead. Murdered. A man who played for your team and helped you get through the season in a position to win it all. What if Maddox's murder is connected to the downfall of the Ravens? What if the police are too late to figure out what is really going on? They seem to think the crime is simply connected to a string of local muggings. Sir Adam believes differently."

"And your money is with Sir Adam?"

"He's never steered me wrong before."

"What is that? More of your macho male-bonding crap?" I looked down at my hands and didn't respond.

"I don't care what Sir Adam thinks." Nina was working herself up into a fury again.

"He is your partner," I pointed out.

"That may be, but only because his money was in the right place at the right time, and it spent like any other. You do what you want with your investigation, Just make sure you make practices and that you don't give up any free goals on game nights."

I looked up at the black veil over Nina's face and remembered how I was before my interaction with Sid Doyle had put my handicap into perspective. It is amazing how sometimes the longest emotional journeys can be accomplished in the shortest of time periods.

I stood up and took the one step needed to bring me into a mirror-image position facing Nina on the opposite side of her desk. We stared at each other. At least I believe we did. Even up close it was impossible to pierce the thick folds of black lace.

With one hand, I reached up and popped back my black patch to reveal the puckered socket underneath. If I wasn't careful, the action could become a habit. I put my hand back flat on the desk and continued to stare.

Nina didn't move, but I first sensed, and then heard her breathing patterns change. She was tense, almost sexually charged. I leaned forward to rest my body against the desk for balance, and reached out slowly with both hands. When there were no cries of outrage at my obvious intentions, I continued my actions and slowly began to raise the veil.

I swallowed hard, trying to steady both myself and my expression, knowing that I was about to reveal the remains of a face which had once been as strikingly beautiful as Nina's sister, Caitlin. The lace rose smoothly and I continued to stare at the top of Nina's head until I had the lace material turned back completely. Then, and only then, did I let my eyes drop.

The horror was no less than advertised. The facial flesh

was folded in on itself in puckered seams like a dried apple. The effect offset the alignment of her eye sockets, and I was startled to notice that one of the eyes was missing. Sir Adam had mentioned that Nina had lost an eye to the shotgun blast, but I had forgotten until now.

A single tear welled up in the remaining eye and ran freely down the mottled color of her skin to disappear between the living purple worms that were her lips.

The suture scars, from the Frankenstein stitching which had held the jigsaw puzzle of her face together, still showed white and livid, and small hairs sprouted grossly in various spots. The whole unsightly mess was framed by lifeless lanks of paste-colored hair hacked off at random lengths.

"Satisfied?" Nina asked.

I waited for a beat while maintaining eye contact. "That isn't one of the words I would apply to the situation."

"Oh? What words would you think appropriate?" Nina still hadn't moved. She was close to hyperventilating.

I sat down again to give myself a second to gather my thoughts. "Perhaps, I would say that I am now more at ease with the situation."

"Perverse curiosity satisfied, then? You show me yours and I'll show you mine. A comparing of war wounds."

"I was thinking more along the lines of a sympathetic sharing of burdens."

Even though she had been giving me a ticking off, I was somehow more at ease around this woman than most others. Maybe because the shared disfigurements gave us a common ground—much like the frank discussion of handicaps with Sid Doyle had helped me come to terms with other facets of myself.

"How far would you be willing to share burdens?" she asked.

"I don't understand."

"Could you make love to this face?"

"Is that an offer?"

"If you feel threatened, you can think of it as an academic question."

"I've never made love to faces, only to women."

"Then you're unlike any other man I've ever known. Tell me—if we were making love would you leave the light on?"

"I honestly have no idea."

Nina pulled the veil back into place, took a deep breath, and sat down. "Then don't think that just because I asked the question you'll get the chance to find out." She pushed herself back more comfortably in her chair before continuing along a different tangent. "You're the first person outside of my immediate family and the doctors who has seen behind the veil. What made you attempt it?"

"Because somebody else recently shared their pain with me and it made it easier for me to carry mine."

"Am I cured now, Doctor? Do I come out of hiding and parade my face around in public? Do I stop being angry?"

"Don't be bloody stupid," I said without heat. "Nothing can ever make right what happened to either of us. But someone who understands can sometimes help us face the next day or the next challenge." Sid Doyle had turned me into quite the philosopher. "It's a valuable lesson I've only recently learned for myself."

Silence stretched again. A clock chimed somewhere in another office. I readjusted my eye patch.

Nina fiddled with her watch strap. There was a slight catch in her voice when she spoke again. "I was born almost two years before Caitlin. I was ten weeks premature and it was a miracle I survived at all. I needed a lot of specialized care during my first few years of life, but my father always said I repaid everything by being a beautiful child with an abundance of talents both musically and socially. I learned quickly how to use my charms and talents to wind adults around my little finger.

"It was an act which caused a great chasm to develop between my sister and me as the years went on. Caitlin was a plain child, although you wouldn't know it to look at her today, and she was all thumbs and feet when it came to the social and artistic graces. The chasm was as much my fault as hers. She was jealous of the attention I was given, and I was greedy for the spotlight.'' She stopped talking to take a deep breath and expelled it as if she were trying to blow cobwebs off past glories.

"Everything changed, of course, when my face exploded.'' She actually laughed when she saw my expression shift with her use of words. "Yes, that's how I think about what happened. My perfect face exploded along with my perfect world. Instantly, I had been transformed into the Wicked Witch of the West, and just as instantly Caitlin seemed to blossom, and Father had a new favorite daughter.

"Seventeen operations later led to what you just saw— what the doctors consider a success.'' She waved her hands around in the air and theatrically raised her voice. "The patient lives. Long live the patient. A testimony to the god-surgeon's skill.'' She lowered her voice again. "I would rather have died.''

The sentiment sounded familiar. I opened my mouth to speak, but it was Nina's turn to cut me off.

"No questions. No condolences. I've had enough for one day. If you want more soul-searching, you'll have to wait.''

"I'll probably need more, especially about your father and other family skeletons.''

"The Irish connection rears its ugly head again.'' She chuckled ruefully. "Like I said, leave it for another day. If it will help solve the mystery of what happened to Maddox and what is happening to this team, I'll tell you what I can.''

She made a gesture of dismissal and I stood up. Her voice, however, stopped me at the door. I had a feeling the crux of the matter was coming.

"I need to win this one, Chapel.'' I knew she was not talking about the play-offs. "I need my father back. I need him to stop loving faces.''

I walked through the door. In my mind, I was remembering her one askew eye welling up with a single tear.

Walking back into the Acropolis complex, I was surprised to hear the continuing sounds of a soccer ball bouncing off the boards even though the regular practice session was long over. I made a quick detour to the locker room to pick up my gear bag, and then followed up on the noise of the bouncing ball.

The scene out on the playing area was as I had expected. When Sticks had not been waiting for me outside of Nina's office, I figured he was off somewhere pursuing his single-minded obsession. I had not been wrong.

On her knees, about eight feet back, Bekka Ducatte was facing the four-foot-high retaining boards. Behind her, Sticks was kicking balls so they ricochetted back off the boards, forcing Bekka to dive from side to side to stop them. Having the balls kicked from behind made it impossible to tell what side or what angle they were going to come from. It was a drill Sticks had forced me to practice over and over until I hated it, but it did wonders to improve reflexes and timing. I could tell from the way she was moving that the drill was playing merry hell with Bekka's knees despite the pads she wore, but I gave her credit for working on without complaint.

Finally, she made a rather spectacular series of dives, saves, and recoveries, and Sticks brought the drill to a close. He always had a knack of ending a session on a high point, judging to the moment when a player had received the most from a routine. Bekka collapsed on her side, breathing heavily. I made my presence known by starting a slow applauding. Both Bekka and Sticks looked around.

"Very impressive," I said to Bekka and she laughed.

"Is he always a slave driver?" she asked.

I nodded. "Now we're in America, I guess somebody should explain to him about your Mr. Lincoln and the Emancipation Proclamation."

"Bah! You're a couple of daft buggers," Sticks said. "Complaining about a speck of hard work."

Bekka and I rolled our eyes at each other. She smiled at me and laughed again. She shook her head slightly, in either amusement or weariness, and the movement tossed her hair gently around her shoulders. It was a simple movement, but something in it touched me and I felt my knees go rubbery. I leaned back against the boards for support, and noticed Sticks giving me a funny look. This was silly. How could this woman be having this kind of effect on me?

Bekka bounced up from the artificial turf when several men from the maintenance crew entered the arena to change it from soccer field to ice rink. There was a game scheduled that evening between Caitlin's Blade Runners hockey team and a Sacramento franchise.

"Thanks for the workout," she said to Sticks. "Can we do it again sometime? It's almost impossible to find a goal-keeping coach in America who really understands the position. I'm sure I could learn a lot from you."

Sticks's smile wrapped around his face from ear to ear. "I'll be around for a while trying to keep this lummox"—he jerked a finger in my direction—"in good enough shape to get down after the low balls. He fell in front of a bus the other day, but everything turned out okay because the bus went under him." Sticks cackled so hard at his own joke that I thought he was going to have a coronary.

Bekka walked over to me and put her hand on my arm. I jumped slightly at the contact, and when I looked into her eyes, I wanted to believe I could see something which indicated she had felt the electricity also.

"Would you wait around while I take a quick shower?" she asked me. "Perhaps, we could grab a bite to eat afterwards? Do you like Mexican food? There's a ton of stuff I want to talk to you about."

I agreed to wait, and Bekka jogged away to the women's locker room. I had wondered at first if there even was a women's locker room—it was not the usual type of consideration for a soccer team—and then I realized there were women on both the volleyball and tennis teams that were part of the Acropolis's other franchises.

Sticks finished putting balls and equipment away before walking up to stand next to me. "You better watch yourself around that one, Ian my lad," Sticks said softly as he looked down the player's tunnel where Bekka had disappeared.

"And what exactly does that mean?"

"Take a look in a mirror at the wistful expression on your face and you'll know what I'm talking about."

"Humpf!"

Before our conversation could deteriorate further, Nick Kronos came out of the player's tunnel. He walked past us as if we were invisible, and continued on to the player's bench, where he retrieved a pair of goalkeeping gloves. Stuffing them in the small duffel bag he carried in his right hand, he turned back toward us.

When he arrived at where we were standing, it looked like he was going to ignore us again. At the last second, however, he stopped and turned to face me.

"You must think you're pretty hot stuff to be stepping into a starting position on a team already in the play-offs." The statement was rhetorical, and since his face was clouded with emotional thunder, I didn't bother even attempting a reply. "But let me tell you, the Ravens don't need you, not while they've got me," he continued blithely. "I'll be playing on the American World Cup team next time around, and there isn't anyone better at playing in goal than me. Especially not you, old man."

I smiled. I knew the bit about the American World Cup team was a load of codswallop. It's great to be confident of your abilities, but no national teams had chosen their line-ups yet. However, arrogance is a wonderful weapon to turn back on its owner.

"I'm sorry," I told Nick. "I didn't realize you were God's gift to goalkeeping. I was under the impression that, until his death, Pasqual Maddox was the Ravens' starting goalie."

Nick glowered, or tried to anyway. His youthful looks, even though they were dark with his Greek heritage, defeated the effect. "Maddox was a miserable, drunken soak who couldn't have stopped a quadriplegic from scoring. His goals against average was almost the highest in the league. If it wasn't for all the game-saving goals scored by Pat Devlin and Danny Castalano, as well as some brilliant defensive players, our season would have been history long ago. Why

do you think I was always called in to handle tiebreakers?''
A tiebreaker was a series of five penalty kicks taken by each
team if a game ended in a tie after two overtime periods.
The team which scored the most goals in the tiebreaker
won the game.

"I played in a total of five games this season, and during
the entire time I was on the field not a single goal was
scored." Nick finished his outburst on a note of triumph.

"Then why was Maddox the team starter?" I asked.

"I don't know!" Nick waved his arms in frustration.
"Maybe he had something on somebody. Maybe there is
somebody who is jealous of me. All I know is, we don't
need you on the team."

"Nick!" The boy stopped his ranting and turned around
at the sound of his name being called. His father was standing at the entrance of the player's tunnel. "Get to the car
before you make a bigger fool of yourself than you already
have." Stavoros Kronos gestured with his arms in a signal
for his son to leave the area.

Nick hissed through clenched teeth. "You better get back
to England before the same thing happens to you that happened to Maddox." He turned away to pass by his father.

"I'm sorry, Ian," Stavoros said to me. He shrugged his
shoulders with a father's resignation. "He is a good boy,
and he will be a good goalkeeper one day if he can learn
patience."

Sticks turned aside Stavoros's proffered olive branch by
blurting out, "All he needs to do is keep his mouth open.
It's big enough to block the whole goal." I nudged Sticks
hard with an elbow and felt sorry for Stavoros, who looked
embarrassed. The coach shook his head and turned to follow his son's passage.

I rounded on Sticks. "Anyone ever suggest you get a
personality transplant?"

"Often, but I'm not one to take other people's advice
seriously."

"What were you trying to accomplish? The man was obviously trying to make peace."

Sticks shook his head. "You don't want peace around here. You'll never find out what's going on unless everything is kept stirred up."

"You have to let some things settle," I corrected him. "Otherwise the water is too murky to see clearly."

Bekka chose that moment to rejoin us. She looked bright and perky in a yellow sundress, which ended three inches above her knees, and low-heeled sandals over bare feet.

"You kids go on ahead without me," Sticks said. "I'm going to get Reeves to take me back to the hotel to catch up on my kip before I fall asleep on my feet." Without further ceremony he tipped an imaginary cap to Bekka and sauntered off.

"What a wonderful man," she said, looking after Sticks's retreating figure.

"Just wait," I told her. "After a couple of his relentless practice sessions you'll be wishing you never laid eyes on him."

Sweet tinkling laughter trickled out of her and she twirled like a young girl, her dress swirling around her, and gave me a happy smile. She suddenly seemed so feminine, I had trouble connecting her with the driven, professional athlete I'd seen during practice.

"Let's get out of here," she said, and took my arm to lead me away.

Out in the parking lot, she led me toward a late-model compact car which stood apart from any other vehicles in the almost deserted lot. Behind us I heard a motorcycle start up and turned to see a helmeted rider on a Japanese crotch rocket pulling away from the side of a column supporting the effigy of Zeus.

I turned back to my companion, but felt the hair on the back of my neck begin to prickle. The noise of the motorcycle became louder, and both Bekka and I turned around again.

The machine was almost upon us.

I pushed Bekka one way and then dove the other way, scraping my hands as I landed hard on the gravel parking surface. The motorcycle zoomed between us as the rider let out a war whoop.

Twenty feet further on, the bike skidded to a halt. The rider turned around in his seat to look at us through the smoke color of the full-face visor attached to his helmet. I picked myself up, wondering if the rider was getting ready to take another run at us, when he raised the visor and stared at me with hatred.

I thought for a split second that Wagstaff was not ready to bury the past, but suddenly I recognized another player in the game.

Liam Donovan was in town.

"The eyes of Mother Erin are upon you," he yelled at me. "And her sons will have their due!" He made a gun shape with his fingers and pointed it at me before popping his thumb down like a hammer falling.

As he accelerated away, his maniacal cackle rang in the wind behind him.

ELEVEN

WE SAT TOGETHER in the restaurant in high, cane-backed chairs on opposite sides of a small table. The motif surrounding us was that of a Mexican atrium garden decorated with terra-cotta floor tile, whitewashed stucco walls, profusions of colorful silk plants, and a small running fountain. Huge windows gave a view of an attractive row of eclectic shops along a busy boulevard.

A Mexican waiter kept running back and forth with an array of frothy drinks, chips and salsa, and the sizzling beef and chicken strips I was told were called *fajitas*. Wrapped in soft tortillas, along with bell peppers, tomatoes, refried beans, and onions, the fajitas made a filling meal to offset the effects of the salty margaritas.

The encounter with Liam Donovan seemed to have whetted our appetites and we ate like starving peasants.

On the way to the restaurant and while we were waiting for the meal to be served, we discussed the motorcycle attack as if it had been an act of random urban terrorism by a local tearaway. Bekka either hadn't completely heard or didn't understand Donovan's cryptic statements and seemed willing to go along with my own protests of ignorance.

As we ate, she had asked question after question about my playing background and my current magazine work. She drew anecdotes and memories out of me that I had thought were long forgotten. She was an animated listener, laughing in all the right places and keeping her face alive with interest, all of which helped ease my usual tongue-tied state. Finally, I changed tracks and brought the conversation around to her and her position with the Ravens.

"The university I was attending had both a women's and a men's soccer team, but the faculty followed the philosophy that never the twain should meet." She took another bite of fajita and chewed quickly. "I protested, believing the only way I could improve my skills was to play against the stronger male players. Chauvinism is rampant in sports, and society gets away with it because everyone points at the physical differences in strength and speed between men and women."

"You don't believe the speed and strength difference exist?"

"Of course they do. The problem comes up in some sports areas, though, where occasionally a woman comes along who can compete with male counterparts. If that is the case, she shouldn't be kept back simply because of her sex. Women have made inroads into some male-dominated sports such as drag racing and even basketball, if you consider the Harlem Globe Trotters athletes as opposed to entertainers, but it isn't enough."

"Are you suggesting all youth sports should be on a . . . What's the American term?"

"Co-ed?"

"Yes. A co-ed basis?"

Bekka thought about that for a few moments as she chewed more food and took a sip from her margarita. "In a perfect world, yes. Perhaps if girls and boys had competed

together from day one, they both would have evolved equally
and would now be able to compete on equal footing."

I shook my head. "I agree with your point that if a woman
is able to compete at a professional level in any sport, she
shouldn't be kept off a team because of her sex. However,
I don't see too many of the top professional women golfers
or tennis players—who might be able to compete in the
men's divisions—rushing to change the rules. And as far as
your views on youth competition in a perfect world, I think
you're full of bull feathers."

She almost choked on her drink, laughing. "Bull feathers? You sure know how to sweet talk a woman, don't you?"

I smiled. "Don't get me wrong. I'm full of admiration
for your playing ability and for your guts to follow through
on what you believe. You are perhaps the exception which
proves a rule. I'm all for equality, but your vision of a perfect world would negate many of the differences between
men and women—differences which I admire."

"If your sentiment about my abilities is true, and not
patronizing, I thank you. As for the perfect world, well . . .
the point is moot. As for the rest? I know I can make it in
the American soccer game, and I want to be the first woman
to break the barrier and play the game professionally."

"Aren't you already playing it professionally?"

"Huh! I'm being paid a very small honorarium for showing up at practices and looking pretty on the bench during
games. I've got a playing bonus, but it has never been ex-
ercised because I've never put one minute of field time in
during a real game. I won't consider my goal achieved until
I actually put in game time."

"Does the part about 'looking pretty on the bench during
games' bother your feminist side?"

"You got the wrong end of the stick. I'm not some raving, radical feminist. I agree with you. . . . Vive la différ-
ence between men and women. But the Ravens were the
only team willing to take a chance on me. If they want to
get some mileage out of the fact that I'm a woman, then

more power to them—because sooner or later they're going to have to play me to validate their hype.''

''What about Nick Kronos?''

''Now isn't he just the thorn on the rose? I wouldn't give the arrogant little twerp the sweat off my panties.''

''Colorful,'' I commented, and Bekka blushed amusingly.

''Ladylike too, I guess, but he really gets up my nose. I know for a fact that his father's coaching contract contains a clause that gives him total control over Nick's playing time. And Stavoros is doing his best to bring the kid along slowly, but the kid just doesn't have it.''

''Nick seems to think he does.''

''He also thinks the sun shines out of his posterior.''

I chuckled. ''Does Nick know about the contract clause?'' I'd never heard of such a thing before.

''Are you kidding? Because of his ego, he'd have a fit if he ever found out. Stavoros was the league's Coach of the Year last season, but the franchise he worked for gave up the ghost—it can happen to even the best of franchises if the corporate and fan support isn't present.

''The Ravens badly wanted Stavoros as a coach, and the only way he would come was if the Ravens also took on his son as the backup goalie. Stavoros has a blind spot where Nick is concerned. He truly believes Nick will make the American national team one day. Old Stavoros played for Greece years ago on their national team, and is filled with the dream of seeing his son repeat the feat in his adopted country.''

''How did you find all this out?''

''I used to date the Ravens' old coach,'' she told me as she pushed her empty plate aside. ''When Ms. Brisbane fired him, he spouted all this stuff off to me one evening in a fit of pique before tucking his tail between his legs and running off to take a coaching job at an Ivy League college.''

I felt a stab of irrational jealousy toward the ''old coach'' and hoped his new team lost every game. "And with him went your chances of getting into a game."

Bekka at least had the grace to look abashed. "These things happen, but this regime too shall pass. Maybe Nick will trip over his own mouth, fall in, and disappear down his own bum hole." She instantly put a hand over her mouth, as if surprised by her own bawdiness, then laughed when I did.

"Stranger things have happened," I said.

A busboy came by and swept up the debris from our meal. Close on his heels, the waiter returned with a dessert tray and steaming cups of coffee. When we were alone again, Bekka began toying with her strawberry cheesecake. I could tell she was building up to say something and I left her alone to get around to it.

"You're not just here to play soccer are you?" she asked finally. "And that man on the motorcycle has something to do with your other agenda, right?"

"What makes you say that?" She'd caught me at sixes and sevens with her questions. I didn't figure anyone on the team outside of Sir Adam and Nina Brisbane would know I'd been asked to do anything more than play in goal. And I thought I had her snowed where Donovan and his motorcycle were concerned.

"The rumor vine is buzzing with the fact that you were one of Sir Adam's tiptoe boys in Ireland. And Sir Adam hasn't exactly hidden the fact that he's not satisfied with the police explanation of Maddox's death."

"Where did you pick up the term 'tiptoe boys'?" I was stalling for time, and Bekka knew it.

She shrugged her shoulders. "I think it was Alan Hardacre who brought it up. He said you'd been some type of super undercover agent, or something, in the British army before you went on to become the hottest goalkeeping property going. He's followed your career closely."

"I'm flattered, but he's quite a bit off the mark."

"You didn't work under Sir Adam in the army?"

"I didn't say that, but Alan Hardacre seems to have been reading too many *Boy's Own* comics."

Bekka held me with a steady gaze and I realized that her eyes were not the ice chips I had first imagined. Now I could see the blaze of heat deep in the center of them, like the fire at the heart of twin diamonds.

"You can trust me," she said.

"So spake the spider to the fly." I was wary, even though I instinctively did trust her. However, if I was going to get anywhere fast with investigating Maddox's murder, I needed an ally who knew all or most of the players.

Bekka had dropped her eyes and had gone back to fiddling with her dessert.

"All right," I said. I reached out and stilled the hand holding her dessert fork. The contact suddenly seemed as intimate as if our lips had touched. "I'll trust you. Sir Adam seems to think I have an advantage over the police, where the investigation of Maddox's death is concerned, simply because of my knowledge of soccer and the fact that I can attack the problem from the inside."

"So he thinks that whatever you find out will be tied to the team in some way?"

"That about sums it up."

Now that we'd started getting the true confessions out of the way, Bekka dug into her cheesecake with gusto. You wouldn't have known she'd just finished a big meal.

"I think Sir Adam is on the right track," she said with her mouth full.

"You do? Why?"

She shook her head. "I don't know. It's just a feeling. Something more than just the animosity between Nina and Caitlin Brisbane. And everyone talks about Terrance Brisbane's ties to the Irish Republican Army, but I don't think that's all of it either. There's something else I can't put my finger on. Or maybe it's a combination of all three—the sisters, Brisbane and the IRA, and something from the unknown."

"Do you have any idea what the unknown factor is?"

"Like I said, I can't quite put my finger on it. Maddox was well past his prime, yet he stayed in as the team's starting goalie."

I drank deeply from my coffee cup, seeking a caffeine fix. "Nick Kronos told me Maddox's goals against average was one of the highest in the league."

"Well, he wasn't exaggerating that point. Maddox also had known problems with gambling and the bottle. On more than one occasion he turned up inebriated for a practice session. Somehow, he always managed to pull himself together by game time—much to the disgust of the more-than-eager Nick Kronos. In fact, Stavoros once caught Nick putting a bottle into Maddox's locker as a temptation."

"So Nick Kronos certainly wasn't put out by Maddox's demise."

She looked up at me sharply. "No he wasn't, but I didn't mean to make him a prime suspect. Nick is a spiteful little bastard, but I think murder is beyond him."

"Based on what?"

"I didn't just play soccer at university. I graduated with honors and a master's in psychology. Another year of internship and I'll have my doctorate. I might want to play professional soccer, but in this country you have to do something else as well in order to earn a living wage. Soccer isn't a sport most Americans think of when you hear about free-agent contract negotiations in seven figures. Or even five or six figures."

I leaned forward and put my arms on the table. "What about Maddox's gambling?"

"It's probably not what you think. The gambling on soccer in America is practically nonexistent. Certainly it isn't enough to make it worth bribing somebody to fix goals. In Maddox's case, a couple of the bent-nose brigade showed up twice that I know of to demand money. They were low key at first, but the second time they tried to get a little physical, which was a bad mistake. He might have been burned out when it came to keeping goal, but Maddox was a big strong man, and he dumped both mob boys on their heads. They never sent reinforcements, so I figure he must have squared the money side of things away.''

We finished dessert and pushed the debris to the side.

''Why are you so interested in helping me?'' I asked her.

The waiter came by at that moment to refill our coffee cups and clear the remaining dishes. He placed the check on my side of the table and made it very clear that he thought it was time for us to vacate the establishment in favor of new diners. I'm very good at ignoring that type of body language, though, and I always adjust the tip downward in accordance with the amount of subtle pressure applied.

Bekka leaned back in her chair. ''I want to help for two reasons. First, I was one of the few people who actually liked Pasqual Maddox. He was that rare male jock who didn't seem to feel the necessity of making a pass at every woman he came into contact with.''

''And your second reason?''

''Much more self-serving,'' Bekka said with a defiant shake of her head which made her hair sway again in the movement I found so delightful. ''As go the fortunes of the Ravens, so go my fortunes as a professional goalkeeper. I told you before that the Ravens were the only team willing to take a chance on me—albeit not much of one.

''If I can help you clear up this mess, then maybe you'll bug out back to your magazine desk next season, and maybe Nick Kronos will drop dead of debauched causes, and ta-da, I'm playing in goal for the Ravens.''

''That easy, huh?''

''Hey, I can dream, can't I? Now, what about this guy on the motorcycle?''

I drank more coffee. I wasn't sure how much to tell Bekka, but I knew I had to give her something.

''Well, I'm not exactly sure how he fits into all of this yet. His name is Liam Donovan, and he is some kind of terrorist attached to an IRA splinter organization. I had a rude introduction to him in England when he requested, in rather strong terms, that I not come to Los Angeles.''

"But how did he know you were going to be at the Acropolis?"

"Whoever sent him after me in England has to be connected with the team somehow. They probably met Donovan after practice to tell him I had arrived and to discuss what to do about me. Liam has a personal axe to grind also, and I think when he saw us in the parking lot, he couldn't resist rattling my cage."

"Is he dangerous?"

"Like a stick of sweaty dynamite."

A shiver ran down Bekka's body, and her eyes flashed.

I picked up the check from the table and slipped a sheaf of bills underneath it before helping Bekka up from her chair.

"Do you want me to take you back to your hotel?" she asked when we moved outside to the parking lot and entered her car.

"Not right away," I told her. "First I want you to tell me a little about the rest of the team, and then I want you to help me run an errand."

"Okay. What do you want to know?"

"Give me a brief rundown on the team's strengths and weaknesses."

She rested her hand against her headrest and closed her eyes in thought. "The weaknesses are easy. We have a major problem with the two styles of play on the field, European and Latin. They don't mix well and neither do the players or even the fans.

"We have a large contingent of die-hard Latin fans who come out to see the Hot Tamales shake-and-bake with their flashy passes and fast and furious play. We also have an equally rabid group of fans who come up from the Santa Monica area, which is a bastion of British immigrants. They love to see Wagstaff and Devlin on the field, and they go as far as throwing trash on the field—which stops the game— when the Hot Tamales come on. We've had more than one fight in the stands between the two sets of fans. And they're both rooting for the same team."

"What about strengths?"

"They can be summed up in two words—Patrick Devlin."

"The little Irishman?" I was surprised.

"Absolutely. He is the only one of our players who can move freely between the two styles of play. He is our one uniting factor, and as a result he's scored more goals and has more assists than any other player. At the end of the regular season, he was named Most Valuable Player for the entire league. Whether or not the Ravens make it through to the finals, Pat Devlin will be there to receive his award at halftime."

"What about Wagstaff and the others?"

"Do you figure Wagstaff as the villain of the piece?" she asked with a mischievous twinkle in her eye.

I grimaced. "I'll not make out that he's my favorite person, but I'd not considered railroading him."

"Too bad. He's almost as big an ass as Nick Kronos."

"He's a hell of a lot better player, though."

"You can say that again. He's tied with Danny Castalano as the team's second leading scorer, and it really chaffs his buns. I've never seen anybody as intense as Wagstaff, but it's a trait which seems to short-circuit him more often than not."

"I see your psychology major isn't going to waste."

Bekka chose to ignore this and continued on. "The other players are the usual mix of over-the-hill or second-rate European or Latin players who couldn't make it in their own countries, or young American players like me who don't know any better."

I laughed out loud at this. "You won't make me believe that you, especially, don't know better. I think you have some grand plan set aside to take Europe by storm someday soon."

I could tell I was hitting close to the mark because she immediately changed the subject.

"What was that errand you wanted to run?"

"I want you to take me shopping for a motorcycle."

* * *

"Why in the world do you want a motorcycle?" Bekka asked after I had given her a slip of paper with the address of a local dealership.

I'd planned on using a motorcycle for transportation even before leaving England, so one of the first things I did when we checked into the hotel was to check out the dealerships in the phone book. Los Angeles and the San Fernando Valley are vast communities, and I felt sure I could find what I was looking for without too much trouble. However, there only seemed to be one establishment within the local area which fit the bill.

"I want a motorcycle," I explained, "because I'm not going to rely on Reeves and his limo to chauffeur me everywhere I want to go."

"You could rent a car."

"I'm more comfortable on a cycle. I ride one at home, and it suits my disability better than driving a car."

"If you say so." She looked again at the address I'd given her. "This is only a little further up the boulevard. We'll be there in five minutes." She started her car, put it into gear, and pulled out of the restaurant lot.

She caught the expression on my face.

"Did you forget something?"

I shook my head. "It's far too late now. I'm out of practice for more than just goalkeeping."

"What do you mean?"

"I just got through telling you what a dangerous man Liam Donovan is, and yet I didn't even think about checking out your car until after you started the engine."

"You mean for a bomb or something?"

I gave an affirmative nod, and Bekka turned a little pale in the streetlights which now streamed through the car's window.

"This game is for real, isn't it?" she asked, slightly shocked.

"Liam Donovan wants me badly. I don't think a few extra bodies one way or the other are going to make any difference to him.'' I didn't want to be melodramatic, but I'd dealt with characters like Donovan before and I knew the word "conscience" wasn't in their personal dictionary. Bekka needed to know what she was getting into by helping me.

I watched her driving and cursed myself for the feelings which were stirring within me toward her. I was giving Donovan, and whoever was controlling Donovan, an edge. Even having known her for what amounted to just a few hours, I was aware she could already be used as a lever against me. Plus my emotions toward her were distracting me. I never would have started a car up in similar circumstances without checking and double-checking if I was running on the cutting edge of cold logic instead of heated emotions. I would have to be very careful or we could end up losing far more than the play-offs. Love, or lust, or insanity, or whatever this was, obviously was a gremlin which delighted in choosing the worst possible moment to assert itself.

When we parked again, Bekka looked at me quizzically. I understood why. Behind us on both sides of the street were the garish lights and gleaming machines of numerous car and motorcycle dealers, but the address we were parked in front of had no machines on display and a rather dingy façade.

In large white letters, a sign on the building proclaimed: EUROPEAN MOTORCYCLE SALES & REPAIRS. Painted flags of the European community surrounded the lettering. A smaller sign told us to enter from the rear, so we hiked around to the back of the dealership and had a pleasant surprise. Rows of bikes could be seen through plate glass windows and the open service bays were bustling with activity even though we were well into the evening hours.

"Can I help you?" a voice from behind us asked.

Bekka and I turned to confront a lanky youth who was wiping his hands on a scrap of cloth. He wore clean, pressed overalls which had a smear of fresh grease down one leg. The youth rubbed it self-consciously.

"I'm interested in buying a cycle," I told him.

He looked at my eye patch dubiously.

"I ride a BMW RS-90 at home, but I need something to get around on while I'm here." This statement launched a conversation about BMW bikes, my reasons for being in America, and exactly what I was looking for in a cycle. It also gave a platform from which the youth introduced me to his father, Spiros Jaul, an Austrian immigrant who knew motorcycles inside out and loved soccer with the heart of a true fanatic. When he found out who I was, he couldn't do enough for us.

It was quickly clear that the front of the business was far from indicative of its status. The service bays were immaculate and crammed with local European cycle enthusiasts, all working to perfect the performance of the oddest assortment of cycles I'd ever seen gathered together.

"They are good people," Spiros explained. "Most of them are from the old countries or are first-generation American and proud of it. By making the bays available to them, it provides good business for me. They are loyal customers and it keeps Mica and his friends off the streets." He affectionately cuffed his son on the head.

"Oh, Papa," the boys said with slight embarrassment. He was in his middle teens and appeared bright and personable.

Spiros took us around into the showroom and through the rows of new and used Motoguzzis, Triumphs, Nortons, Husqvarnas—the top Swedish dirt bikes—Ducatis, and various other esoteric European manufacturers. He didn't have a BMW RS-90 in stock, and he refused to sell me any of his other similar BMWs because they had not yet been reconditioned to his satisfaction.

"Couldn't you settle for something normal, like a Honda Gold Wing, or a Suzuki, or maybe a good old American Harley?" Bekka asked in frustration after we had seen most of the cycles in stock.

Spiros looked at her with deep sadness in his eyes. "You have a lot to teach this one," he said to me cryptically, and then turned away to whisper in his son's ear. Mica moved quickly away.

"The Honda Gold Wing is basically a two-wheeled Winnebago," I told Bekka, referring to a popular brand of motorhome. "The other Japanese rocket bikes have too much power and not enough sureness of handling for my one-eyed liking, and Harley-Davidsons are basically reserved for rebels without a clue."

Spiros laughed, but Bekka sniffed. "I'd be careful where you spread such blasphemies," she told me. "Those are fighting words if I've ever heard them."

In the back of the shop an engine turned over and settled into a distinctive rumble. I instantly looked at Spiros, who flashed his teeth at me when he knew I recognized the sound.

"A Laverda," I said to him.

"Yes, yes," he said, clapping his hands. "I thought it might interest you. It is a 1978 in beautifully restored condition."

"Three cylinder, 1000 cc engine?"

"Absolutely. Nothing else sounds like it."

"What's the cylinder alignment? Two up and one down, or one up, one down, and one in the middle."

"The latter. It made for better optimum horsepower."

"Orange or black?" I asked. The Laverda had been manufactured in the two colors by an Italian tractor company whose owner and sons dabbled in motorcycles as a sideline. It handled better than most Japanese bikes and was much faster than the British cycles.

"Come and see for yourself," Spiros said, and led the way.

We walked quickly through to a small room at the back of the shop. Mica was standing near the beautiful black Laverda. His smile was a duplicate of his father's.

The cycle had twin disks on the front and the typical sport style handlebars for leaning into the wind. It was also taller than most Japanese cycles because of its higher ground clearance.

I wanted it immediately. "Find me a helmet," I said, and sealed the deal by taking out a thick book of traveler's checks.

There was another reason for the motorcycle, which I hadn't discussed with Bekka. If I spotted Liam Donovan again, I wanted a two-wheeled chance to catch him.

TWELVE

FOR MOST OF that night, I slept the sleep of the dead. I'd ridden the Laverda back to the hotel after saying good night to Bekka and acquiring a stack of local maps from Spiros. After the events of the day, I had reveled in the feeling of power I always keyed into when riding a motorcycle. The wide city streets were a dream, and I'd found my way back to the hotel faster than I would have liked.

One of the hotel's parking valets was a bike fanatic, and he fell in love with the Laverda as quickly and I had done. He promised to park it in a nearby protected area. I over-tipped him, happy with the arrangement since it would keep the bike handy as well as safe. I entered the hotel and made my way up to my room.

Sticks was already sawing logs with the rattling sounds which can only be produced by the true mouth-breather. I had to close the doors to both his bedroom and my own in order to cut the noise of his snoring to a reasonable level.

I had planned to lie in bed and think through the events

of the day, to decide what steps I was going to take next, but the instant my head hit the pillow, I was off to the land of nod. I didn't actually go to sleep. I passed out instead.

Ten hours later, as my jet-lagged sleep receded, I dreamt mixed-up dreams filled with images of Nina Brisbane lifting her veil to reveal Bekka's face, only to have it explode like a cartoon character's demise. My agitation over the dream affected my breathing, which woke me up as 8:15 A.M. clicked over on the digital clock.

I am a firm believer that whoever invented mornings should be taken out and shot, so it was a cranky Ian Chapel that I dragged out of bed and put through a half-hearted exercise routine. My body had stiffened up from the flight with Wagstaff, and even after a twenty minute hot shower, it hurt to raise my right arm above shoulder level.

Sticks, knowing well my morning moods, had gone out after leaving me a note stating he would see me at the Ravens' afternoon practice. Left to my own devices, I eventually wandered down to the Marriott's dining room for breakfast. The waitress was young and pleasant, and I ordered something called the lumberjack special, orange juice, and a pot of coffee. She smiled and bounced away full of light and joy. I really hate morning people.

The lumberjack special turned out to be a tall stack of pancakes topped with three eggs, a side of sausage, and enough hash brown potatoes and toast to feed an army. I was just taking the first sip of juice when Caitlin Brisbane stepped up to my table. She looked trim and sultry, with a knowing expression on her face beneath perfect makeup.

"Do you mind some company?" she asked, and slid into one of the three empty chairs without waiting for an answer.

Ancient habits die hard, and I had purposely sat facing the entrance to the dining room, but I had not seen Caitlin enter. She must have been lying in wait for me at another table or booth, and I wondered what she would have done if I had ordered room service. She placed an elegant eelskin handbag on the table between us.

"To what do I owe this honor?" I asked. I gave the rest

of the room an unobtrusive scan to see if she had brought along any other company. There was some furtive movement in a rear corner booth.

"Oooh," she faked a shiver and ran her hands up and down the sleeves of her pink cashmere sweater, making her breasts bounce around like bear cubs fighting under a blanket. "If the temperature in your voice drops much lower, we're going to have to move this conversation closer to the equator."

I ignored this. "How long have you been waiting for me?" I said, not raising the temperature any.

"About two hours," she said. At least she was not going to try to con me that this was a chance meeting. "But I think you'll be worth the wait."

"That probably depends on what you're waiting for."

The radiance of her smile spread slowly across her face, and I could almost feel her turning up the heat of her raw sexuality. It made me think, though, of the emotional electric shock I'd experienced when I first laid eyes on Bekka. I knew immediately that there was nothing this woman could offer me beyond the physical.

At some other point in my life a physical spark might have been enough. However, at the moment I still hadn't had a chance to come to terms with what I was feeling toward Bekka. I hadn't even been able to consider what she might be feeling toward me. All I knew was that Bekka had definitely thrown a spanner into my emotional works; so much so that the sexual sparks flying off Caitlin Brisbane were having as much effect on me as a hammer on an anvil.

While Caitlin watched, I dug into the breakfast in front of me. She poured coffee into one of the extra cups on the table and allowed me to struggle with a full mouth when the waitress came by to ask if everything was okay.

Oblivious to the fact that we were sitting in a nonsmoking area, Caitlin took a slim cigarette out of her handbag and used an inlaid pearl lighter to set flame to it. She released smoke through flared nostrils, an action which immediately negated any sexual pull she might have tried to exert.

She put the lighter back in the handbag and pulled out a fat envelope. She placed the envelope on the table near my left hand and left the handbag open. I stared at the envelope.

"I won't beat around the bush," she told me. "My sister thinks I don't have the brains of an earthworm, but she's wrong. I have an MBA degree and I am a certified public accountant. I know my father's sports businesses from the inside out, and when he retires or dies, I am determined to take over from him. I deserve it. All the time everyone spent coddling Nina over her face, was time that I had to help keep Father and his enterprises together. He was a basket case for a long time after Nina was shot. If it hadn't been for me there would be no spoils to fight over. Just because Nina is Daddy's favorite little girl, his poor wounded bird who needs to be protected, is no reason why I should be cut out of things."

I wondered which of the two sisters really was Terrance Brisbane's favorite. Each one thought it was the other, and it was easy to see how the bitter gulf between the two women had developed. Perhaps, I thought, Terrance Brisbane nurtured the feuding between his daughters as his revenge for neither of them being sons.

I also wondered what Mother Brisbane made of all this and figured I'd set the cat among the pigeons by asking.

The question made Caitlin laugh nastily. "Our mother was thrown out on her ear years ago when Father became convinced she was incapable of giving him a male offspring. There has been a succession of step-mommies since then, but not one of them has produced any further siblings for us to squabble with. Life would be a lot less expensive for him if my father would just admit he's become sterile instead of blaming each successive wife."

As often happens when I hear the horror stories of other people's upbringings, I felt blessed a thousand times over for the loving family which I came from. When Gerald and I fought, it was always out of love, never from hate or jealousy.

I shrugged as I finished my breakfast. "What does all this have to do with me anyway? I'm a goalkeeper, not a probate solicitor."

"You know damn well what this has to do with you. I'm sure my sister has explained how my misguided father plans to make a decision regarding his business interests. Everything is based on the success or failure Nina and I experience with the teams he's given us to run."

"From the look of things, I would have thought you had the upper hand. Hockey and volleyball over soccer and tennis?"

"Under normal circumstances, perhaps, but not at the moment. The Blade Runners have little chance of climbing out of the league cellar before the end of the year. That type of position makes fan support an oxymoron. And as far as volleyball is concerned, the team indoor game has not yet developed the following that the two-man beach game has.

"Nina has gotten lucky. Tennis has always been a big draw in this town, and her LA Rackets team tennis group has done well. And even with their own fan support problems, the Ravens have done even better. By getting into the play-offs, the Ravens are starting to develop a following. The death of Pasqual Maddox and the fighting in the crowds have also brought the team additional notoriety which is catching the public's attention.

"The competition for crowds in Los Angeles is tough. The teams which were established before my father opened the Acropolis are still the big crowd-pleasers. Nina and I are left fighting for the dregs. If the success of the Rackets and the Ravens keeps building, I'm in danger of losing what crowds I am getting. Everyone loves a winner, and Nina's teams are the ones doing the winning."

The Acropolis looked like a healthy concern. Even the dregs Caitlin was bemoaning could still add up to a good-sized gate. Still, I could see Caitlin wanting to attribute her sister's successes to fate rather than hard work.

I stared pointedly at the envelope which was still on the table.

"Look for yourself," Caitlin said, catching my gaze.

I picked up the envelope and hefted it in my hand. "Is this how much a one-eyed goalkeeper is worth?" I asked.

"You tell me."

I opened the envelope and with exaggerated movements I allowed the wad of thousand dollar bills to fall onto the table. I picked one up, held it by my face to examine the beautiful artwork splayed across the green bill, and smiled. I was enjoying myself. I even knew what I was doing.

"How much is here?"

"Fifth thousand."

"And what exactly do you expect for your fifty thousand?"

"How about a sudden muscle tear before the next game?"

"Stavoros will just replace me with Nick or Bekka."

Caitlin snorted like a stallion in heat. "That would be like replacing Babe Ruth with some sandlotter."

I picked up all the bills and tapped them into a neat pile. "Is this how much you paid Maddox to maintain the highest goals against average in the league?"

"He wasn't in your class as a goalkeeper. He took what he could get to feed his vices, and he was happy to do that well."

"Fifty thousand isn't in my class either," I said. I was interested to see how far she would go.

"A hundred thousand," she offered without hesitation.

"Three hundred thousand." I had the pleasure of seeing her blanch.

"Don't price yourself out of the market," she said.

"We're talking millions and millions of dollars on the line here if your father leaves control to you. What's a few hundred thousand between friends?"

"A hundred thousand now, and two hundred thousand when the Ravens are eliminated from the play-offs."

"I want something else also," I told her.

Her sexual antennae suddenly quivered as she interpreted the quickening of interest in my voice. This was something she understood very well. It was also something she enjoyed holding over her sister—using her beauty to get the physical reactions which would forever be denied to Nina.

"I can't imagine what else you could want," she said, and moved her body under the table so one of her thighs rubbed up against me. She also leaned forward so the ∨ of her sweater lowered to reveal creamy cleavage. She was as subtle as a bricklayer.

I put my left hand on her thigh. "Oh, I think you can imagine," I told her.

"Tell me," she said. One of her own hands was busy below table height.

"All right," I said. "I want the tape recorder in your handbag."

I was quicker than she was. My right hand shot into the handbag and came up with the miniature recorder before Caitlin had changed gears from sexual assault to the realities around her.

"You bastard," she hissed. She swung a hand to slap my face, but I caught it before it finished its arc.

"If you knew my mum, you'd realize there isn't a chance I'm illegitimate."

There was movement behind me, and I knew Caitlin was trying to keep me distracted. I put my foot on one of the extra chairs around the table and shoved it for all I was worth.

The chair skittered over the dining room's beautiful tile floor, collided with a scrawny man in jeans and a bulky sweater, and knocked him to the floor. The camera around his neck spat out its innards as it smashed against the tile.

I released Caitlin's hand and turned to the man. Heads in the restaurant were turning our way. "I'm terribly sorry," I said, helping the man to his feet. I reached over to brush him down and at the same time, I popped open the back of the camera to expose the film. "What a shame," I said, in a solicitous voice. "I hope your holiday snaps weren't on this roll."

"I'll sue you, you prick."

"Take your best shot, mate." I turned back to face Caitlin, but she was on the move out of the restaurant. I left my newfound friend to follow her.

Reeves and the Acropolis limo were waiting out front. I thought Reeves only drove for Nina Brisbane, but it was becoming clear that he was a general dogsbody. It would be interesting to talk to him further at some point in the future.

I stopped behind the hotel's glass doors to watch as Reeves opened the limo's rear doors for Caitlin. When he did so, I saw another man in the interior. At first I thought it was Terrance Brisbane and then realized the man was too small. The only connecting factor had been the head of white hair. The door closed again before I could get a better look at the man. Reeves saw me and tossed off a friendly salute along with a roll of his eyes. I wondered who he was impersonating today.

I walked back into the Marriott's dining room, still holding Caitlin's tape recorder and the roll of film in my hands. My new friend with the camera had departed and my table had been cleared of dirty dishes.

The fifty thousand dollars was gone too. I wondered if Caitlin had picked it up, or if the waitress just thought I was a good tipper.

The blackmail attempt had been clumsy, but then it was clear that Caitlin, whatever her educational background and business skills, was not real polished when it came to dealing with people. Her beauty and her money had spoiled her, like an overripe fruit that had been given too much sunshine and water. She was to used to getting her own way and couldn't understand that she was not the center of the universe.

In her mind, if I couldn't be seduced over to her side by her beauty, I could be bought off by her money. And if I was stupid enough to resist her charms, bodily or monetary, then I would have to be blackmailed into thinking her way.

She might not have even needed to resort to blackmail. If I wouldn't play along, the photos alone could have been mysteriously delivered and could put me in a difficult position with Nina Brisbane. The Ravens would have had a tough time replacing me with a top goalkeeper before the play-offs.

The photos could have also placed me in a criminally prosecutable position with the American Indoor Soccer League. But I didn't think that was a factor Caitlin was going to lose sleep over.

Caitlin wouldn't have appeared in the pictures of course. Just me, picking up heaps and heaps of money I didn't have an explanation for. Just me, mugging for the camera with a thousand dollar bill next to my smile, and forty-nine others as a side order with my pancakes. However, Bekka had said there was more going on than the feud between sisters, and I felt she was right.

If, as Caitlin had intimated, she had bought off Pasqual Maddox, it only muddied the waters surrounding the question of who murdered him. Had Pasqual backed out of his deal with Caitlin, and had she decided to eliminate him? Or had Nina found out Caitlin had the fix into her goalkeeper and had him killed for revenge? There was also the possibility that the bent-nose brigade, which Bekka had mentioned, had indeed come back for a round-three knockout.

For my part, I would have loved to find a way to put Liam Donovan in the picture. And there was still the police mugging theory to contend with. In the real world the rozzers are rarely wrong when it comes to murder. Due to procedural glitches or lack of evidence, they might lose a case in court. However, in cases where there are any clues at all, the police don't often find themselves barking up the wrong criminal tree.

I looked at my watch. There were still three hours before the scheduled two o'clock Ravens practice. Contending with the police theory was not something I was looking forward to, but it might be best to get it out of the way. I used the lobby phone to call the number Sir Adam had given me. He had said he would use what influence he could to smooth the legal way for me, but if experience proved my fears correct, then influence would only breed contempt.

I got passed through the desk officer to Detective Gill, via two other disembodied voices, without being cut off. Gill sounded gruff and hurried. I wondered briefly if it was an attitude he cultivated. He said his partner would be back in an hour and they would see me then. It was obvious he was doing me a favor.

I had an hour to kill. I decided to do what I'd wanted to do all morning.

I called Bekka.

THIRTEEN

MY PHONE CALL caught Bekka just as she was going out the door. She sounded bright, breezy, and excited—glad to hear from me, but in a hurry. She was on her way to an early practice session arranged for her by Sticks. We agreed to meet again for dinner that evening after the regular practice. It would be our last night in town before flying to Houston, Texas, for the first play-off game with the Houston Alamos. Now there was a team name a publicity manager could love; built-in rallying cry, ready-made headlines, instant fan identification.

After hanging up, I sat in the lobby and spent some time with the maps Spiros had given me. I familiarized myself with the directions and names of the local streets. The layout was so much clearer and more straightforward in American cities than in English. I pinpointed the police stations, hospitals, small airports, and the Acropolis complex.

Recovering the Laverda, I zipped on the leathers I had brought with me from England. Then I left the hotel and headed for the police station in a roundabout manner to gain a feel for some of the area.

Knowledge of the battleground is one of the most important standards of any war, and I had no doubts about being engaged in a war. Small scale it might be, but with the presence of Liam Donovan complicated by Terrance Brisbane's supposed IRA ties, the animosity between Nina and Caitlin, and one death already, whatever Sir Adam had dumped me into was still a war.

I was also aware of the adrenal glands in my system telling me that the Ravens were in a war. Every professional athlete knows that the line between the game they play and the struggle for life and death is erased on the trail to a championship. Even though I'd only had one practice with the Ravens, I could sense the play-off tension. There was an instant identification with our dark-horse chances. Everyone loves an underdog. I always play to win, no matter what the odds. I don't know any other way to play the game; whether it be the game of soccer or the game of life. In my case, I often found it difficult to separate the two.

With five minutes to spare before my appointment, I parked the Laverda in front of the Los Angeles Police Department's West Valley station. It was a small building, matching in architecture the library and city offices which extended to one side of the police building. There was a small park on the opposite side. Apartments and older houses filled in the surrounding streets like peasants crowding around a castle for safety.

Inside the swinging glass doors, a uniformed desk officer directed me down a hallway to a small office where the bottom half of a Dutch door kept the public at bay. Inside the office was a cramped jumble of desks, files, business machines, files, men in shirtsleeves and ties, files, and ringing telephones. The phones seemed to ring incessantly even though every man in the office seemed to already be talking on every available instrument.

I waited until a detective grudgingly noticed my presence. With marked irritation, he asked me what I wanted.

I was not going to have somebody tell me to "have a nice day" here. Apparently, nice days came around in police work as often as rain in the desert—and with about as much effect. I gave my name and said I had an appointment with Detective Gill. I was told to wait, so I sat on the hard wooden bench outside the office door and waited.

For twenty minutes I watched the odd parade of humanity which walked up and down the corridor. There were suspects in handcuffs and victims in shock. A few members of each category were bleeding. There were confused witnesses and outraged parents, and there were all manner of police officers. Some of the cops were in uniform, others in suits, and still others whose looks differed from those of the suspects only by the addition of police badges or ID cards. Everyone shared a communal agitation. Eventually, a knife-faced man called my name from the Dutch door. I stood up and he looked at me like I was lying about who I was.

"Ian Chapel?" he asked again, as if seeking confirmation.

"Yes." I wondered if he was making snap judgments based on my motorcycle leathers. It had happened to me before.

"I'm Gill. This is my partner, Briggs." He indicated another man behind him who was talking on the telephone. Briggs continued his conversation without acknowledging me. Unlike the thin, sharply dressed Gill, Briggs sported a beer belly held in check by a wide belt and the latest in lime-green polyester attire.

Gill opened the bottom half of the door and ushered me inside. With his hand he indicated a smaller office that couldn't be seen from the Dutch door opening. He seemed very put out with having to deal with me, and I couldn't think for the life of me what I could do to put him at his ease.

Inside the smaller interior office soundproof tiles kept the ringing of the telephones at bay. There was a table and three hardback chairs seemingly thrown into the room at random.

In one of the chairs sat a man of my own age and build. He wore a black sweater over black jeans, and shining black cowboy boots. A police ID card was clipped to the sweater's crew neck. I had seen him come come up the hallway and go through the Dutch doors shortly before Gill had called me in.

The man stood up and smiled. Youth was still in his face, but it was hiding beneath the crinkles brought on by stress, sunshine, and time. He was blond and his eyes were very hard under the surface twinkle. I'd seen eyes like that before, when I ran with Sir Adam's crowd. I'd seen them in my own mirror. They were warrior's eyes.

Gill backed out of the room without a further word and closed the door behind him.

"Ian Chapel?" the man asked. I wondered if this constant questioning was supposed to make me break down and confess to lying about my name.

"Yes. And you are?"

"Ethan Kelso. Detective Kelso if you prefer, or plain Ethan if you want to make things easy. Can I call you Ian?"

"Yes, of course, but I thought Briggs and Gill were the detectives handling the case I'm interested in."

"They were. That's why they've had their noses put out of joint. Although with Gill it's hard to tell. He is always surly. Something to do with his hemorrhoids. Still, nobody likes to have an open case taken away from them. It makes them suspect that you're either going to steal their thunder, or that somebody is questioning their competence."

"Which is it in this case?"

"Briggs and Gill are topflight homicide investigators, but to mix a metaphor or two, this case could take them out of their depth and into my ballpark. However, the last thing I want is publicity. To do my job successfully, you have to make out like you're pissing in a dark blue suit. It feels warm and good, but you hope nobody notices."

"What exactly is your job?" I asked, slightly confused.

"Oh, sorry. I'm a spook."

A sudden shape became clear in the dark waters.

"Has Sir Adam Qwale been pulling strings in high places?"

"Who?" Ethan looked coy.

"Ah, I see. I'll take that as a yes. Are you part of the Los Angeles Police Department? Or are you attached elsewhere."

"I'm true blue LAPD, all right," Ethan said with pride. "But I'm assigned to a special unit which I like to refer to as The Emperor's New Clothes Division. I don't think anybody, not even us, knows exactly what we do, but everyone still says we're doing a hell of a job at whatever it is. One day somebody will notice that the emperor isn't wearing any clothes, but until then I have job security."

I looked blank, waiting for Ethan to get to the point in his own good time. I had him pegged as some type of intelligence officer, and I'd dealt with his kind before in Ireland. The best of them were mavericks with their own way of doing things, and it was difficult to rush them.

"We deal with terrorism as it relates to the city of Los Angeles," he continued. "Domestic. International. Narco-terrorism—that's the current catchphrase which has everyone's bowels in an uproar—and all kinds of other think tank issues. We're analysts from hell. We watch. We track. We investigate. We try not to violate anybody's rights under the Constitution, and we abide by the most convoluted set of manual guidelines this side of Satan's deal with God."

I was only a little less perplexed, but I thought I could see what was coming. "And suddenly you're interested in the supposed mugging murder of a professional goalkeeper."

"Yeah. Isn't it great, the fun you can have when you aren't expecting it?"

I chuckled slightly, but I doubt Pasqual Maddox would have found any hilarity in the dark humor.

"What is it about the Maddox case that interests you?"

"You tell me."

I stood up and turned to leave.

"Where are you going?" Ethan asked, reaching out and putting a hand on my sleeve.

In actuality, I hoped I wasn't going anywhere. What I was trying to do was cut through the surface flack he was firing at me.

"I don't have time for larking about," I said, playing my hand out. "I'd rather deal with down-to-earth cynics like Gill and Briggs than trade bon mots with a naked emperor's emissary who wants to screw around with word games."

Ethan tugged harder at my sleeve and waved his free hand at me. "Sit down," he said with a smile. "Sir Adam said you could be prickly."

Since he gave ground by acknowledging Sir Adam's influence, I turned back and sat.

"I'm sorry," said Ethan. "Sir Adam, through my boss, asked that we extend to you all the help we can, and I intend to do so. Intelligence work, however, even on a local level, tends to get you into the habit of talking in circles. If I start doing it again, you can call me on it, okay? Truce?"

I nodded and waited.

"Great!" His face reanimated with a smile. "Your Sir Adam, who my boss seems to hold in Godlike awe, has led us to believe this whole thing with Maddox might have something to do with the IRA. He told us about this Liam Donovan character and we've opened an investigation on him and the Sons of Erin. . . ."

I interrupted. "I saw Donovan yesterday."

Ethan looked alarmed. "When? Where?"

I told him about the run-in Bekka and I had had with Donovan in the Acropolis parking lot.

He didn't take notes of any kind. I doubted he ever did. If the need arose ten years down the line, he would probably be able to quote our conversation verbatim. True intelligence types aren't made, they're born.

When I was done, he left to make a phone call. He was gone about five minutes before he returned carrying two cups of abysmal coffee.

"Right," he said, and I detected a slight accent somewhere in his voice. "I've let our crew know Donovan is around and they'll do what they can to locate him. There'll be questions asked in high places about how he got into the country, but that's not our worry. We have to find out why he's here."

"Are you English?" I asked.

He looked genuinely surprised. "Who's been telling tales out of school?"

"You still have a slight accent on some words. And your speech is peppered with English idiom."

"You never get it out of your blood, do you?" he said rhetorically. "Not that I want to, mind," he added quickly. "I came here with my parents when I was eight. It was an age where all the other kids make fun of you if you talk funny, so I lost my accent as best I could. However, I get home every couple of years and the second I step off the plane my English accent rushes back."

"You still consider England home?" If he had come here when he was eight, I judged that he'd been in America for over three quarters of his life.

He nodded. "I love America. This country has been very good to me, but for some reason England is still 'home.' You can't deny your roots. But I guess I'm on safe ground . . . at least until the Prime Minister decides it's time to declare war on the Yanks."

"Does your English background have any bearing on why you're working the IRA investigation?"

He nodded. "Typical, isn't it. The English haven't been able to figure out the Irish since the island separated from the mother country during the primordial ooze, so they give the only Englishman on the terrorism squad the chance to continue screwing things up."

"I like it. It has a certain warped logic."

Ethan turned serious again. "So, do you have any ideas what the hell is going on?"

He was still trying to get something from me without giving anything up, but two could play that game. "Why don't we start with you telling me what you have on Maddox's murder?''

He had apparently tired of the game because he settled back in his chair, downed the dregs of his coffee, and made a face. ''A couple of homeless alcoholics found Maddox's body near the Acropolis's dumpsters. They were looking for a place to doss down and split a short-dog. When they saw the body, they thought it was one of their buddies sleeping off a drunk. Then they saw the blood. I'm actually surprised they bothered to call it in. Most of their type are very wary of dealing with the police—often with good cause. The first uniformed coppers on the scene secured the area and all the usual homicide procedures were followed, but we didn't come up with diddly.'' The crossing of English and American in Ethan's speech was unique.

''The coroner's report,'' he continued, ''stated Maddox was kicked to death by at least three assailants. From the marks on the body, the coroner could definitely identify two brands of American-made soccer cleats and an unidentified pair of steel-toed boots. It was the boots that did the final damage to Maddox's head, face, and throat.''

''What made Briggs and Gill think it was a routine mugging? I would have thought being kicked to death by soccer boots was a little unusual.''

Ethan shrugged. ''Briggs and Gill are currently working thirty-five murder cases in various stages of investigation and prosecution. If there was any way they could have proved Maddox committed suicide by kicking himself to death, they would have done. Anything to clear the books and get the stats down.'' He gave an eloquent shrug. ''That isn't to say they are absolutely wrong in this case. In homicide, the easiest answer is almost always the right one. Maddox's wallet was missing, and there has been a string of muggings around the Acropolis area committed by a group of soccer hooligans—an English import, like punk music and skinheads, which should be immediately eradicated from the face of the earth.''

Soccer hooligans are the curse of English soccer. They

are fans who came to games strictly to fight and cause aggro. They are rabid supporters of the teams they choose to align themselves with. They dress in team colors, travel in packs, and destroy everything in their wake. Their joy is not in the game, but in the violence they themselves bring to the sport.

Soccer violence in England has become so bad that the phenomenon is referred to as "the English disease" and is considered fodder for study in many major British universities. Soccer hooliganism has been responsible for over three hundred deaths and uncountable injuries at games both in England and in Europe, where English teams often travel to play games. Things became so bad at one point that English teams were banned from European competition.

To combat the violence, sixty million dollars was allotted by the English government to form the National Football Intelligence Unit within the English police force. With the cooperation of the courts, the NFIU uses every trick in the book to identify and prosecute the perpetrators of soccer violence. Crowds at games are constantly scanned by remote control cameras for the first signs of trouble or for known soccer hooligans. Once an individual or a concerted action has been located, mounted police officers and other officers with dogs, or on free foot-patrol, move in to take charge of the situation and either evict or arrest the troublemakers.

Other stringent methods are also employed by the police. Prior to entering a soccer stadium to watch a match, fans from the visiting team are herded into a human crocodile to be searched for weapons and identified. If anyone steps out of the crocodile, they don't get in the stadium. The true fan has to suffer these indignities the same as the troublemakers, which causes debates in the House of Parliament regarding the infringement of human rights. But the bottom line is that soccer violence has to be stopped—at any cost.

"I didn't think Americans were fired up enough about soccer to be fanatics like the English soccer hooligans."

"For the most part they aren't, but you know as well as

I do that the game is only an excuse for the violence. The loyalty to the soccer teams is fanatical, but it is the thirst for fighting and blood that binds the soccer hooligans together.''

I thought about that statement and couldn't find fault with it. Soccer hooligans would delight in stopping a game by running onto the field to attack a player from an opposing team—even if it would cause the team they supported to forfeit the game.

''Does this firm of local soccer hooligans have a name?'' I asked.

In response to my question, Ethan dug into his back pocket and produced a piece of cardboard about the size of a business card. He flipped it onto the table between us. Displayed in the middle of the card was a crude drawing of a raven sitting on top of a soccer ball. A German SS-style dagger ran at an angle through the ball. Above the logo was the statement: LA RAVENS RULE—OK. Beneath the logo was the firm's chosen name: *The Hardbirds*. The sexual innuendo was juvenile and typical.

''These cards have been found scattered on the floors of stadiums where the Ravens have played and fights have broken out between groups of fans.''

''The cards indicate the Hardbirds were the cause of the violence,'' I told Ethan. ''In England the hooligan firms leave them behind to let everyone know who was in town. It's the same as your gangs writing graffiti on the walls on another gang's turf.''

''I figured as much,'' Ethan said. ''As far as we can tell, the Hardbirds' leader is a kid named Archer. The most we've been able to find out about him is he is the twenty-year-old black-sheep son of a titled English family, and he's in this country on an expired visitor's visa.''

''How about the rest of the firm? How large do you figure it is? The firms back home have ranking structure with a general leading the group. In this case that sounds like Archer, but in the English firms they have transport captains, armorers, intelligence officers, and the like.''

"There's probably only three or four other core members in the Hardbirds, so it wouldn't be as big as most of the English firms." Ethan's expression was one of detached cynicism. "But we still believe they are responsible for the violence which has been occurring in the crowds during the Ravens games, both at home and away, as well as for the series of muggings in the Acropolis area. It seems the Hardbirds aren't adverse to a little fag-bashing, or to the extorting of protection money from the local merchants."

I picked up my coffee cup, looked at the remaining contents, and set it back down on the scarred table. I was a bit puzzled and gave voice to my misgivings. "This still sounds like normal crime. Nothing beyond the experiences of Briggs and Gill, and certainly nothing for any sort of terrorist intelligence division to be interested in."

Ethan nodded his head in agreement, but also raised his right hand and index finger as if to make a point. "All too true if it wasn't for the fact of Terrance Brisbane's connections to the Acropolis and the IRA."

"You're investigating Brisbane?"

"I'm going to have to play semantics with you again to stay within the department's legal guidelines. We are investigating a new source of money which is making the IRA coffers overflow. International terrorist sources tell us the money is coming from Los Angeles.

"Locally, Terrance Brisbane is one of the most vocal supporters of the Irish Republican Army, and he is a major fund-raiser for IRA front groups in America. He is high profile in a time when the support of terrorists is unpopular. However, many people still do not see the IRA as terrorists. Instead, they are viewed in many quarters as freedom fighters, and they are not of concern to most Americans because they have never attacked American targets."

"Some people never learn, do they?" I said.

"Especially Terrance Brisbane. After what happened to his daughter, you would think the last thing he would do is continued to support the IRA. But his self-image is too important to him to ever admit he's wrong, so he has rationalized the whole incident to relieve his own guilt. He even openly maintains a defense fund for Duncan Finlas.''

''Who is Finlas?''

''The triggerman who destroyed Nina Brisbane's face and murdered a whole family. Terrance Brisbane is trying to get Finlas's status changed to that of a political prisoner instead of the murdering scum he is.'' Ethan sounded angry.

''There has to be more.''

''There is. I'm convinced Terrance Brisbane is the source of the new IRA money. It is flowing from somewhere in his sports empire, and I'm determined to stop it. I don't have any hardcore evidence yet, but I believe Archer's firm of soccer hooligans is part of Brisbane's team. I think they've graduated from violent yobs to terrorists. There is precedent in the case of the Chicago street gang, the El Rukans, who were convicted a couple of years ago of receiving money from Libyan sources to commit terrorist acts on American soil.''

''And Maddox's connection?''

''I've been through everything in his personal effects and everything in the investigative evidence, and I'm still running on gut instinct alone. But I'm telling you that Maddox wasn't mugged for a couple of bucks in his wallet. He saw something or heard something that made him a liability to Brisbane, so Brisbane turned Archer loose. Maybe Maddox was trying to blackmail Brisbane with what he found out. I don't know yet. But I will, and that's where you come in.''

''Me?''

''Our division is still going to be continuing the police investigation from the outside, but Sir Adam has convinced us of your qualifications . . .''

Damn that man!

''. . . and we want to use you as an agent in place. I want you to be my eyes and ears inside the Acropolis. Anything you can come up with on Archer, Donovan, or Brisbane, I want to know about. If Maddox found out something while playing for the Ravens, then maybe you can still discover what it was.''

I was not a happy camper. "From journalist, to goal-keeper, to investigator, to spy in one easy lesson." I shook my head. "No, it's too much."

"What are you talking about?"

"Look, here. If . . . and it's a big if. If I discover anything to do with Brisbane and the IRA, I'll pass it along. My brief from Sir Adam is to get the Ravens through the play-offs and try and maintain the integrity of the team and keep the sport of soccer as unsullied as possible. I've got more than I can handle doing just that.

"I came to see Briggs and Gill more out of courtesy and curiosity than any belief that they were going to be able to do anything for me. Now I'm here, and you're laying some kind of James Bond trip on me." I stood up. "I'm a goal-keeper, not an agent in place. If something happens that I think will interest you, I'll get in touch."

A slow smile spread across Ethan's face like an expanding oil slick.

"What are you grinning at?" I asked.

"That was a pretty speech. But I'm not convinced. You'll figure this caper out. You can't help yourself. I can see it in your eyes."

Before walking out of the office, I gave a wry grin of my own back to Ethan and told him not to hold his breath. But, damn it, the man was probably right. The suspicions he'd planted would roam around in my subconscious, seeking confirmation and driving me mad until I had everything in its place. It is one of the curses of my nature not to be able to leave anything undone.

I had come to the police station in the hopes of eliminating or confirming one of the possible motivations for Maddox's murder. I'd hoped to at least put into place the pieces which outlined the puzzle. What I had done was discover that the puzzle was far larger than I had imagined, and I didn't even have a picture on the top of a box to guide me.

FOURTEEN

A**S I DROVE** the sweet-riding Laverda to the practice session at the Acropolis, my mind was filled with murder and motives. It should have been filled with what side of the road I was driving on. Twice, car horns sent terrifying surges of adrenaline coursing through my body as I almost drifted into oncoming lanes of traffic. My body might be in Los Angeles, but my subconscious driving habits were still back in England.

I parked by the player's entrance to the Acropolis and hopped off the bike. There were several advertising flyers scurrying around on the ground in the warm breeze, and I noticed there were copies of the same flyer stuck under the windshield wipers of all the cars in the parking lot. Normally, I would have ignored the advertising except that I recognized one of the black-and-white photos on the front of the flyer. It was a portrait of Terrance Brisbane. I put my foot down on a copy to secure it and then bent down to pick it up.

As I stood up, I heard a noise and turned to see Pat

Devlin coming up behind me. He was carrying a sports bag with a Nike logo in one hand. Hanging from his other hand was a pair of indoor soccer boots tied together by the laces. He was short with a slender build. Thin legs with knobby knees protruded out through a pair of tan shorts like the appendages of a stick man drawing. It was hard to believe those sparrow's legs had carried him to the position of the league's MVP.

He looked over my shoulder at the flyer.

"That bastard gives Irishmen a bad name," he said, nodding down at Brisbane's photo. "The troubles will never end as long as men like him support the IRA scum back home."

I was startled at the venom in Devlin's voice, and I quickly took a closer look at the paper in my hand to see what he was talking about.

Aside from Brisbane's photo there was another shot of a gaunt-faced man with raggedly cut straw hair and a nose which was sharp enough to core apples. The name under the photo was Niall Emmanon.

Big black letters centered below the photo captions declared that the Irish/American Benevolent Association was proud to present sports entrepreneur Terrance Brisbane and recently released freedom fighter Niall Emmanon, speaking on "The Politics Of Soccer." The event was a fund-raiser for the Irish Widow's and Orphan's Fund. It was scheduled for seven o'clock that evening at the Golden Harp pub in Santa Monica.

The bottom half of the page was taken up with a political cartoon showing a motley group of English soccer hooligans driving a British armored car and firing soccer balls into an Irish Republican Army stronghold. The caption read: *Run for it lads! This time they mean business.*

"Widow's and Orphan's Fund, my granny's bum." Pat was getting heavy into sarcasm, his Irish accent full and rich on every consonant. "The closest any money they collect tonight will get to a widow or orphan is after it's converted into guns or explosives and the widow or orphan knows how to pull a trigger or rig a timer.''

"I'm not following you," I said, although I had a very good idea what Pat was talking about.

"Don't act like you've just stepped out of the bog. The Irish/American Benevolent Association is nothing more than a front to fund the IRA. They stroke idiots like old high-and-mighty Brisbane and other money men or media stars with talk of fighting the good fight and how Ireland must be united. They fill them full of all kinds of patriotic twaddle that hides the fact that innocent citizens are dying every day because of the people the association supports.

"The IRA has killed twice as many people in Ireland as the bloody British army has, and twelve times as many as the incompetent RUC. But the bleeding heart liberals still open their wallets and pocketbooks, and the next thing you know there is blood all over their hands and they don't even know it.''

"If you feel that strongly about it why do you work for Brisbane?'' I asked as I pushed open the door to the player's entrance.

"I don't work for Brisbane. I work for his daughter and she knows firsthand what the costs of civil war are. She's one of the victims. And you should know better than anyone that soccer can transcend any war. I play the game because it's what I am." He pointed a finger at the flyer I was still holding. "If you come by the Harp tonight, though, you might see that I can also fight the war at the same time.'' He did his best to give me a cryptic grin, and slid past me into the building.

We spent the next hour in a cramped and overheated projection room watching films of the Houston Alamos destroying almost every opponent they came up against. The Ravens had already played the Alamos twice during the season. Early in the year, the Alamos had outscored the Ravens 10–2 with a very weak showing on the part of Pasqual Maddox. Six weeks later, though, the Ravens came away victorious after a shoot-out at the end of a 4–4 tie. Nick Kronos had been in goal for the shoot-out, and he smirked at me as we watched the replay.

It was very strange watching Maddox on video. He was dead. Murdered. But he was still playing the game in a celluloid hell that showed his betrayal over and over and over. And it was a betrayal. After years of playing the game, and years spent analyzing the moves of other goalkeepers, I knew every angle there was. Now, watching the ten goals the Alamos scored in the first game against the Ravens, I knew Maddox was dogging it.

Eight of the ten goals could have been stopped. Of those eight, six should have been stopped. And of those six, two were absolute blatant go-bys. Maddox just got out of the way and let the shots go by. He betrayed the team, himself, and the fans. But most of all he betrayed the game.

I don't understand why he allowed the game to turn into a rout. It would have been just as easy to let the Alamos win by a goal. Whatever his reasons were, though, I still hoped he was roasting in hell.

In the second game it was the same story. The score was closer only because our Ravens defense didn't allow the Alamos to get anywhere near as many shots on goal. I had no doubt we would have lost the game if Maddox had remained in goal for the shoot-out. Like it or not, Nick Kronos had saved the game.

Now, we were set to go up against the Alamos again on their home turf. Only this time, I was going to make damn sure they didn't have an extra man on the field in a Ravens uniform.

After the films, we stayed in the projection room while Stavoros gave us a straightforward chalk-talk on what our tactics would be. However, he apparently wasn't much on pep talks. That chore fell to Pat Devlin, who stood up in the center of the room and gave an electrifying speech about team unity and how the Ravens as a team were something special.

He talked about putting differences between ourselves behind us and overcoming the obstacles which had been thrown in our path. He spoke of rising to a higher level of play through belief in ourselves and the purity of our effort.

I'd heard these kind of speeches many times before. Sometimes they fell flat and did little to spark a team's enthusiasm. Most often, they calmed nerves and rallied a feeling of kinship with your other teammates which lasted until kickoff. Every so often, though, the ritual of raising a team's espirit de corps became something special, and Pat Devlin had the ability to bring it off. His rich Irish accent seemed to touch something deep in all of us. The Latin players were also responding. For some reason they viewed Ireland as another struggling third-world country like the ones that still held their roots.

Even Wagstaff was caught up in the oratory. He caught my eye and gave me a hard stare. It wasn't antagonistic, however, as there was no malice in it. His look acknowledged equal status, one predator recognizing the ability of another. I wasn't sure how I felt toward him. Anger still surged in me, but it could be dealt with later. After the Houston game was won.

When we finally broke out of the projection room, we were in high spirits and hurried to get changed. Reporters from the local press were waiting for us in the locker room. They quickly got busy rounding up quotes for their next editions. We had all been told to be on our best behavior with the press, and after Devlin's speech we even felt like cooperating fully. There was a lot of humor flying back and forth between the two groups which was a good sign.

Stavoros was holding court in one corner of the locker room with his two assistant coaches, Brian Doogan and Larry Durrell. Both assistants were expatriated Englishmen who had played in the English leagues before my time and loved the game more than life itself.

Standing apart from all the activity, seemingly unaffected by the noise and confusion, was Nina Brisbane. She watched the proceedings with what I could only assume was an air of satisfaction. It is amazing how out of touch with a person's emotions you can become when you can't see their face. It was almost impossible to tell what was going on behind Nina's veil. You had to work at it, use whatever other subtle signs of body language you could pick up on to read her mood; hand movements, muscle tenseness, leg position, tone of voice, etcetera. By standing quiet and still, Nina was almost invisible. An omnipresent being, or a Greek chorus.

At my locker, I was cornered by Alex Bowman, a feature writer for the top American sports slick. He'd been a middling-to-good pro golfer before turning to writing, and we hit it off right away. With my own sports and writing background, we had a lot in common. He picked my brains while I changed, but he didn't bother with unnecessary questions about my prior history or about my accident. That was the type of stuff he could pick up from other sources by doing his homework.

He did, however, ask a couple of pointed questions regarding my feelings toward playing on the same team with Wagstaff. He obviously already knew about my accident and who had caused it. I verbally bobbed and waved, not giving direct answers to the questions. Alex gave me a look which told me he'd let me off the hook for now, but he'd be back for the straight scoop later.

Nobody asked about Maddox. This factor I put down to the American public's lack of interest in soccer and their being anesthetized to crime in general. One goalkeeper or another didn't make any difference, and neither did one murder or another. Overall, though, I was impressed by the politeness of the reporters when compared with what I was used to from the Fleet Street scribes.

Eventually, the well-orchestrated but casual press conference broke up and the players and coaches exited the locker room to get on with the final tune-up practice.

I found Sticks and Bekka already out on the practice area. Sticks was being his usual cantankerous self, and Bekka appeared to be a joyous ball of enthusiasm. She had two or three reporters around her and was obviously enjoying the attention. She seemed to glow from an inner power source, and I was struck anew by the effect she had on me.

When she saw everyone else enter the playing area, she broke away to join us and Sticks followed behind her.

"This man is incredible," she told me excitedly, and nodded toward Sticks. "We've been practicing all morning, and I've already learned more in one day from him than from all my other so-called coaches put together."

"Don't let Stavoros hear you say that or you'll never get in a game," I warned her in half-seriousness.

I heard Sticks mumble something about Stavoros under his breath which I didn't quite catch. He obviously hadn't been fatigued by his early session with Bekka because he started right in with me on a vigorous series of stretching exercises. He also seemed to have come to an unspoken agreement with Stavoros to take over as the goalkeeping coach. He roped a reluctant Nick Kronos into our group. Within no time, Nick and I had both broken a sweat, and I could feel all of my joints and muscles getting into the groove. Bekka joined us as soon as we were warmed up, and practice went into high gear.

While Stavoros and the assistant coaches put the offense and defense through a light, pregame workout designed to bring them to the cutting edge of their abilities, Sticks drove the three of us with a relentless determination that was tough even by his standards.

Sweat poured in rivulets as Sticks put us through one routine after another. I wondered at first what in the hell he was up to, but then it dawned on me that he was trying to determine who was the better goalkeeper; Nick or Bekka. Ability-wise, I would have put them on an even keel. Nick had the strength, but Bekka's reaction time and anticipation were incredible and more than compensated. Attitude, however, was making all the difference in the world between them.

Bekka put everything she had into the practice. Her desire was obvious to anyone. She wore it on her sleeve in place of her heart.

Nick, on the other hand, tried to cruise through the practice as if the whole idea of effort was beneath him. He did as little as possible and alternated between whining and sneering. He was about as fun as a canker sore.

Eventually, Sticks put the two of them into head-to-head competition. The practice had been running for almost two hours, and the other players were about to be cut loose to the showers, when Sticks had the team's equipment manager set up two indoor soccer nets about six feet apart. Both nets faced out toward the center of the field.

Stavoros came up to stand next to Sticks. He looked worried. "I hope these will do the trick for you," he said, and indicated two contraptions being wheeled onto the playing field. "Ms. Nina borrowed them from the Rackets tennis team."

The two contraptions turned out to be tennis cannons. There was a bucket of tennis balls at the back of each one which fed into the contraption's innards before being fired out of a long tube. On a tennis court, the balls would fly across the net so a player on the other side could practice service returns, ground strokes, or other shots, over and over until they became second nature.

The two cannons, which were quickly set up about twenty feet away from the two side-by-side goals, were state-of-the-art. They could be adjusted to fire balls not only to the same spot time after time, but also to random spots at varying speeds.

"Get in one of the goals, Ian," Sticks said to me, "and show them how this works."

In England, I'd played a version of this drill, only without the high-tech approach of using the tennis cannons. Players would line up at the edge of the penalty area and throw tennis balls for me to stop. To succeed in the drill, reaction time and concentration had to be tuned to their highest peak. Strength and endurance would also be tested to the maximum as you were required to bounce off the ground again and again, flinging yourself around the net with abandon.

I waited in the goal for Sticks to get the hang of the

remote-control box which operated the cannon. When he finally got himself set, he hit the trigger button. The first two balls zinged straight by me and into the back of the goal net. I saved the next three straight, and by the time twenty balls had been fired I was into the rhythm and my concentration was pinpointed.

The movements of my head, which I used to supplement my depth perception, were second nature now. I couldn't believe that out of embarrassment I had spent a year trying to hide them. Cages of our own making are always the hardest to escape.

When the last of the bucket of eighty balls was fired, I was wrung out like a limp dishrag. I had nothing left. There were twenty-eight balls in the back of the net. I'd saved forty-two, and ten had gone wide. It was a tough exercise, but I knew that any saves over fifty percent were an excellent showing. Sticks gave me a rare smile.

The other players had gathered around to watch the odd proceedings, and they catcalled and yelled encouragement as Nick and Bekka were called down for their turn.

Nick gave Sticks and Bekka a dirty look. I could tell he felt he was being set up, but didn't know what to do about it. Both he and Bekka took positions in one of the goal mouths and faced the tennis cannons as if they were to be the victims of a firing squad. It was clear that this exercise was a showdown. High noon on the soccer field.

On my way off center stage, I passed Bekka. "Don't get mesmerized by the cannon tube," I told her in a quiet voice. "Wait for the balls to fire before you react and use your body to block them when you can instead of trying to catch them. You don't have to worry about the rebounds, so it's safer." The advice wasn't much, but it was the best I could do. Nick saw me talking to Bekka and gave me his standard sneer. I would have given him the same advice, but I knew he would ignore it.

Sticks gave the remote-control box for Bekka's cannon to Stavoros, who was looking very apprehensive. I had a feeling that the Ravens' head coach knew his son was not going to fare well in this drill. He might appear on the surface to be blinded to his son's shortcomings. What parent isn't? However, he was also an experienced enough coach and player to recognize he was about to be slapped in the face with a dose of reality. Even the mood of the other players was a telling factor. Nick had not endeared himself to the team with his attitudes, and he was about to be made painfully aware that he was going to have to do more than be the coach's offspring if he wanted professional acceptance. I almost felt sorry for him. Almost, but not quite.

Stavoros shot out the first ball, which caught Bekka off guard and flew into the back of her net. While Nick was busy sneering, Sticks fired a ball past him. Bekka gave a little laugh which brought high color to Nick's cheeks, but after that they were too busy flinging themselves at the tiny green spheres to pay attention to what was happening in the net next to them.

By the time ten or so balls had been fired by each cannon, both Bekka and Nick and the crowd were beginning to get into the spirit of the drill. The other players oohed and aahed as the cannons fired ball after ball at the goals. Stavoros was desperate to put the balls past Bekka and kept the machine moving at top velocity and firing speed. Sticks on the other hand, was sending the balls more skillfully at awkward angles toward Nick.

After twenty balls, Nick had only stopped eight, but Bekka had only stopped four. After forty balls, though, Bekka had captured the rhythm and pattern of Stavoros's firing. She had started to stop more and more balls and had evened things up with Nick.

With sixty balls fired, the crowd was really getting into the act. Every time Bekka made a save they shouted and cheered her on. Nick's natural ability, though, was pulling him through. If he had put his heart into the drill, I think he could have put Bekka away. She was tiring and getting sloppy, the constant bombardment of balls almost overwhelming her. But Nick couldn't stick with it. At seventy balls fired, he cracked, his pride, not Bekka, defeating him.

"This is stupid!" he yelled as two balls in succession bounced into the net just out of his reach. Nobody paid any attention to his outburst and a third ball zipped past him. The crowd was cheering Bekka on as she kept her concentration and stopped another tennis ball.

"Screw it!" said Nick, and he gave Sticks a rude two-fingered gesture before storming away and down the player's tunnel toward the locker room.

Stavoros continued firing balls at Bekka, but Nick's capitulation had given her a second wind and she stopped seven of the last ten balls. Meanwhile, with a self-satisfied grin, Sticks fired every one of the last seven balls in his cannon into the back of Nick's unguarded net. When Stavoros's cannon ran empty, Bekka fell to the ground, exhausted. She was quickly surrounded by myself and the rest of the team as we helped her up and patted her on the back in congratulations.

There were forty-three balls in the back of her net. There were fifty-two in the back of Nick's. Even without the last seven freebies which had gone directly from Sticks's cannon into the back of Nick's net, Bekka had still beaten him by two.

"Viva La Gata Blanca!" called out Pepe Brazos. He used the occasion to pat Bekka's backside.

The rest of the team cheered in response, "Viva La Gata Blanca!"

The White Cat. It looked like Bekka had earned herself a nickname. She had definitely arrived.

FIFTEEN

AT DINNER THAT evening, Bekka was animated and full of laughter. Her victory over Nick during the practice session had left her on an emotional high. The congratulations showered on her by the other players had been hugely gratifying. Payment for her long hours of effort.

I could remember what it was like to be at the beginning of a career with a world of glory stretched out before you for the taking. I didn't pop her bubble. Reality would do that soon enough. It would take more than winning one drill to secure her a place as the backup goalkeeper. Nick was a vicious little bastard, and he'd quickly find some way to strike back.

After practice, Bekka had left her car at the Acropolis and thrown her long, jean-clad legs over the back of the Laverda. Her hair was still pulled back into a ponytail, but she had applied a light touch of makeup which accentuated her features. The lipstick on her full lips was a rich, deep red which stirred something inside me.

I'd felt very comfortable riding the Laverda with her arms wrapped around my waist and the heat of her breasts pressing into my back. She was a natural on the bike, riding as smoothly as if she were an integral part of the machine. She put all her confidence in my abilities as a driver, and we flowed like mercury along the twilight streets. She made the short ride to the restaurant a joy. My heart was racing faster than the bike's engine. I tried to remember that there is no fool like an old fool. However, neither love nor lust has a conscience.

"All I have to do now is get you on a plane back to England, and I've got myself a starting position," Bekka said over the dessert. She finished the sentence with a light laugh.

I couldn't stop my emotional reaction to the statement from flickering across my face. Bekka saw it and reached out to touch my hand, which was resting on top of the table.

"I meant that purely from a professional standpoint, not a personal one. I've only known you two days, but I've watched you on film so many times you were already in my dreams before I met you. Don't worry, I like having you around in the flesh."

I felt myself blush, and Bekka laughed again. "That's delightful," she said. "I don't think I've ever made a man blush before."

I knew I was turning even redder. The tips of my ears were burning. "Are my feelings that obvious?"

"Not at all," Bekka said. "I just feel tuned in to you. And I can't say I've ever felt that with anyone before."

I brought my eyes up from where they had been focusing on her hand touching mine, and met her steady gaze. The ice color of her eyes had changed to smolder with white heat.

The restaurant she had chosen was a casual eatery called The Mainsail. It specialized in seafood. The atmosphere was red-checked tablecloths, antique ship's wheels and bells on the walls, and hundreds of oil sepia photographs of whalers doing battle with the sea's giant mammals. The lighting was subdued, made romantic by red candles which flickered shadows across the faces of the diners.

I shifted verbal gears to break the silence stretching between us.

"I had a proposal this morning," I said and offered up a mischievous grin. I often run for the cover of humor when I find myself involved in intense situations with women.

Bekka caught my mood and pulled her hand back in mock offense. "Oh, really?"

I proceeded to tell her about my encounter with Caitlin Brisbane. I overplayed the circumstances to comic proportions and by the time I was done we were holding hands across the table again. Bekka was laughing so hard, tears were rolling down her face. Every man loves to have a beautiful woman laugh at his jokes, and I am certainly no exception. I felt wonderful.

When we had regained our composure I asked, "Does what you said last night about wanting to help me with my other agenda still hold true?"

"You bet. What do you have in mind? Something to do with Caitlin?"

"No, not yet." I shook my head and asked, "How far is Santa Monica from here?"

"About twenty minutes by freeway if the traffic is light. Why?"

"Well, I'm not sure, but I want to follow up on this meeting." I took out a copy of the flyer advertising Terrance Brisbane's speech in honor of the Irish/American Benevolent Association. Bekka took it from me and looked at it with interest.

"What makes you think this has anything to do with the Ravens?" she asked.

I told her about the scenario Pat Devlin had described; that the Irish/American Benevolent Association was possibly a front for the IRA. I then went on to tell her of Devlin's cryptic statement about being able to play soccer and fight the war at the same time.

Bekka shrugged her shoulders. "If you want to go, I'm game," she said.

Her statement reminded me of the old joke about the two hunters who came across a naked woman in the woods. The woman looked at the hunters with lust in her eyes and said, "Hello boys, I'm game." So the two hunters shot her.

I hoped that whatever I was getting us into wouldn't end up the same way.

The Golden Harp pub dominated the ground-level end unit of a rundown building on the corner of Santa Monica Boulevard and Seventh Street. The ocean was only a few blocks further west and the sea breeze filled the night air with its saltiness. The logo on the sign over the entrance to the pub made the politics of the place very clear. It displayed a huge, ornate golden harp with the strings replaced by iron prison bars and a shadowy figure lurking behind them.

Inside, the pub was three-quarters full. The mass of humanity was swilling down Guinness like the taps were about to run dry. The smoke of pipes and unfiltered cigarettes battled with the smells of fried food coming from a small kitchen in the rear. A wooden bar formed a square in the middle of the room, and behind it three bartenders poured liquid courage nonstop.

Flush with the west wall was a low rectangular platform obviously acting as stage. On the wall itself were blowups of the photos and political cartoon featured on the flyer. Against another wall three separate dart games were in progress, and a jukebox was pounding with the sounds of the rock group U2.

I entered the pub and muscled my way to the bar with Bekka following behind me. A bartender shoved two pints of Guinness at me without asking, snatched a ten dollar bill out of my hand, and didn't return with the change. In our turn, we were elbowed away from the bar. We found our way to two chairs that had been pushed back from full tables. As we sat, a somber-looking youth with a two-day growth of beard and a dangling earring took the stage. Feedback wailed from a pair of beat-up speakers when he attempted to talk into the microphone.

As the youth turned to work on the sound system, I took a quick look around the room. I couldn't spot Pat Devlin or anyone else from the Ravens. However, standing in front of the stage, facing the audience in a military at-ease posture, was a rough-looking quartet of youths sporting knit scarves in the Ravens' colors. One of them turned to say something to the one next to him, and I caught a glimpse of Terrance Brisbane and the other speaker, Niall Emmanon, sitting on the stage behind them.

I took a closer look at the four young men. They appeared cocky and dangerous, all muscles and anger, as if they would like nothing better than a punch-up to break out. One of them was obviously the leader by dint of his stature. He was tall and wiry, about twenty-five years old, with a long aquiline nose and strong features. He had shiny black hair pulled back into a ponytail which rivaled Bekka's for length. He was clean shaven and wore a crisp white shirt with a green tie which snugged up under his scarf. Suspenders held his pressed Levis up over his slim hips, and high polished boots extended from the bottoms of his stovepipe trouser legs. I was willing to give odds-on that the boots were steel-toed Doc Martin's.

I looked at the other three. They were all dressed similarly, although without the crispness of their leader's demeanor. Instead of Doc Martin's, they wore black soccer boots with yellow stripes slashed across them. I wondered if Ethan Kelso was anywhere around. I had the gut feeling that these clowns were the core of the Hardbirds firm of soccer hooligans led by Archer, the royal bad boy.

Before I had the chance to make any further observations, the youth on the stage got the microphone working properly and attempted to get everyone's attention. His brogue was so thick it was hard to understand. He must have put his point across because the audience started applauding politely and Niall Emmanon stepped up to the mike.

In person, Emmanon's nose seemed even sharper than in the picture on the flyer. His straw hair and gauntness were also emphasized. He had the haunted look about him of a man who was constantly looking over his shoulder, yet I also sensed a steel inner core marking him as a very dangerous being. The hardness emanating from him wasn't the flashy viciousness of the character I had pegged as Archer. Archer was the type of petty bullyboy who was only dangerous when backed up by the lesser animals in the pack. Strip Archer of the pack and you would break him like a twig. Emmanon, though, was a true hard man. To go against him one-on-one would be the most dangerous thing you had ever done.

Emmanon's speech started out hitting the usual Irish political catchphrases, designed to whip up the crowd's sympathy. He spoke of the ''Irish struggle,'' the battles he had fought and paid the price for in prison time, and his dedication to the cause. He pleaded the case of the widows and orphans left behind by those who had made the ultimate commitment for the cause, and the lonely women and children whose men were locked away but not forgotten.

When he wound down there was a loud round of applause and several voices took up the verses of an Irish fight song with most of the crowd joining in on the tear-jerking chorus. When it looked like the singing was going to continue unabated, the youth who had introduced Emmanon regained the stage and called for quiet. When he had a relative response to his request, he introduced Terrance Brisbane, who was received with a swell of applause and cheering. It was obvious Brisbane had worked this crowd before and that they liked him. It quickly became clear why he was so well liked, because the first thing he did was order a round of drinks for the house.

When everyone was served, Brisbane half turned and dramatically pointed a finger toward the blowup of the political cartoon on the wall behind him.

''British soccer has become synonymous with violence over the past few years,'' he stated in a sonorous voice as he warmed to his subject. "In 1985 British soccer hooligans rioted in Turin, Italy, and trampled thirty-nine innocent people to death. In 1986 hooligans in London went on a mad rampage, destroying buildings and attacking innocent people in the streets after their team lost a football match. Later that same year, hooligans stabbed a nineteen-year-old man to death after he merely shouted his support for another team.

"More recently, English soccer hooligans were responsible for the horror at Heysel Stadium in Brussels, and the disaster last April at the Liverpool–Nottingham Forest FA Cup semifinal in Sheffield where ninety-five people died. Stadiums everywhere have been destroyed by the 'English disease.' Players have been terrorized, neighborhoods vandalized, and referees threatened with death over controversial calls.

"The soccer violence in Britain has come to rival the death statistics run up by the drive-by shootings and turf clashes of the gang warfare in urban American streets." Heads in the audience began to nod in agreement with this as Brisbane continued his oration. "The British ruling class states its outrage at this turn of events. It professes shock at the actions of the working-class soccer fans, but does nothing to alleviate the source of the problem, which is the oppression and exploitation of the working class. In point of fact the British ruling class, as always, even encourages this exploitation."

The audience applauded these statements with enthusiasm. Nobody seemed inclined to question Brisbane's own "ruling class" roots, or the fact he appeared to be employing his own soccer bullyboys for protection. As long as he was hitting the right notes of outrage, the crowd was willing to listen to him. And drink his booze, of course. It made me sick. Brisbane had no idea about the rot he was talking. But he still kept talking.

"The British government is expert at exploiting working-class rivalries to its own advantage. Soccer provides a diversion from the poverty and unemployment suffered by the working class while maintaining rivalries between working-class factions. Problems that the British government is unwilling, but not unable, to solve.

"The violence that erupts is almost inevitable, given the fortress-like conditions that prevail at soccer stadiums, where fans are herded into steel-encased pens, like so many cattle, to direct their anger and frustration toward a rival group of fans. And the situation promises to get worse as the British government threatens to implement a soccer fan ID card scheme as part of the Football Spectators Act forced through the Parliament last year. This action is just another example of the ruling class attempting to take away the freedoms of the working class in order to keep them repressed and in their, quote, proper place. We should not and will not stand for this!" Applause rang through the pub.

"The situation is analogous to the conditions in Northern Ireland where the working class is sequestered into ghettos and pitted against one another like rival teams in the name of national security! The God Forsaken British Empire . . ."

"What the hell do you know about Northern Ireland, you stupid git?"

Every head in the pub suddenly swivelled to see who the owner of the blasphemous voice was. I was no exception, and I spotted a masked figure standing on the bar. Surrounding him were seven or eight hardcases who had brought axe handles out from under long coats. They all had bandanas pulled up to hide the lower part of their features and baseball caps pulled low on their foreheads.

I was only able to recognize the masked figure's voice as Pat Devlin's because I had been warned to expect trouble.

In one hand, Devlin held a red balloon that looked to be filled with some kind of liquid.

"Get off the stage, you blithering idiot," he yelled at Brisbane. "You've no idea how many people's blood you have on your hands so here's a sample." With that, he threw the balloon with deadly accuracy. It caught the top of the microphone and ripped open, sending a thick red substance spraying across the pale gray of Brisbane's suit front. I caught the offal smell instantly. Animal blood.

The pub had broken into pandemonium. Pat Devlin had to have a very personal stake in he Irish troubles to take this kind of action, but there was no time to worry about what it was. Devlin's cohorts with the axe handles had started to wade into the crowd with indiscriminate swings, and Archer and his bullyboys were headed into the fray for a major confrontation. It was time to get out.

I grabbed Bekka's hand and pulled her up out of her seat. We weren't fast enough, though, and one of the axe handle-swinging thugs was bearing down on us. I dodged under his first swipe and hit him as hard as I could over his heart. He went down in a heap. Pain lanced through my fist and I prayed I hadn't broken anything.

I reached back behind me to grab Bekka's hand again and started to plow through the crowd. There was a sudden explosion at the front of the room and I glanced up to see Niall Emmanon waving around the biggest pistol I had ever seen. Where he'd kept it while he was speaking I had no idea, probably in the small of his back. It looked like he had fired into the air to clear the space around him, but I didn't wait to see if he was going to start picking out targets.

I felt a hand grab my sleeve and I spun around to lash out with my fists again, but I recognized the features of Ethan Kelso just in time.

"What the hell are you doing here?" I asked.

"It's my job! What the hell are you doing here? And who's this with you?"

A beer glass flew between us and shattered against a chairback. The pub was in a full scale punch-up.

"Can we save the reunion and introductions till later?" Bekka asked urgently. "We've got to get out of here!"

Ethan changed my initial direction and pulled us toward the back of the pub. I felt like a trout swimming upstream since we were moving against the tide of humanity trying to get out of the pub's front door. There was a back door, but everyone seemed to have forgotten about it. After much pushing and shoving, Ethan suddenly dragged Bekka and me off to one side and into the men's restroom.

"Always have a plan of retreat," he said, as he propped open a small window. He punched out the wire screen covering the opening and stood back to help Bekka up and out. I climbed through next, and then reached back in to help pull Ethan through. Police sirens could be heard arriving at the front of the pub.

"Let's blow this pop stand," Ethan said, and started to jog down the alley we'd found ourselves in.

We'd only gone a few steps when I put my hand out to stop Ethan.

"Wait a minute," I said. "I think that motorcycle parked against the wall is the one Liam Donovan was riding when he tried to run us down at the Acropolis."

Ethan stopped to look at the bike I was pointing out. It was parked almost directly behind the back door of the pub where patrons were now spilling out like lemmings running for a cliff. There were several cars also parked in the alley, but the bike stood out because of the bright yellow gas tank which I remembered from the night before. I know bikes, I've been around them and studying them for years. Makes, models, and features stay with me like suspects' faces, names, and methods must stay with Ethan. The bike was the same make and model of Japanese crotch rocket that Donovan had been riding, I was sure of it.

"Damn. We don't have time for this," Ethan said. "We've got to get clear before the uniforms close off this alley. Are you sure?"

I nodded.

Ethan looked undecided for a second until a black-and-white police car turned into the far end of the alley.

He pushed me urgently in the opposite direction. "The bike will have to wait. We have to get clear of here."

All three of us started to run down the alley.

"I've got a surveillance team set up to follow Emmanon. If he got clear of the pub, I've got to be clear to stay with him."

We exited the alley, but continued running until we reached the parking lot where I'd left the Laverda. Ethan pulled a radio transmitter out of his back pocket and within seconds a black, unmarked coupe had curbed itself alongside of us with its passenger door open. Ethan jumped in.

"Thanks," I told him.

"Just get clear of here and call me tomorrow."

"Don't you want to say I told you so?"

"Why? Because I said you'd get involved in this thing?"

"Yeah?"

"Okay. I told you so. Now get out of here." He pulled the car's door closed and the black vehicle moved away with alacrity.

"Who was that guy?" Bekka asked.

I watched the black car disappear into the night.

"Bond," I told her. "James Bond."

The interior of the Acropolis was dark except for the light coming from the player's tunnel and the twinkle of a red bulb on each side of the scoreboard cube. The arena seemed vast and cavernous, echoing my footsteps.

"I knew you'd get by here sooner or later, laddie." The familiar voice came out of the darkness close by.

"Old superstitions die hard, Sticks. You know how it goes."

Sticks was sitting on the player's bench on the home side of the arena. I had just wandered onto the playing surface and was standing at the midfield point. Directly above me was a huge overhead scoreboard cube. One long support stretched from the top of the cube into the darkness of the ceiling. The effect gave the scoreboard the appearance of a huge, square, alien eye suspended by a straight optic nerve.

"Is Bekka with you?" Sticks asked.

"No, this is a solitary vigil."

I imagined Sticks nodding his head. "Aye. Well, I won't be keeping you long, laddie. I just wanted to make sure you were feeling ready for tomorrow."

"I appreciate it. I think I'm okay."

"You getting anywhere with this Maddox thing?"

"The only thing I seem to be getting lately is trouble. As far as solving Maddox's murder and finding out what's happening with the Ravens, I feel like a pigeon set amongst the cats. I'm simply wandering around wondering where the next attack is going to come from." I brought him up to speed on Liam Donovan and the events of that evening at the Golden Harp.

After escaping from the pub, Bekka and I had headed back to the Acropolis parking lot where she'd left her car. We'd been unable to talk while on the Laverda, but Bekka had held on to me tighter than ever. The warmth and feel of her body against me communicated something beyond words.

Standing at her car, I told her about my morning interview with Ethan Kelso. We discussed my theories about Archer and the Hardbirds, but we still couldn't put anything coherent together that fit all the facts. There were still far more questions than answers. Was Maddox's murder connected to Caitlin Brisbane's bribery scam? Or was it somehow connected to Terrance Brisbane and Archer's firm of soccer hooligans? Was Terrance Brisbane supporting the IRA financially, as Ethan Kelso and Pat Devlin appeared to believe? And if so, why was Pat Devlin so enraged as to jeopardize his entire soccer career? And how the hell did Liam Donovan fit into the grand scheme of things?

It was this last question which bothered me the most because the answer could prove to be fatal to my continued health. Donovan was a wild card. He had shown up in England before my involvement in this mess started, and because of my actions, he now had a personal score to settle. I'd have to watch my blind side very carefully.

I'd been busy espousing all of this to Bekka when she leaned forward, put her hand behind my neck, and kissed me full on the lips in midsentence. I felt my knees go weak.

She pulled away after a second, looking like a scared kitten whose curiosity was about to kill it.

"I'm sorry," she said, misinterpreting my stunned silence.

I reached out with both my hands and grabbed both of hers. "Don't ever be sorry for something as wonderful as that," I said when I found my voice. I bent forward slowly and kissed her gently. Suddenly, the kiss turned fierce as the passion between us erupted. We held each other tightly and our lips felt seared together.

When we broke the clinch, we were both breathing heavily.

"I . . . uhm . . . ," we both started to speak at the same time and then laughed.

"You first," I said.

"Not fair."

I looked around the parking lot. We were alone. I pulled Bekka to me and kissed her again. It was as good as the first time.

"Whew!" she said when we parted.

"Yeah," I said, slightly breathless.

Neither of us seemed to know what to do or say next. Not an unusual state of affairs for me when I'm around a woman I have feelings for.

Bekka seemed as flustered as I was.

"Uhm . . . I guess I'll see you tomorrow at the airport?" she said.

"Airport?"

"Yes. For the flight to Houston."

I shook my head to clear it. "Oh, yes. Of course."

"Uhm . . . Well, good night. It was . . ."

"Different?"

She gave a suddenly natural and relaxed laugh. "Is that what it's called when your date almost gets you killed?"

I laughed too and we kissed again before she slid into her car and drove off with a wave.

I stood in the parking lot for a long time, not thinking about anything but the feel of her lips on mine. Why is it that romance always seems to spring up under the most inconvenient circumstances? According to my brief from Sir

Adam, I was supposed to be tracking down an insidious threat to soccer in America, but here I was, pursuing Cupid's promise. I never said I was smart.

When I finally got my act together, I entered the Acropolis through the player's entrance. It was time to play out my ritual of visiting the playing field on the night before a game. It didn't matter that the Ravens' home field wouldn't be the one we were playing on, or that the field was set up tonight for a hockey match instead of a soccer game. It was the ritual that was important because it gave me time to focus myself and prepare mentally for the game to come. Sticks knew my pregame habits and had waited for me to show up.

Sticks stood up in the shadows and came over to stand in front of me. He rested one of his frail hands on my shoulders. The light from the player's tunnel spilled around me and played across his face, showing me the compassion in his features.

"Tomorrow night will be a long way from an international confrontation at Wembley," he said quietly.

I nodded, suddenly unable to speak with the enormity of it all. I was going back between the goalposts. It was a feat that only days earlier seemed an impossibility.

"Do you believe in reincarnation?" I asked, my voice choking. Too many emotional swings in too little time. From anger to hope. From lust to love. From despair to . . . to what? Life, perhaps.

"No. But I do believe in you, Ian. You were the best I've ever coached. Maybe the best anyone has ever coached. You can be again."

"No. I'll never be the best there is again." Tears sprang to my eye. Sid Doyle popped unbidden into my mind. "But I can be the best that I can be."

The following day would quickly show if that best was good enough.

SIXTEEN

THE HOUSTON SPORTS PALACE was rocking and rolling with a packed house of thirteen thousand fans eagerly awaiting the quarter-final game kickoff. I was waiting in the player's tunnel with my stomach in knots. The rest of my teammates were ahead of me in the tunnel, each one running out onto the playing field as his name was called over the loudspeaker. We all carried cheap soccer balls with us that we would kick up into the stands when the introductions were finished.

Finally, I was at the tunnel mouth. I could see the other players lined up at center field. I began to pray that I wouldn't trip over my own feet as I ran out to join them.

The arena announcer continued his hype-filled introductions. ". . . and playing in goal for the Ravens, wearing number eight, returning to goalkeeping for the first time in over a year . . . IAN . . . CHAPEL!"

I was rooted to the floor until Stavoros gave me a gentle push from behind to move me out into the arena. My heart was in my mouth, and the second the full force of the crowd noise hit me I felt like I was going to throw up. Then somebody in the crowd yelled, "Go home Cyclops!" and I knew everything was as it should be.

I stood with the rest of the Ravens as the crowd yelled their enthusiasm for their home team player introductions. We then fidgeted through the national anthem, and finally exploded into action by kicking the soccer balls we were carrying into the stands.

Jogging over to the player's bench, I picked up my gloves, stuffed my hands into them, and pulled the Velcro closures tight at the wrists. I didn't normally wear gloves, but then I didn't normally wear a lot of the gear I had covering my body. My long-sleeve jersey came complete with padding quilted into the shoulders and under the forearms, and my sweatpants had knee pads permanently sewn in. I'd learned the hard way during practices that these items were essential to the survival of the indoor soccer goalie. The hard inside playing surface was nowhere near as forgiving as the outside turf.

"Good luck," Bekka said from where she sat on the bench next to the Hot Tamales and the coaches. In the first row of audience seats behind the player's bench, I could see Nina Brisbane, prominent in her black veil, and Sticks sitting side by side. They both nodded to me.

"Get yourself ready," I said to Bekka. "I might let four goals get by me in the first four minutes and you'll find yourself called into action real quick."

Bekka laughed, but Nick cut her off. "I'll be put in before she is," he said, and glowered at me.

"Nick," I told him disdainfully, "you're simply a legend in your own mind."

Impulsively, I gave Bekka a quick pack on the cheek and trotted out to take my position.

The Ravens' European line was on the field and Wagstaff came back to have a brief word with me.

"Get the ball to me in the middle of the field as much as you can. I want to score early and put this game away."

"Good luck to you too," I said.

Wagstaff grunted and, to my surprise, smiled. "You and me, we're too good to have to rely on luck." He turned on his heel and glided back to center court.

The referee blew the whistle and we were under way.

There was something vaguely familiar about the referee. He was a short, stocky man with a shock of white hair above and heavily muscled thighs below. I didn't know the man, so I could only put the familiarity down to the white hair which was as full as that possessed by Terrance Brisbane. The mind association with Brisbane made me wonder if he'd been able to get the stains from Pat Devlin's blood balloon out of his suit.

Devlin himself certainly appeared no worse for the wear from the near riot he'd caused. He'd greeted me as we boarded the plane earlier in the day with a Cheshire grin and a copy of *The Outlook*, the local Santa Monica paper. It was folded to a half-page article detailing the events at the Golden Harp. Pat had stuffed it in my hands without a word and moved off to find his seat.

Now it seemed he had put the previous evening behind him and was concentrating strictly on soccer. He glided across the field like a wraith full of fury and power. I'd looked up his statistics in the form book and they were impressive. He'd scored forty-three goals over the course of the season and had been credited with thirty-three assists for a combined total of seventy-six points, the highest in the league. Now, watching the power of his play, it was easy to see the genius that lurked inside him.

It was only seconds after the kickoff that I had my first opportunity to get my hands on the ball, and my first indication that there was something out of kilter with the referee. The Alamos were renowned for their physical style of play, often drawing criticism from opposing teams. I found out firsthand how physical they could be when Bronco Powell, their captain and center forward, shoulder charged me while I was still in the air trying to gather in a high cross.

Instinct made me secure the ball between my arms and chest, but the air had vacated my lungs and there were dark spots before my eyes as I crashed to the carpet. The only thing missing from the tableau was the sound of the referee's whistle. I looked up from my fetal position to see him signalling angrily at me to play on and mumbling something about delay of game. Delay of game? The game should have been delayed right down his throat! I'd never been the victim of a more flagrant foul. I dragged myself to my knees, rolled the ball to Birch Bloodworth, and tried to prepare for the next onslaught.

It was about here that the differences between indoor and outdoor soccer became exceedingly clear. The indoor game was not merely a substitute for its more popular outdoor relative, nor was it some second-rate sport for broken-down footballers. I learned rapidly that indoor soccer demands that every skill learned in outdoor soccer be speeded up and honed to perfection. There was no margin for error.

The game also demanded additional skills as players rebounded passes and shots off the boards with consummate perfection. Set plays were used far more often than in outdoor soccer, and defensive players were expected to constantly push forward on offense as well.

Goalkeepers, in particular, had a far more demanding position to play. Within three minutes, I'd already been called on to stop five shots. In some outdoor games, I wouldn't have been called on to stop five shots during the whole ninety minutes. The pace of the game was tremendous, like being inside a giant soccer pinball machine being played by an expert.

I was also amazed to see the Houston goalie often come out of his net and dribble the ball a third of the way up the field with his feet before passing off and running back to cover his goal again. In outdoor soccer this move, while legal, would have been suicide. In indoor soccer, though, it was all part of the game. I began to wonder if I had really bitten off more than I could chew. I had enough on my hands just keeping up with my traditional goalkeeping duties without worrying about developing new field-playing skills.

Shortly, I was rudely introduced to another tricky aspect of indoor soccer, the shoot-out. Often a series of shoot-outs are used to determine the winner of a game tied at full-time, but a shoot-out in indoor soccer is also in place of a penalty kick.

Indoor soccer is played in four fifteen-minute periods, as opposed to the more traditional forty-five-minute halves of outdoor soccer. About ten minutes into the first period, the referee blew his whistle to call our fullback, Alan Hardacre, for a hand ball in the penalty area. Alan nearly went spare. There was no way, he insisted, that he had intentionally touched the ball with his hand, and I can't say as I disagreed with him. Bronco Powell had made a long, left-footed shot which had caromed off of Alan's side, striking his arm and hand through no fault of his own. The referee would hear nothing of Alan's protest, though, and sent him to the penalty box for two minutes while awarding Powell a shoot-out penalty shot.

I had practiced for this with Sticks, but this would be my baptism under fire. The shoot-out was different from a regular penalty kick in several aspects. It was still a one-on-one confrontation between the keeper and the penalty shooter, but that was where the similarities ended. In a shoot-out, unlike a penalty kick in outdoor soccer, the goalkeeper is able to move as the penalty shooter dribbles towards him from the red line located thirty feet from the center line in each half. The penalty shooter tries to dribble the ball, or shoot the ball, around the keeper and into the goal for the score.

When Bronco started toward me, I came out cautiously to cut down the angle. His sprint in was hard and fast, and he sold me a dummy like I was some wet-behind-the-ears rookie. I went one way, and Bronco easily ran the ball around me in the other direction and hammered it home for the score. The red light above the goal blazed to life, and a siren wailed over the cheering of the crowd. Bronco, fist clenched in the air, ran to accept the congratulations of his teammates.

I was again surprised when Wagstaff came over to help me to my embarrassed feet.

"So, they draw first blood and you are no longer a virgin." His clipped Germanic accent always reminded me of something out of a bad movie. "Now, you will relax and play better than ever."

Here was the man I'd hated with such intensity giving me a pep talk. It was seemingly incongruous, but I accepted his hand-up in the spirit it was given. Our fight during the first day of practice had taken a lot of hate out of the both of us.

The Alamos were soon coming back at us again. With Powell scoring on the shoot-out, Alan Hardacre was immediately released from the penalty box. It wasn't long, however, before another Raven took his place.

We'd finished the first quarter down by one goal and switched ends of the carpet for the start of the second quarter. The Hot Tamales were on the field. Pepe Brazos took the ball from Chico Juarez and streaked down the field in a dazzling one-man display of footwork. From six yards out, he fired a rocket shot that rebounded off the glass above the crossbar.

Danny Castalano had been following Brazos in on the play. In a spectacular display of gymnastic ability, he leapt into the air and executed a picture perfect bicycle kick which sent the rebounded ball streaking into the back of the Alamos' net. Lights and sirens exploded and we all ran out to embrace Danny.

It was all for nought, however, because the referee was blowing his whistle and disallowing the goal

"What the hell is he talking about?" Danny exploded when he realized what was going on.

"Dangerous play. High kicking in a crowd of players," the referee stated flatly. He had his palms up in the air as if to ward off our anguished arguments. "Two minutes in the penalty box for Castalano," he said, and then tried to walk away from all of us who were clustered around him.

At the timekeeper's table he briefly explained his decision to one of the two assistant referees.

We argued and raged, but the outcome remained unchanged. When order was restored, the goal was disallowed and Danny Castalano went off to spend two minutes in the penalty box.

I gave the referee a hard look. There was something wrong, out of kilter. I'd felt it at the beginning of the game and put it down to the similarity in hair color with Terrance Brisbane, but now I couldn't shake the feeling that there was something more to it. I didn't know what yet, but there was definitely something.

I didn't have time to think about the problem, however, because the next two minutes were a solid blur of action. With Castalano in the penalty box, the Alamos turned the pressure up with a ferocious power-play offense. Bronco Powell was backed up by Jaime Estevez and Emilio Orantes, two of the league's top strikers, and Erik Greenspan and Johan Luft, two brilliant defenders who also possessed strong striking skills. Between them they fired shot after shot on goal.

Playing a man short meant that we could do little more than fight back with a tight-knit zone defense. Stavoros had substituted our line to put the best defenders and penalty killers on the field. Wagstaff was the field general. Pat Devlin might have more goals and assists than Wagstaff, but he wasn't the leader that the German was and that's why Wagstaff was the team captain. Our backs were Blockhead Bloodworth on the left and Alan Hardacre on the right. Mitch Dakota, one of the American defenders, had been moved up to play opposite Wagstaff.

With myself in goal, we fought vainly to keep the Alamos from scoring. We would have had an easier time of it, though, if we hadn't been hindered again and again by the referee's whistle. Every time we turned around it seemed we were being penalized for some real or imagined infraction of the rules. The Alamos received gifts of free kick after free kick, but we fought on grimly and refused to let them penetrate the goal net.

When Castalano was released from indenture, he sprinted onto the field and we were suddenly on the attack again. Stavoros immediately substituted the line to bring in fresh legs. Brazos and Juarez joined their fellow Hot Tamale on the front line, Hank Decker replaced Bloodworth, and Dakota dropped back to his normal defensive position.

For the next few minutes, the Hot Tamales went into their shake-and-bake routine. Their play brought the crowd to its feet in admiration. Not one of the Latins kept control of the ball for longer than three seconds before passing it off to another teammate.

They seemed to know that they had to keep the ball moving to avoid getting called for false fouls. Their passing and control was so brilliant they dazzled the Alamos into confusion. Everything was two-touch; one touch to control the ball, and another to pass it off. Once the ball was passed, the passer would run to an open zone to receive the ball back again for another two-touch.

Their play was like fine Swiss clockwork, cleanly executed and precise to the second. Brazos to Juarez to Castalano and back, over and over again. The Alamos were getting desperate, jumping in and colliding with one or another of the Hot Tamales in vicious sliding tackles which drew no attention from the referee. And then suddenly, when it appeared that the Hot Tamales were going to do nothing but play keep-away with the ball for the rest of the period, Danny Castalano let loose a first-time volley shot off a pass from Juarez. The Alamos' goalkeeper never saw the ball as it flashed past him and jammed into the back of his net. This time the lights and sirens couldn't be stopped by the referee's whistle, the goal had been pristine, and the score stood at 1–1.

We battled on with the Alamos for the remainder of the period without further scoring, a situation that didn't come about from lack of trying on the part of the referee. I was really getting narked. I'd been beat about by so many knees, fists, elbows, and feet that I felt like I'd been run through a blender. However, not one single foul had been called against the Alamos' players as a result of this treatment. When the halftime whistle sounded, I was a weary and sodden mess as I dragged myself off to the locker room.

The halftime break ran for fifteen minutes. I knew that I was going to have to find some way to fix the referee before we went back to start the third period or there was no way we were going to survive the game. In the locker room Wagstaff was ranting and raving, fit to be tied. Stavoros, Danny Castalano, and the other Hot Tamales were also all trying to talk at the same time. I couldn't think because of the noise, so I grabbed a handful of orange slices and stepped outside into the corridor.

Sticks was standing out there along with Nina Brisbane.

"Tough game, old son?" he asked.

"Any game is tough when the other team constantly has an extra player on the field."

Sticks nodded, but before he could speak further, a voice came from further down the corridor.

"Ms. Nina? Where do you want me to pick you up when the game is over?"

Nina, Sticks, and I all turned to find Reeves in his chauffeur's uniform, waiting for an answer. He had flown with us on the plane and had taken charge of the limo that was waiting to pick Nina up at the airport. The team might be having financial troubles, but Nina still had the wherewithal to travel in style.

I took one look at the young black man, and the penny dropped into place. "Quickly, come with me," I said to him before Nina could reply to his question. I grabbed him by the arm and hustled him down the hall. Sticks and Nina followed in our wake, obviously as baffled by my actions as Reeves was. I, however, knew exactly what I was doing.

When we arrived at the small locker room that the referee and his assistants used for changing, I pulled Reeves to a halt. "Yesterday, when you picked Caitlin Brisbane up from outside my hotel . . ."

"What . . . ?" Nina tried to interrupt, but I waved her down.

"Do you remember?" I asked Reeves.

"Yes, of course."

"There was a man in the back of the limo. A man with white hair. Do you know who he was?"

"No idea. The back of the limo is soundproof. I'd picked him up earlier in the morning at the airport at Ms. Caitlin's request. He waited in the car while she was at your hotel. After we left the hotel, Ms. Caitlin had me take him back to the airport."

"Have you been watching the game at all?" I asked.

"No. I've been cleaning the car and refilling the champagne coffers. The service we rented the car from really did a lousy job. . . ."

I cut him short impatiently. "Look through there," I said, pointing at a small window in the locker-room door. "Tell me if you recognize anyone."

Reeves turned his face to the window and peered inside. "Absolutely," he said a second later. "The guy with the white hair is the guy that was in the back of the limo with Ms. Caitlin. Who is he?"

"Just what is going on here?" Nina was demanding to know. Her voice was strident, and I put a finger to my mouth to quiet her down.

"Your sister tried to buy me off yesterday, but she had another plan waiting in the wings in case, as it turned out, I didn't want to join her party. It should be real clear to anybody watching this game that the referee has been about as unbiased as a South American election. When I followed your sister out of the hotel restaurant and watched her get into the limo, I caught a glimpse of a man with white hair in the backseat. I thought it was your father at first, but then realized the man wasn't big enough.

"All game long I've been trying to figure out what it was about the referee that was familiar, but it wasn't until Reeves showed up in the corridor that I put two and two together."

Nina's veil was vibrating like her head was on a launching pad.

"I swear I'll cut that little bitch's heart out." She spat the words out like a vicious epithet.

Always practical, Sticks asked, "What are you going to do about the situation?"

I thought for a moment.

"I'm going to run a bluff."

Nina's program listed the referee's name as Leo Crider, and I wanted a word with him.

As the team made its way down the player's tunnel for the start of the third period, I slowed everyone down until I saw Crider exit his locker room with his two assistant referees. Working to my instructions, all the Ravens players surged forward to overtake them.

With the precision of German engineering, Wagstaff cut off Crider and isolated him from his cohorts like a cowboy cutting a rogue calf out of the herd. As Wagstaff kept Crider pinned back, the rest of the team members swept the assistant referees along with their tide.

"Get out of my way," Crider said to Wagstaff in an imperial manner. He tried to poke Wagstaff, but the German grabbed Crider's hand and bent the offending finger back painfully.

"If you scream or call out," I told Crider calmly, "I'll let him break it."

I pushed open the door and Wagstaff walked Crider backwards into the referee's locker room. The door swung shut with a quiet shushing noise. Wagstaff was keeping enough pressure on Crider's finger to keep the man up on his toes in pain.

"What do you want? This is an outrage!" Crider was fuming mad, but he didn't cry out. That in itself was a good enough indication that he knew he'd been caught with his hand in the biscuit tin.

"I'll tell you what we want Mr. Crider. We want a fair game. Not this rigged carnival sideshow you've been running . . ."

"I don't know what you're talking about. Let me go before I have you slung out of the game."

I nodded to Wagstaff who applied more pressure to the finger. Crider crumpled down to his knees, his bent finger still in Wagstaff's sadistic control. When Crider started to scream, I grabbed a dirty sock off a bench and shoved it in his mouth.

I squatted to put myself on the same level as Crider. There were tears in the man's eyes. "The only person who is going to be slung out of the game is you, mate," I told him in reasonable tones. "I know all about your little cozy chat with Caitlin Brisbane. If that becomes public knowledge, then you're going to be at least banned from soccer for life and maybe prosecuted." If it was possible, Crider turned paler than ever at my words. He still had some fight in him though, and spat the sock out of his mouth.

"You can't prove anything," he said with contempt.

We didn't have much longer before someone came looking for us. It was time to play my ace bluff card. I pushed open the door to the locker room and pulled Reeves inside.

"Is this the man?" I asked him.

"That's the scumbag all right." Reeves had the collar of his shirt and jacket turned up and a pair of futuristic Ray-Bans wrapped around his face. He looked like a casting call reject from "Miami Vice," which I'm sure was his intention.

"This gentleman was your chauffeur in Los Angeles when you flew in yesterday for your meeting with Caitlin Brisbane. He overheard your entire conversation with that lady through the limo's intercom system. He is willing to testify against you. I'm also sure it won't be too hard to get the passenger lists for the airlines to corroborate his evidence regarding your presence in LA."

Crider's attention was definitely riveted. He couldn't take his eyes off of Reeves as he considered the implications.

"Now, we're not asking you to call the game in our favor. We can beat this team without your help. But if you so much as make a single bad call against us for the rest of the game then we will immediately file a protest and you can kiss your ass good-bye. *Capice?*'' I threw in a little Italian in memory of Maddox.

Crider nodded his head up and down, but that wasn't good enough for Wagstaff. ''If we lose, little man,'' he said evilly, ''I will come back and break all your fingers. . . .'' He would have said more, but I put my hand on his shoulder and tugged him gently away.

Wagstaff released the finger and followed me to the door. However, he hesitated there and turned back to face Crider. ''Remember what I promised,'' he said, and then followed me out the door and down to the field.

The third period was ten minutes late getting under way and the crowd was getting restless. Eventually, though, Crider came down the player's tunnel with one of his assistant referees who had gone back to look for him. He had a little color back in his face, but he refused to look at either Wagstaff or me.

The whistle blew and the bloodbath began.

Crider had gone from turning a blind eye to fouls committed by the Alamos to turning a blind eye to all but the most flagrant fouls committed by either team. This put us back on even footing with the Alamos, but at a very high cost.

Halfway through the third period, Danny Castalano was carried off the field. He was lost for the season with a knee injury. Mitch Dakota took an elbow in the eye and had to leave the game, and Jackson Bopha, the third striker on Wagstaff's offensive line, was run into the boards and slightly concussed. Those were the worst of our injuries but all of us suffered from various trips, elbows, fists, knees, and slammings. The audience ate it up.

At the end of the third period the score was 3–3. Two more goals had been slipped past me by the Alamos' strikers, but Wagstaff had kept us even with two punishing goals of his own. He'd played like a madman unleashed, even refusing to come off the field when Stavoros signaled him. I'd seen him play this way enough times in outdoor soccer to know what he was capable of and I sent the ball his way as often as possible. It was nice for a change to have him as a weapon instead of an adversary.

During the short break before the last period, I quickly took stock of our condition. Overall we were battered and bloodied but unbowed. We'd also dished out a fair share of physical punishment to the Alamos. As we sucked oranges on the sideline, I looked over the see a satisfying profusion of ice bags being put into use on the Alamos' bench.

I turned my attention back to our batch of warriors and looked for Wagstaff. He was icing down a nasty turf burn on his left thigh.

"Fifteen minutes left to win this thing," I said to him as I discarded an orange rind. "How are you holding up?"

He grimaced. "I'll make it."

I watched him for a second and then asked, "If I get everyone to feed you the ball, can you score?" I was well aware that Pat Devlin might be our top scorer, but I knew Wagstaff of old and there was nobody better in a game like this. I only gave fleeting thought to the irony inherent in my current relationship with this man.

The German gave me a shrouded look from under his brows. "I'll make you a deal," he said. "You keep the ball out of the back of our net, and I'll make sure it gets into the back of theirs."

"Done," I said, and moved off quickly to pass the word on to Pat Devlin. I also spoke with Pepe Brazos, who was now playing on the line with the two Europeans because of the injuries to Castalano and Bopha.

On the field again, the Alamos came out with all their guns firing. Their front line of Powell, Estevez, and Orantes came at us like the Four Horsemen of the Apocalypse minus one. They kept the pressure on full-bore. Shot after shot blasted toward me, but I'd suddenly found an old familiar groove and there was no way they were going to get by me. I was so tuned in to the ball that every time it came near me I gathered it in as easily as if it were attached to me by a string. I felt like I had wings on my feet.

A great joyfulness was welling up in my chest, almost bringing tears to my eyes. I'd thought I would never feel this way again. It was like being reborn. Resurrected. It had taken me a lot longer than three days, but the result was the same. The rock had been rolled away from my crypt and I lived. By the grace of God and all that was true in the world, I lived!

If we stayed strong and cool, I knew we could break the back of the attack. I could sense the Alamos' show of force was all bluff and bluster, a fragile front like a movie studio's back lot. It looked good from a distance, but there was no substance behind it.

Once again I gathered in the ball as Alamos' players crashed around me. Quickly I threw it overhand to Wagstaff, who was streaking up the field. Instead of coming back on defense, he had been continually staying in the area of the Alamos' red line, looking to penetrate their defense with a fast break.

With inborn skill, he trapped my pass with his chest and dropped the ball down to his feet. A simple sidestep faked the one Alamos defender who was close to him, and then it was off to the races.

Gregor Dunforland, the Alamos' goalkeeper, came gamely out of his net, but he was no match for the determined German. Moving at top speed, Wagstaff ran around one side of Dunforland while passing the ball to himself around the goalkeeper's other side. Dunforland didn't know which way to go, tried to go both directions at once, and self-destructed. Behind him, Wagstaff calmly regained the ball and belted it into the top of the empty goal.

The shot was so powerful, the red light on top of the goal was knocked flying into the audience.

We screamed and cheered and I ran down the field to embrace Wagstaff in a bear hug. 4–3. We were one goal up and only three minutes left until the end of the game.

When order was restored, the game was restarted. How-

ever, the remaining moments were merely ritual. The game
had ended with Wagstaff's goal. The Alamos were left
leaden-footed and dispirited. When the final whistle blew,
the charade of the last minutes was over and we went happily berserk.

Bekka rushed off the bench and threw her arms around
me, and I suddenly felt like it was the most natural thing in
the world. I might have been bold enough to kiss her full
on the lips, but the moment was broken as other Ravens
players swarmed onto the field and wrapped their arms
around us.

The celebration slowed down long enough for us to shake
hands with some of the Alamos players. Then the backslap-
ping and joking continued as we made our way down the
player's tunnel to the locker rooms. Bekka had to separate
from us to go into the women's facilities, and I realized
how lonely her quest was to insinuate herself into an all-
male sport. I admired her tenacity.

In the locker room you would have thought we'd won the
World Cup. It was incredible. We still had two tough games
ahead of us to worry about, but the relief of making it
through this game against the rough play of the Alamos was
an almost tangible thing.

There was only one small incident which marred the celebration. After showering, I was getting dressed in front of
my locker and talking over the game highlights with Pat
Devlin when the local reporters were allowed in. With them
was a young boy about ten years old. He gave off the air of
being attached to one of the reporters, although it wasn't
very clear which one. I had a suspicion he wasn't with anyone in the room, but he scammed his way through the door
in a quest for autographs.

He was a clean-cut lad with an impish smile that lit up
his whole face. After a few minutes of hanging around with
the reporters, listening to the informal press conference, he
broke loose from the crowd and made a beeline for me.

"Please, Mr. Chapel, can I have your autograph?" He

held out a grubby notebook and a pen with a chewed end. "You were terrific tonight."

Polite and complimentary. How could I resist?

I took the proffered notebook and pen. "What's your name, son?"

"Billy, sir. I want to be a professional goalkeeper too when I get out of college. I'm already the goalie on my AYSO team. We were undefeated this year. State champions!" He was bubbling over with enthusiasm, and the fire of the soccer fanatic burned brightly in his eyes.

I scribbled something appropriate in the notebook and handed it back.

"Thanks, Mr. Chapel."

Something about the boy's open enjoyment of everything going on around him touched me. "Wait a minute, Billy," I told him. "I've got a better idea."

I walked across the locker room to the ball rack. Miles Norton, the Ravens' equipment manager, had restocked it with the inexpensive balls we kicked into the crowd at the beginning of the game. I noticed, however, that these new balls had red markings instead of black. There were about twenty balls on the stand. I picked one up to give to Billy. It felt a bit mushy, so I put it back on the rack and squeezed another one. They all seemed short of air. I put it down to the cheap quality used for promotion and settled for the best of the bad bunch.

I took the ball back with me to where Billy was waiting. I borrowed his pen to scrawl my name on one of the leather pentagons which made up the stitched fabric quilt of the ball, and tossed it to Billy. His face came alive like that of a kid surveying his wrapped booty on Christmas morning.

"Gee, Mr. Chapel, this is great. Thanks."

"You're welcome, Billy." I turned to Pat Devlin, who'd watched the interchange with amusement. I handed him the chewed pen. "Sign the kid's ball and quit grinning your fool head off. You were ten years old once too."

"Oh aye," said Pat taking the pen. "And don't I just wish I was again."

"Here! What's going on? Give me that!" Miles Norton snatched the ball out of Billy's hands as he was handing it to Devlin.

"Where do you get off stealing this ball?"

"I, I, I . . ." Billy stammered, shocked.

"Cool down, Norton," I said, putting my hand on Billy's shoulder to reassure him. "I gave the kid the ball. He didn't steal it. It's only one of the ones we kick into the crowd."

"Well, he can't have it!"

"Why not?"

"We've given enough free soccer balls today. That's why not." Without further explanation Norton stormed off with the ball.

I looked askance at Devlin, but he just shrugged at me. "Must be his time of the month," he said.

"I'm sorry about that, Billy," I told the boy. "But don't worry about it. How would you like a sweaty goalkeeper's jersey instead?" I handed my jersey to the boy, who reacted like I'd given him the Holy Grail.

"Wow!" he said, with his eyes as big as moons.

Billy went off to make his autograph rounds, and the excited celebration around the locker room continued. Someone broke out a case of champagne. After the death of Maddox and the uncertainty surrounding it, the team had been thrown off its stride. Winning this game had restored the team's confidence and esprit de corps. More than anything else, that was what the celebration was about.

We had four days before the next game, when we would have to put it all on the line again. But right now, for this instant in time, we Ravens were invincible.

SEVENTEEN

INVINCIBLE IS A relative term. By noon the next day, events had shattered the spell of our victory and had brought stinging reality into harsh focus.

Five of us were gathered in the sitting room of the Marriott suite that Sticks and I shared. Bekka was draped over an easy chair while Sticks was slumped in its matching counterpart. Nina Brisbane, trim and mysterious in black pants, black silk blouse, startlingly white pearls, and the ever-present, shoulder-length, black veil, sat on the couch. I stood with my backside resting on a small writing desk while our surprise guest, Sir Adam Qwale, paced the plush carpet.

The previous evening, Sir Adam had been waiting at the airport when our plane arrived back from Houston. It was no secret that money was tight in the Ravens franchise, so there were no overnight accommodations for the team in Houston after the game. The closest we came to being splurged on were the two free drinks in the coach section of the red-eye flight back to Los Angeles.

Other business had kept Sir Adam from being at the game, but as half-owner of the Ravens, he was still excited to be part of the winning performance. After all, the thrill of vicarious victory was the main reason owners took the financial risks inherent in running a sports franchise. Prestige and love for sport were also elements, but winning was the big rush. Sir Adam's jubilation, though, like that of the others gathered in the room, had been blasted to hell by the morning newspapers.

The front pages had the whole mess smeared across a banner headline: SEATTLE GULLS GOALKEEPER MURDERED. In smaller type beneath the banner was a second eye-grabber: *Tom Sweet, Second AISL Goalkeeper Killed This Season.*

"If anyone has any bright ideas, now is the time to air them out," Sir Adam commented flatly. He seemed to suddenly tire of his pacing and flopped down on the couch next to Nina Brisbane. With an angry gesture he snatched up the disarrayed newspaper pages from the floor in front of him. We had been hashing over the news in them for the past two hours and were no more settled than when we'd started.

Earlier in the morning, Nina Brisbane had been having breakfast with Sir Adam in the Marriott's dining room when she spotted a photo on the front page of the *Los Angeles Tribune* that had been left behind on their table. Shocked, she had shown the photo to Sir Adam, and they had immediately rushed to find me.

When they had pounded on the door to the suite, I was already being interrogated over the phone by Ethan Kelso. Bekka, who had come over to take me out on a long training run, answered the door.

I put my hand up to cut short any outburst from Sir Adam as he stormed into the room, and then spoke back into the phone. "Yes, all right, Ethan, I'll come by first thing tomorrow and talk to the Seattle detectives. I don't think there's anything I can tell them, but I'll come anyway."

I listened some more and then answered again. "Yes. Like you, I have no doubt it's Donovan, but I have no idea what he plans to do next. That's your job to guess, not mine. Okay. I'll see you tomorrow.'' I hung up and turned to Sir Adam. He thrust out the front page of the paper at me.

''Have you . . .''

''No, I haven't seen the papers,'' I interrupted, and took the outthrust pages, ''but Ethan Kelso . . .''

''Who's Kelso?'' Nina Brisbane asked.

''He's the detective in charge of Maddox's murder. He told me that one of the reporters on the *Seattle Times* is an indoor soccer fan. . . .''

''One of the few,'' mumbled Sticks as he came into the room to sit down opposite Bekka.

I gave him a quick glance and continued. ''Anyway, the reporter connected this new mess up in Seattle with the Maddox murder down here. Now the Seattle police are looking for a direct tie between the two incidents.''

Newspapers always seem to be the bearers of bad news and today was no different. The story had hit the front page of the *Los Angeles Tribune* in the form of a captioned photo with an allusion to a short article on page three's ''Around the Nation'' section. Sir Adam had arranged for a copy of the main Seattle paper to be immediately faxed to the hotel.

Tom Sweet was the AISL's rookie of the year. Before joining the Gulls, he had been a goalkeeper at Notre Dame University where he'd been majoring in physiotherapy and female physiotherapists. His stellar performances this season had kept the Gulls at the top of their division. The previous evening, while we had been playing in Houston, Sweet had been flawless as his team went on a 5–0 rampage against the Vancouver Totems in the other west coast quarter final.

The Gulls game had been played on their home turf before a good-sized crowd. After a brief celebration, Sweet had returned to his upscale townhouse and gone to bed with a soccer groupie. According to her statement, quoted in the newspaper, she had experienced numerous orgasms before passing out on Quaaludes and could provide no further details.

While the couple languished in sexual unconsciousness, somebody had entered the townhouse and put an end to Sweet's career by dropping a concrete slab on his chest.

Apparently, the first impact had only paralyzed him. The police believed the slab was dropped three more times before he died. The murderer, however, hadn't laid a finger on Sweet's passed-out bed partner. She was left to come out of her stupor in the morning and discover the eighty-pound, three-inch-thick slab of concrete embedded in Sweet's chest like a misshapen tombstone.

In an attempt to bulk up the meager facts about the murder, the Seattle paper had gone on to cover less important information. The story finished with the statement that the Gulls were scheduled to play the AISL semifinal game against the Ravens in LA on Wednesday.

The New York Lights and the Chicago Wind had won their respective quarter final games. They would now be paired off in the east coast semifinal game the same night. The winners of the semifinals would then battle it out on Sunday. Los Angeles had been chosen a year earlier as the site for the AISL's 1990 Super Soccer Bowl.

Nina Brisbane appeared distraught by the news of Sweet's murder. Sir Adam, on the other hand, was startled by it, but had quickly accepted and assessed the situation. It had angered him and started him pacing, but he'd accepted it and had immediately started to look for options.

"Is there any doubt in your mind at all that Liam Donovan is the slab dropper?" Sir Adam now asked me from his position on the couch.

"None at all. I also believe he wants us to know it's him. Why else would he use Sean Brody's signature killing method? Donovan swore he would hold me accountable for his partner's death. By using the concrete slab on another goalkeeper, he's sending a message that he hasn't forgotten about me. Whatever other motives are behind his actions, you can bet that I'm still somewhere high on his list."

"I don't understand any of this," Bekka said in exasperation. "What is really going on? Are you saying that Maddox's murder wasn't an isolated incident? That this Donovan character is some kind of madman running around killing off goalkeepers?''

I shook my head. ''Liam Donovan is definitely a murderous loose cannon, but I don't know yet if we can say he's responsible for Maddox's murder as well as Sweet's. You're far from alone in not understanding everything that's happening.'' I turned to face Sir Adam. ''What about pulling back and leaving the whole situation to the police? Maybe the rest of the season should even be cancelled. Or at least postponed until Donovan is either captured, killed, or chased out of the country.''

Sir Adam looked back at me sharply. ''We can't cancel the rest of the season. Soccer is bigger than the actions of any one man. It has often proven to be bigger than countries. The game is above politics, above wars. The game, like the show, has to go on. It has to endure.''

''Even at the risk of human life?'' I asked. In actuality, I agreed with Sir Adam's sentiment, but I couldn't help pushing the issue. I'm a perverse devil's advocate at heart.

Sir Adam didn't answer me, but his features turned morose.

The room itself seemed caught in a state of limbo at this juncture in the conversation until Nina Brisbane rose from her position on the couch. Appearing to have regained much of her normal composure, she walked the few steps to where I was standing. She placed her right hand on the intersection of my crossed arms, as if her touch could transmit her feelings better than her words.

''Ian.'' She paused after saying my name. Perhaps it was only my imagination, but I could somehow sense the horrible slash of her mouth trying to twist into a gentle smile behind her dark veil. ''The bottom line is that if the Ravens do not receive the gate revenues and league bonuses for the remaining play-off games . . . if we do not, in fact, reach the finals . . . then the franchise will be bankrupt. We are hanging on by the slenderest of financial threads, like the league itself.'' She pulled on my arms, gently rocking them back and forth as if to shake some sense into me.

''I know this sounds terribly cold and self-serving, but we have to make this situation work for us. Maddox and Sweet are dead. If there was any price I could pay that would change that, I would pay it, but there isn't. And meanwhile their deaths are bringing public attention to the league like never before. We can't afford to squander that attention if the team and the league are to survive.''

I didn't know how to respond. Her reasoning made no sense to me. ''Quite the humanitarian, aren't you?'' I asked with obvious sarcasm.

''I'm a businesswoman,'' Nina retorted. The level of her voice hadn't changed, but there was a different kind of steel in it. ''Any humanity I had was stripped from me years ago.'' She jerked her hand off of me and put it to her veil. The depth of her sudden anger and frustration seemed to physically reverberate around me like the ringing of a gong.

I looked at her and realized I could never understand what went on in her mind. Even knowing what my own handicap had done to my mental outlook, I couldn't conceive of what had happened to this woman's inner being after her outer shell had gone from princess to gargoyle. My trials and tribulations seemed trivial by comparison, and I felt a sudden and deep compassion for her.

''I've never known you to run from a fight, Ian,'' Sir Adam said quietly.

''And I'm not running from this one.'' I shrugged my shoulders and sighed. ''I'm just trying to consider all the options. I told you back in England that I would play the hand out, and I will.''

I also knew that I didn't have much choice but to continue. Cancelling the season wouldn't stop Liam Donovan's personal quest for revenge. I was also struggling against the fact that it wasn't in my nature to sit around and wait for the axe to fall. Or in this case the slab to drop. I didn't know what was behind Donovan's actions, but if I kept trying to push the buttons of whoever was controlling him, I might get a crack at settling the situation.

As melodramatic as it appeared, it didn't change the fact that Donovan and I would end up confronting each other in a final showdown. Even if Donovan would let me walk away from the situation—no harm, no foul—I knew I couldn't. Moral outrage is an odd concept, perhaps, but two men were dead and the existence of something I loved was threatened. I was the individual who had a chance to rectify that situation. Not anyone else. Just me.

I looked away from Sir Adam, and back at Nina Brisbane.

"Thank you," she said, sensing my decision. Her hand reached out again for my folded arms. She seemed to have forgotten her outburst.

Turning her head away from me, she spoke to Sir Adam. "I have to meet with my father, but perhaps we could get together again later?"

"Yes, yes, of course," Sir Adam replied, and he stood up to see her out the door.

When she was gone, he looked at me. "I'm sorry for getting you involved in all this."

"Don't be."

"Why ever not?"

"Because last night, I was given back something in my life I never thought I'd have again. If the cost I have to pay is facing down Liam Donovan, then I'd consider it cheap at twice the price."

"Does this mean you won't be going home at the end of the season?" Bekka asked, and I turned to see she was attempting to lighten the mood.

"Don't worry too much about it, lass," said Sticks in his usual droll manner. "If Donovan doesn't get him, age will. You'll be playing first-string over him by next year."

"Thanks for the vote of confidence."

Sticks winked at Bekka and she laughed.

"Can we get back to a serious look at what's happening here?" Sir Adam requested. "If what you told me is true, about Caitlin Brisbane putting in the fix with the referee last night, do you think she could be directing Donovan's actions?''

"I don't see it," I said, and shook my head in the negative. "Caitlin Brisbane is about as subtle as a television preacher. Her attempt to blackmail me and her fixing of the referee were clumsy, both in their conception and execution. Donovan is being kept in check by a far stronger force.''

"And even if she was running Donovan," Bekka chimed in, "why would she have him kill Tom Sweet? With him out of the picture it only increases the Ravens' odds of beating Seattle in the semifinals. That's just what Caitlin doesn't want. She wants the Ravens to be defeated.''

"I must say, I have to agree," Sir Adam mused. "But if not Caitlin, then who? Terrance Brisbane?''

We all thought about that for a minute.

Bekka looked at me. "You did say it was Donovan's motorcycle parked behind the Golden Harp on the night old man Brisbane spoke there?''

"Aye," I agreed. "But we didn't see him inside, and I don't see Donovan mixing with the likes of Archer and Brisbane's other bully-boys. There could be a money connection between Terrance Brisbane and Donovan, though. After all, Ethan Kelso believes Brisbane is sending heavy financial aid to the IRA.''

"But we know that Donovan is no longer with the IRA," Sir Adam said. "He's broken away and joined the Sons of Erin.''

"Perhaps Brisbane doesn't know Donovan has splintered off. Or perhaps he's decided to knowingly support the Sons of Erin because he's tired of sitting back and waiting for the IRA to start a full-scale war. On the other hand, perhaps Donovan simply followed us down to the Golden Harp. Maybe looking for a chance to take another run at me like he did in the Acropolis parking lot.''

"That's a little too scary to even think about," Bekka said, her voice quiet. "Do you really believe Donovan is stalking you?''

"I'm going to start acting that way. He was after me in

England when I first went to visit Sir Adam. He swore revenge during our little punch-up on the docks after Brody was killed. And then he tried to run me over at the Acropolis on my first day here. If he isn't out to get me, then he's doing a good impression of someone who is."

Sweat kept dripping into my good eye from the band that held my eye patch in place. The salt from the sweat stung irritatingly and blurred my vision. I tried to wipe my forehead dry, but the cotton wristbands I was wearing were already soaked and virtually useless. Bekka and I were almost four miles into our five-mile run around Balboa Park, and the unseasonably warm California sunshine was taking its toll on me.

The Balboa Park area, adjacent to the Acropolis, was like a recreational oasis within the close-packed, middle-class city environment surrounding it. The route we were running circled the major parts of the park, starting from the intersection of Balboa and Burbank boulevards.

Burbank ran east and west, parallel to the Ventura Freeway, and Balboa ran north and south. We had begun our run north on Balboa for a mile and a half to Victory Boulevard, then east for a mile to Woodley. At Woodley, we'd turned south to pound our way down the mile-and-a-half ribbon of pavement that would lead us back to Burbank Boulevard. There we would start the home stretch.

Inside the outline of our route were the grass and trees of the recreation area, three golf courses, and a wildlife preserve. To the east of us, as we ran down Woodley, was the Sepulveda Dam reservoir area, and ahead of us, I could see the cars racing along busy Burbank Boulevard. At Burbank, I knew we would turn west to get back to our starting point at Balboa.

On the opposite side of our route down Burbank Boulevard was the looming structure of the Acropolis. I had learned from Sir Adam that Terrance Brisbane had been given the permits to build the Acropolis in return for his large monetary contributions to the upkeep of the Balboa Park recreational facilities.

Brisbane certainly knew how to make his money work for him, but I had been wondering, while running, exactly how solvent Terrance Brisbane really was. How could he afford to see either of his daughters allow the professional teams they owned to go bankrupt? I would have thought that the Acropolis, like any other sports center, needed a full complement of pro teams if it were to remain a going concern.

Sports complexes are like huge money sponges, soaking up currency like there was a never-ending supply. How Brisbane kept it all going and still had money to supply to the IRA was an interesting conundrum—one that Sir Adam or Ethan Kelso might want to attack in a search for answers.

After the powwow at the Marriott, Bekka and I had decided there was no reason why we shouldn't go out on our training run as originally planned. I needed to work out the kinks from the game the night before, and Bekka was obsessive about her workouts.

Now, she was running smoothly in step beside me. The moisture on the golden skin of her arms and legs glistened in the sunlight. She seemed to move with effortless feline grace in high-cut, peach-colored running shorts, a matching singlet, and white Nikes. The muscles in her legs stretched and flexed with each stride. Even though we were keeping up a good six-and-a-half-minute-mile pace, I felt she could run away from me anytime she wanted. Sticks was right. If Donovan didn't get me, age would.

As we rounded the corner onto Burbank Boulevard, Bekka looked over and asked, "How are you doing?"

"I was just thinking that I'm not as young as I used to be."

She laughed, a tinkling sound that was like music to my besotted ears. "I was thinking the same thing," she said.

"What, that I'm not as young as I used to be?"

Bekka laughed. "No silly. I don't care what they say. This running stuff never seems to get any easier."

"Do you want to back the pace down a notch for this final mile?" I asked, hoping for a respite.

"Please," she said. Her next two strides slowed the pace and then she yelled, "Last one back buys the beer!" and with a loud laugh she was off like a flash, catching me flat-footed as I tried to change gears from slowing down to giving chase.

"You little minx. I'll . . ." I didn't have enough breath to finish the rude sentiment. I was going to need all the oxygen I could get if I was going to catch the pair of tan legs dashing away from me.

The stretch of pavement we were on was flanked on the right by a six-foot chain link fence. On the other side of the fence was the golf course that I had seen from Nina Brisbane's office window. On our left was a four-foot expanse of dirt that ended in a concrete curb. Beyond the curb were the cars moving down the boulevard in a congested ribbon. The dirt area dipped in the middle to form a wide ditch with eucalyptus trees growing tall from the middle of it.

Within a dozen strides, I found myself surrounded by a cacophony of noise comprised of speeding traffic, the blood pounding through my head, the throbbing of my missing eye, and the gasping of my lungs as they sought desperately for oxygen. Bekka had gained a good five or six yards on me and was threatening to pull further away. I tucked my elbows in and began pumping my arms like the driving rods on the outside of a steam locomotive. I lengthened my stride and went after her.

My concentration was so intense that the noise of a motorcycle closing in on me from behind didn't register in my brain until it was almost upon me. The roar of the engine suddenly invaded my sensory department, but it was too late for me to react. Far too late.

I tried to turn to face the threat, but a searing line of pain suddenly stung across my shoulders. I arched in agony. A split second later another whip-cut lanced across my face and I stumbled forward, momentum almost tripping me over my own feet.

I'd thrown up my hands in an involuntary and useless gesture to cover my face when I heard Bekka scream. I dropped my hands and looked through blurred vision to see Donovan turning his motorcycle around for a second pass. Where had the bastard come from?

I only had the width of the pavement and the four-foot stretch of dirt ditch in which to maneuver. There was no time to climb the chain link fence to my right, and no way to escape into the busy traffic on the left without being killed. Geographically, Donovan had planned his attack well. I'm sure he'd even taken into account the fact that I would be feeling the effects of the run by this point.

With the bike stopped and both feet on the ground, Donovan revved the throttle. A second later he opened the clutch and surged forward. He removed his left hand from the handlebars and sliced an extended length of the car antenna back and forth with vicious threatening strokes. It was this ugly weapon that had cut into my shoulders and face.

Two things occurred to me almost simultaneously. The first was the irrelevant thought that somebody might be able to check the flight schedules from Seattle to Los Angeles that morning and be able to place Donovan on one of them. He would have had to fly back to LA after murdering Sweet, in order for him to be back in town so quickly.

My second thought was more germane to the situation. Donovan was still playing games. This attack was little more than the act of a cat playing with a mouse—painful, but not quite deadly. If he'd meant to kill me, he wouldn't be messing around with car antennae.

My musings were cut short as my own personal madman continued to race forward. Time seemed to slow down, and I could see Donovan's ugly ferret face and protruding teeth twisted into a sadistic grin of enjoyment. I tried to duck and weave, but Donovan was too expert a rider to let me escape so easily. At the last second, I threw my arms up over my face and took the brunt of the antenna's biting slash across the soft skin on the back of my upper arms. I instantly rolled away as Donovan roared past, and managed to avoid his second backhand slash.

"Run," I yelled at Bekka, and started to sprint toward

where she was standing. Behind us, I knew Donovan was readying for another run at me.

"Where the hell did he come from?" Bekka asked.

"The Acropolis parking lot. Just like the first time," I said. It was the same question I'd asked myself, and it was the only logical answer. My brain was racing furiously. "Who the hell is he tied to over there?" I demanded in frustration.

I shot a look over my shoulder and saw Donovan accelerating again. The fire of the blows I had received was cutting deep into me and I felt blood running down my arms. The swelling welt on my face had split my lips, making it difficult to talk, and there was the taste of blood in my throat.

"Over the fence," I said.

"No way! I'm staying with you." Bekka saw what I had in mind and obviously didn't like it.

"Don't be stupid, and don't argue. There isn't time. He'll use you to get to me. Don't become his pawn!"

Donovan was suddenly on top of us. Bekka was on my right, closest to the chain link fence. I turned my back on Donovan and forced Bekka against the fence, trapping her there and protecting her with my body. My hands clawed a hold on the chain link on either side of her.

I heard Donovan's high-pitched laughter as he raced by and cut two more lashes across my exposed back.

Other runners and bicyclists were backing up in amazement on the sidewalk as they observed the action, and there were the sounds of a fender bender on the boulevard as drivers were distracted by the action.

"Over the fence," I repeated to Bekka. "Before he comes back again."

This time, she didn't argue. Instead, she ducked out from under my arms, backed up a short distance, and then took two quick strides forward. She placed one foot into my cupped hands and with the boost, she sailed over the six-foot fence like a quail breaking cover. On the other side of the fence, she landed lightly on the manicured green of the sixth hole and shoulder-rolled to break her fall.

I probably had time to zip over the fence as well, but I was angry and tired of being hunted. My mind was clear and I could find no fear in it. I wasn't going to run from Donovan. If he wanted to play, then it was okay by me. So far he was up on points, but the round wasn't over yet.

As the motorcycle accelerated toward me again, I shifted down into the middle of the dirt ditch and put my back to one of the eucalyptus trees. The dip of the ditch was only about two feet deep, but it was enough to give Donovan a more difficult approach.

When the yellow motorcycle was about four yards away from me, I crouched down and picked up a fist-sized dirt clod that had been baked as hard as a rock by the California sun. Donovan clearly saw what I was doing, and when I threw the clod at his head, he ducked and swerved. I had missed, but so had he. The swinging arc of the antenna had sliced through the air without connecting with anything that belonged to me.

As Donovan roared past, I heard Bekka yelling my name. "Ian!"

I looked at her in time to see her chuck a golf club, javelin style, toward me. Behind her a startled duffer was counting the clubs in his bag.

I grabbed the club in midair and pulled it down behind my right leg. I turned back to the action and saw, as I had hoped, that Donovan was still turning his bike around. He hadn't seen Bekka toss me the nine iron. If I had my way, though, he'd see it soon enough.

The motorcycle leapt forward toward me again, Donovan spewing forth a rebel yell at the top of his lungs. I had the feeling this was going to be his final pass. He was pulling out all the stops. His speed was faster, his expression of demented malevolence etched more deeply across his features. He would go for my face again when he cut with the car antenna.

I stood my ground, and Donovan maneuvered to pass me on my left, swinging the car antenna with his left hand. At the last second I brought the golf club up in my own left hand and whipped it forward with all the power I could muster. My reach was easily four inches longer than Donovan's, and the golf club was a good ten inches longer than the antenna in Donovan's grip.

Before Donovan could start his cut at me with the antenna, I planted the flat head of the club smack in the middle of his chest and saw his body fold in around it. The antenna dropped from his grasp and he howled in pain as the motorcycle passed me.

The momentum of Donovan's passing tore the club away from me and spun me around and to the ground. From my prone position, I watched Donovan waver atop the bike and then suddenly lay it down on its side. I tried to scramble to my feet, but nothing seemed to be working right. The air had been driven out of me when I'd landed hard, and my body was screaming for oxygen.

Donovan couldn't have been much better off, but somehow he got to his feet, picked up the still running motorcycle, climbed on, and threaded his way into the boulevard traffic. I wanted to race after him, but there was no way I was going to catch him on foot. I slumped back down to the ground.

Suddenly, Bekka was beside me. She had climbed back over the fence and rushed to help me to my feet. She went to let go of me when I was standing, but I held onto her. I pulled her against me and refused to let her go. She seemed to approve of this, so I kissed her. Hard. My split lips complained, but she didn't. When our mouths parted, I kept my arms around her and kissed her again. She tasted delicious, and for the first time in ages I felt the tides of passion rising inside of me.

The onlookers, who had been shocked by the actions of the idiot on the motorcycle, seemed to think this was appropriate behavior because they all started to applaud.

EIGHTEEN

I LOOKED AT my face in the mirror. It was a real mess. The welt raised by Donovan's backhanded antenna lash ran diagonally from the bottom of my eye patch to the small cleft in my chin. It just touched the side of my right nostril and had split open both lips. It looked red, angry, and painful. It also felt red, angry, and painful. The backs of my arms had stopped bleeding, but had decided instead to ache intolerably in time with the throbbing of the lash welts on my back.

Still naked and dripping wet from the shower, I dried my body and then used the nap side of a fresh towel to gently pat the moisture from my face. Looking in the mirror again, I peeled my lips back to check my teeth. The ivories were okay, but the movement of my mouth caused the splits in my lips to reopen. I winced and looked away.

After Donovan had ridden off with his tail tucked between his legs, Bekka had helped me to cover the final mile back to her car. Our six-and-a-half-minute-mile pace had certainly gone up the spout, but we finally managed to get there under our own power.

Bekka had wanted to call the police immediately, but I'd told her I would call Ethan Kelso when we got back to the hotel. It didn't make sense to involve the uniform boys when Kelso was already handling the investigation.

While Bekka drove us back to the hotel we didn't say much, but we held hands like a couple of school kids. I felt about fourteen years old, and figured I would break out in a pubescent rash of acne at any second. Either that or my voice would crack.

"I have to go home to clean up and change," Bekka told me in the hotel's parking lot. "And then I'll come back and get you."

"Great," I told her.

We tried to kiss again, but by this time the split across my lips had gone from numb to agonizing and I drew back cringing after the lightest of contact.

Bekka laughed. "I finally find a man to care about and I can't even kiss him," she said.

I tried a weak smile. "I care about you too," I said. "In fact, I think I'm beginning to care a whole lot."

"How long does it take lips to heal?" she asked.

"Fingers and knuckles and eye sockets, I can tell you about. I'm not sure, however, about lips."

"Quickly, I hope."

I slid out of the car and she drove off with a wave. My heart thumped happily.

Sticks was not in the room when I entered, so I didn't have to explain what had happened to my face. I snatched up a washcloth, filled it with ice from the hotel's ice machine, and kept it pressed against my face for thirty minutes while I lay on top of the bed covers. I should have been thinking about Donovan or the coming semifinal game with Seattle, but my thoughts kept being overwhelmed with erotic images of Bekka.

Eventually, I hauled myself off the bed and dumped the remaining ice into the bathroom sink. I ran the shower and climbed under the hot, stinging spray until I felt somewhat revitalized.

It was just before drying that I had checked my face in the mirror for the first time. Between my eye patch and the red welt, I looked more like a pirate than ever. All I needed to complete the ensemble was a gold hoop earring and a hook for a hand. Or a peg leg. It would be hell trying to play goal with a peg leg. Amused by the mental picture of a peg leg goalkeeper, I thought that things could be worse.

And then suddenly they were.

I walked naked out of the bathroom while trying to dry my hair without further aggravating the welts on the back of my arms. The towel was still over my head when I heard a noise and realized I wasn't alone.

"Is that you, Sticks?" I asked, sure that it was.

"Hardly, mate," said a strange voice.

I snatched the towel off and saw Archer standing in front of me. I recognized him from the night at the Golden Harp. Behind him, one of his followers had pushed a large laundry basket into the room.

Without another word, Archer viciously swung his right foot toward my unprotected groin. I reacted, trying to twist and take the brunt of the blow on my thigh. I wasn't quite fast enough, though, and my testicles suddenly felt like they had been jammed up around my armpits. Nausea hit me like a freight train and I doubled over.

I tried to make the best of a bad situation by rolling to the floor and then continuing to roll, like a bowling ball, until I knocked Archer over for a strike. If the fight had simply been between the two of us, I would have eventually come out on top. Archer was a good street fighter, but I had been trained by some of the best instructors in the SAS. However, Archer had brought his backup with him, and they fell on me like a pack of wild dogs.

I tried to fight back, but the wealth of numbers over-whelmed me. They kicked and punched me until I thought I was destined to suffer the same death as Maddox. Before that happened, though, a sweet-smelling cloth was slapped over my nose and mouth. I tried to hold my breath, but it was a losing prospect. In seconds I was off on a trip to oblivion city.

Gradually, I discovered that inhaling chloroform produces a hangover from hell. I didn't have the nerve to open my eye. Things were bad enough while I was still in the dark. I could feel the world spinning around and my whole body was wracked with cold and nausea. My head pounded to the beat of an internal jackhammer, and my mouth was as dry as a sawdust sandwich. Every muscle was throbbing to its own discordant rhythm of pain and agony.

I don't think I've ever felt so sick. Not even when I came back to consciousness in the hospital after losing my eye. Then I had simply felt like I wanted to die. Now I felt like I had died and was already in hell paying for my sins.

I was on my side with my arms stretched out in front of me. I groaned and tried to roll over, but I couldn't. My arms wouldn't cooperate. They were wrapped around something and I couldn't pull them free.

I must have passed out again because I came awake for a second time with a jolt. I still felt deathly ill, but at least the room seemed to have stopped spinning. I tried to open my good eye and panicked when it would not respond. Frantically, I rubbed the orb against my bare shoulder and felt dried blood peeling away. When I tried next, the eyelid slitted partially open and I peered out into a blur of light. When my vision cleared, I closed the eye again. The effort hadn't been worth it. I hadn't liked what I'd seen.

I was lying on the concrete floor of what appeared to be a small utility storage area. I was still naked, and the reason I couldn't get my arms to respond was because they were handcuffed around a concrete-filled steel pipe that was anchored between the concrete floor and the room's concrete ceiling.

The pipe was about four inches in diameter and showed as much promise of being moveable as I did of becoming a prima ballerina. There were two other similar support pipes in the room, which on second glance appeared to be little more than a six-by-ten-foot concrete womb.

One wall sloped outward at about a forty-five-degree angle, and there was a metal door set into it that gave the whole setup a surreal effect. A rough blanket had been slung on the floor underneath me, but it did little to hold back the cold that was seeping up through the concrete.

At the base of the pipe, near my hands, were two one-gallon plastic jugs of water. There was no food that I could see, and I literally didn't have a pot to piss in. I felt a wan smile touch my lips. If my brain waves were still producing bad puns then perhaps there was hope.

At the furthest end of the room there were several coiled hoses and two wheelbarrows. Next to them was a small, paint-splattered, wooden shelf unit filled with pots and cans. Some of the cans had thin wire handles attached. Others had their contents liberally splashed over their sides. What looked like a well-used sandblaster was tilted over on one side where its axle was missing a rubber wheel. There was nothing tangible to identify the room, which was lighted from above by a naked, low-watt bulb encased in a metal cage.

I yelled out "Help!" and felt stupid. My voice seemed to flatten against the walls and go no further, and there was an odd feeling of being in a pressurized chamber.

I yelled again, and again, and then realized that I had been put here because I was safe from discovery. No self-respecting kidnapper would put his victim somewhere where they could be rescued simply by calling out. I laid back and thought for a minute, and then yelled another dozen times to be sure. I was still too befuddled to think of anything more constructive to do.

Sleep overcame me again, and when I woke up next my mind was clearer. I was thirsty as hell, and from somewhere I found the strength to sit up and open one of the jugs of water. I took slow sips, finding it awkward to drink with my arms wrapped around a pole. The chloroform-induced nausea had passed and the construction crew in my head appeared to have knocked off for the day. I decided to make another inspection of my surroundings.

The handcuffs around my wrists were not tight, but there was no way to slip my hands backwards through them. They had been double locked so they couldn't tighten up on me either, which was a small blessing to be thankful for. The pole I was attached to was as solid as first impressions had indicated.

On the floor behind me, I discovered another rough blanket folded into a square. On shaky legs, I stood up and used my feet to pull the blanket closer to the pole. I then stooped to pick up the blanket I had originally been lying on and wrapped it around my shoulders. Wearily, I dropped down to sit cross-legged on the second blanket. Being folded, I hoped it would keep me better insulated from the cold concrete floor. Exhaustion overcame my efforts and I leaned my left shoulder forward into the pole for support. I wanted to take another nap, but sleep was now elusive, so I sat and thought. Again, there was not much else I could do.

I thought a lot in the next few hours. I also worried quite a bit. How long was I going to be kept here? Would somebody come to bring me food and more water? Was I going to have to sit in my own waste? Was anybody coming back at all? Did anybody know I was missing yet? Why the hell had I been kidnapped in the first place? And what the hell had I gotten myself into? To relieve the boredom and take my mind away from the aches of my body, I concentrated on trying to think up answers.

Somebody hadn't wanted me to come to Los Angeles in the first place and had sent Sean Brody and Liam Donovan to discourage me. Whoever was behind that attack must have had some kind of a tie to the IRA—how else would they have known how to contact Brody and Donovan? They must also be tied to the Ravens and, possibly, to Maddox's murder.

Donovan had twice attacked me in the vicinity of the Acropolis, and I was still sure it was his motorcycle I had seen behind the Golden Harp on the night Terrance Brisbane had spoken there. If Donovan was tied to the Acropolis, was he also tied to Terrance Brisbane? Or was he possibly tied to the Acropolis through Pat Devlin?

After all, it was Devlin who had caused all the trouble in the pub. Donovan could have been one of the other hooded troublemakers. Devlin was violently anti-IRA, but Donovan was also against them since he had changed his allegiance to the Sons of Erin. Pat Devlin was a loose end that would need tying up if I ever got clear of this mausoleum in which I was currently interred.

Archer and his firm were another puzzle. At the Golden Harp, they had appeared to be working as muscle for Terrance Brisbane, but why would Brisbane want them to kidnap me? Had they killed Maddox? I certainly had the bruises to prove they were capable of it. The autopsy report showed Maddox had been kicked to death by a pair of steel-toed boots and two different pairs of soccer cleats. That factor also pointed to Archer and his firm of Hardbirds.

But if the Hardbirds had killed Maddox, why not simply kill me too? Why kill one goalkeeper and not another? The fact that two water jugs had been provided for me indicated there was at least a possibility I would be released in the future. How long till that future, though, I wondered?

This thought brought me to Caitlin Brisbane. Now there was a viper done up with a pretty bow. She definitely knew how close to the edge her sister's sports franchises were. By pushing one or another of them over the edge, Caitlin, according to the edicts of Terrance Brisbane's plan, would gain control of her father's vast sports empire. Her own teams were in deep trouble also, and she was bound and determined not to lose the power and money of the Brisbane fortune to Nina.

Three times, that I knew of, she had tried to put the fix in with the Ravens. Caitlin had tried to buy me off, and at the same time had admitted to paying off Maddox to blow games. When she couldn't buy me off, she bought herself a referee. Was she blowing wind about Maddox to impress me, or had he really been in her pocket?

I wondered if, perhaps, Maddox had been stringing Caitlin along. Taking her money to pay off his gambling debts, but not blowing the games as he had agreed. After all, the Ravens had made it into the play-offs. If Caitlin had had her way they would never have made it that far. Perhaps Caitlin had Maddox murdered because he was double-crossing her.

I didn't particularly like that scenario because, while Caitlin was an underhanded bitch, she was not adept at crime. I didn't see her putting the boots to Maddox herself, and I didn't see her having access to the type of people who would. Unless, of course, she had access to Archer and the Hardbirds firm through her father. The Hardbirds could be dancing to the tune of more than one master; protecting Terrance Brisbane when he wanted to put on a display of muscle and running murderous errands for Caitlin in their off hours. Now there was a thought that brought me full circle back to square one. I wasn't getting anywhere.

I stopped the whirl of my brain for a moment and took a few more swigs from the first water bottle. I put the bottle down and closed my eyes again. This time sleep came.

Cold haunted my dreams, and I awoke at one point in a semidelirious trance to find I had fallen sideways off of the pole and onto the floor. I had also twitched off the blanket which had been around my shoulders. Still feeling spaced-out, I reorganized the folded blanket beneath me into a larger, but thinner, rectangle on which I could lay in a fetal scrunch. Battling the frustration of having my hands restricted, I pulled the other blanket over me. I trapped it beneath my body as best I could, and allowed the delirium to fully consume me again.

Later, I came back to consciousness feeling as cramped and slimy as a snail who had outgrown its shell. I had no way to tell how much later it was. It could have been five minutes, five hours, or five days, as my surroundings were timeless. I thought depressing thoughts about loneliness and starvation, about dying, and about love.

I concentrated on love because love is supposed to keep

you warm. I thought about Bekka and what I had felt when I first saw her. Was that love, or was that simply a stirring of lust set off by a glandular reaction? Could love be an instant response, bursting into life in full bloom, or could love only be looked at in retrospect, after time had proven the emotion existed?

One thing I was certain about was that love is never convenient. It never pays attention to circumstances, or considers the consequences of its actions. It is an emotion that is both animate and inanimate. Those it strikes are filled with joy and life, yet in and of itself love possesses no feelings.

In that lonely room, on the cold floor, I thought about love. I was from a loving family. I had felt love from them, the type of love that goes beyond platonic because it deals with the pull of bloodlines and creation, but stops short of the depths of love that a man and a woman can feel for each other. I wondered if I had the beginnings of that kind of man-and-woman love with Bekka? I thought yes, and that scared me.

Time passed. Relentlessly. Slowly. Infinitesimally. At least I think it did. I felt like a lab rat in some kind of existential experiment. Did the world outside my concrete womb exist, or did it only exist while I experienced it? If a tree falls in the forest and nobody is there to hear it does it make a sound?

Beyond driving myself to distraction with unanswerable philosophical questions, I had come back to the conclusion that I was to be kept in captivity until after the Ravens–Gulls semifinal game on Wednesday. It was the only scenario that made sense.

If ransom was the goal, there were a lot of other more appropriate targets for kidnapping. Ransom did not make sense in my case. If Archer and company were out for ransom, they could have gone after Caitlin or Nina, or Terrance Brisbane himself. Those targets would have the ability to command a high price.

However, by keeping me away from the game on

Wednesday, the chances were that the Ravens would blow the game. The team was already in a state of upheaval over Maddox's murder. My disappearance would only add to the pressure. That thought put Caitlin back on the top of my suspect list as to the power behind Archer since she appeared to have the most to gain.

Or did she?

Somewhere in the back of my brain the evil shadows of another idea began to germinate. There was somebody else who would benefit from my absence at the semifinals. Somebody who was as impatient as Caitlin to reach the heights of fame and fortune.

I had tried to fit Donovan into the overall scenario. He was like a part from another jigsaw puzzle which had been inadvertently put in the wrong box. His presence niggled at me and niggled at me, and then suddenly the clarity of inspiration struck me.

I had been trying to put all of the puzzle pieces I possessed into one picture. This was not the brightest of moves since life itself rarely presents us with one picture at a time. In all of our lives there are many different scenarios taking place, connected only by the single thread that they are taking place in our lives.

Perhaps the puzzle pieces I had been given to play with could not all be put together to form one pretty picture. Perhaps I had pieces from two or more separate puzzles, connected only by the factor that the Ravens organization was a part of each picture.

I brought my manacled hands up to eye level and took a close look at the handcuffs themselves. I had to get out of this tomb. I was tired of letting events happen to me. It was time to stop playing defense and to go on the attack. A renewed determination was welling up inside of me despite, or perhaps fueled by, the cold and my discomfort. I closed my eye and tried to conjure up a mental image of how handcuffs worked.

In my mind, I imagined the ratchet end of the handcuff that slides into the locking section of the cuff. If there is no wrist inside the cuff, the ratchet end can be pushed straight through and brought around again. However, once into the locking part of the cuff, the ratchet end catches on a pin and can't be pushed backward unless the pin is raised by unlocking the cuff. I wasn't Houdini, but there still had to be a way out of the cuffs.

An SAS instructor once demonstrated to me how anything, from a piece of paper, to a credit card, to a paper clip, could be turned into a weapon. I didn't need a weapon at the moment, but I needed a key or a tool, and I wondered if the same principal could be brought to bear.

While I mulled this over, I stood and began to jog in place to warm up. I had avoided exercise before because I knew I would only cool down again and end up colder than when I started. Now, though, I had the beginnings of an escape plan and I needed to get blood and warmth to my fingers to make it happen. Calling my thoughts an escape plan was perhaps a bit grandiose. They were more like the glimmerings of an idea borne up on the wings of hope, but I needed all the confidence I could muster.

To begin with, I felt like an idiot dancing around with the pole as my partner. I must have looked like an ugly, oversized, naked nymph circling a maypole, but the blood began to course through my veins, and my battered and scarred fingers began to tingle as I flexed them painfully open and closed. The warmer I became, though, the better I started to feel.

I still had no way of telling how long I had been in captivity. My body was out of sync and there was no way to judge time by my usual bodily function schedule.

I'd finished drinking the contents of one of the water bottles before I had been forced to start filling it up with my bladder voidings. Now I looked at the remaining bottle of water. It was still three-quarters full. If I emptied it out, I would have no water left to drink. I could have emptied out the waste in the other bottle, but what I had planned would involve chewing, biting, and tearing the plastic container.

The prospect of using the refilled bottle didn't sit well with my fastidious habits.

I weighed the pros and cons of my escape idea and decided there were definitely more cons than pros. I drank my fill, and then emptied out the rest of the clean water bottle anyway. The idea would simply have to work.

I sat down on my blanket and stuck my index fingers into the top of the empty plastic gallon jug and tried to tear it apart. The area was reinforced and it didn't give. My hands and fingers are battered and knobbled and prone to arthritis, but they are strong, so I tried again. It still didn't tear. I had kind of expected it wouldn't, but I could have done with the break.

I bit into one of the rounded plastic corners and chewed. The plastic flattened out, but it didn't split. I chewed on it some more to no effect. I bit into a different part of the plastic, and then another part, and then another. I worried the plastic jug like I was a dog with bone. My jaw began to ache and my gums to bleed. I chewed on. I returned to previously chewed parts and chewed on them again and again.

After what seemed like hours, I felt one area of the plastic puncture under pressure from my right canine tooth. I felt a surge of relief, and began to chew furiously. Before long, I had made a hole big enough to stick my fingers through. This time when I pulled, the water bottle split wide open.

I went back to chewing and tearing with my teeth. The torn edge of the plastic cut into my tongue and lips until blood was flowing freely. Eventually, though, I chewed free a rough rectangle of plastic about three inches long by one inch wide. I held my newly fashioned possession in my hand and closed my eyes to rest.

Not only did my mouth hurt, but my shoulder, arm, and side had been rubbed raw by their constant contact with the pole to which I was shackled. I'd tried using a blanket as a buffer, but it constantly slipped down, or bunched up, until I preferred the chafing over the effort of keeping the blanket in place. I was exhausted again and I would have loved a swallow of water. However, I now had a tool.

When I could rouse myself again, I folded my strip of plastic in half and in half again. I used my teeth to flatten the creases of the folds. The plastic was now a sturdy strip that was thin enough to slip into the hole of the handcuff where the ratchet end entered. My idea was to push the plastic strip in over the top of the ratchets, raise the pin which stopped them from backing out, and then slide the cuff open.

It was a good idea. It should have worked. But it didn't.

I tried everything. I tried pushing the plastic strip through from either end. I wiggled it. I twisted it. I screamed at it. I prayed to God about it, and God answered. He said, "No."

Finally, I gave up. In frustration I threw the plastic strip across the storage room and wept. I was cold to my bones, and I ached in every joint. Tears coursed down my face in a lopsided torrent because I only had one eye to cry from. I was angry and frustrated and feeling sorrier for myself than I ever had before. God had said no to my prayers.

Or had He just said, "Not that way?"

Had he simply told me I was trying to open the cuffs the wrong way? There was a new idea in my head. I had no idea where it came from. Had God said, "Not that way; this way," and then put the new way into my head?

I looked for my plastic strip. There was no way I could have faced biting off another. It was about four feet away from me to one side. I stretched out one leg and tried to reach it with my toes. I was a few inches short, so I laid down on my side and stretched out. By performing like a circus contortionist, I brought the offending piece of plastic back to where I could pick it up with my hands.

I kissed it. "Oh, you little darling," I told it. My voice sounded strange in the room, and I realized it was the first time I'd spoken actual words since I'd recovered consciousness.

"You're going to work this time, my love," I told the

plastic. I was talking to build my confidence. At least that's what I like to think.

I unfolded the plastic and, at one corner, I carefully bit free a quarter-inch tab. I then rolled the plastic lengthwise and peeled the tab back with my fingers. I now had what looked like a short straw with a quarter-inch tab sticking out sideways from one end. What I actually had was a crude handcuff key. I held it tightly in my right hand and inserted it into the lock on the left cuff.

The lock on a handcuff has a small pin sticking up in the middle of it. The hole in the center of my straw fit tightly over this, and the tab of the straw stuck down into the lower part of the keyhole where it belonged. I twisted my crude key. Nothing happened. I twisted it the other way. The cuff fell open.

I was dumbfounded. I sat with my arms up in the air staring at the left cuff swinging free beneath the still attached cuff around my right wrist. I changed hands with the plastic straw and tried to work the same magic on the right cuff. This time, though, no matter which way I twisted the straw, the cuff would not unlock. I kept trying, and then realized I was being an idiot. It didn't matter if the right cuff would come off or not. I was free from the pole. I could get out of my concrete womb.

I stood up and walked over to the door set in the angled wall. No key was needed on the inside. The door handle had a twist lock set in it. I put my ear to the door, but all I could hear was a faint swishing sound which I couldn't identify. I twisted the knob of the lock, then turned the door handle and pushed the door open.

I had no idea what to expect.

What I found was freedom. The door opened into the night and it was raining outside. Rain in Southern California. I stepped out into it and nothing had ever felt so good as standing naked in that darkness with the rain pouring down on me.

I looked around me. I was standing on the top of a huge concrete dam. Below me, on either side the of eight sluice gates, the dam sloped steeply down to the concrete basins of the control reservoirs. The empty reservoirs stretched away into the rainy darkness in either side. So, too, did a long concrete control channel which did have water in it. It was a surreal concrete world of phosphorus gray highlighted everywhere by the garish paint swirls of graffiti.

Behind me, set into another sloping concrete wall, was the little maintenance room that had been my prison. The maintenance room itself was attached to the back of the much larger dam-control building like a barnacle on the bottom of a boat. Half a mile away, the headlights of cars flowed down a freeway, their tires swishing in the accumulated water from the rain.

I quickly recognized where I was as the Sepulveda Dam, east of the Acropolis in the Sepulveda Basin. While running, Bekka and I had seen the dam shortly before Donovan's second attack, but we had turned away from it in the opposite direction.

I was sure the entire area around the dam was deserted. Bekka had told me that the dam was never used except in years of exceptionally heavy rainfall when the recreation areas in the basin were threatened with flood. I wondered if the rain now coming down was the precursor to a flood, or simply a shower which wouldn't even be remembered in the morning.

Knowing my location cheered me greatly. I knew I could get from the dam to safety without too much trouble. After all, if everything I'd heard about California was true, a naked man walking through the rain on a dark night shouldn't even be a cause for comment.

I started to wonder who would be the most surprised to see me.

NINETEEN

"**Y**OU DO LOOK a sight," Ethan Kelso said when he entered the small doughnut shop where I was waiting for him. "Are you sure you didn't run off to join a religious cult and sell flowers at the airport while the rest of the world has been going crazy looking for you?"

"Your sense of humor is less appreciated than your prompt arrival," I told him. I was still shivering despite the oven warmth of the doughnut shop.

"You can't have one without the other," Kelso said. "Love me, love my warped sense of humor. It's a package deal."

"How about I like one and tolerate the other?"

"You drive a hard bargain for a man who I still say looks like a Hare Krishna reject."

Ethan's derisive comments about my appearance were justified. After my initial exaltation over being free had moderated, I had thought twice about traversing the land-scape in my birthday suit. With an effort of will I had re-entered my prison. I made sure to leave the door open behind me, and grabbed one of my trusty blankets.

With the aid of a snapped knife blade I'd found on the shelf with all the various pots and cans, I cut a rough hole in the center of the blanket. I slipped the resultant fashion statement over my head like a poncho. If I had been able to reach the knife blade while I was attached to the pole, I could have saved my mouth a whole lot of grief. But you have to work with what you've got. While I was attached to the pole, I hadn't even known the knife blade existed. Score another point for existentialism.

Finding more work for the broken knife blade, I'd hacked a strip of cloth free from the second blanket and used it as a sash to secure the first blanket around my waist. I thought the style of my garb was reminiscent of Clint Eastwood in his early spaghetti westerns when he wore a poncho with panache. Ethan obviously felt I looked closer to a casting call hopeful for the role of Jesus. He was probably right.

Once I was sartorially acceptable, I'd bugged out of the concrete maintenance room, locking and closing the door behind me. Without further hesitation, I had made my way across the dam toward Burbank Boulevard.

The rain outside was continuing to course down and it immediately began to soak into my blanket. I didn't care as much about getting wet as I did about the rain turning the steep bank which led up to the roadway into a muddy quagmire. Twice I slipped when I was only halfway up and slid back to the bottom. On the third try, though, I scrambled clear and started the long trudge down the sidewalk to find a phone. Cars slipped by me down the boulevard, but nobody stopped to offer me a lift. I can't say I blamed them.

The Acropolis was full of bright lights and the parking lot was about half filled with cars. One of Caitlin's or Nina's other teams must have had a game going on. However, I avoided entering the sports complex, as I wanted to keep my freedom a secret for a while longer.

By this time the rain had washed off some of the mud I'd picked up while climbing the bank, but my poor, pale, soft,

English feet were paying the price of their barefoot adventure. Limping on as best I could, I eventually made it to the corner of Burbank and Balboa where Bekka and I had started our training run in what seemed like an age ago. I remembered that kitty-corner to our starting point was a small shopping complex. I shuffled across the street against the lights to see if I could find shelter and a phone there.

The complex housed a half dozen small shops, with a row of offices above them, and a large medical building. Everything was closed for the night except for a tiny convenience market and the doughnut shop. Hot smells of pastry wafted through the raindrops. Back in my concrete prison, I'd ignored my hunger pangs by sheer dint of will. I hadn't realized how hungry I was until the aroma of fresh doughnuts penetrated my sniffer. My stomach did flip-flops, and my salivary glands started to work overtime.

Inside the doughnut shop a lone man was working in the heat of the back room. He was a Pakistani with a slight build, wearing a T-shirt and jeans and a flour-covered apron tied around his waist. He came out to the counter when a bell rang to announce my entrance. After one glance at me, though, the look in his eyes changed from friendly to wary. I noticed he was wearing a name tag with *Singe* emblazoned on it.

"I know I look like a weirdo," I said. "But I'm not." I couldn't have been too convincing because there was no change of expression on Singe's face. I could see him checking out my eye patch and the handcuffs which still dangled from my right wrist.

"Please, I need help," I tried again. "Can I use your phone to call the police?" I didn't want the police to come, I wanted them to contact Ethan for me, but that was too complicated to explain right then. I needed to gain this man's confidence. "I'm not going to hurt you. I just want to use the phone and then I'll wait outside for the police to come. Please."

Singe continued to stare at me. Then, for whatever reason was valid in his own mind, he decided to help me. He showed me the phone and I called the West Valley station desk. I impressed upon the officer who answered the importance of getting a message to Ethan and asked him to use Ethan's pager to get him to call me back at the doughnut shop. I was surprised when I didn't get an argument and after I'd hung up I wondered if he would actually do as I asked.

Singe had gone back to preparing doughnuts and he didn't comment when I stayed waiting by the phone. Twice he came out to serve customers, and twice he went back to his baking without asking me to leave. Finally, the phone rang and I grabbed it off the receiver. Singe looked up at me. The call might have been for him, but I was too on edge to care. However, it was Ethan on the other end of the line.

I quickly explained where I was and that I wanted Ethan to come and get me. I'm sure he was busting with curiosity, but, good cop that he was, Ethan didn't bother asking questions. He knew he'd get all the answers he needed when he picked me up. He told me to put Singe on the phone. I called Singe away from his baking and he took the receiver from me. He listened for a almost a minute, mumbled something into the phone, listened again, said, "Okay," and then hung up.

Singe turned to me with a smile on his face. "Come sit down, Howard," he told me.

"Howard?" I asked.

Singe ignored my question and guided me by my arm to a small table near the doughnut display case. "Your policeman friend. He said to give you as many of my best doughnuts as you wanted. And coffee. Lots of coffee." Singe began piling a plate full of goodies.

My stomach convinced me not to question him further. The doughnuts were delicious, and the coffee was strong and hot. I was still shivering, but I was on the road to recovery. Singe hovered around me like a mother hen. I couldn't think for the life of me what Ethan could have told him to gain this kind of response.

I didn't want to break the spell of Singe's cooperation by

asking him what day it was. Instead, I plucked a discarded newspaper off of another table and looked at the date. If the paper was current, then today was Tuesday. Tuesday night to be precise. I'd been imprisoned since Sunday!

Fortunately, I'd picked up the sports section of the paper. In between bites of doughnut, I flipped through it quickly and located an article previewing the upcoming AISL semifinals. In a sidebar article there was a discussion about the lack of police progress in the murder of Seattle goalkeeper, Tom Sweet, as well as the fact that the Ravens' goalkeeper, your truly, had done a disappearing act. The murder of Maddox was also rehashed, along with speculation about the incidents that was much more sensational than factual.

Ethan finally arrived and after greeting me, he held up a wait-a-second finger. He walked to the back room where Singe was busy baking. I saw Singe nodding his head and smiling happily when Ethan handed him something.

When we were in Ethan's car I asked him about it.

"I told him on the phone that you were Howard Hughes."

"Howard Hughes? But he's been dead for years."

"Yeah. I told him you had faked your death, had a face-lift, and were running around loose in the area."

"And he believed you?"

"No. But he did bite when I told him I'd give him a hundred dollar bill if he treated you right until I arrived."

I started to laugh and then suddenly I felt like I was going to cry. Whether the emotion was from relief or exhaustion, I didn't know. I put my head back on the seat and closed my eye. It was all too much.

The next thing I knew, Ethan was shaking my shoulder to bring me out of a dreamless sleep. It was still dark outside and the air was filled with a salty tang. The rain had turned to a heavy mist. Through the windshield of the car, I could see the masts of docked boats bobbing as the water beneath the boats moved with the storm.

"Where are we?" I asked.

"The Santa Monica Bay Marina. I live on a boat here. Fortunately for you, my domestic arrangements are currently in a cohabitive state. And since there is only room for me on the boat, the cohabitating is taking place elsewhere.''

"Does all of that gobbledygook mean I can lie low here until I decide what to do next?''

"Only if you tell me what the hell is going on, and why you don't want anyone to know where you are. You've got one little lady ready to move heaven and earth to find you.''

"Bekka?''

"If you have to ask then you don't have as many smarts as I gave you credit for.''

I felt my stomach flip-flop when I thought of Bekka being worried about me. I knew that if the situation had been reversed, I would have been taking apart the town to find her. I had never had a woman care about me in that fashion, and it was a warm and glorious feeling to know that one did.

"I'll let her know very soon. Before the game tomorrow,'' I said. "But right now I need time to think and time to recover.''

In the darkness, I saw the vague motion of Ethan nodding his head. "Come on, then,'' he said. "Let's get you aboard and you can tell Uncle Ethan all about it.''

Ethan's boat was a thirty-two-foot Hammond sloop called the *Corrienearn*. Through the darkness and the heavily misting rain, I could see its design lines were low and sleek. Even at its stationary dock it exuded a feeling of free-flying movement, a racehorse waiting for the gate to burst open.

The interior of the main cabin was immaculately tidy and fitted with teak paneling and fixtures.

"This must have cost you a fortune,'' I said in admiration.

"And on a cop's salary, too,'' Ethan replied. The note in his voice was cynical, and I looked sideways at him.

He caught my glance and shrugged his shoulders. "The department's Internal Affairs division took me to task over the boat. An officer can pay a half a million dollars for a house or pick up a fancy car and nobody questions him, but when you start getting into fancy boats everybody assumes you're on the take." He shrugged again. "This boat is my home. It is the one luxury in my life. I drive a five-year-old Honda and pay my bills on time, but I still had to account for every last penny I put up for the *Corrienearn*."

"Do I detect a trace of bitterness?"

"No. You detect a whole manure-load full. Now, if you think we've had enough foreplay, quit teasing and get on with the main act. Where the hell have you been since Sunday afternoon?"

I was dog tired. Fatigue was washing over me in drowning waves, but I took a deep breath and began to relive my tale.

At noon the next day, I stepped out onto the deck of the *Corrienearn* and stared up into the beautiful sunshine. Everything was clean and fresh and there wasn't a trace of the rain from the night before. The news reporter I'd just listened to on the radio had promised more rain for the early evening hours, but the Southern California weather gods appeared to be conspiring to make him into a liar.

After I'd finished telling Ethan my story the night before, I'd drunk my fill of water and wolfed down a steak and baked potato whipped up in the galley. I'd then slept for twelve solid hours. I had no recollection of going to sleep, and no idea when Ethan had left the boat. When I awoke, however, there was a note from him saying he'd be by to pick me up about one o'clock.

My body was rested, but it still felt jangly and uncoordinated. It was as if the muscles in my arms and legs had turned into old rubber bands that were no longer able to fully contract when released. My bones were acting like they were all disconnected. I rummaged around in Ethan's clothes locker and commandeered a pair of nylon running shorts and a ragged T-shirt. I needed to sweat and get the natural lubricants in my joints flowing again.

Barefoot, I hopped onto the dock and began to jog out of the marina and down to the beach about a half a mile away.

I took it easy to start, stretching everything out slowly and listening to my internal rhythms.

I have no idea how people jog or run with radios plugged into their ears. They can't possibly hear what their body has to say to them, and they are still bound by the mundane, pressurized, world of civilization. The radio keeps them a prisoner. They are moving, but they aren't running. They are still tethered to the earth.

Running is a savage and primal experience. It removes the conscious mind from the body and allows the body to become in-sync with the nature of being. It is the purest form of human movement, and in the wake of its purity it brings serenity. A battery-powered hip-hop rap throbbing through your brain while you plod one foot down in front of the other isn't going to bring you to a higher level of consciousness.

When I hit the beach, I lengthened my stride and picked up speed along the water's edge. My feet began to tingle from slapping on the sand, but the cold ocean water periodically rushed soothingly around them. It was the wrong time of year for sun worshippers, but a few die-hard surfers were riding the chop, and a smattering of beach people walked or frolicked as I passed.

Two wet, shaggy dogs joined me when I was about two miles into the run. They looked well fed, but ownerless, and seemed to enjoy having someone to follow. I felt like the leader of the pack, and that thought brought Archer and the Hardbirds to mind. As humans we like to think we are different from animals, but we are not. We are simply a more evolved species that quickly reverts to kind when needs must. The traits of all animals can be found within the various examples of the human form. Archer and the Hardbirds were just the human equivalent of hyenas.

I turned around at the pylons that supported the Santa Monica Pier. The carnival atmosphere above me on the pier itself acted like a Greek chorus to my actions—laughing and reveling at my problems while looking for a way to complicate them. The dogs barked at me, but kept going, not understanding why I would want to return the way I came.

Halfway home, I felt my body suddenly clicked into rhythm. Sweat was streaming out of my pores, and I felt my movements become smooth and effortless. I picked up my pace again and found a full reserve of energy.

Closer to the marina, within view of the *Corrienearn*, I could no longer feel the ground beneath my feet. Water swirled around my calves as I splashed into the ocean, the blood in my veins singing. In my heart I knew I was only one step away from flight. I took that step and dove into the air. My body flew forward, suspended between the earth and the sky. I was unbound by all that was earthly for the split second out of time before gravity took over and I crashed down into the ice-cold waves.

I came up for air, swimming hard against the undertow. I did two hundred strokes toward Hawaii, turned, and did two hundred strokes back to the mainland. The last strokes were finished in a rush as a wave threw me forward onto the beach in the reverse of a fisherman throwing back a fish. I guess I wasn't big enough be a keeper. Either that or the ocean thought I should be thrown back for Liam Donovan to catch.

I did a hundred sit-ups and a hundred push-ups on the sand, rinsed off again, and jogged slowly back to the *Corrienearn*. Ethan and Sticks were waiting for me on the dock.

"Pretty impressive," Ethan said. They had obviously been watching my antics on the beach.

"Hello, Sticks," I said.

"Hello, yourself," he said in a gruff voice. "Who do you think you are, running off to have a good time while the rest of us sit at home and worry?"

"I'm sorry, Dad. I'll try not to let it happen again."

"He caught me in the hotel room while I was trying to round up some clothes for you," Ethan told me. "In fact he damn near took my head off with a baseball bat before I could explain who I was and what I was doing."

Sticks shrugged. "I thought he was part of whatever had

happened to you. I'd been waiting for someone like him to turn up.''

"You were waiting?" I asked.

Sticks shrugged again. "Bekka was taking care of making all the noise to get others to try and find you. Waiting to see if anyone would come after your things for some reason seemed like the only other thing I could do.''

"Even after I was able to get him to believe who I was, he wouldn't let me take the clothes unless I brought him back with me. He's a stubborn old coot," Ethan said.

"Who is he calling old?" Sticks asked.

I laughed. "Old or not, it's good to see you," I told him.

"It good to be seen. Are you okay?"

I briefly filled him in as we went on board and I took a sailor's shower and changed into my own clothes.

"I suppose you have something up your sleeve," he said when I finished, "but can I let Bekka know you are okay? She's going crazy.''

I thought for a second. "Okay. Let her know, but tell her not to let on to anyone else. I've got plans to make a grand appearance in the locker room before the game tonight and I want to check the reactions of someone there.''

"So what are you going to do now?" he asked.

"Try to find some evidence that will corroborate the reaction I expect to see tonight." I looked over at Ethan. "Hopefully, we already have it.''

"I don't understand," Sticks said.

"While I was playing *Escape From Alcatraz* I began to wonder about Maddox being in gambling trouble with the local bent-nose brigade. Bekka told me that when a couple of collectors tried leaning on him, Maddox dumped them on their heads. Bekka also said that to her knowledge the mob boys didn't come back, so she assumed Maddox had squared things away.''

The scenario bothered me because mob collectors don't run away with their tail between their legs. And according to Ethan, Maddox didn't have the scratch to pay off his light bill let alone a heavy gambling debt.

"You think the collectors killed Maddox? You think it's unrelated to what is going on with Liam Donovan?"

"No, I don't think the collectors killed Maddox. That would have been killing off the goose that laid the golden egg. Maddox couldn't pay them if he wasn't breathing anymore. However, I don't believe Maddox's murder is related to Liam Donovan's actions. I think somebody picked up Maddox's markers and that's why the mob boys backed off. I also think that Maddox double-crossed whoever paid off his debts, and that's why he ended up a dead man."

"And how does Donovan fit in?"

"As I said, I don't think he fits in with Maddox's murder. I think we've stepped into the middle of two separate games, both of which are getting people killed."

When I paused, Ethan jumped in. "Early this morning," he said. "I went over the Maddox murder file again. Bekka's statement is in there regarding the leg-breakers who were giving Maddox a bad time. I showed the descriptions to a friend on the organized crime squad and he recognized one of them as Jackie Casio—a collector for Max Turner, who runs much of the action in town."

"Can he be located?" I asked.

"He already has been. He didn't fancy trying to explain to Max Turner why the cops came and kept him from making his duly-appointed rounds, so he coughed. He figured the information we wanted wasn't any big deal anyway since Maddox's markers had been bought in full, two weeks prior to Maddox turning up stiff."

"Who bought them?" I asked.

Ethan smiled. "You had him picked. It was that second-string goalkeeper and charming man-about-town, Nick Kronos."

TWENTY

THE BALL TOOK a funny slide across the artificial turf, but I put my body down behind it and gathered it in safely with my arms. The Seattle Gulls' striker faked a kick toward my head to see if he could bluff me into letting go of the ball to protect myself, but I'm too old of a dog to fall for that one. Instead, I let my momentum carry me forward and took the striker's feet out from under him. The referee blew his whistle and awarded me a free kick. I should have received an Oscar for my performance. I'd committed the foul, but had made it look like the striker had.

"If you ever try that again," I whispered in his ear while we were still in a tangle on the ground, "I'll knock you down so hard you'll wake up in the next time zone."

"Screw you," came the muffled reply from the head that I was accidentally on purpose compressing between my body and the turf.

Ah, sportsmanship.

Earlier, when I had walked into the Ravens' gloom-laden

locker room, I was flanked by two uniformed police officers and followed by Ethan Kelso. The effect was everything I could have hoped for.

The team was having a final strategy meeting. Bekka was in the room along with everyone else. Though she was always fully clothed, Bekka had long ago put behind her any embarrassment over the various states of undress of her male teammates, and once they had gotten over trying to impress her with their physiques, the situation had become no big deal. After the shock of women journalists being allowed to invade the once male-dominated locker rooms, everything became possible. Nina Brisbane, wearing a designer peach dress and matching veil, was also present. I didn't think there was anything that could embarrass her.

Even though Sticks had let Bekka know I was safe, she bounced out of her chair like a demented Jack-in-the-box and threw her arms around my neck. Several of the other players let out whoops when they spotted me. Suddenly, I was so surrounded by bodies clapping me on the back that I almost missed the reaction I was banking on. But it wouldn't have been possible to miss it. Nick Kronos, the starting goalkeeper's jersey stretched across his shoulders, was glued to the bench he was sitting on. His mouth hung open like that of an unhinged puppet.

"Surprise," I said, waggling my fingers at him.

He looked suddenly deflated. "I . . . I . . . I'm starting tonight. . . ." It was the most he could force out in a harsh whisper. He sounded like a child trying to bargain with God.

Ethan had explained to me that there wasn't nearly enough evidence to even arrest Nick, let alone get actual criminal charges filed against him for anything. However, there was nothing to stop Ethan from questioning Nick.

"A little pressure, a little con, a lot of luck. I'll get him to cough," Ethan had said. He'd also told me about a sign over his office door that stated his motto: YOU CAME IN HERE WITH A PRETTY FACE AND INFORMATION. YOU CAN'T LEAVE WITH BOTH.

What we were trying to do through my unexpected arrival

was soften Nick up, make him vulnerable to the pressures Ethan planned to apply.

The two uniformed officers went over to stand by Nick.

"What is this?" Stavoros Kronos asked. "You can't just walk back in here like this and expect to play. Nicky is starting tonight."

There was something in Stavoros's voice which ran along the jagged edge of hysteria. Ethan picked up on it even before I did. It was like watching a round of cards being dealt. First one player looks like the best bet, and then another card falls and the player sitting next to him is an even better bet.

Stavoros was suddenly a new player in the suspect game. A player with a strong hand. His hole card was the fact that he had the same possible access to Archer and the Hardbirds as Nick did in order to get them to kidnap me. And the card he'd just thrown on the table held the fact that he hadn't bothered to ask me where I'd been for three days. All he wanted to do was tell me I couldn't expect to play and that Nicky, his pride and joy, was going to be the starting goalie in the coming game. Which is exactly what would have happened if I was still intimately connected to the pole in my concrete prison.

Nina Brisbane had pushed her way through the crowd of players around me. Her body language showed she was mad enough to spit nails. "Chapel, would you please explain where you've been for the last three days, and exactly what these policemen are doing here?"

I changed suspect gears as fast as I could, processing the responses my appearance had created. "Why don't you ask Coach Stavoros? Now that he's over the shock of my turning up like a bad penny, he's probably as up-to-date as I am on where I've been and what's going on. While you're at it, you can ask Nicky-boy who bought Pasqual Maddox's gambling markers and then tried to blackmail Maddox into faking an injury so Nick could step in and take the starting goalie spot." I was taking an educated scattershot at the truth. Some of the points might still be distorted, like an image in a fun house mirror, but I was hoping my analysis would still come close enough to score.

"You can also ask Nick about what happened next when Maddox laughed in his face. After all, Maddox had to keep playing. Your sister was paying him to let goals slip by, to lose a game here and there, and he needed the money to keep up with his gambling debts." I was making a giant assumption about Caitlin bribing Maddox, but the theory fit together nicely and if it wasn't true it was as good a bluff as any.

"If it hadn't been for the high-scoring ways of Devlin and Wagstaff, there's no way this team would be in the play-offs. Between the two of them, they scored more goals than Maddox could let by, and that's what's made the difference to the Ravens' season." I was relying on Ethan's interrogation techniques to clean up the rough edges around all of this.

"This is preposterous," Stavoros Kronos yelled, dismissing my whole statement with a Greek wave of his arms. "Nick is starting in goal tonight and that's final. I am the coach. Not you, Mr. Chapel. Nor you, Ms. Brisbane. I am the coach. I make the decisions."

"What is it, Stavoros?" I asked. "Are there going to be scouts for the American World Cup team in the stands tonight? You figure Nick will make enough of an impression to get a place on the team."

"Once they see how he can play, Nick will start on the World Cup team." Stavoros puffed out his chest. He was looking to relive old glories from his youth, but he was too paternally blind to see that the talent wasn't there.

"Do you mind leaving some of the blood and thunder to me?" Ethan asked sardonically from the edges of the crowd.

Nina looked at him. "I suppose you have warrants?" she asked, annoyed.

"Warrants will come later. Right now I'm simply here following up investigative leads. There are a number of questions I need to ask of father and son Kronos."

"Don't you realize this team has a very important game to play in a few minutes?" Nina asked Ethan.

"Do you really want this team to go into that game being led by someone who doesn't have the team's best interests at heart? If I were you, I'd get the worms out of the apple before they do any more damage."

There was a moment of charged silence before Kurt Wagstaff spoke up. He had been watching the whole scenario unfold while keeping his own counsel to this point.

"We can win this game," he said, "but only if we have Chapel in goal and a coach who can keep his mind on the game. Even if he's as pure as the driven snow, Stavoros will be distracted by all that has happened here. I suggest you exercise your contractual right of final say in the team's well-being, Ms. Brisbane, and put Stavoros on temporary hiatus."

"And what do you propose we do for a coach?"

"Let Sticks lead the team," Wagstaff said in an offhand manner.

Stavoros looked panicked. Sticks looked surprised.

"You seem to know an awful lot about Coach Kronos's contract." Nina's eyes flashed at Wagstaff. You could almost see the gears turning in her head.

Wagstaff merely shrugged.

The bottom of Nina's veil twitched angrily as she shook her head. "I'm sorry Stavoros," she said, "but I don't see that I have any other choice."

After the bluster and flurry of activity that followed Nina Brisbane's decision, Ethan moved Nick and Stavoros out of the locker room. The two had not yet started yelling for lawyers, and that was something Ethan wanted to avoid. He was at his commanding, yet soothing, best as he started to manipulate his two suspects into a proverbial corner from which they could not escape.

For my part, I took it upon myself to whip the team spirit up into something resembling a positive mind-set. With the help of Bekka, Wagstaff, and Pat Devlin, we brought the team's focus back to the game ahead. We would win this game if we all pulled together. If each one of us believed in his own abilities and supported his teammates, then we were unstoppable. All of this was nothing more than emotional fuel, the mumbo jumbo of the jock as magician, but it worked. You could feel the mood in the locker room lighten. In reality, our problems were just beginning, but with my safe return and the labeling and clearing out of Nick and Stavoros, the illusion was that we had put our problems behind us.

Sticks too rose to the occasion by sliding easily into his new position as a temporary replacement for Stavoros. The assistant coaches, Brian Doogan and Larry Durrell, seemed too overwhelmed by events to make any sort of organized protest about Sticks's unprecedented promotion over them.

I wondered briefly why Wagstaff made the suggestion of making Sticks head coach, but, God help me, I had come to trust the man's judgement in these issues. I still had trouble equating the Wagstaff that I had hated for so long with the Wagstaff that I was coming to know. Perhaps he felt that if Stavoros was dirty then the corruption could have spread to the assistant coaches. By putting Sticks in the position of head coach, it could short-circuit anything else that was going on.

We hit the playing field with a fury. The agitation of waiting through the introductions and the national anthem boiled within each of us until it exploded into a fireball of energy at the starting whistle. For the first period our opponents, the Seattle Gulls, didn't know what had hit them. I was only called on to stop two shots during that first fifteen minutes because the rest of the action was concentrated deep in the Gulls' half of the field.

Sticks kept substituting players with dizzying speed, and the difference between his approach to the game and Stavoros's was quickly apparent. Sticks didn't give a toss for playing lines that were separated along ethnic styles. With abandon, he split up the members of the Hot Tamales and inserted them into the game with Pat Devlin and Wagstaff.

Later, after pulling him for a brief rest, Sticks put Wagstaff back into the game alongside Pepe Brazos and Chico Juarez. The result worked like a charm. Danny Castalano, his injured knee propped up painfully in front of him, cheered from the sidelines along with everyone else when this new combination of Ravens players scored two beautiful goals in as many minutes. The Ravens were coming of age under fire.

Even the defensive players were getting into the action. The American players, Hank Decker and Mitch Dakota, individually substituted with Alan Hardacre and Birch Bloodworth without concession to which front line was on the field. Everyone on the bench, except for Bekka, was able to fly into the fray, and I felt compassion for her plight. Goalkeepers are rarely substituted except in case of injury. With Nick gone tonight, she was one step closer, but she still wasn't in the game.

Another factor in our favor was the crowd. Nina Brisbane's promotion machine must have been working overtime because there were few empty seats in the Acropolis, and the positive noise was louder than the Ravens had ever encountered before. It fed us like applause feeds a show business performer.

Having more time to myself in goal than I wanted, I was able to spare a few glances toward the crowd. I was looking for Archer and the other Hardbirds, as I knew Ethan's men would be looking for them. I couldn't imagine them not showing up for the game, as fanatical as they were supposed to be about the Ravens. Of course that didn't seem to apply when it came to kidnapping me, because I, immodestly, didn't see how that action could be construed as being in the team's best interest.

I wondered at what monetary price Archer placed his loyalty to the team. And then I knew that was a silly thought. Archer and the Hardbirds didn't give a damn about the Ravens. They were only interested in the pursuit of their own warped antisocial behavior. Rebellion and anarchy for their own sake. Where was the next thrill, or the next punch-up, to come from? These things were their only touchstones. Still, they should have been in the crowd tonight looking for trouble, and yet there was no sign of them. Ethan needed to get his hands on them. He needed to play them against Nick and Stavoros, and vice versa.

In the game's second period, Kyle Ridgway, the Gulls' top scorer, began to bring the game into my domain. He was equally deadly with either foot and could play a re-bounded ball with infinite finesse. We clashed several times before I ended up getting the free kick called in my favor while I was sitting on Ridgeway's head.

My mistake was in concentrating on Ridgeway. I was being set up and I should have known it. Ridgeway kept up his one-man assault on me for almost the entire second period. Taking advantage of any chance, he took shot after shot, even if they were of low percentage. He made one-man dribbling runs from midfield that more often than not ended in a clash of arms and legs with yours truly.

I was getting into the rhythm of his play, anticipating his next move with absolute alacrity. I had no trouble handling his longshots, and I enjoyed the physical tussles which were the end result of his dribbling runs. All of this led to me being suckered as time ran out in the half.

Ridgeway gathered in the ball at midfield and started a dribbling run. He left Alan Hardacre tied up in a knot and faked Hank Decker out of his shorts. I came off of my line to challenge Ridgeway, as I had been doing all of the second period. I was sure of what he would do next. I was sure, but I wasn't right. As I committed myself to diving for the ball, Ridgeway flipped a soft pass off to the left—something he had not done all game—and his fellow Gulls striker, Clayton Mahoney, was there to drive the ball into the net. The period ended 2–1 in our favor, but the momentum was swinging to the Gulls.

During halftime, while we were trying to pull ourselves together and stuff orange slices down our gullets, the Acropolis announcer spread the news that the other semifinal game, which was being played that night, had been won by the New York Lights. The news meant that whoever won the game here tonight would meet the Lights in the Soccer Bowl on Sunday.

While all of this was going on, I caught a glimpse of movement out of the corner of my eye. I turned to look into the middle of the field, not at all sure what had attracted my attention. After a few seconds, I noticed that the huge electronic score cube was being telescoped up toward the ceiling. The cube had run into some kind of electronic glitch during the first half of the game and was not working properly. It was obvious that the Acropolis maintenance staff was trying to fix it before the game started again.

I was fascinated to see that part of the ceiling had been rolled back to expose the room that the score cube's long support pole telescoped into. It had never dawned on me that there had to be some way to service the cube. Also, the cube needed to be out of sight when the Acropolis hosted concerts or other nonsporting events. I found it fascinating to watch the heavy cube disappear. I began to think about the possibilities of other hidden rooms within the Acropolis providing hidden living quarters for Archer and the Hardbirds.

As the third period began, Pat Devlin began to show why he had been chosen as the league's most valuable player. Working in concert on the front line with Jackson Bopha and Chico Juarez, Devlin took the game to the Gulls and stole back the momentum they had begun to build. He directed his teammates like he was an army field general. He set up plays, organized attacks, and stole the ball away from Gulls and left them standing flat-footed. He alternately shot or passed off depending on what move had the best chance of resulting in a goal.

Devlin was a brilliant player. I was not too sure where his off-field politics stood, but on the soccer field he was a solid and powerful leader. Sticks kept substituting the other field players, but he left Devlin alone because he had obviously become the team's lynchpin. All of the other Ravens responded to him and began to raise their own levels of play. We'd started out the third period with a one goal lead, but by the end of the period we were up by five, the score standing at 6–1 in our favor.

On the bench during the short break before the fourth period, Sticks turned to Bekka. "Go check in with the referee. I'm taking Chapel out to save him for the final. You're on."

Bekka looked shocked. She didn't move from the bench.

"Get a move on, Ducatte," Sticks growled at her. "Stavoros was an idiot not to give his other goalkeepers actual game experience. If Chapel gets injured, I don't want to have to put in a keeper who's a virgin to game conditions."

Bekka looked at me. I can't say I was pleased to be taken out, but I was very happy for her. "Good luck," I said to her. "And watch out for Ridgeway. He'll try to intimidate you if he gets the chance." She bounced up without another word and went to notify the referee of the change in keepers. I knew her heart must be in her mouth.

When the teams moved back on the field, the crowd went nuts when they saw Bekka in goal. Half of the crowd was cheering her, and the other half, not believing a woman belonged on a professional soccer team, jeered her. It didn't seem to make any difference to Bekka. She smiled and waved to the crowd, did a few stretches to warm up, and took up her position. Her face was full of color, and if her emotions ran any higher I thought she might take off like a rocket.

The Gulls came out shooting, looking for a couple of quick goals off an inexperienced keeper to get them back in the game. They had taken the substitution of the second-string goalkeeper as an insult, as Sticks had known they would, and they threw everything but the kitchen sink at Bekka in an effort to get the ball by her. However, La Gata Blanca held her ground and kept her net inviolate.

After one particularly nice save, where Bekka took a rough roll at the hands of Kyle Ridgeway and came out on top, the crowd warmed to her and began to chant her nickname, which had been mentioned in the newspapers and program, in three distinct beats. "La! Gata! Blanca! La! Gata! Blanca!" If she became any more popular I was going to find myself out of favor.

In the end, the Gulls pulled their own goalkeeper in order to put in a sixth offensive player. This is always a desperation move, and almost always ends in disaster for the team that initiates the move.

Knowing there was no trained goalkeeper in the Gulls net, Pat Devlin and Wagstaff went to work at a fever pitch. Together, they began running up the score like there was no tomorrow. When the full-time whistle blew, we had destroyed the Gulls by a score of 12-1. We were so charged up that if we could have continued on and played the New York Lights in the final right then and there, we would have slaughtered them as well. Hell, we were so ready we could have taken on the world. But for tonight, we had to be satisfied with the scalp of the Gulls under our belt and the promises of the future.

''I don't think I'm ever going to calm down enough to get to sleep,'' Bekka told me as we walked along the dock area near where Ethan Kelso's boat was kept.

Bekka had become an instant star during the last period of the game, and the hustle and bustle of the postgame revelry revolved around her. All the news hounds, who had more often than not taken a very lackadaisical approach to anything having to do with the Ravens, swarmed around her yelling questions and demanding more of her than she could possibly give. However, like she had handled Ridgeway and the Gulls on the field, Bekka took all of the attention in her stride. She gave witty, intelligent answers to all the questions that deserved them, and she came up with devastating put-downs to all the questions that didn't. The press ate it up and came back for more.

Eventually, Sticks had to shove the reporters out of the locker room so he could have his own say about the evening. He kept his comments short and sweet, basically telling us we'd played a hell of a game, but there was still the final to come. He set a practice session for the following afternoon. Sick bay report, for anyone with aches and pains, would be at ten in the morning.

Nina Brisbane also put in her two cents worth. She was vibrating with pleasure at the team having made it to the finals, and promised a modest bonus to everyone if we beat New York. Her smoky, sensual voice purred like a cat's. I knew she had to be gratified by the coverage Bekka had brought the team as well as by the night's gate receipts. She might stand a chance against her sister yet.

When all was said and done, Bekka came over and grabbed my arm. "Let's get out of here," she'd whispered urgently in my ear. "Take me somewhere quiet before I jump out of my skin."

Taking her car, we'd escaped and driven to the Santa Monica Bay Marina. I still had the key to Ethan's boat. I wanted to be somewhere where Bekka and I could have privacy but Ethan could get in touch with me. On the drive down, I'd brought her up to date on everything that had happened over the last few days, including the reasoning behind Ethan's questioning of Nick and Stavoros.

Now, we were walking along the docks trying to wind down as the clock ticked close to one in the morning.

"We'll all have plenty of time to sleep when we're dead," I told her. "So don't worry about the sandman now. Enjoy what you're feeling and be thankful that you've become one of the few to experience it."

'Mmmm . . .'' Bekka hugged herself against the cool breeze that was coming in off the ocean. She did a dancer's twirl. "I can't believe I've actually played in a professional game."

"You didn't just play in a game," I told her. "You made the start of a legend for yourself while damn near putting me out of a job."

"Oh, Ian," she said, suddenly nervous and apprehensive. She put her arms around my waist and hugged me tightly against her. "I'm so sorry, I've only been thinking of myself. . . . How stupid of me . . ."

I laughed. "Don't be ridiculous, woman. I couldn't be happier for you. I never thought I'd hear myself say this, but I've had my fifteen minutes of fame. I'll still take the limelight when I can get it, but I've come to accept how fleeting the feeling is. Enjoy it while you can and savor the memory when it's gone. It's all you can do in the long run.''

''Wow,'' said Bekka. ''You go into solitary for three days as Ian Chapel and you come out as Socrates.''

I grabbed her by the waist and started to tickle her while growling fake anger deep in my throat. She pushed away from me, laughing, and started to run down the deserted dock and out onto the sand.

I gave chase and we eventually ended up in the wet sand in an out-of-breath heap. Bekka had maneuvered herself on top of me, with her hands pushing my shoulders down into the sand. With deliberation she brought her mouth down on mine and kissed me deeply. Small waves made shushing noises in the background as they peaked and tumbled.

''I was so worried about you. . . .'' she said softly when she relinquished my lips.

''Don't talk,'' I said, and putting my hand behind her neck, I brought her lips down to meet mine again.

We held the kiss for a long time, our tongues darting and entwining. There was the sound of a larger wave breaking and then water flooded over us. Taking her mouth from mine, Bekka started to laugh, and water poured down my throat and up my nose. I rolled over, retching and choking. The water was freezing.

We dragged ourselves back to the boat in fits of giggles that must have irritated even the deepest sleepers amongst our marina neighbors.

When we were inside, I dug out a couple of thick white towels. ''Next time I run into Burt Lancaster, I'll have to ask him for a few tips. He didn't seem to have any problems making love along the water's edge in *From Here to Eternity*.''

''You are some piece of work, Ian Chapel. I've never met another man who makes me laugh like you do, or who makes my emotions do flip-flops like you do.''

The cabin was dark except for the moonlight that poured through the portholes. Throwing her towel aside, Bekka slid into my arms again. My hands moved of their own accord under the cotton top she was wearing and up to caress the swells of her breasts. Bekka moaned into my mouth.

Her nipples were cold and hard against my palms and she raised her arms for me to slip her blouse and bra over her head. I tasted her skin with my tongue, and the salt residue left behind by the ocean that had flooded around us was tangy and full of enticement.

Her skin was beginning to heat, and she arched her body against me in a demand for response. Somehow she had shed the jeans she had been wearing, and as my hand slipped down over the taut muscles of her belly she shuddered deeply. She placed her own hand on mine and guided it swiftly to the center of her heat. There was a soft growling in the back of her throat, and I felt myself start to ache with wanting her.

I guided her gently from the main cabin into the state-room, and we lowered ourselves onto the bed. As she lay on top of me, she tore open my shirt and we laughed as the buttons popped away all over the room.

Naked together, she poured herself over me like warm honey. Her hair was still damp, smelling of the sea and the faint traces of her perfume that hadn't been washed away. It tickled against my chest as she nipped at me gently with her teeth. I ran my hands the length of her back and then down to the taut cheeks of her buttocks.

Her body was elegant and strong, hungry for me. I rolled on top of her, and she opened her arms and herself to me with a gasp of joy and pleasure. We seemed to fit perfectly together like two halves of a whole, intimately complete and perfectly right.

Lying motionless, for fear of disturbing the unbelievable sweetness of our symmetry, we stared for a long time into each others eyes in the moon-pierced darkness. And then the hunger and need overtook us, and we began to move to the beating of an inner metronome that drove us deeper into each other, past all physical barriers, and into the heart of passion.

TWENTY-ONE

A T FIRST LIGHT the following morning, still tangled in each other's arms, we were rudely awakened by Ethan. He came on board as loudly as a drunken sailor—his polite way of making sure everyone was decent before handshakes were exchanged. He looked tired and haggard-eyed, but if he disapproved of the sleeping arrangements currently on board his boat, he didn't let it show.

He dumped the morning's newspapers down on the small table in the main cabin alongside a bagful of doughnuts and six Styrofoam cups of coffee.

"I know you would probably prefer tea," he said to me by way of greeting. "But I also know how picky the English are about the way it's brewed. Trust me. You're better off with coffee while you're in America."

"Good morning to you, too," I said. I felt groggy from lack of sleep. "Did you sleep well?" I asked nastily.

I was peeved at having my beauty rest disturbed, however I was interested in what news Ethan had brought with him about Nick and Stavoros.

Ethan yawned dramatically. "Is sarcasm a strong suit of yours in the morning?" he asked. "I feel like I haven't seen a bed since sometime last month."

"What happened with Nick and Stavoros?"

"In a while," he said. He flapped his hands toward the coffee and doughnuts. "I want to put the *Corrienearn* through her paces first. I need to be rejuvenated by the smell of the salt air and the touch of sea spray at speed."

"Great," said Bekka as she came out of the small forward stateroom. "Can I help? I used to sail with my father when I was younger." After less than three hours' sleep, she looked bright and alive, and I saw the first glitch in our relationship appearing on the horizon. She was a morning person and I was a night owl. I was having trouble getting the lid off my first cup of coffee, and she was ready to take on the world.

"I'd be glad to have you lend a hand," Ethan told her. "But I'm sure you'll want to see these first." He opened the two daily papers he'd brought with him to the sports pages.

The coverage was good. Bekka's smiling face was plastered all over the front of one sports section, and it made page two of the other. Together, we ate doughnuts and read the articles about the semifinal games out loud to each other.

Nina Brisbane's publicity machine had obviously been in action again, and Bekka was providing them with a good hook. Such was the current local awareness of indoor soccer that the removal of Nick and Stavoros from the Ravens lineup didn't even cause a single comment. In any other American sport, if a head coach and one of the players had been replaced right before a play-off game, sparks would have flown in the press. However, indoor soccer was only now beginning to come into its own, and the players and coaches were hardly household names, even to the press.

When we'd finished basking in the reflected glory from the newsprint, Ethan and Bekka disappeared out of the cabin hatch with the intention of getting us into open water. I know very little about boats. I understand what makes them float only a little less vaguely than I understand what makes planes fly. I simply accept boats floating and planes flying based on the Emperor's New Clothes theory of science . . . you don't want to ask too many questions in case you destroy the illusion.

Ethan and Bekka, however, seemed to have no problems with all the little rituals and operations required for casting off, motoring out of the marina, hoisting the single sail, and setting the *Corrienearn* running before the wind.

The sea was calm and colored with opaque blues, grays, and greens that split into a foamy white as the sloop's hull sliced through them. I'd initially worried that I might get seasick, but when no symptoms appeared I made my way up on deck. It was quite cold, and both Bekka and I were wearing extra bits and pieces of Ethan's on-board wardrobe for warmth.

Ethan, already looking refreshed, was alternately puffing on a stubby burlwood pipe and sipping from his second container of coffee. He was somehow managing to handle both activities with one hand while the other steadied the tiller. Sitting next to him, Bekka had her head back and her eyes closed in enjoyment of the moment. Her hair was pulled back again into a tight ponytail that streamed away behind her.

I was quickly finding my sea legs and didn't make too much of a fool out of myself as I crossed the deck and sat down on the opposite side of the tiller to Ethan.

"Do you want to take her?" he asked.

"I don't think I have a license that covers this type of activity."

"Don't be silly." Ethan reached over and put my hand on the tiller, and suddenly I was sailing a boat for the first time.

"What do I do now?" I asked.

"Keep the wind in her sails and relax," Ethan told me. "It's not like you're going to have to battle rush-hour traffic out here."

He seemed content enough to trust my abilities, so I settled back to try and enjoy myself.

After a minute, Ethan refilled his pipe and began to unfold his tale.

"Your little shenanigans have put me in dutch with my bosses," he said to start.

"Really? In that case I'll try not to get kidnapped again."

"Just sail the boat, landlubber. I can tell this story without any help from the peanut gallery."

"Yes, Captain, my Captain."

"The problem, as my boss sees it, is that I'm dabbling in ordinary everyday crime. Stitching up kidnappers and murderers is all well and good, but if that were all this case was about, I should have left it in the hands of Briggs and Gill. My brief is antiterrorism and I've got to find some way to make all of this apply."

"Are you telling me that Stavoros and Nick admitted to murdering Maddox and to kidnapping me?"

"Not so fast. I've been at this thing all night and I'm still analyzing how it all gets put together." He paused to get his pipe fired up again and to adjust my hold and reposition the tiller before continuing.

"The information about Nick buying up Maddox's gambling markers was on the money. So was the fact that, as quickly as Nick bought him out of debt, Maddox began gambling again with his original bookie. Jackie Casio, the leg-breaker for Max Turner, put me on to the bookie. It turned out to be a guy who owed me a couple of big ones from the days when I was working vice. He told me that Maddox had the fever bad and was losing big on everything from the ponies to cockroach races. The difference this time was that Maddox was keeping up with his bills. Now, whether that money was coming from Caitlin Brisbane or not remains to be seen, but I can't find any other source of income for Maddox that would cover this kind of action."

"Did Nick let you in on why he bought up Maddox's original markers?" I asked testily, trying to jump to the car chase.

"Are you always this cranky in the mornings?" Bekka asked. "Let the man tell it."

"Thank you, ma'am," Ethan said as he adjusted the tiller for me again. "Nick's first story was that Maddox came to him and asked for help, and out of concern for his fellow teammate, he paid off Max Turner's goons in an effort to get Maddox back on the straight and narrow."

"What a guy," Bekka put in. She still had her eyes closed, but it was obvious she was listening intently.

"Yeah." Ethan gave a half laugh. "I told him to pull my other leg since it had bells on, and he got all upset and bent out of shape. However, by the time I finished with him, he admitted that he tried to use the markers to force Maddox out of the starting goalkeeper position."

"How did he find out about Maddox's gambling problem?" I asked, trying to get a handle on all the angles.

"The same way Bekka did. Nick saw Maddox take out the leg-breakers who were sent to rough him up. He went further than Bekka did, though, because he traced the collectors back to their source."

"I take it we were right in assuming Maddox told Nick to pound sand."

Ethan nodded. "Maddox was an old hand at this type of game. When he found out Nick had the markers, he simply took them away by force and destroyed them. He then walked away, leaving Nick out of pocket and hanging in the wind."

I continued to try to anticipate the sequence of events. "And out of revenge and a desire to knock Maddox out of the starting goalkeeper position, Nick pays Archer and the Hardbirds to provide Maddox with a career-shattering injury. Things get out of hand and Maddox ends up dead."

"It works for me," Ethan said. "But Nick says it ain't so. I wrung the boy dry, but he still denies any contact with Archer and company. I could have forced him into admitting he hired Archer. . . . Hell, I could have forced him into admitting he killed JFK, Jimmy Hoffa, and Elvis. . . . The problem with doing that is I deal in truth, and the truth is Nick didn't have anything to do with Maddox getting dead.''

"What about Stavoros? He wants Nick as a starting goal-keeper as bad as Nick wants it, but he couldn't justify the move as long as Maddox was part of the team. Maddox was a far superior keeper even if he was on his way over the hill. Stavoros dreams about his boy making the next American World Cup team, and that isn't going to happen if Nick doesn't get the right kind of experience and exposure.''

"Again, I agree with you. But there's the rub.''

"What do you mean?''

"By the time I got to Stavoros, he had a whole flock of high-priced lawyers throwing around injunctions and other legal paper airplanes. The nasty thing about all that is Stavoros didn't make any phone calls. The lawyers simply showed up like someone had turned on the Bat Signal. Somebody knew Stavoros was in police company and jumped to the rescue. Someone with money. These types of legal boys don't come cheap.''

"So, what are you telling us?''

"I'm telling you that Nick and Stavoros are both back on the bricks, and until I can get my hands on Archer and his crew, or some other kind of evidence, they're going to stay there.''

"What about your boss?''

Ethan shrugged. "There's still something going on here that we're not seeing. I've managed to talk my boss into accepting that there still might be something terrorist-related, but I need to come up with firm evidence soon.

"You were talking about a two-handed game yesterday, and I think you're right.'' Ethan puffed his pipe into a billowing smokestack. "Maddox's murder is only one of the problems surrounding the Ravens and the Acropolis. Somewhere in the rest of the mess, Terrance Brisbane is making big money for the IRA, and somewhere else Liam Donovan is playing out some other kind of action. Caitlin and Nina Brisbane are muddying the waters with their own battles. And Archer and the Hardbirds are making things even more murky. Meanwhile, you're still the big stick I need to stir the pot.''

"Thanks, heaps.''

"Hey, if you can't take a joke, you shouldn't have joined.''

By the time we were alongside the Santa Monica Bay Marina dock again, Ethan had related the lack of success his men or contacts had had in trying to track down Archer and the Hardbirds or anything of consequence regarding Liam Donovan.

"What about searching the Acropolis from top to bottom and trying to locate the Hardbirds' crash pads?'' I asked when we were all secured.

Ethan shook his head. "I don't see anyway to justify a warrant, and even if we were able to get permission to search the Acropolis, I don't think I could muster the manpower to do it properly. The place is just too big. We might come up with the Hardbirds' crash pad, like you say, but I'm sure they've got that place wired like you wouldn't believe and we'd never catch them inside.''

I had to agree with his assessment. "So, we just hang around and wait for the other shoe to fall.''

"No. I keep plodding along like a good little policeman, and you keep making as much of a nuisance out of yourself as you can. You're almost as good at that as you are at being a goalkeeper.''

"Thanks. I'll get a letter of recommendation from you next time I'm putting a resume together.''

"You have a better plan?''

"If I did, you wouldn't hear me bitching about this one so much.''

Bekka decided to put her oar in the water. "Don't forget, we've also got a league final to prepare for.''

I cocked my head at her with my eyes on Ethan. "Anybody would think she'd beaten the Gulls single-handedly last night.''

"Given half a chance, I think she could have done it,'' was Ethan's reply.

* * *

The most interesting thing about that afternoon's practice, beside the new tortures Sticks had designed to put us all through our paces, was an argument in the stands between Nina Brisbane and her father. Terrance Brisbane was coming down hard on her for her decision to remove Stavoros from the head coaching position. He was demanding Stavoros and Nick both be reappointed, but Nina was standing firm.

The whole flare-up was like a bursting firework, in that it exploded fiercely but quickly disappeared as Terrance Brisbane stalked away in a still smoldering huff. If you hadn't been watching you would have missed the whole gist of the argument and put it down to a father-and-daughter spat.

As it was, I was very intrigued by Terrance's insistence on Stavoros's and Nick's return. Terrance Brisbane certainly had the money to cover lawyers of the type Ethan had described. Terrance Brisbane also had a direct connection to Archer and the Hardbirds. He might not admit to it if confronted, but he was definitely using them as security during his speech at the Golden Harp. Logic from that point ran that if Stavoros or Nick had direct ties to Terrance Brisbane, they could easily have access to Archer and the Hardbirds through Brisbane. It was the kind of thin thread Ethan was looking for, but I didn't yet know how to unravel it.

After practice, I had arranged to meet with Sir Adam in the Marriott bar. Bekka dropped me off since I'd not yet recovered my Laverda from the hotel parking lot.

"Can I leave you alone for five minutes without you disappearing on me?" she asked, only half kidding.

"I'll try to be good."

"Just don't let me turn around again and have to start looking for your face on the back of milk cartons."

I kissed her and we parted with promises to meet for dinner. There was so much to talk over between us, but so little chance to do it with everything else going on. I watched her drive away until she turned a corner and was out of sight.

Sir Adam was waiting at a corner table. The bar was well lighted and decorated with white wrought iron tables with glass tops, wicker chairs with thick cushions, and pastel drapes and carpet. The drinks all came with fruit skewered on plastic swords, or little paper umbrellas shading the liquid below them. Sir Adam had an umbrella. I ordered a large orange juice and found it came with a savaged slice of the real thing.

Sir Adam took me through the whole of my kidnapping and escape again with infinite attention to detail. When I explained to him how I'd used the plastic container to make a key he nodded his head in approval, but I was also sure he felt I should have thought of the method sooner.

Next, he took me back through everything that had happened since I'd arrived on American soil. When I was done, we went over it again. I didn't mind. I remembered being debriefed in the same way by Sir Adam after returning from undercover assignments in Ireland. It was an excellent way of making sure no stitches were dropped and that all angles had been covered. Sir Adam had an agile mind and I could almost feel the intellectual power emanating from him as he mulled over everything I was telling him.

Eventually, there were three more orange juice glasses lined up in front of me and four discarded umbrellas in front of Sir Adam. I don't know what he'd done with the glasses, but they were nowhere to be seen. Perhaps the waiter was more attentive to Sir Adam's side of the table than mine. I'm sure he could tell which pocket his tip was coming from.

"If Terrance Brisbane is acting as a conduit for funds to the IRA, I want to know how. He might think he's a big fish in the pool out here, but I can get people who wouldn't even consider him bait."

"Feeling our oats a bit are we?"

"I don't like terrorists and I don't like people who support terrorists."

"Your terrorist is somebody else's freedom fighter," I said just to jerk his chain. It worked.

"Poppycock!" Sir Adam's voice suddenly rose to the point that it attracted the attention of several other patrons in the bar. He noticed the reactions and dropped back to a much more subtle decibel. "A terrorist by any other name is still a terrorist."

I held up my arms placatingly and slapped a mischievous smile on my face.

Sir Adam realized I'd been going after his goat and trailed off with, "Well, yes then." He harrumphed. "As I was saying, Brisbane will take the fall if we can find out what's going on, but I'm still as concerned about what is happening with the team, and that means Liam Donovan figures in this somehow."

There was something that had been nagging at the back of my mind for a while. I had first come up with it while sailing with Ethan earlier in the day, but I hadn't wanted to say anything until I'd had a chance to think it out. Sir Adam, though, would be a good guinea pig for the thought since he might have the contacts to follow it up.

"I've been wondering some about Pat Devlin," I said.

"Oh, yes." Sir Adam looked interested. One of his strongest points as a leader was his willingness to listen to any theory, no matter how far out.

I still didn't have it all clear, but I decided to take a stab at it. "We know that Liam Donovan has strong IRA connections. He's splintered off now with the Sons of Erin. If he's connecting with Terrance Brisbane, you can bet it has something to do with money for the cause. It might be a more violent cause now, although a group more violent than the IRA is tough to swallow, but it's still a cause."

"Go on."

"Well, if Brisbane found out through his daughter that I was not only being brought in to play goal, but also to investigate Maddox's murder, perhaps he called in a favor from Donovan and stuck him on me in England because he didn't want me stirring up a hornet's nest here and maybe stumbling onto the source of his funding for the IRA.''

"Maybe, but what does that have to do with Pat Devlin?''

"I'm not sure, but Devlin seems to be the other side of the coin, here. He is opposed to Brisbane's politics, as evidenced by his actions at the Golden Harp, but what is the basis for his feelings? As far as I can tell he should be on the side of the devils. He tells me he's a good Catholic boy, so he's not in with the radical Protestant Orangemen. So what is he? He's a loose cannon on the deck and we need to find out more about him.''

Sir Adam shook his head. "Agreed. I'll get someone on it right away. In the meantime, can you trust this Ethan Kelso fellow?''

"Do you mean can I trust him to keep a low profile when it comes to any scandal that may affect the team?''

"Exactly.''

I thought about that. "I believe I can. His brief is to keep a low profile in everything he does. I know he isn't looking for any personal publicity, and hc's told me his boss has an absolute aversion to it. Between the strings that you can pull and Ethan's own reluctance to step into the spotlight, I think we can keep things pretty quiet. The big problem remains, though, that we still have to uncover what's going on before we can shut it down and cover it up again.''

"I have faith in you, my boy.''

"I'm glad somebody does.''

Another drink had miraculously appeared in Sir Adam's hand. He removed the little umbrella and added it to his collection.

"By the way,'' he said, toasting me with the glass before taking a sip, "you played a hell of a game last night, but you better be looking behind you because that young filly has got what it takes.''

"So much for your faith in me,'' I said.

Fifteen minutes later, after rehashing the Gulls game and musing about the upcoming final against the New York Lights, Sir Adam and I went our separate ways. I was feeling sleepy again and figured I had time for a couple of hours kip and a shower before I was due to meet Bekka for dinner.

Taking the elevator up to the floor of my suite, I unlocked the door and stepped inside. I called out to Sticks, but there was no answer. He was probably still out taking care of details concerning the team and Sunday's final.

I threw the dead bolt on the room door and secured the burglar bar. I did not want a repeat of my tussle with Archer. One trip downstairs in a laundry basket was all I cared to participate in during this lifetime.

I pulled the rugby shirt I'd borrowed from Ethan over my head and stepped into the bedroom. As I did, I also stepped into the trap of a far deadlier adversary than either Archer or Liam Donovan.

I stopped dead in my tracks. Perched on the edge of my bed was Nina Brisbane. She wore a red lace veil over her head. The bottom of the veil was tucked into the turned up collar of a white fur coat that flowed down to just below her knees. Her bare legs were tucked back under her on the bed, and she was practically vibrating with a terrifying mix of sexual energy and nervous tension.

TWENTY-TWO

NEITHER OF US said anything for what could only have been seconds but seemed like eons. I stood, bare-chested, in jeans, high-top tennis shoes, and my black eye-patch. I stared at Nina, a lump forming in my throat. I could sense what was coming and could see no easy way out.

Everything about her screamed sexual seduction, but the effect was blunted by a self-esteem destroyed by her years behind the veil. She was like a child desperate for approval.

A braided red silk cord secured the flowing lace around Nina's forehead. She looked attractive and alluring, but I could tell she was on the ragged edge of her emotions. It must have taken every ounce of courage she had to run the risk of rejection by confronting me this way.

"Have you been waiting long?" I asked. It was a stupid thing to say, but I'd never encountered a situation like this before and I was scrambling to find the proper way to respond.

"I knew you would return sooner or later." The smoky

throatiness of her voice was even more pronounced than usual. A tremor ran through her and I thought for a moment that she was going to pass out.

"Ahhmm . . . I don't know if this is a good idea, Nina. Sticks might come back at any time."

"No he won't. He is attending a press conference and then he will be handling a coaching meeting. He will not return for several hours."

"Ahhmm . . ."

Nina stood up and her coat swung open to reveal a clinging red silk sheath underneath. The dress revealed every line of her magnificent body. The physical effort she must have to extend to maintain her shape would put most athletes to shame. Her rounded breasts tapered down to a tiny waist, and her tummy and abdomen were as taut as a trampoline. Her exposed legs were long and slender, her tiny feet painted red on the nails to match her dress. She had the body of a beauty queen, but I knew it was topped by a dried, worm-eaten apple of a face. I felt like crying for her.

"Do you like what you see?" she asked, moving closer to me.

"You are incredibly beautiful," I told her truthfully, for at that moment she was. I don't know if I would have verbally responded the same way had her veil been removed. However, the veil was in place and she did look beautiful. I thought of Bekka.

"You are a brave man, Ian Chapel."

"Why do you say that?"

Nina reached out with her right hand and ran a perfectly manicured finger across the surface of my eye patch. "The first day you were here, when you removed my veil, you were the first man to ever attempt to do so for the right reasons." Her other hand was sweeping slowly across my chest, and I felt myself physically responding.

"Right reasons?" I was as jumpy as a cat trapped in a kennel's dog run.

The finger on my face moved across my lips and then traced the line of my jaw. The fingers of her other hand traced the loose waistband of my jeans. "Yes. You were not curious. You weren't a freak collector—a man who has a fetish about women who are deformed or handicapped . . ."

"Oh, come on," I broke in.

She moved her finger back to silence my lips. "No, it's true. There are men who live to put freak notches in their bedposts. I should know, I've been pursued by several of them. They think you should be grateful to have someone take a sexual interest in you. But I hated them; hated their motives; knew instantly what they were all about—no feelings, no emotion, only perverted lust. They are mental freaks looking to take advantage of physical ones."

"You are not a freak, Nina." I tried to imagine what life was like for Nina Brisbane. It was a futile effort. My own physical problems appeared to pale by comparison. An ugly, scarred man can be said to have character, but an ugly woman is simply written off as ugly. We are a shallow people, who rarely look beyond appearances.

"You were different, though," Nina said, as if she had not heard my last comment. She had moved both hands to my face now, and I had the impression she was trying to see me with her fingers, like a blind person.

It was a type of intimacy that is very hard to describe. I stood still and let her touch me. I felt more exposed than if I had been naked in the hotel lobby.

"When you lifted my veil it was a gesture of compassion. I didn't know what I was feeling inside. You confused me. I responded by making snide remarks, but you absorbed them without anger."

"I remember," I said. And I did remember the scene in her office all too well.

"Do you also remember that I asked if you could make love to this face?" One of her hands briefly touched her veil before moving back to my face. "And you told me you made love to women not faces?"

We were entering very dangerous ground.

"I also remember asking you if you were making an offer, and you told me not to think I'd get the chance."

"Well, I'm giving you the chance. I want you to make love to me." I could feel her trembling against me. "Nobody has ever made love to me. Even before my face exploded, I was saving myself for the right man. I think you are the right man." Her voice caught in her throat, her emotions laid bare. "Will you make love to me with the lights on?" The desperation in her voice was like fingernails dragged across a chalkboard. She had driven herself to this seduction. She had worked herself up for it, planned it, and somewhere inside she had found the nerve to act it out.

My heart was hammering around in my chest. I wanted to swallow, but couldn't. Nine had molded herself to me and her body felt like it was on fire. Millions of tiny neurons exploded in my brain and raced instant images through my mind.

I thought of Bekka, of making love to her and what that had meant to me.

I thought about how short a time I had known Bekka. What did I owe her? What did I want her to feel toward me?

I thought of my unspoken commitment to one woman.

And I considered what my declining of this simple, beautiful request would do to the woman next to me, who had already known so much pain in her life.

"Nina." I took both her hands in mine. "I can't."

She tore away from my grip.

"No," I said imploringly. "Not for the reasons you think."

"Shut up!" she screamed.

I grabbed her hands again, but she fought against me. "Please, listen to me. I want to make love to you with every fiber of my physical being, but I can't because I am committed to somebody else."

"Who? That Ducatte bitch?" She pulled away from me again, her voice rising to a squeal. "I asked you to screw me. I didn't ask you for any kind of commitment."

"Don't ruin what you asked of me by making it cheap."

"This is the nineties. Everyone screws everybody else. Commitment has nothing to do with lust."

"Nina. Stop it!" I took a step toward her, but she slapped me across the face and backed away from me.

"Stay away, you bastard!"

Her fingerprints felt hot on my face. "You didn't ask me to screw you. You asked me to make love to you. This might be the nineties, but I don't just screw for the sake of screwing. I never have. And making love carries commitment with it, whether you want to admit that or not. I don't know where the relationship between Bekka and me will lead," I said, impossibly trying reason against emotion, "but if I made love to you the relationship would eventually wither."

"Why? Would you tell her you screwed the team's owner? Would you laugh about it in the dark?"

"You would never have asked me to make love to you if you believed I would act that way."

"She would never have to know." Nina's voice had taken on a pleading tone, one last appeal.

"But I would know," I said quietly, my head down.

Nina wrapped the fur coat around her, closing herself off from me physically. "You are either a fool or a prime bastard," she said. "You're just like all the rest."

She stepped forward, confronting me in her pent-up anger, and snatched the veil from her head. The horror of her face was screwed up even further with spitting hatred.

"Take a good look at me," she screamed. "Look at what my father and those IRA bastards did to me on the outside."

I was silent, maintaining a one-eyed locked stare with Nina's single askew orb.

"That's right. It's a nightmare what they did to me on the outside, but it's nothing compared to what you just did to me on the inside."

"I'm sorry. . . ." Again I was saying stupid things, but what else was there to say?

"You will be sorry," Nina hissed at me. "You'll all be sorry. My father, you, that bitch you're sleeping with, and others." Her lips twitched. I think it was a wicked smile. "Oh, yes, there'll be others.'

I kept her gaze for a beat longer, and then she pulled back. "Get out of my way," she said.

I stepped aside and she stormed past me. At the door to the bedroom, she turned back. "Everything will be on your head, Chapel. You had the one chance."

She left the room and a second later I heard the locks on the front door being turned, the door opening, and then the finality of the slam.

I didn't know that Nina was talking about in the end, but I did know she was wrong about one thing. Her interior scars had been there for a long time before I came into the picture. Maybe I had ripped them open again, for which I was incredibly sorry, but I had not created them. That had been done at the point of a shotgun and through a father who thought the shotgun was justified.

I wondered if Bekka would think I'd done the right thing. I sure didn't know.

I went into the bathroom and vomited up every one of the orange juice drinks I had consumed with Sir Adam.

The next two days passed in a flurry of preparation for Sunday's final against New York. Nina Brisbane was noticeable only by her absence. I would have thought she'd been kidnapped, as I had been, except Sticks was in contact with her and was acting as a conduit for her wishes.

Neither Nick nor Stavoros Kronos had made a reappearance. Terrance Brisbane had passed through once to talk in an almost clandestine manner with Miles Norton, the equipment manager.

Sticks made no comment about any activity other than the coming game. He was like a man possessed. I'd never known him to have ambitions to lead a team. Goalkeeping and goalkeepers had always been his passion, but now he was like a whirlwind of intensity—a man who had discovered a consuming passion late in life and was racing to catch up with something that had almost passed him by.

Bekka and I worked out together, not talking about the possibility of her starting in goal instead of me. There was no doubt in my mind that Sticks would start me, but the papers and the crowd wanted to see Bekka in action again, and who knew what Nina Brisbane would demand? She could override Sticks as easily as she overrode Stavoros.

Outside of training, my relationship with Bekka continued to blossom. As I had told Nina Brisbane, I had no idea where the relationship was leading, but if I had my way I wanted a long future for it.

I hadn't told Bekka about the scene with Nina. I hadn't told anybody about it. I felt I owed Nina that discretion. But did Nina know that, or was she staying away out of fear of laughter behind her back? I wanted to contact her, to tell her she had nothing to fear from me, but I couldn't think of any way to break through and convince her. I felt helpless, so I let the situation lie.

On Saturday morning Sir Adam had caught up with me at breakfast in the Marriott dining room.

"Your thought paid off, but I don't know what it means," he said, sitting down and pouring himself a cup of coffee from the plastic hot pot on the table.

"I had a thought?"

"Yes. You remember, don't you? Surely it's not that rare an occurrence in your life."

"Har, har, har." I spoke deliberate laughter notes. "To which particular thought on my part are you referring?"

"The one about Pat Devlin."

"Ahh. Okay. I'm with you now. What have your found out about the darling of the Ravens and the league's soon-to-be-honored most valuable player?"

"You do go on," Sir Adam said.

"Humor me."

Sir Adam sipped his coffee and took a sheaf of teletypes out from the inside pocket of his well-cut blazer. I knew the papers were only a prop, something for Sir Adam to do with his hands. Once he had read something, he could spit it back at you verbatim even years later.

"It seems our young friend has a very interesting and

diverse background. He is illegitimate. Born to a Protestant woman but raised Catholic.''

''What?'' I'd never heard of such a thing in Ireland, where views on religion are cast in iron.

''I know. It's very odd, isn't it?''

''Do we know why his mother bucked the system?''

''Apparently, Devlin's father was a Catholic, and an IRA man to boot. His mother, the bonny Peggy Devlin, worshipped the ground her Catholic lover walked on. She couldn't give up her own beliefs, but she made sure that her son honored his father. She even christened him with his father's name, but Devlin later changed it to his mother's family name.'' Sir Adam rifled through his stack of papers and pulled out a faxed document. ''It appears that Pat Devlin didn't care for his father's politics or activities.''

''Did he know his father?''

''Only through the wire fence that separated them on visiting days. And that was only until his mother died. After that the lad never went back to the prison. By all accounts he blames his father for not being there to raise him or to take care of his mother when she became sick. And on top of it all he blames the IRA for turning his father into a murdering terrorist.''

''I take it we know the identity of this paragon of fatherly virtue?''

''Aye, that we do.''

Sir Adam shoved the fax copy of the document in his hands toward me. It was upside down and turned around, so it took me a few seconds to identify it as a copy of Pat Devlin's birth certificate. His mother, Peggy Devlin, was duly noted, and in the space for father's identity was the name Duncan Finlas.

I looked up sharply at Sir Adam. ''I know that name.''

''Aye.''

''Let me think, let me think . . .'' I closed my eye and wrung my brain. I knew the name. It churned inside me with an excitement that let me know we were on the verge of something. And then I had it. "Duncan Finlas! He's the IRA hit man who destroyed Nina Brisbane's face!"

"I never said you weren't sharp," Sir Adam said.

"Sweet Mary," I said in a half whisper, as I considered the consequences of the information. "Does Devlin know his father was responsible for Nina's injuries? Hell, does she know she has the son of the man who disfigured her playing on her team?"

Sir Adam shrugged. "I'm quite sure Devlin knows. He has a scrapbook that he takes everywhere with him. It has the newspaper reports of the entire incident and the subsequent trial. Playing his heart out for Nina Brisbane, and taking the war to idiots like her father, are what Pat Devlin thinks of as ways to make up for his father's sins."

"How do you know that?"

"The same couple of tiptoe boys who went through Devlin's possessions and found his scrapbook also found his private journal. It made interesting reading."

"I'll bet, but aren't there laws against burglary in this country?"

"We didn't take anything."

"Just Devlin's privacy."

"Come on, Ian. Grow up, man."

I nodded. Sir Adam always believed there was one set of rules for some people and another set for others. I never could figure out how he defined the difference.

"How about Nina? Does she know."

"Hard to tell," Sir Adam said. "I can't find her to ask her."

"I thought she was in touch with Sticks."

"She is. She calls him. Nobody has any way to get in touch with her."

"Curiouser and curiouser, said Alice," I said.

"Are you related to Lewis Carroll, or do you just like to misquote him?"

I ignored the remark and moved on. "Any of this tie to Liam Donovan?"

"I'm having it worked on, but nothing yet. We're trying

to backtrack Donovan's movements since he hooked up with the Sons of Erin.''

We both sat and thought about that for a few minutes while we polished off the dregs of the coffeepot and I munched the last of my toast.

I didn't like the trails my thinking was leading me down. I didn't want to talk about what had happened between Nina and me the previous day, but all theories had to be aired.

''I think Nina Brisbane is fully aware of who Pat Devlin's father is. I also think she possibly has something planned that none of us are going to like. The damage from Duncan Finlas's shotgun blast might not be finished.''

''Tell me all about it, son.''

I did. I told Sir Adam about the attempted seduction and the threats which it degenerated into.

His eyes took on a sorrowful cast. ''The poor woman.''

''I still don't know how I could have handled the situation any differently.''

''You could have screwed her. We might have been better off all round. You've killed for your country, I would have figured this would have been far easier.''

''It's unlike you to be crude, sir,'' I said coldly.

He flapped his had. ''I'm sorry, son. I wasn't thinking. It was crass of me. You did what you thought was right at the time. And who knows—if the woman is unbalanced, you could have even more problems on your hands. If you had made love to her, and she kept expecting more, any little rejection might have set her off.''

I replayed Nina's threats through my head again. She said we'd all be sorry. Her father, me, Bekka (I didn't like that part at all), and the others. Who were the others? The Ravens? Pat Devlin? His father, Duncan Finlas? Or perhaps the whole bloody IRA—who knew?

The waitress came by and put the bill on the table. I signed it and added my room number.

''It's time to start tying up loose ends,'' I said, after wiping my mouth and putting my napkin down. I stood up. ''The season final is tomorrow. If we can't clean this up between now and then, we will have to wait for the beginning of next season to start at square one again.''

"And during all that time, you're going to be waiting for Liam Donovan to drop the axe."

I shook my head. "No. I'm not going to wait. I'm going to find a way to crack this open one way or the other. And I think I'm going to start by cracking Archer and the Hardbirds."

"A good trick if you find them."

"I'm not going to find them. They're going to find me."

Saturday afternoon practice was light physically, but heavy on the mental exercises. Sticks played film after film of games featuring the New York Lights, and we all were mesmerized by the level of their play. They had been the champions of the league for the last three years running, and were the odds-on favorites to repeat a fourth time. We weren't only a dark-horse team, we were pitch-black plow nags.

The Ravens had played the Lights three times during the regular season and lost all three games. The last game, a 6–7 squeaker, was the closest we had come to beating them. At least it had been an improvement over the first game, when they had beaten us 10–2. Pasqual Maddox had been in fine form that day. It showed in the films if you were looking. Goals that he should have saved went by him easily. Oh, he made it look like he was trying hard, but it was all flash and no substance.

When all was said and done for the day, I joined Kurt Wagstaff in the steam room. We were alone, everyone else having bugged out for an early evening.

I poured some more water on the stones and climbed up on the wooden slat benches mounted on the wall across the small room from Wagstaff. He opened his eyes and looked at me without saying anything. I stared back. There was communication that went beyond the verbal plane.

"It's funny," I said after a while. "I never thought I'd be able to sit across a room from you like this and not be consumed by a black hatred."

I saw Wagstaff nod his head through the steam. "Nor I you, England. Only my hatred was always red."

I felt shocked. "You hated me?"

"But of course."

"Why? What did I ever do to you?"

"That is part of why I hated you. You never knew what you did to me."

"I don't understand."

"You ruined me! Ruined my career! Even stole my family from me!" His voice had filled with repressed anger, but his body language was still relaxed, limp from the steam.

"What the hell are you talking about? You were the one who ruined me. My career. My eye!"

"Ah, yes. Your eye. You lay in hospital, and everybody rallied around you. Everybody gave you their support and love. You were the mighty hero struck down in your prime by the filthy *Boche*. I was the villain of the piece."

Wagstaff sat up on the wooden slats of the tier he was perched on and leaned toward me. "Ian . . ." His voice trailed off, and then he tried again. It was the first time I'd ever known him to use my first name. "Ian. I don't care what you think. I don't care how inconclusive the films are. I did not kick you in the face on purpose."

I didn't say anything.

Wagstaff reached out a hand and grasped my arm. "I did not kick you in the face on purpose," he repeated. "I am a physical bastard of a player. Putting the ball in the goal is my only reason for existence, but I did not kick you in the face on purpose. The game is the most important thing in my life, and kicking people in the face on purpose is not part of the game."

"That still doesn't explain why you hated me."

Wagstaff released my arm and sat back. "I hated you because everybody else thought I kicked you in the face on purpose. Every referee in every game I played after you lost your eye kept me tied up in knots. The slightest contact I made with another player got me called for a foul. Other players, especially your English teammates, targeted me for revenge. The young players thought they could make their reputations by going up against me physically, like western cowboys going up against an ancient gunfighter.

"The first season I played after you lost your eye, I suffered more injuries than in the rest of my career put together. Even my wife believed I kicked you on purpose. When I came home to lick my wounds she laughed, told me that what I had done sickened her and that I deserved the treatment I was receiving. She left me at the end of the season. Took my sons with her.

"My career continued to falter until I ended up here on this broken-down excuse for a soccer team, in a country that doesn't even know the sport exists. I love this game. But, like my wife, it no longer loves me."

"I had no idea."

"No. And that made my hatred of you even stronger. That first day when you showed up for practice, I thought I would kill you. But now . . ." He shrugged his shoulders in the European way that spoke volumes. "Now, I find that hatred is useless. I saw that you had lost as much as I had. That all the support of your friends and family couldn't give you back the game."

"Not the game as we knew and played it."

"No. Neither one of us will ever play at the top again."

I thought about Sid Doyle. "I once had a friend who told me the only way to always be a winner was to go out each day and do the best that you can do. He said if you always do the best that you can, then you will always win no matter what the score of the game was."

"A wise man, your friend."

"No. A wise boy."

"If wisdom is coming earlier in life, then perhaps there is still hope for the human race."

Wagstaff stood up and poured more water on the heating stones. Steam billowed around us, and he regained his perch.

"Do you still hate me?" he asked.

"No. I've come past that point. I no longer see you as a

nonperson, a nonfeeling, inhuman being to vent my inner poisons on. I see you as a man.''

''And do you still think I kicked you on purpose?''

I paused before answering. Steam billowed around the room in gray clouds. ''If I'm honest with myself, which is very hard to do, I don't think I ever did believe you kicked me on purpose. I wanted to believe it. I let everyone know that I believed it. I needed somewhere to put my anger and my frustration. If I could believe you kicked me on purpose, then I could put all of that on your shoulders. When I came face-to-face with you again . . . when we fought . . . and later when we played together, I knew I had only been fooling myself.''

I saw something very strange make its way across Wagstaff's face. I could have sworn it was a smile.

''Is that a grin of triumph or relief?''

''Believe what you will,'' he said lightly.

I laughed. ''You're still a bastard.''

Wagstaff nodded his head. His voice became serious again. ''Now, tell me what it is you want from me.''

''You know I want something?''

''I may be a bastard, but I'm not deaf and blind. It is obvious that there is something going on with the Ravens team, and you are involved in it up to your eyeballs . . . excuse me, eyeball.''

''Don't push your luck with bad jokes.''

''Look, Chapel. You didn't come into the team room to compare demons. Explain to me what is happening. Tell me what I can do to help. The Ravens might not be much, but they're the only connection with the sport I have left.''

''In that case how would you like to help me save them?''

Wagstaff leaned toward me again. ''You mean between us we are going to do more than win the final tomorrow?''

The plan that I had started forming at breakfast with Sir Adam began to come together in my mind.

TWENTY-THREE

THE INTERIOR OF the Acropolis rang with an empty hollowness. It wasn't quite a sound, more a feeling that involved several of your senses at one time without allowing you to pin it down specifically. It was late Saturday night. Almost Sunday morning. Bekka and I had said good night several hours earlier. Since then, I'd been aimlessly driving around on the Laverda, killing time until I knew the Acropolis would be deserted.

The arena had played host to a professional wrestling match earlier in the evening. Now, however, the cleanup crews had been through and the maintenance teams had taken down the wrestling ring and set up the indoor soccer boards. Once the preparations for Sunday's Super Soccer Bowl were completed, everyone had gone home. Everything was locked down, an only the amber safety lights illuminated the tunnels and hallways.

There had been a security guard sitting in his car when I'd walked through the middle of the parking lot. He had been engrossed in a paperback novel and hadn't even seen me when I used a key to enter through the player's entrance.

Ethan Kelso believed the Hardbirds were hiding out in the Acropolis and using it as a base. With the See No Evil Security Company on the job it was no wonder they could come and go as they pleased.

Inside the Acropolis's main arena, the giant score cube had yet to be lowered over the middle of the field. I thought again about the room that housed the cube for maintenance, and wondered how many other small rooms the Acropolis might have for a variety of reasons that would never occur to the man on the street.

Since I had arrived in America there hadn't been a chance to search the structure myself, a fact I was rapidly coming to regret. Knowing your battlefield is of prime importance. If Archer and the Hardbirds had taken up squatter's rights in the Acropolis, they would know every in and out of the building and its complex maze of utility tunnels, delivery entrances, storage areas, equipment rooms, locker rooms, cash room, administrative offices, maintenance expediators, and garbage dumps.

I made my way back down the tunnel from the arena to the home team locker room. There was a panel of switches on the inside wall closest to the door and I flipped them on. What had been dark became light, but there were no monsters lurking. Empty benches stretched out in front of the lockers that lined two walls. In the back, I could hear the dripping of a leaky showerhead. I picked up a loose soccer ball and carried it away with me.

I found another panel of switches in the player's tunnel and flipped those on too. I had no idea how to light up the arena itself and no convenient panel of switches presented itself. However, the glow from the player's tunnel cast noir shadows over the boards, through the goal nets, and across the artificial turf; enough light for what I needed.

Entering the field through an opening in the boards, I bounced the soccer ball on the artificial turf and caught it again with both hands. I do not like artificial turf. It is far more unpredictable than sod and provides no cushioning effect when you fall. Taking my time, I began to walk the perimeter of the field. I was bouncing the ball and catching it in my hands over and over every few steps.

I'd been walking the home field on the night before a game ever since the start of my career. The habit had started when I was a kid and couldn't sleep before my first big game. I had climbed out of bed and trotted all the way down to the school field. Once there I'd walked around and around the playing area until I felt tired and sat down with my back against one of the goalposts. The Games Master had found me there the next morning, snoring my head off. He'd sent me to see the Headmaster with a flea in my ear about sleeping at school.

Although sleeping with my back against a goalpost was not an experience I wished to repeat, I still found that walking the home field on the night before a big game helped to center my concentration. It was part of my own ritual for getting ''up'' for a game.

I wasn't superstitious to the point where I believed I would have a bad game if I didn't walk the field, but whenever I did I found I was better prepared. It really wasn't much different than a Grand Prix race driver walking a course. The exercise put my mind on the game. I imagined myself diving after shots and saving them. I thought about all the movements my body would make in the air, straining to reach a ball that looked impossible to stop. I imagined myself stopping that impossible shot. I made every thought during the process positive, and I knew I would play better for having taken the time to do it.

As I gradually made my way around the outside of the field, I began to bounce the ball off the boards. The sound of the ball hitting the boards echoed like gunshots. I threw the ball harder, making louder sounds on impact. Again and again. Harder. Louder. Each time I threw the ball, I moved fast enough to gather the ball up in my arms like making a save. I imagined the crowd shouting, cheering, applauding.

Clap . . . Clap . . . Clap . . .

Applauding?

Clap . . . Clap . . . Clap . . .

I snatched the ball up in my arms a final time and turned to look behind me. A figure was silhouetted against the glow from the tunnel lights.

Clap . . . Clap . . . Clap . . .

In the seats stretching away to either side of me there was more slow, deliberate applause.

Clap . . . Clap . . . Clap . . .

Behind me now, in the seats behind the far goal, a fourth pair of hands joined in.

"Archer," I said. It was an acknowledgment instead of a question.

"In the effin' flesh, mate," confirmed the silhouette.

"I see you brought some friends with you again to the party," I said.

"Too bloody right, mate. We always run in a pack, and this time we ain't gonna give you the chance to do an effin' Houdini."

"Tell me," I said affably. "What do you get out of all the aggravation you cause?"

"Aggro is wot me and the 'ardbirds is all about. Some peoples, they likes to smoke. I don't smokes. Some peoples likes their drink. I don't drink. Me? I likes to fight. Fighting and punching lets everybody know you ain't gonna be pushed around. We does what we wants, when we wants. And ain't nobody gonna stop us. You come on our turf and we're gonna make sure you remember who's top of the heap."

"That's what all this is about? You being the top hammer?"

"Peoples respect you when theys got to answer to your fists."

"You have it all wrong, old son," I told him. "People might fear you, but they are not going to respect you."

"Fear's good enough."

"What are you going to do about me then? I don't fear you."

"You will do before we're done 'cause we're gonna bash you into the ground. Just like we did wif effin' Maddox."

"What in God's name did that poor bastard ever do to you?"

"Nuffin'." I saw the shoulders of the silhouette shrug. "We did him for kicks."

"No, I don't think so." I shook my head in disagreement, and I wondered how clearly Archer could see me. "There is more to Maddox's murder than that," I said. "And I know there is more to your story than simply bashing for kicks. I think you're dancing to Terrance Brisbane's tune. He pays and you lick his boots. You imagine yourselves to be a bunch of tough guys, but you're nothing but a bunch of suck butts who can't make it in the real world."

"Who gives a tinker's fart what you think?"

"The police for one."

"Yeah? Well, I don't see no effin' filth anywhere around here. Nobody is 'ere 'cept you and us. And we don't likes anybody who don't run with the pack. So, maybe you're thinking of dialing nine-one-one. You gots a phone in your shoe?"

What Archer didn't realize was that I didn't want the police. I'd told everyone, including some of the press who were doing last-minute write-ups for the late Saturday edition, about my habit of walking the field alone on the night before the game. I'd hoped the grapevine would get the information to Archer.

I'd made a big production out of obtaining the key from Terrance Brisbane to let myself into the Acropolis. I knew Terrance had contact with Archer and the Hardbirds because he'd used them as bodyguards. I wanted him to see my being alone at the Acropolis as the perfect chance to set them on me again. I was also running the risk that he would set Liam Donovan on me, but somehow I didn't think that Donovan was connected to Terrance Brisbane. I'd come around to believing that Donovan was connected to another Brisbane.

After letting myself into the Acropolis, I'd made enough noise to raise the ghosts of the great goalkeepers of the past. I'd hoped that if Archer and the Hardbirds were using the Acropolis as their base, and if they hadn't picked up my message via the grapevine, that they would come to investigate if they heard the commotion. I'd wanted Archer and his crew to come after me. I was ready for them. But I wanted them alone for a while without the police.

I was operating by Sir Adam's rules, which meant that anything goes. The ends justify the means. The taking of the law into one's own hands. I had only this chance to break things open, so double standards be damned. I was going to start smashing the rules like everyone else. If that dragged me down to their level, then so be it. I wasn't going to wait to be kidnapped again. Or for Donovan to come after me at his leisure.

"Archer," I said, starting to walk slowly toward him. "You are nothing but a spoiled brat who suddenly found the royal teat turned off back in England, so you came over here to raise hell for a while. You've got yourself a bunch of losers who think you're King Kong because you dress funny and butcher the Queen's English. . . ."

I heard a footstep behind me. I had been waiting for it and I pivoted fast with my left arm outflung in a spinning back fist. I connected squarely with the face of the Hardbird who had originally been in the stands behind me. He staggered backwards with a grunt of surprise.

He was a big lad, about eighteen years old, but he was slow and stupid. I grabbed the front of his shirt with both hands, pulled him toward me, and smashed my forehead into his face. His nose exploded and blood flew everywhere. I nutted him again for drill, and then let him drop. He went down without a sound.

"Not real impressive," I said, turning back to face Archer.

"Get the sod!" he yelled to the other Hardbirds. He

started to run toward me. As he ran, he let out a primal scream, but it didn't quite drown out the sounds of his compatriots clambering out of the stands and over the bards.

"Wagstaff!" I yelled at the top of my lungs, and then I dropped the ball I was still holding and charged toward Archer. If the boy wanted to fight, then I was going to teach him what it was all about. I'd grown up fighting, defending Gerald and the other kids in the neighborhood. The SAS had turned me from a fighter into a killer. And I embraced fear as a friend. Archer was in for a shock.

In the steam room earlier in the day, Wagstaff had agreed to stay hidden in the Acropolis after everything had been closed down for the night. He would stay inside so that if Archer and the Hardbirds appeared as I hoped and prayed they would, he would be there to back my play. Now, as I rushed toward Archer, I had a brief image of Wagstaff sprinting down the player's tunnel to join the battle.

When I was close enough to Archer, I threw myself down like I was going one-on-one with a striker who had broken free with the ball. The big difference in this situation was that I wasn't playing the ball, I was playing the player. If there had been a referee present, I would have been red carded out of the game.

As my momentum carried me forward, I raised one leg and planted it viciously in Archer's groin. He let out a howl of pain, and I allowed his motion to carry him over me and crash him down onto the turf. Giving credit where credit is due, I will say he was tougher than I had expected. Even with his testicles planted somewhere up around his stomach, he unbent himself and came back at me.

Through the shadows in the arena, I could make out Wagstaff mixing it up with the two other Hardbirds. I wanted to get in and help him, but I had to finish dealing with Archer first. When he came at me again he was more careful, wary that I might have other tricks up my sleeve.

The light from the player's tunnel washed over his face as we circled. I again placed his age at around twenty, as I had when I'd seen him in the Golden Harp for the first time.

The five years between us should have given him the physical edge over me, but he wasn't even close to being in the league of hard men that claim Liam Donovan and his kind as members. A league that I had once held my own place in.

Archer was a charismatic enough leader for the young yuppie losers who ran with him as the Hardbirds. He led them in a pack to prey on the weak and the defenseless, but being confronted by somebody who knew how to fight back was a whole new experience. I wondered how they had managed to take out Maddox—a man who had bounced around a couple of mob enforcers—and decided to add the question to the list of others I was going to ask.

In a street fight patience is truly a virtue. You keep your defenses up and wait for your opponent to make a mistake. Archer did not have what it takes. He wanted to mix it up immediately and get everything over and done with as quickly as possible. I had been this route before, so I covered up and let him come at me.

I absorbed a flurry of rights and lefts, with my forearms up to protect my head. The blows landed ineffectually on my shoulders while stealing energy from Archer. He quickly became frustrated by his inability to break through my defenses, and decided to see what kind of damage he could do with his steel-capped boots. His kick landed hard on my shin, but I had come prepared for this kind of fighting and was wearing a pair of bamboo soccer shin guards.

Archer was surprised when his action did not elicit the usual reaction; the victim crying out and falling over in pain. I took advantage of his confusion to launch my own attack. I hit him hard over one ear with my open palm, and then over his other ear with my opposite palm. He flinched, and I clouted him on the nose with a downward-striking fist.

Archer cried out in pain and threw himself at me. He clawed at my face, going after my good eye, but I stepped back and fended him off with two more blows over his ears and another bash to his nose. The blows disoriented him,

but he still continued to strike out blindly in my direction.
I turned aside one of his blows and drove my stiffened fingers into his ribs, twice, and then kicked his left knee out
from under him. He went down in a heap and I dropped
knees first onto his back. The fight went out of him like a
fish giving up the ghost on dry land.

Roughly, I pulled his hands behind his back. Moving
quickly, I reached into my pocket and pulled out a length
of strong twine and used it to tie his thumbs together. I
stood up and stepped back, feeling like a cowboy who had
just roped a cow in a rodeo.

Archer wasn't going anywhere, so I sprinted to where
Wagstaff was still doing battle with the two other Hardbirds.
On the way, I passed the first Hardbird I had taken out. He
was just beginning to stir, so I kicked him hard in the stomach and he flopped out again.

Once at Wagstaff's side, I grabbed the ponytail of the
Hardbird closest to me and pulled him backwards. I swung
him around and around until he fell to the floor in an uncoordinated tumble. Keeping hold of his ponytail, I yanked
the youth over onto his stomach and used another piece of
twine to secure his thumbs in the same fashion as Archer's.
By the time I was done, Wagstaff had controlled the last of
the four Hardbirds and had subjected him to the same treatment.

Both of us were breathing hard, but we felt satisfied.
Wagstaff held his hand out to me, open palm up. I slapped
my own palm across it.

"Nice work," I said.

Wagstaff smiled. "I enjoyed it."

Together, we walked over to the only one of the four
Hardbirds who was unsecured. He had vomited from my
passing kick to his stomach. We pulled him clear of his
mess and trussed him up with a last piece of twine. We then
took the belts off of three of the Hardbirds and used them
to secure their feet. We had other plans for Archer.

"They won't be going anywhere for a while," I said.

"They haven't been going anywhere since they slipped

out of their momma's wombs,'' Wagstaff said with contempt.

I snorted and then shook out my shoulders and arm muscles. The last thing I needed was to be sore for the upcoming final with the New York Lights.

"Let's get on with it," I said.

We walked back to where Archer was lying. I squatted down and grabbed hold of his hair. I twisted his face to make him look up at me. Even in the poor light, I could see the hatred smoldering deep in his eyes.

"We're going to have a little chat," I told him amiably enough. "And you're going to tell me everything I want to know."

Blood had run down from his nose into his mouth, and he spat a gout of it at me. It splattered disgustingly across my shirt. I bounced his head off the turf and then grabbed his hair again.

"You don't want to make me mad, old son," I said through clenched teeth. "I've been taught how to cause pain by the best of them. If you don't tell me what I want to know I might start practicing again on you."

"Bugger orf," he said.

"Let me deal with this." Wagstaff's gruff voice cut in. Bending over, he grabbed Archer's arms and started to drag him toward the end of the field closest to the player's tunnel. Archer tried to struggle, but I reached down and dug my fingers into his injured knee and effectively controlled him through the use of pain and compliance. As long as he complied he didn't feel any extra pain.

When we reached the boards by the entrance to the player's tunnel, Wagstaff threw Archer against them and let him sink down to a sitting position.

"Now we will have more light to work by," Wagstaff said, since the spillover light from the player's tunnel provided more illumination in this area. He stood over Archer with a wide-legged stance, his hands on his hips.

"I would let the Englander do this," he said in the theatrical German accent that I knew was his normal speech pattern. "But, like all of his kind, he would be too soft on you. I, however, am made of sterner stuff. We Germans can always make insects like you do whatever we want. Everybody knows about the German SS, right?" He didn't wait for a reply. "You just wait here a minute," he continued immediately. "I'll be right back."

Without further verbiage, Wagstaff turned and moved quickly down the player's tunnel.

"I don't know what he has in mind," I told Archer truthfully. "But I know it won't be pleasant. The part that bothers me the most is that my friend seems to be enjoying himself. A lot. I don't know how much I'm going to be able to control him."

"You can't do anything to me. It would be against the law."

"You're a contemptuous little bastard," I said. "I don't see any policemen here. Do you? What do you want to do, dial nine-one-one? Or perhaps your shoe phone is out of order?"

"I ain't telling you nuffin'." Archer was still defiant, but his voice had adopted a new quaver. He didn't know what to expect and it was putting him on edge.

I heard a commotion coming from down the tunnel. It was a smashing and splintering sound, and I wondered what Wagstaff was doing. Shortly, though, the German was back with us. Over his shoulder was slung a large nylon net bag of soccer balls.

"I don't know where they keep our supply of game balls," he complained. "But I broke into a wooden storage cabinet in the equipment room and found this bag of promotion balls." He was referring to the balls we sometimes kicked into the crowd before the start of a game. "They are cheap pieces of crap," he continued, "but they will do for what I have in mind."

"Last chance," I said to Archer. "How about answering a few questions, then we can all have a cup of tea and call it a night?"

"Oh, come on, don't be a spoilsport," Wagstaff said to Archer. "Hold on a bit longer and let me have some fun."

Archer didn't speak, but his eyes didn't leave Wagstaff for a moment as the German spilled the balls out of the net and onto the turf. I bent down and picked up one of the balls. It was soft, ever so slightly underinflated. It felt like the one I had autographed for Billy in the locker room in Houston before Miles Norton had taken it away from me. It was also slightly heavier than a regulation game ball. It was like the ball was waterlogged. Wagstaff was right, the balls were cheap pieces of crap. The were put together in Mexican sweatshops and shipped across the border for a quick profit. I didn't remember the balls we kicked into the stands feeling this way, but they were the same brand.

Gently passing one of the balls back and forth between his feet, Wagstaff backed up until he was about ten feet away from where Archer was slumped against the boards.

"Start asking your questions," he told me.

"All right," I said to Archer. "Let's start with an easy one. Why did you kill Pasqual Maddox?"

"This is effin' bogus," Archer said nastily. "You can't do this to me. I gots rights you know."

From ten yards out, Wagstaff fired off a shot that blasted into the boards by Archer's head. It hit with a noise like a cannon shot.

Archer screamed. "Bloody effin' hell! Are you trying to kill me?"

"Why did you kill Pasqual Maddox," I asked again in an even tone of voice.

When there was no reply, I passed another ball back to Wagstaff. Wagstaff cocked his leg and booted the ball first time. His power and accuracy were amazing. The ball was not kicked as hard as the first one, but that was only because it was aimed at Archer's chest.

It slammed into our captive and drove the breath out of him. He slid sideways until he was lying on the floor in agony. I walked over and hauled him back up by his hair to a sitting position.

"We've got all night, old son. How much more of this can you take? You've proven you're a tough guy. Now tell us what we want to know. If he wants to, Wagstaff can break every bone you've got."

Archer was gasping for breath. His face was pale and sweat was beading on his forehead. I stood up and backed away again.

"Why did you kill Pasqual Maddox?"

"It was an accident," Archer sputtered. "We were only supposed to duff him up. Make it so he couldn't play for the rest of the season. We took him by surprise by ambushing him outside of the Acropolis. He'd been drinking—thought we were working for the mob and kept telling us he was paid up. He tried to fight back and busted up one of the boys. Nobody does that to the Hardbirds, so we put the boots to him. It was his own fault."

The logic of that argument escaped me for the moment, but there you are. It is a strange world, filled with strange people, and even stranger motives.

"Who told you to do it?" I asked.

Archer was slow to respond and Wagstaff fired off another cannon shot. It rebounded off the boards right beside Archer's head.

"All right! All right! Give me a second," he screamed. "Effin' Stavoros Kronos gave us five 'undred dollars to do the deed."

"How did he know how to contact you?"

"Through Brisbane."

"Which one?"

"Terrance Brisbane. We was working for him as bodyguards when he was doing his fund-raising for the Irish. He thought it was a big laugh having an Englishman around who'd turned his back on his country. He used to get me to make speeches about how the British army is all a bunch of wimps and fags who go to Ireland to beat up on women and babies."

"How did you hook up with Terrance Brisbane in the first place?"

"Some of his security people caught us sneaking into the Acropolis one night and held us for him."

That was a little hard to swallow, considering the quality of the security in the parking lot when I'd entered tonight. Of course tonight could have been a laid-on job.

"Instead of turning us in," Archer continued, "Brisbane hired us on because of our anti-English image. He was real quirky about it. He let us have the run of the Acropolis and do whatever we wanted. It was a big kick bashing people in the crowds and getting into pub punch-ups when Brisbane gave his fancy speeches."

I felt like I was on a roll, but Archer was beginning to sound cocky again. We weren't in the clear yet.

"Why did you kidnap me?" I asked.

Archer laughed. It was high-pitched and girlish. "What a laugh that was. We took you easy," he said.

"Why?" I insisted.

Archer laughed again. "You still don't get it do you, you stupid sod."

Wagstaff fired another ball from behind me. This one scraped the side of Archer's face.

Archer screamed. "We did it for money," he yelled out. "We did everything for money! Stavoros wanted his son to get the starting position in goal. He was furious when you got called in to take over for Maddox, but Brisbane wouldn't let him do anything about it because of the screwup with Maddox. Brisbane didn't want any more heat. But after you showed up at the Golden Harp Brisbane figured you were doing too much snooping for your own good. We were told to get you out of the way for a while."

"Why just for a while?"

"Brisbane had a big business deal going down. Stavoros and some of the other Raven personnel were in on it with him."

"Nina Brisbane too?"

"No. She didn't know nuffin' about the deal. Daddy kept her in the dark. Brisbane didn't want you killed because he didn't want another murder investigation screwing up the deal with cops swarming all over the team. When it was time to release you, Brisbane was going to pay us off, and we could fade away. The filth would never have caught up wif us. You mucked everything up by escaping.'' He sounded like he expected me to apologize.

I paused to gather my thoughts.

"What do you know about Liam Donovan?"

"Who?"

Two balls in quick succession blasted into the boards on either side of Archer.

"I don't know from Liam Donovan," he shrieked. "Keep that German bastard under control, Chapel. He's going to kill me!"

Wagstaff might at that, I thought. The use of his heavy German accent and the stereotypical terms, like "Englander" and "Ve have vays of making you talk" were strictly put-ons, lines stolen from bad World War II movies. However, by the way he was firing the soccer balls at Archer, I could well imagine one of them killing him. I also remembered Wagstaff breaking my ribs with a well-placed penalty kick right before he kicked my lights out.

If Archer didn't know about Liam Donovan, I would have to try another approach.

"How about Pat Devlin?" I asked.

"He's a striker for the Ravens."

"If you don't want me to turn Wagstaff loose, you better try a little harder."

Archer was sobbing now and it was making it hard for him to talk. "Devlin's the son of the man who shot up Brisbane's daughter." He gasped for breath.

I knew that, of course, but I was surprised Archer did. "How do you know that?"

"I heard Brisbane talking about it after the punch-up at the Golden Harp. He was telling Niall Emmanon about it. Brisbane knew Devlin was one of the blokes who caused the trouble. He was furious because he had set it up for Devlin to come and play in America at the request of Devlin's father. Devlin doesn't know, of course. He thinks he's here of his own accord to do penance to Ms. Nina, the silly sod.''

Brisbane's reasoning was beyond me.

''Why does Brisbane insist on supporting the man who disfigured his daughter?''

''How the effin' hell should I know?'' Archer complained. ''He's got a screw loose or something. He can't accept the fact that he'd supported the people who were responsible for shooting up his baby girl. He'd rather live in an effin' fantasy world where the whole thing was a British plot. He maintains the IRA and Devlin's father were set up, made victims like his daughter. He keeps sending the cause money to maintain the fantasy in his mind.''

This was really one for the books, but no one can reason with a fanatic, and Brisbane definitely qualified on that account.

''Where does he get the money from for the IRA?'' I asked.

''I don't know.''

Wagstaff shot off another ball that rebounded close to Archer's head. Archer screamed and tried to scrabble away, but his injured knee prevented his movement.

''I swear I don't know,'' he yelled at the top of his lungs.

Wagstaff fired off two more balls. Hard shots capable of smashing bones. Archer screamed again and again. Tears ran down his face.

''I don't know. I don't know,'' he sobbed.

I was turning toward Wagstaff to tell him to hold his fire when he loosened off another shot. It was his hardest one yet, and it impacted directly above Archer's head. The sound it made when it hit was like the crack of a sonic boom, an explosion of sound and power. The ball, however, didn't rebound. Instead, it seemed to disintegrate as it burst its cheap seams against the boards.

From its interior a thick white cloud of dust billowed in every direction.

Cocaine.

TWENTY-FOUR

Wagstaff had been surprised and shocked by the discovery of the cocaine. I was surprised too, but not shocked. I knew about Ethan's strong suspicions that Terrance Brisbane was sending financial support to the IRA. If those suspicions were correct, then the money for that support had to be coming in from a clandestine source that Ethan and his contemporaries had not yet been able to trace. And in this day and age the largest supply of illicit, hard-to-trace money comes from dugs. When the dust had literally settled, I left Wagstaff to keep an eye on Archer and the other Hardbirds while I went back to the locker room and used the phone.

My first call was to Sir Adam Qwale. My initial responsibility was to him, no matter how much Ethan Kelso wanted me to think I was his agent provocateur. I was not a police officer and so was not bound by their rules of professional ethics. If Sir Adam wanted to handle the situation without involving the police, it was fine by me. In the army, I'd worked for him long enough to have faith in his decisions.

As it was, however, Sir Adam told me to notify Ethan Kelso immediately and let him handle the situation. It appeared that Sir Adam and Ethan had an understanding that went far beyond my knowledge of the situation.

I called Ethan's pager number and punched in the number of the phone I was calling from. When Ethan had originally given me the number, I'd written it down on a piece of paper. However, after the fiasco of my naked kidnapping and escape, I decided I'd better memorize it or have it tattooed on my body in case I needed it again. I'm not much on needles, so I settled for memorization.

Unlike Sir Adam, who, no matter what hour you phoned, always sounded like he was wide awake anticipating your call, Ethan sounded like a groggy bear coming out of hibernation.

"I knew you were going to be a curse to my life the first time I laid eyes on you," Ethan told me wearily. "I've just finished putting in fifteen hours of fruitless surveillance on a group of domestic extremists, and I just bet you want me to come out and play again."

I commiserated with him for a few seconds and then got to the point. "How would you like to close down Terrance Brisbane's source of money to the IRA, clear up Pasqual Maddox's murder, and nip soccer hooliganism in America in the bud all in one fell swoop?" I asked.

Ethan instantly came alive. "You're playing my tune."

I figured I would pique his interest. "Well, if you want to dance, why don't you meet me at the Acropolis as soon as you can?"

"I'll be there with bells on."

I had another thought. "Use the player's entrance when you come in and bring the security guard from the parking lot with you. We don't want him to report to Brisbane that his plans have gone astray." I smiled to myself before adding, "And, on second thought, take your time getting here."

"Why?"

"Because I'd rather see you arrive wearing something other than bells."

* * *

When Ethan entered the locker room thirty minutes later, Sir Adam was also on the scene. Ethan was wearing a pair of rumpled black sweats, and had brought three of his partners with him. I didn't know any of them, and Ethan didn't make any move to introduce them. They all had the same steely-eyed look of professional hard men everywhere. Their movements were smooth and economical, and they listened closely as I ran down the situation for Ethan and Sir Adam.

I showed them the ball Wagstaff's kick had burst open. Using his pocketknife, Ethan cut open another of the promotion balls. Inside was a plastic-wrapped, quarter-kilo package of cocaine.

Ethan used the locker room phone to talk to an on-call District Attorney. The DA, in his turn, talked to an on-call judge who called Ethan back and gave him a telephonic search warrant for the Acropolis premises.

When this was done, Ethan's partners all moved off in different directions. No words had been exchanged between them, but they were like parts of a well-oiled machine, each of them knowing exactly what was expected of them and how to accomplish it. While two of them dealt separately with Archer and the other Hardbirds, Ethan and his other partner searched for and gathered up all of the promotion soccer balls. All of the balls were marked with the trade name "Mizak" and a red or black lightning bolt logo. One by one the balls were cut open. All of the balls with the red lightning bolts had cocaine inside them.

We had kicked the balls with the black lightning bolts into the stands. There had been no dope in those balls. However, before the end of the game Terrance Brisbane's contacts had replaced the give-away balls with a batch of dope-filled balls with red lightning bolts. These had been mixed in with the remaining black lightning bolt balls to be transported and distributed in the cities where the Ravens played.

When Brisbane was ready to hand over the dope at its final destination, he was able to easily identify which balls contained the dope because of their red lightning bolts. A new batch of the innocent black lightning bolt balls was then supplied for kicking into the stands. Neat and simple.

The dope-filled balls had been the perfect smuggling device until I'd almost given one away in the locker room. It wasn't any wonder Miles Norton had been so upset, and his actions that day certainly implicated him in the scheme. None of the players on the team, however, necessarily needed to have known what was going on under their noses.

Ethan placed a sample of the narcotics into a small, clear plastic holder. Inside the plastic holder were two chemical vials. Ethan broke one vial, shook the contents about, and then broke the other vial. The contents turned a vivid pink.

"Test positive. Real positive," he said. "I don't think this stuff has even been stepped on yet. I'd say it's about eighty to ninety percent pure. Right off the rock."

"How much is it worth?" I asked.

Ethan looked around him at the stash. "With what's here? A hundred balls . . . A quarter key of coke in each . . . Twenty-five kilos of coke this pure . . . You're looking at maybe three million dollars wholesale. Ten million by the time the stuff hits the streets. I figure Brisbane is the middleman. His cut would probably be close to five million. Small change by the standards of some operations today, but certainly enough to keep the bloody IRA boys in beer, guns, and explosives for a while. And that's just this shipment. Who knows how long this has been going on."

While Ethan's crew continued their flurry of activity, Wagstaff and I sat in the locker room with Sir Adam and rehashed the events of the evening. Because of Wagstaff's involvement in the discovery of the dope, Sir Adam had allowed me to bring him up to speed on the other aspects of the situation. If Wagstaff had been shocked by the discovery of the cocaine, he was truly astounded by the full breadth of what had been occurring more or less under his nose. He looked slightly sad.

"How are you going to handle Terrance Brisbane?" I asked Sir Adam eventually.

He shrugged slightly. "I'm not quite sure yet. Our people are in touch with the big boys who run Ethan's unit. Brisbane has already been unobtrusively picked up. Perhaps we'll be able to turn him to our advantage. Perhaps not. But for now we'll be keeping him on a very tight leash. We've got him by his John Thomas, and I have no doubt he'll see things our way in the end."

"What about Miles Norton, the equipment manager? I'm sure he was in on the smuggling caper."

"Norton and several others," Sir Adam agreed. "Once we get a handle on the scope of the operation, we'll handle them all."

"And these Hardbird idiots?" Wagstaff asked. I could tell he wasn't used to the way things were handled in Sir Adam's world.

"I wouldn't worry too much about them," Sir Adam reassured him. "Justice will be served. Right now, I'm sure they are spilling their guts to Ethan's partners. There'll be some minor publicity when their arrest is announced, followed by a quick court proceeding where they'll all plead guilty to manslaughter. They'll go down for Maddox's murder without a whimper."

"How can you be so sure?" Wagstaff pushed the point.

Sir Adam looked at me.

I shook my head. "You and I are playing out of our league here," I told Wagstaff. "Justice is different for some. I don't know if that's wrong or right, but it's the way things are."

Ethan Kelso had warned me when we first met that his unit operated a lot differently than the rest of the police department. "Like no other place on earth" was how he'd put it, and I believed him. I'd seen Sir Adam operate this way before.

Wagstaff continued to look slightly stunned, but after a moment he asked, "And the game goes on?"

"The game goes on," Sir Adam confirmed. "I will not allow soccer in America to become a victim of Terrance Brisbane or anyone else."

Wagstaff nodded his agreement with this, but he still asked, "And you have the power to do this?"

Sir Adam's smile was his only reply.

After a few seconds of introspective silence, Sir Adam spoke up again. "There are loose ends about this situation that bother me."

I knew exactly what he meant. "One of them is that nothing here tonight ties in with Liam Donovan, right?"

"Exactly." Sir Adam stood up and began to pace back and forth with his hands behind his back. "Why did he come after you in England, and what game is he playing here? Why did he kill the goalkeeper in Seattle? And why is he playing cat and mouse with you?"

I walked over to the watercooler and used a paper cup to retrieve a few mouthfuls of water. "I've had some thoughts in that area," I said, when I'd finished drinking. "I don't like where they lead, but I don't see any other answers."

Ethan Kelso wandered over. "Any thoughts you've got would be better than what I have," he said. "Because I'm as stumped as Sir Adam."

I rubbed two fingers under my eye patch and then ran my palm over the rest of my face. I was tired, and from what Sir Adam indicated there was still going to be a soccer final to play.

"Has anybody located or been contacted by Nina Brisbane yet?" I asked Sir Adam.

"Not that I'm aware. If Archer and his followers weren't in custody, I could believe she'd been kidnapped like you were. However, I'm still very concerned." He gave me a hard look. "Do you think Liam Donovan has her? Do you think he's working for Caitlin Brisbane?"

"No, that's one thing I don't believe. Caitlin certainly has enough Irish contacts through her father to find someone like Donovan, but her goal was to stop the Ravens from winning. I could believe she sent Donovan after me in England to stop me from coming to Los Angeles, but then why not have Donovan kill me when I arrived here? And why would she have Donovan kill the Seattle keeper? That action only made the odds more in our favor when we played against the Gulls.''

''Where does that leave us?'' Ethan asked.

''It leaves us with Nina Brisbane as Donovan's control,'' I said.

''How does that figure?''

''When we talked before,'' I said, turning back to Sir Adam, ''I told you I believed we were involved in a two-handed game—two separate agendas with only the Ravens in common. After what Archer has admitted, I think we are actually looking at a four-handed game: Terrance Brisbane using the Ravens and the Hardbirds as a front for the narcotics he was selling to fund the IRA; Stavoros Kronos, who was involved with Brisbane in the narcotics smuggling, but had his own priorities when it came to using the Hardbirds to help get Nick a starting position with the Ravens; Caitlin and Nina Brisbane's struggle for control of their father's sports empire; and Nina Brisbane's personal agenda for revenge.''

''Revenge?'' I could practically see the gears whirring in Sir Adam's brain.

''Yes. I think the tragedy which resulted in the destruction of Nina's face has finally pushed her trolly off the track. Between her father's continued support of the IRA, and the power struggle with her sister, Nina has gone over the edge.''

''She told you she was going to make everybody pay, didn't she?'' Sir Adam remarked thoughtfully.

I was embarrassed by the memory of the seduction scene, but it was the one event which had given me a glimpse of Nina's cards.

''How much did you tell Nina about me before you asked me to come and play for the Ravens?'' I asked. ''Did you tell her how reluctant I might be to accept the offer?''

Sir Adam scratched his head. ''Yes. I also convinced her that you were the only goalkeeper available who was good enough to get the Ravens through to the finals. Anyone else who was any good was already being used in the league, or was committed to outdoor teams."

I nodded. "Okay. Stay with me on this for a second. Nina's objectives were two-fold. First she had to get the Ravens through to the finals in order to stand a chance against her sister in the struggle for the Brisbane sports empire. On one hand, she desperately wants her father's approval—she told me she lost him to Caitlin after the destruction of her own face, and Caitlin's blossoming beauty. On the other hand, she hates her father for continuing to support the IRA and Duncan Finlas, the man responsible for the nightmare of her injuries."

"Are you saying," Ethan began to ask, "that Nina Brisbane is plotting to revenge herself on her father?"

"Not only her father, but also Finlas's son, Pat Devlin, the IRA, me, and anybody else her confused mind has targeted as victimizing her."

"And Liam Donovan?" Sir Adam asked.

"Give me a chance. I'm getting there," I said. "We agreed that Caitlin Brisbane could have had enough access to her father's Irish contacts to find someone like Liam Donovan. If Caitlin had that kind of access there is no reason that Nina couldn't have found Liam Donovan, or someone like him, as well. I'm sure the fact Donovan and his partner, Sean Brody, were IRA outcasts appealed to Nina. The pair of them would have no qualms about screwing up the flow of money from Brisbane to the IRA because they were no longer a part of that team."

"They would have wanted the money for the Sons of Erin," Sir Adam said when I paused.

"And I'm sure Nina promised it to them."

"But why did they go after you in England?"

"Wait for it," I said. "Nina had everything on schedule. Pat Devlin was on the team where she could get to him whenever she wanted. The Ravens were headed into the play-offs, and she had two very hard men to do whatever she had planned."

"And then Maddox got bumped off," Ethan said.

"Right," I agreed. "With Maddox out of the team the odds were against the Ravens getting through the play-offs."

"That is true," Wagstaff interjected in agreement. "Nick Stavoros didn't have enough experience to take over for Maddox, and nobody had any idea Bekka was as good as she is."

I filled up my water cup and took another drink before continuing. "So, Nina was in danger of losing the Brisbane sports empire to her sister. She felt she'd already lost her father to Caitlin, and she believed by beating her sister in the business competition she could win him back." I took a pause to see if everyone was with me. Nobody jumped in with any questions. "Not willing to take the risk that I wouldn't agree to play, Nina sent Donovan and Brody after me. Their brief wasn't to kill me, just to make it appear that way and make the threat to the Ravens appear even stronger than it was. She was using reverse psychology—believing the actions of Donovan and Brody to discourage me would only add fuel to Sir Adam's arguments to convince me to play."

"And the goalkeeper in Seattle? What was his name?"

"Tom Sweet," I said. "After the game with Houston, where Caitlin bought off the referee, Nina became more than willing to play hardball. Caitlin had already shown herself capable of taking drastic steps to stop the Ravens, so Nina decided to take out a little insurance for the next game. She ordered Donovan to kill Sweet. With their first-string goalkeeper gone, the Seattle Gulls were an easy mark for the Ravens at full strength. When I went missing, Nina probably believed Caitlin was behind the disappearance. She must have felt even more justified about the murder."

"Likewise," said Ethan, "she's kept Donovan reined in from killing you because she still needed you in goal for the Ravens."

"Right. After the season was over she'd turn Donovan loose on me. However, after I turned down her advances it's hard to say if she still has the same priorities."

Everyone thought about that situation.

"Okay. I'll buy it as a scenario," Sir Adam said. "But what kind of revenge is she planning that is going to take out everyone she has in her sights?"

"I'm afraid that's the point where I run up against a brick wall," I said. "I have a bad feeling, though, that we're going to find out real soon."

And I knew none of us were going to like it.

TWENTY-FIVE

I WAS EXHAUSTED by the time Ethan and his crew were ready to wrap things up. Wagstaff was curled up on a padded bench in the physical therapy room taking a catnap. Ethan woke him up and told him to go home and get some proper rest. I needed sleep too, and getting my head down on a soft pillow for a few hours was the most important thing on my mind.

With Wagstaff and Sir Adam tagging along, I followed Ethan out through the Acropolis player's entrance and into the parking lot. Ethan's partners had already hustled Archer and the Hardbirds away and into what remained of the night.

After calling back the on-call judge he had spoken to earlier, Ethan told him what the search of the Acropolis had turned up. He also detailed for the judge the admissions Archer and this buddies had made to the other police officers. According to Ethan, once their lips had been coerced into moving, Archer and the Hardbirds couldn't seem to tell their story quick enough.

In the parking lot, I straddled the Laverda and then started it up. My missing eye was throbbing to beat the band. It seemed to be keeping pace with my pulse, and the beat reverberated through my entire body. If Donovan had chosen that moment to kill me, I think I would have been happy to let him do it.

I rode slowly back to the Marriott, where I parked the bike and made my way up to the suite. Inside, I could hear Sticks snoring through his open bedroom door, sleeping the sleep of the righteous. I envied him. I thought of the method I had employed to break Archer, and I wondered who had appointed me God. Was there any difference between Liam Donovan and myself, or were we simply a one-eyed Jack and a two-eyed Jack at opposite ends of the same facecard? Was I to be considered on the side of the angels only because the people who supported me were in the current position of power? I hoped not, but I was too tired to argue the morality of the point with myself any longer.

I wanted to call Bekka to let her know everything that had transpired, but one look at the clock told me that sane people were still off in the land of nod. Still in my clothes, I flopped on my bed and joined them.

When I woke up, I found someone had thoughtfully removed my shoes and covered me up with a blanket. Someone was also moving about in the suite's living room, and there was the smell of bacon and coffee. I rolled over, dragged myself off the bed, and made my way out there.

"Good morning, Sunshine," Sticks greeted me. "Did you sleep well?"

"Mmph," I grumped. I'm not good when I first wake up. Sticks ignored me.

"The papers have given the game decent coverage for a change," he said, rustling the pages of the Sunday sports section from the *Los Angeles Tribune*. He spread them out on the small table in front of him.

There was a room-service cart next to the table and I began to investigate the contents of the covered dishes on top of it—eggs, bacon, hash browns, pancakes, toast, pots of tea and coffee.

"Is all this for me?" I asked.

"Say thank you," Sticks said. "I had to think of some way to bring you back from the dead."

"Thank you. It smells good. What time it is?"

Sticks checked his watch. "Eleven o'clock."

"Has Bekka called?"

"No."

I shoveled food into my mouth and poured a cup of tea. As I chewed, I picked up the phone and dialed Bekka's number. There was no answer. I told myself not be to concerned, but my heart didn't want to listen to what my mind had to say. I've never put much faith in precognition, but my heart was racing.

As I put the phone down it suddenly rang, making me jump. I snatched up the receiver and at the same time sent up a quick, silent prayer: *Please let it be Bekka.*

"Hello," I said into the receiver. My voice sounded funny. There was still food in my mouth and I was having trouble swallowing.

"I told you I'd get you, you bastard," a gruff voice said. It was filled with gloating. The voice of a nightmare. "Your girlfriend is real cute, Chapel. Gorgeous red hair. Long legs that go all the way up and make an ass out of themselves."

"What do you want, Donovan?" My insides had turned into a glacier.

"I want to tear your beating heart out of your chest, but before I do, I'm going to make you wish your mother had aborted you before you ever saw the light of day."

"You have Bekka?"

"How many other girlfriends have you had time to develop since you've been in America?"

"You're out of luck, mate. She doesn't mean anything to me." The statement was the hardest I have ever had to make and I could not stop the lie from creeping into my voice. I felt physically sick. My empty eye socket began to throb with lightning stabs of pain.

Donovan laughed. "You're a pathetic liar, Chapel. I saw the stars in both your eyes at the Golden Harp. And I was watching the two of you together on the beach and in your little floating lovenest." The thought of Donovan watching the *Corrienearn* while Bekka and I were aboard making love scared the hell out of me. "If she means nothing to you," Donovan continued, "you're not going to care that I'm going to cut off one of her fingers for every goal you let by you during the game tonight."

"You're crazy, Donovan," I said with venom in my voice. "If you harm her in any way, you'll be signing your own death warrant. I won't rest until I kill you." I saw Sticks looked at me across the table and I turned away from his gaze.

"You don't scare me, Chapel. You were with the bastards who killed Sean. Now it's your turn to squirm. After the final, after I'm done having my fun with your girlfriend, I'm coming after you."

"Why wait till after the final?" I asked, desperately trying to push any of Donovan's buttons. "Won't Nina Brisbane let you off your leash before then?"

"I'm being paid to do a job of work. When that job is done, sending you to hell will be my sole obsession. Nina Brisbane will have her revenge, and then I'll have mine. If you do anything that stops the game going off as scheduled tonight, your bird will die immediately." Donovan laughed nastily. "Remember, though, once the game starts, it's one finger for every goal you let in. We'll be close, and I'll be watching." He hung up the phone.

I put the receiver down and took a deep breath. By pushing Donovan, I had learned two things. First, Donovan was working for Nina Brisbane and Nina was after some form of revenge. And second, Donovan, Nina, and Bekka would be somewhere close during the game. It wasn't much, but it would have to be enough.

I closed my good eye and put my head in my hands. After a few seconds, I felt Sticks come up behind me and put his arm around my shoulders. He obviously knew something was up.

"Whatever has gone wrong, son, we'll get through it together."

I used Ethan's beeper number to contact him. When he called, I quickly filled him in and arranged to meet him at Bekka's condominium. I hadn't been to the condo before, and Ethan had to trace Bekka's phone number through a contact at the phone company to get her address. Fortunately, it was located very close to the Marriott in a complex referred to as Warner Center. The Laverda sped me there in short order, and after knocking repeatedly on Bekka's door and getting no answer, I was forced to wait on pins and needles for Ethan to arrive.

Larger than apartments, but smaller than most houses, the condos were groups of three or four look-alike residences connected to each other by a common wall. The complex which housed the development was fairly new and the landscaping was well maintained. There was a communal pool and a recreation room. Both appeared to be used extensively by the twenty- to thirty-year-old newlyweds and singles who seemed to make up the majority of the complex's residents. While waiting for Ethan, I knocked on the doors of the condos on either side of Bekka's. None of the occupants had seen Bekka, or anything out of the ordinary.

Ethan finally turned up with one of the blackclad men from the night before at the Acropolis. Knowing Donovan's expertise in explosives, we took things very carefully opening the door to Bekka's apartment in case of a booby trap.

Ethan's partner had brought an explosives sniffing dog with him. When the dog gave off no positive indications after sniffing around the doorjamb, Ethan took a slim packet out of his jacket pocket. From the packet, he extracted several thin pieces of metal and proceeded to pick the two locks with skilled speed.

The door was eased open a crack and then Ethan's partner

sprayed an aerosol around the opening. The aerosol was designed to show up any trip wires that could be lurking in deadly earnest. When the door was fully opened, the dog was brought into play again, entering and searching the premises before coming back to the door without giving any indications that explosives or booby traps were present.

Fortunately, the entrance to Bekka's condo was secluded from the main parts of the complex and our actions hadn't attracted attention. After the dog had finished his duties and had been fussed over by his handler, we entered the dwelling to complete a search of our own.

The interior was inexpensively, but tastefully decorated in cool pastel colors and soft fabric. Everything was neat and tidy except for the bathroom off the master bedroom where there were obvious signs of a struggle. Makeup containers had been knocked off the countertop, a hair-curling brush was still plugged into a socket near the sink, and a hand mirror had been smashed against a wall.

"Seven year's bad luck for someone," Ethan said as he picked the mirror's frame up of the floor.

"I'm going to make damn sure that someone is Liam Donovan," I said. Stabs of anger burst in my stomach like gastric flames.

"We have to find him first," Ethan replied. I was surprised he didn't give me a lecture about taking vigilante action, or staying out of the way of the police investigation, but then I knew Ethan wasn't a standard type of policeman. His unit had its own agenda that seemed to tie in closely with the efforts of Sir Adam and his cloak-and-dagger connections. Because of my connections to Sir Adam, Ethan appeared to regard me as an equal, a fact for which I was grateful.

We continued to look through the condo with Ethan and his partner for any indications of Donovan's intentions. I don't know what it was we were expecting to find. Perhaps a treasure map with "X" marking the spot where Donovan had taken Bekka. What I did find, though, only served to add to the stress of the situation.

Bekka had plopped her purse and a stack of miscellaneous bills, mail, and papers on her kitchen table. Flipping through them, I came across a plain lavender envelope with my first name scrawled across the front in large cursive letters. The envelope wasn't sealed, and inside was a contemporary greeting card.

The picture on the front of the card was of a couple walking hand in hand along a beach. The sun was low over the water, lending a golden glow to the scene. Printed across the bottom of the card was the sentiment: *Every time I think of love* . . . I opened the card to where the sentiment was continued: *. . . I think of you.* Beneath the printed sentiment, Bekka had added words of her own: "I found love when I found you." She had signed her name in the same scrawling freehand she had used to put my name on the front of the envelope.

I'd often received cards from family, friends, and fans, but this was the first time in my life a woman I cared about had ever expressed herself in this manner. My heart felt like it was being squeezed into a knot, and I was terrified I would never see her again.

"You find something?" Ethan asked.

I held out the card to him and he read it.

"I'm sorry," he said, handing the card back. "I won't tell you not to worry, and I'm not going to offer you false hope. If we're going to find Bekka, we're going to need time and luck, so you better get prepared to stop everything that New York throws at you tonight."

"And now introducing our own Los Angeles Rrrrrrravens!" The voice of the public-address system announcer echoed down the player's tunnel where I waited with the rest of the team. Minus Bekka.

The surprisingly large crowd was capacity for the stadium. They came through with a heartwarming roar, and for the first time since I came to America, I thought soccer might stand a chance of surviving. I just didn't know if Bekka would. Or if I would.

Ethan and I had gone directly from Bekka's condo to the Acropolis, where a team meeting was scheduled prior to the game. We found both Sir Adam and Wagstaff before going into the meeting and filled them in on what was happening. Like everyone else they were concerned but had no ideas about how to handle the situation besides progressing in the hopes that Ethan could work a miracle.

We discussed cancelling the game and throwing the whole situation open to a full-scale investigation, but Donovan's threat to immediately kill Bekka if the game didn't go on as planned was enough to douse the flames of that idea.

In the meeting, Sticks had made an excuse for Bekka's absence to the other players who weren't in the know. After that, he'd kept things short and sweet. If we weren't already prepared for the game with New York, we never would be. Tonight was our chance to shine, to show the world what we were made of. For some of the players tonight was also a final chance to impress scouts from European teams looking for American bargains.

Sir Adam had Terrance Brisbane under his thumb, but could get nothing useful out of the man in regard to Bekka. Ethan and his crew had searched the Acropolis as best they could, but the only thing they had turned up was the makeshift living quarters used by Archer and the Hardbirds. No Donovan. No Nina Brisbane. No Bekka.

In the player's tunnel, waiting for our introduction, Wagstaff had turned to me and placed both hands on my shoulders.

"Never give up," he said to me in a quiet voice. "It is the single most important trait that has made you English unbeatable in any war. You never, ever, give up, no matter what the odds. Don't give up tonight. You and I will each play like ten men. We will be indomitable."

I forced a smile and then it was spotlight time. Wagstaff's name was announced over the PA system, and he turned away from me and ran into the arena. Five seconds later, my own name was called and I jogged out into the blaze of lights and the roar of the crowd.

* * *

For all my apprehension, I felt ten feet tall in the goal and faster than anything that could be thrown at me. The crowd was reacting with the phenomenal presence that gave them the force of an extra player on the field. This was what the promise of American soccer held—the same symbiosis of team skills and fanatical fan involvement which lifted the game above the level of a sport and onto a plateau usually reserved for religions, a plateau where gods and miracles are commonplace.

Bekka's chances were now in the hands of the soccer deities, and the only way for me to plead my case was to display my skills to the limits of my abilities and beyond.

When I had entered the arena to the cheers of the crowd, I had jogged to the center line to join my teammates. Ravens team flags had been handed out to the fans as they had arrived. All of the flags were waving, giving the impression of a flowing stream of alternating colors.

As the national anthem played, I looked to our bench. In the seats directly behind it, I saw Sir Adam sitting next to a very pale and drawn Terrance Brisbane. If I had ever doubted Sir Adam's continued involvement in clandestine activities, one look at the power he was now obviously exerting over Terrance Brisbane was enough to make me a believer.

Sir Adam saw me looking at him and nodded his head. He also pointed to his left and my eyes tracked the direction of his movement. A dozen or so seats further down, with the best view of the field, were some surprise guests. My brother Gerald and his wife Zoe waved wildly at me as the national anthem ended. Next to them was an even bigger surprise—Sid Doyle. His cheeks were flushed with the excitement of the evening and he was grinning at me like a happy madman.

I ran over and tapped the Plexiglas extending from the boards in front of them. They were yelling words of encouragement at me. However, all but the obvious sentiment was lost in the noise of the crowd. I moved down to the bench to pick up my gloves. My heart struggled between the elation of the movement and desperation concerning Bekka. Sir Adam came down to the bench enclosure and caught my ear.

"We're doing everything we can. Ethan and his entire crew are continuing to comb the Acropolis. We've got an additional man up with the security cameras scanning the crowd. If Donovan and Nina Brisbane are here with Bekka, they'll find them."

Donovan had told me on the phone, "We'll be close, and I'll be watching." With soccer being what it was at this point in American history, tonight's game was only being carried live over the radio. An all-sports cable TV channel was there to film the game, but it was for delayed broadcast in a time frame for insomniacs. If Donovan was going to be close and watching, then he had to be somewhere in the stadium. I looked at the capacity crowd. Where could you sit with a terrified woman and cut off one of her fingers every time her lover let a goal slip by him?

On the field, a ball launched itself at me from midfield as New York tried to work a fast break. I came out of the goal and out of the penalty area to boot the ball back down the field.

Wagstaff, who had been dropping back quickly on defense, patted me on the butt as he passed behind me. "Don't get carried away," he told me. "Stay in the goal. Leave the field to me." He was right of course, but I was so full of energy I wanted to ram the ball into the opposite goal myself.

Gunner Torenson was New York's main scoring threat. A big muscular German, he was a contemporary of Wagstaff's. I'd been warned by Wagstaff that Gunner was an enforcer, and I'd already experienced one of his elbows trying to bury itself in my neck outside of the referee's view.

New York began to attack again. Gunner brought the ball quickly up the middle and then played it off to Trent Marlon, an American-bred winger whose ball-control skills rivaled those of many European and South American play-

ers. As New York hustled down the field, we were caught
on the hop during a line change and found ourselves short-
handed in the backfield.

Hank Decker moved to cover Marlon, but he was no
match for the more skilled player. Marlon beat him flat-
footed and shot the ball in a hard low line drive across the
goal. Gunner bulled his way past Bloodworth and crashed
into me as I dove out to scoop the ball into my arms. The
referee blew his whistle for the foul, but the damage had
been done. There was no air in my lungs, and I lay on the
carpet alternately dry heaving and gasping for breath.

The referee showed Gunner a yellow booking card, which
the big German simply smirked at while our trainer and
Sticks came off the bench to attend to me. They couldn't
take me out of the game, not only because of Donovan's
threats, but because there was nobody to replace me. Bekka
was missing in action, and Nick Kronos still hadn't returned
after being in police custody.

Bobby Rogers, our trainer, put me in a sitting position
and lifted my arms up over my head. Air seeped slowly
back into my lungs. Eventually I was able to stand up on
my own accord and limp back to the goal. My eye patch
had been twisted around. I pulled off a glove and adjusted
the black triangle of cotton back to its normal position.

Before New York could take another crack at me, the
whistle blew to end the first period. Sticks immediately hud-
dled with the offensive players and I sat on the bench sucking air and orange quarters. I looked over to Sir Adam who
shrugged his shoulders and gave me a hang-in-there gesture.

When play resumed, I was still not fully recovered and
New York renewed their assault with fresh determination.
They were looking to take advantage of my weakened con-
dition, but they had not reckoned on dealing with Kurt
Wagstaff. Exploding in a fury of activity, Wagstaff appeared
to be everywhere at once. When he wasn't cutting Gunner
down at midfield, he was intercepting passes between Trent
Marlon and New York's other forward, Randall Newman.

In between defensive maneuvers, Wagstaff combined with Pat Devlin for our own all-out assault on New York's goal.

Sticks kept freely substituting Chico Juarez, Pepe Brazos, and Jackson Bopha on the front line, but he left Wagstaff and Devlin alone as they were playing like demons. In the backfield, Sticks didn't substitute as freely, but he still kept Decker, Hardacre, Dakota, and Bloodworth rotating if they showed signs of fatigue.

As I regained my strength, I began to ache for the touch of the ball. I got my wish when Trent Marlon hit a first-time volley that came at me like a rocket. I only had time to knock it down, and was then forced to scramble for the loose ball. I dove after it and at the same time caught sight of Gunner's foot as it viciously slashed toward my head. *Not again*, my brain screamed. My fingers wrapped around the ball and I rolled away. I felt the slipstream of air as Gunner's boot missed me by a fraction of an inch, and then I swung my legs around to collide with the single leg he was standing on. He crashed to the carpet in agony.

The referee's whistle blew. I figured the foul was being called on me, but it was Gunner who was again called for dangerous play. I was hoping he'd be red carded and thrown out of the game, but the referee wasn't of the same mind.

The tit-for-tat foul was sometimes the name of the game. By taking Gunner down, I'd served notice that I was not going to be messed around with anymore. Gunner would think twice now before trying to intimidate or bully his way through me again.

I heard a cry from up the field and blasted the goal kick out to Wagstaff. He was right at the midfield line, and as I kicked the ball, he caught New York's defense on the square. He ran past them and controlled my pass beautifully.

Running forward, he drew New York's goalie, Deke Theakston, out of the goal mouth. Theakston moved confidently to cut down the angle, but Wagstaff was the better man. With consummate skill he stepped one foot over the ball, brought his rear foot up to trap the ball between it and

the heel of his front foot, and then flicked his heels up
in the air.

The ball popped up behind Wagstaff, arched over his
head, over Theakston's surprised, outstretched hand, and
then dropped neatly down in front of the goal where Wagstaff was waiting to meet it and pound it home. Lights
flashed, buzzers blared, alarms sounded, and the crowd
came to its feet in an astounded mass to give tribute to a
beautiful display of skill. The Ravens swarmed down the
field to embrace Wagstaff, who ran to meet them with his
fist upraised in triumph.

There was a short flurry of activity in midfield after the
ensuing kickoff, but before New York could mount a coun-
terattack, the referee blew the whistle for halftime.

One to zero. I had kept a virgin net for the first half of
the game. And, hopefully, Bekka had kept all her fingers.

In the locker room, I was too wound up to concentrate
on what was going on around me. I had congratulated
Wagstaff, but he was now grouped together with Sticks and
the assistant coaches as they went over second-half strategy.

I slunk out of the room and made my way back down the
player's tunnel. I stood at tunnel mouth and stared out into
the arena.

In the middle of the playing field the halftime activities
were in full swing. A square, two-tiered platform had been
set up over the center circle, and various dignitaries from
the league were making short speeches. Several presenta-
tions were being made to the accompaniment of crowd applause.

Sir Adam was standing in front of the player's bench at
one side of the field. Next to him was Terrance Brisbane,
holding the silver plate that was to be awarded to Pat Devlin
as the league's outstanding player of the year. Devlin himself was standing on the other side of Sir Adam, waiting for
his turn to be introduced into the hoopla.

I saw Ethan standing in the player's penalty box. He was
looking up at the score cube that loomed over the square
presenting platform. I followed his stare.

HOME-1 VISITORS-0

The score was spelled out in lights on all four sides of the cube, surrounded by advertisements, period indicators, foul statistics, and timers.

I looked back down at the crowd as they watched the awards ceremony, waiting patiently for the third period to start. I heard footsteps behind me and turned to see Wagstaff approaching with a ball under one arm and a water squeeze-bottle in the other. He stopped in front of me and extended the squeeze-bottle. "Anything?" he asked.

"Not yet," I said, and took the bottle from him. I took a long draw from the straw.

Wagstaff looked out into the arena. "What's with him?" he asked.

"Who?"

"The detective. Kelso."

I looked back at Ethan. He was still staring at the score cube.

I looked back up at the cube. The score hadn't changed. I looked above the cube to the long telescoping pole that supported it. About halfway between the pole and the ceiling there was a bulge in the pole that I did not remember seeing before. Trying to piece the gloom above the lights, I noticed for the first time that each of the ceiling doors, which slid back to accept the score cube when it was pulled up for servicing, had a small inset window.

I looked down at Ethan. He was looking at Sir Adam, who was making his way to the awards platform after being introduced over the PA system. As co-owner, he was due to say a few words on behalf of the Ravens in place of Nina Brisbane. Terrance Brisbane would be introduced next. As owner of the Acropolis and a founder of the league, he was scheduled to present the Most Valuable Player of the Year award to Pat Devlin.

Pat Devlin. The man whose father rotted in a jail in Ireland beyond Nina Brisbane's reach. The son. The only way for Nina to strike at the father.

In a few seconds all of Nina's possible targets would be

in the same place at the same time on the awards platform. Except for me. And with Bekka in the hands of her hire gun, Nina was already seeing her revenge toward me coming full circle.

I look again from the huge electronic score cube to the awards platform beneath it. Aside from intimidation and sadistic torture, explosives had been Liam Donovan's specialty in the IRA. I saw Ethan begin to move and I immediately knew what he was thinking and where he was headed.

"Come on!" I shouted at Wagstaff, pushing him back down the tunnel.

I slid past him and started to run.

TWENTY-SIX

THE STEPS UP to the Acropolis's second level seemed endless. The stairway we were in ended at that level, and we burst through the unlocked access door. Wagstaff still had the soccer ball with him, carrying it in the crook of his left arm.

The offices along the corridor were deserted and all the lights were off. I fumbled in the dark for a bank of switches on the wall, but couldn't locate one. The only light came from the stairwell through the access door Wagstaff was holding open. Footsteps pounded up the stairs and Ethan was suddenly with us.

"This way," he said, seeing we were confused as to which way to turn. "There is a maintenance stairway off this corridor that leads up to the next level and the roof." He pulled a small flashlight out of his pocket and turned it on. I wondered how many other little gadgets he had tucked away and if he always carried them with him.

Wagstaff had not bothered to ask any questions when I'd started running. He apparently trusted me enough to catch up with what was happening as we went along. Now, though, he threw out a question as we quickly followed the pinpoint of Ethan's torch along the corridor.

"Where are we going?" he asked. I was huffing and puffing, but from his voice, Wagstaff didn't appear out of breath at all.

"Center room over the ceiling of the arena. It's where they pull the score cube up for maintenance."

"What do you expect to find there?"

"Salvation, perhaps," Ethan answered cryptically. It was all the explanation we had time for as we had reached the entrance to the maintenance stairway. He brought out a ring of keys and inserted one into the door. "We searched the upper maintenance areas earlier today, but it was impossible to keep them all covered. Nina and Donovan could have slipped in behind us. Especially as Nina has access to all the keys. We didn't have time to change the locks."

"Come on," I said. "We don't have much time." I pushed past Ethan and ran up the stairs two at a time. At the top, however, I had to let Ethan through again, as I had no idea which way to go.

Moving quickly through the maze of service corridors, Ethan led us to a door with a faint light showing under it.

"Locked?" I whispered the question.

"Who knows?" Ethan said. I sensed him shrugging in the darkness. "And we don't have time to play this straight," he added. "Stand clear."

My eyes were adjusting to the deep gloom, and I saw Ethan pull a handgun out from a shoulder rig under his light jacket. It looked like a cannon. Ethan later told me it was a .45, which only his unit and the department's SWAT team were authorized to carry.

Flames blasted back the darkness and the sound of the gunshots in the confined space were both startling and deafening. Before Wagstaff or I had a chance to recover our wits, Ethan had shouldered his way through the door to the score cube maintenance room. The lock he had shot off had offered no resistance. He was frozen in the doorway with his gun extended.

"Damn!" he said.

The room was empty of human inhabitants.

We looked all around.

Nothing.

A big, square room with a telescoping pole running from a black gearbox mounted on the ceiling, down through a slot in the floor, to the score cube far below. Several metal lockers stood against the entry wall behind us, and a low counter ran the length of the opposite wall. The light we had seen coming from under the door had been filtered through the viewing windows from the arena below.

We looked through the viewing windows. They were set in the middle of each of the floor panels which slid back to accommodate the scoring cube. On the stage directly below, Sir Adam was handing the microphone over to Terrance Brisbane, whose short speech would lead to Pat Devlin's presence on the stage with them. The view of the stage was partially obscured by the score cube, and it was easy to imagine the damage and death that would occur if the huge electronic cube were dropped.

"Put the gun down, old cock," came a voice from the destroyed doorway.

The voice was familiar to me, because I was the only one to have heard it before, but I believed we all instantly knew to whom it belonged.

Donovan sensed something in Ethan's hesitation to release his gun and fire spat from the doorway. I yelled out as Ethan was thrown backwards by the impact of the bullet.

The gun from Ethan's hand sailed through the air and landed at my feet. I looked at it stupidly.

"Don't even think about it," Donovan said. "You can either die now or later, and I'm sure both of us would prefer it to be later."

I glanced over at Ethan's body. He hadn't moved. I wondered where the rest of Ethan's crew were. It was clear he'd come up the stairway alone, but I wondered if he'd taken the time to contact them via radio.

I wanted to say something to Wagstaff, but I suddenly realized I couldn't see him in the diffused light of the room. It was like he'd done a disappearing act. One moment he had been in the room with us, and the next it was like he'd never existed. The strange thing was that Donovan didn't appear to notice that Wagstaff was gone. Had he even seen him to begin with?

"Come on, let's go join the party," Donovan said to me. He gestured with the gun in his hand and I walked out through the doorway. Donovan shoved me with the barrel of the gun as I moved past him, and then followed after me. Wherever Wagstaff was, Donovan obviously was unaware of his presence.

As Donovan followed me down the corridor, my brain was racing. I knew Donovan had only fired once, dropping Ethan, but was my mind playing tricks on me? Had he fired twice, the shots so close together they sounded like one? Was Wagstaff also lying on the floor of the cube maintenance room, somewhere in the shadows where I didn't see him due to the night blindness caused by the muzzle flash?

I must have slowed my walking pace while I was thinking because Donovan gave me another shove. "You've put explosives on the score cube support, haven't you?" I said, half asking, half accusing. "What detonates it? A radio beam signal?" It would have to be. There were too many variables to set a timer accurately.

"You get full marks for your deductions, Sherlock." The satisfaction in Donovan's voice was evident. "But what gave you the idiotic idea we'd be sitting in the room right above the explosion? The damn floor in that place could disintegrate from the shock waves traveling up the support pole."

It hadn't seemed idiotic in the desperation at the time, only in retrospect. "We'll be close, and I'll be watching," Donovan had said over the phone. The cube maintenance room had appeared to be the perfect spot.

Donovan stopped me with a hand on my shoulder, and

then pushed me against a corridor wall as he unlocked the door to another room. Inside, it was dark except for the glow of the television screens picking up the broadcasts from the Acropolis's in-house security cameras. The man Ethan had left there to scan the crowd was a lump in one corner of the room. Another lump was made by the security guard who usually monitored the screens. Donovan had been busy plying his violent trade. He pushed me in, following closely on my heels and leaving the door open behind us.

In the flicker of the bank of security screens, I saw Bekka. She was strapped to the arms of a swivel chair and the panty portion of a pair of her pantyhose had been stuffed in her mouth. The legs of the pantyhose were tied tightly behind her neck, but she was alive. Her eyes looked intently at me and then twitched away to where Nina Brisbane was standing.

The first thing I noticed about Nina was she didn't have her veil covering her face. Her grotesquely twisted features looked even more hideous in the flickering lights of security t.v.'s

She cackled when she saw me. A witch sound. Not human any longer. She extended her hand toward me. In it was a small metal box with a red button on top. The detonator.

"Hello, Ian." Her smoky voice was pitched a full octave above what I remembered as normal. "I told you I would have my revenge, but you didn't believe me. Too bad," she said. Her eyes turned back to the security screens. I looked too. Pat Devlin had just been introduced and was making his way up onto the stage. The crowd was applauding enthusiastically, the sound tinny as it came through security screen speakers. "Soon," Nina said quietly, more to herself than to anyone else.

I moved to Bekka's side, ignoring the threat of Donovan's gun behind me. He wouldn't kill me yet. "Are you all right?" I asked her, putting my hand on one of her arms. She gave an affirmative nod of her head, but her eyes pleaded with me to do something. What the hell could I do? There was no time.

"You played well during the first half," Donovan said mockingly. "I was disappointed. I didn't get a chance to use my knife." He tapped the wicked looking blade strapped to his waist. "She still has all her fingers. At least for a while."

On the main security screen, Pat Devlin was holding the silver plate he'd received as the league's most valuable player high over his head. On one side of him, Terrance Brisbane stood with a false smile and a very pale face. On the other side, Sir Adam grinned hugely and genuinely. Nina had brought the telephoto capabilities of the security camera down as far as it would go, holding the three faces in close-up.

"Why, Nina?" I asked loudly. I knew it was a stupid question, but I didn't know what else to say. "You've beaten your sister. The Ravens are in the final. Your father will see you're the better candidate to take over his empire. This isn't going to solve anything."

She turned on me savagely. "Look at me! My father hates me. He'll never let me run the business. Everything will go to Caitlin and he'll continue to support the monsters who did this to my face!"

"Okay, I understand about your father, but Pat Devlin had nothing to do with your injuries."

"The sins of the father are carried on to the next generation," she said. "I can't get to Duncan Finlas, but I can get to his illegitimate bastard son. The son will pay his father's debt, and Finlas can feel the pain of the loss."

"This won't fix your face," I said desperately.

Nina's eyes were back on the security screen, her arm extended, the detonator aimed at the screen's images. "No, but it will make it a lot easier to live in."

There was no way to jump at her. She was out of my reach and there was a bank of screens protecting her. Only her head and neck showed above the screens, like a floating gargoyle head. Out of the corner of my good eye, I saw a movement in the open doorway. Wagstaff.

There was a sudden thump and a split second later, Nina's head snapped backwards and she collapsed to the floor. The soccer ball that had hit her rebounded across the room like a ricochetting bullet.

Donovan whirled round to fire at the open door, but Wagstaff had already jumped to one side. I hit Donovan with a rugby tackle which drove him to the ground and bounced the gun out of his hand. He twisted in my grip like an angry eel and sank his teeth into my left shoulder. I howled in pain and pushed him away from me. He hit me two sharp blows to the head, and I fell back stunned.

Donovan rolled to his knees, then his feet. His gun had disappeared into the dark shadows on the floor. He went for the knife at his waist, but his instinct for survival took over and he bolted for the doorway. Wagstaff tried to grab at Donovan's flying form, but he might as well have been trying to grab smoke.

I was having trouble getting my feet under me. "Let him go," I yelled. "Get the detonator from Nina."

"The what?" Wagstaff came into the room.

"Small black box with a red button on the top. Whatever you do, don't push it."

Wagstaff moved over behind the bank of security screens and bent down. "This thing?" he asked holding up the box.

I staggered over and looked down at Nina. She was out cold. Wagstaff's shot had taken her square in the face. Her nose was bleeding, spreading gore over her features. On the main security screen, everyone on the stage was smiles and handshakes, totally oblivious of the drama taking place above them. The second half would be starting soon.

"Where did you disappear to in the other room?" I asked.

"When I heard the voice at the doorway, I knew I was out of the speaker's line of sight. I just stepped further back between two of the lockers against the wall. I stayed there until he took you away."

Bekka was making muffled noises behind us. I turned to her and untied the gag.

She coughed, and when she spoke her voice was hoarse and scratchy. "Don't let that bastard get away," she said urgently. "He won't rest until he kills you. Stop him now!"

"The game . . ." I said, but Bekka cut me off.

"Screw the game. I'm not hurt. I'll go in goal. Just get after Donovan!"

I hesitated, unsure.

"Go! Go!" Bekka said loudly. Wagstaff was freeing her arms.

"If I didn't know better," I said half-jokingly, "I'd think you were trying to get rid of me so you could play in the final." I grinned at her, more relieved that she was okay than I could have believed possible.

"I'll bash you," Bekka retorted angrily to the mock charge, and began looking around her.

I figured she was looking for something to throw at me, so I got on my horse and ran from the room on unsteady legs.

"Be careful. I love you," I heard her call after me.

"And I love you," I called back, knowing I did.

Making my way down the dark corridor, I tripped and almost fell over a body near the door of the score cube maintenance room. The body grunted.

"Ethan?"

"God, my chest feels like it's been caved in." His voice sounded weak, but that it sounded at all was a miracle. "What kind of cannon was Donovan using?"

I dropped down on my knees next to him. "How can you be alive? I saw you go down."

"Bulletproof vest," Ethan said ruefully. "Always wear the damn thing, but I never thought I'd need it."

"Did Donovan pass by you?"

"Seconds ago. I tried to stop him, but he went through me like I was a child. I was too weak to do more than slow him down a little."

"Wagstaff and Bekka will be along in a second. They'll
get help for you. We stopped Nina."

"My radio was damaged when I got blasted." Ethan was
struggling for breath. We were communicating, not con-
versing. The bulletproof vest had stopped the shot, but the
trauma had probably broken a rib or two. "Couldn't call
for the others to stop Donovan."

"I'm going after him," I said.

Ethan grabbed my arm as I started to move away. "Make
it permanent," he said.

I didn't comment on the execution order, just gripped
Ethan's hand reassuringly and then started after Donovan
again.

I raced down the stairs and out into the Acropolis parking
lot. It was raining again, another light misting that damp-
ened the ground and made yellow halos around the street
lamps. I couldn't believe this was the southern Californian
land of endless sunshine I'd heard so much about.

To try and pick up Donovan's spore, I'd followed the line
of least resistance through the Acropolis. He would want to
get clear of the area as quickly as possible. I tried thinking
like I would if I were in Donovan's position. Where would
I run? How would I get clear?

My legs were feeling stronger underneath me, and my
head was clearing from the blows Donovan had delivered.
In the damp night air I looked and listened for any clue.
Then I heard the motorcycle.

Speeding down the main parking lot access road was a
black motorcycle with a long-haired, helmetless rider. Donovan. Motorcyles appeared to be his transportation of
choice. He had either traded in the bike he had originally
been riding for the new black one, or some citizen was
going to be very disturbed after the game to find his ride
missing.

I vaulted over a low retaining wall and sprinted the short
distance to where I'd parked the Laverda earlier in the evening. I was still in my uniform and the keys to the bike

were in my locker, but that type of situation had stopped being a problem when I was around fourteen. Within seconds, I had the motor revving and was roaring after Donovan.

I hightailed it diagonally across the parking lot, making one of the attendants jump clear. As I approached the entrance, I was more than surprised to see Donovan idling, waiting for me. He gave me a rude two-fingered salute, twisted his throttle, and zoomed away, daring me to follow.

He still had a good lead on me, but I was the better rider, and he was unable to make use of his bike's extra power due to the wet streets.

From the Acropolis, I turned onto Burbank Boulevard and raced eastward after the fleeing Donovan. Traffic was light. There were only two passenger sedans separating us. I blew past them to close the distance. I figured Donovan was heading for the freeway on-ramp, but as he approached the entrance, he turned off the road and dropped down the other side of the dirt shoulder.

This was an area I was familiar with. I had crawled out of it under similar weather conditions a few days past. I followed my quarry, standing up on the pegs as the Laverda's wheels spun through the mud. Ahead of me, Donovan was sprinting for the base of the dam. I poured on the speed and went after him.

The cracked and weed-riddled concrete that formed the dam's basin was a wet and dangerous surface to be fooling around on. However, it was showdown time and Donovan had chosen the site without consulting me.

As he reached the base of the dam wall, he turned his bike around to face me. I slowed and came to a stop fifty yards from him. We faced each other as the rain became a little heavier and the lights of the freeway cars made constantly changing shadows across the killing ground.

"I've lusted after this moment," Donovan yelled at me. "And don't think that your girlfriend is safe. After I'm done with you I'm still going to have my fun with her. I wanted it to be the other way around. Make you suffer. But you can't have everything in this world."

"It's going to end here, Donovan," I yelled back over the rain. "You can go down easy or hard. It's up to you."

Donovan laughed at me. I knew it was useless to expect anything else.

"It's dying time, Chapel!" Donovan hit his throttle and roared towards me.

I gave the Laverda gas and leaned down over the gas tank. If Donovan wanted to play chicken, he was in for a surprise. When we met twenty-five yards later, the bikes were up to fifty miles an hour. Donovan broke first, cutting to my left, but as he flew by me I felt a horrible stinging across my back. I had forgotten about Donovan's knife, the one he had been planning to use on Bekka's fingers, but had now used to slash down my back instead. He'd kept it hidden until the last moment.

I turned the Laverda around to find Donovan coming at me again. I accelerated straight at him. He cut to my left again and I tried to kick out at him, but my timing was off. He'd reversed the knife blade and the flat of it caught me across the base of my neck. My head snapped back and I felt myself losing control of the Laverda.

Trying to save something out of the situation, I sought to lay the bike down with some manner of form. I was only half successful. I went down straight, the concrete below me tearing up my left leg, but the bike got completely away from me. It slid straight for a few feet and then the front wheel twisted and the bike jumped into the air in a somersault, smashed down again, and tumbled across the wet concrete.

I lay with the rain falling into my open mouth. I was gasping for breath, my head feeling like it had been cut off by a blunt guillotine. My left side was a mass of agony, and I couldn't move my left arm. I tried for feeling in my legs, but it was tough.

From a long distance away, I heard the roar of Donovan's motorcycle. He was coming back to finish the job. From

somewhere, I found the preservation instinct to roll out of
the way as Donovan raced his bike over the spot where I
had been lying. His high-pitched laugh echoed over the
sound of the rain and the bike's exhaust. The bastard was
really feeling his oats.

I was able to roll out of the way twice more, but I realized
Donovan was only playing with me like a cat with a mouse.
He could kill me anytime he wanted, but savoring the experience was half the fun. I had to do something, or I was
going to die.

Dragging myself to my knees, I groped around on the
ground for anything I could use as a weapon. I found a fist-
sized chunk of concrete that had cracked away from the
basin floor. Standing, I waited for Donovan to come at me
again. Vision in my good eye was almost obscured. I wiped
the back of my hand across the socket and cleared away a
thick warm substance. Blood.

Donovan sprinted forward on the black bike, and I threw
the rock with all the strength I could muster. It was a wasted
effort. The rock was way off target, and Donovan's booted
foot kicked out and drove into my stomach. I went down
again.

I tried to roll out of the way of Donovan's next pass, but
this time the rear tire of his motorcycle crunched over my
left ankle. I screamed. An eye and an ankle. I was becoming a hopeless cripple in bits and pieces.

Anger welled up within me. I knew the rage Nina Brisbane felt. I knew the rage that had driven her actions, pushed
her over the edge into madness. It lived within me like a
caged beast. It was a rage screaming to be released, a rage
that wanted to destroy everything with indiscriminated hatred. It flowed out of me now in waves, unstoppable after
being repressed for so long. I would not die here. I would
not let Donovan destroy me a piece at a time.

The rage propelled me up onto all fours like a wild beast.
I scrabbled around on the cracked concrete basin, blindly
searching for anything, anything. There were small concrete

chips and paper trash. Odds and ends of miscellaneous nothingness. Nothing I could use as a weapon.

As Donovan zoomed by again, his booted foot kicked out into my midsection and tumbled me over and over. My hands hit something hard. I wrapped my fingers around it and pulled it toward me. It resisted at first and then pulled free. I looked down through the blood curtain in my eye and found I was holding a splintered wooden spar broken off from a loading pallet. How the pallet came to be abandoned in the basin was beyond my reasoning, but how does any debris get anywhere? I didn't question providence. I only blessed it.

The spar was a good two feet long. It was roughly pointed at one end, about three inches wide at the other, and about three quarters of an inch thick. I liked the feel of it in my hand. It was a primitive weapon suitable for a primitive rage.

I dug deep and found some reserves of strength and prepared myself for Donovan's next pass. He approached at about thirty miles an hour, and I lay doggo, waiting for my chance.

Moving with a speed I didn't know I had left inside me, I whipped my body around and thrust the spar out toward the motorcycle's front wheel. It jammed into the spokes and tore out of my hand, slicing off a layer of flesh and snapping two fingers.

I rolled away as the spar jammed behind the motorcycle's front forks without snapping. The front wheel locked up and there was a screeching and rending sound as the motorcycle swerved uncontrollably. It hit a crack in the basin floor and bounced up. Donovan went over the top of the handlebars, sailing through the rain and night air like an arrow in flight. He howled my name, "Chapellllll!" like a banshee screaming in the jungle.

The motorcycle's gas tank ruptured as the bike spun wheel over wheel into the darkness, and burst into a fireball with a physical *whummmmph*!

But the sound of Donovan's neck snapping when he hit

the ground cut through all other noises like the loud, clear
ringing of a bell.

I rolled over on my back and let the rain wash down on
my face. The anger seemed to be flowing out of my every
extremity, fingers and toes, like electricity. It dissipated with
a crackle into the night. I cradled my crippled hand.

The flames from the bike died down quickly.

I closed my eye.

There was the sound of sirens in the distance.

I wondered how Bekka was doing in goal.

And then, feeling peaceful, I didn't wonder anything anymore.

EPILOGUE

I HATE HOSPITALS, but as hospitals go, this one was better
than most. The private room assigned to me was nicely
decorated and featured a picture window overlooking
the hospital's rose garden. The nurses and orderlies bustled
with polite efficiency, and the doctors complemented their
top-notch surgical skills with compassionate bedside manners. It all must have cost a bomb. I was sure my VIP
treatment was due far more to Sir Adam's money than to
my American celebrity status.

There were several sprays of flowers and clusters of
helium-filled balloons brightening up the ambience. But the
best thing about the room was the figure of Bekka standing
next to my bed holding my uninjured hand. Sticks, Gerald,
Zoe, Sid Doyle, Sir Adam, Wagstaff, Ethan, and a host of
others had all been through earlier, and would be returning,
but right now Bekka and I had the room to ourselves.

The Monday papers were spread all over the bed covers,
and Bekka's photos were spread all over the sports pages.
Everyone loves a winner. The headlines of the *Los Angeles*

Tribune sports page read: LA GATA BLANCA WOWS 'EM AT THE ACROPOLIS! And in smaller bold print: *LA's Ravens put out New York's Lights 3-Zip.*

The accompanying prose glowed off the page.

. . . Bekka Ducatte, known to her fans and teammates as La Gata Blanca, was called into action for only the second time this season, due to the injury sustained just prior to halftime by starting goalkeeper Ian Chapel. Ducatte is the first woman ever to play in a men's professional soccer league, and she gave the crowd a fireworks show of skill that had them on their feet cheering!

Ducatte's appearance in the third period sent the New York team into an explosion of offense. Ducatte, however, proved herself to be more than up for the challenge as she continued the shutout begun in the first half by starting keeper Ian Chapel. Backing up Ducatte's efforts was a dynamic trio of goals by forward Kurt Wagstaff. The feat was Wagstaff's first hat trick of the season and paced the way for the Ravens' 3–0 victory . . .

"You're certainly the Ravens' star now," I said with a big smile on my face. "And you've set yourself a high standard to maintain."

"Don't be silly," Bekka said, giving my hand a squeeze. "You're still the Ravens' starting keeper."

Still smiling, I shook my head. "Not anymore. My contract has run out, and nobody is going to want a slow, one-eyed goalkeeper with a limp." I raised my ankle slightly under the hospital bed's light covers. According to the doctors there was a hairline fracture and some bad bruising. The ankle was wrapped tightly in about a mile of stretch bandage. It still hurt like hell.

My other injuries included two splinted fingers, an ounce of gravel picked out of various road-rash sites, eighteen stitches to close the gash on my back from Donovan's knife, an assortment of bruises and aches, and a possible concussion.

However, I was still luckier than Donovan. He was dead.

Donovan made the newspapers as well. There was a small article buried on page six. The story was two paragraphs long, covering the fatal accident of a man who lost control of his motorcycle on the wet streets and crashed down into the Sepulveda Dam basin. There was no mention of my involvement. I had wondered briefly what had happened to my Laverda, but I was sure it had become another victim of Sir Adam's and Ethan's manipulation of the facts. Damage control was the term they used. Cover-up was closer to the truth.

"If it's true that you're putting your playing days behind you, and I don't believe that for a New York second, then why are you smiling?"

I thought about that for a minute and then realized something. "The anger is gone," I said. "After losing my eye, I thought I'd never play again, but I did. I played the best I could and I came away a winner. The ankle will heal, but between it and my eye, my moment in the soccer spotlight has come and gone. It's time to move on. Somehow, though, I don't feel cheated like I did when I first lost my eye. The things that have happened to me in the last few weeks—confronting Wagstaff, playing in goal again, meeting you—have changed me. When I was lying in the ran last night, after it was all over with, it was like letting go. I felt . . . I don't know . . . free, I guess."

We were both quiet for a moment, Bekka still holding my hand gently.

"What will you do instead?" she asked. I knew the question was loaded with much more than curiosity.

"I'm not sure. There's still *Sporting Press* to run, but I don't think I need to bury myself in that kind of nine-to-five world again to escape from the past. I might still write for Gerald occasionally, but I don't think I want the full editor status again." I put my head back on the pillow. "Now that Sir Adam is taking over as full owner of the Ravens, maybe he'll offer me a job in the head office."

At that Bekka's eyes lighted up, making me laugh. I

pulled her down to the bed on top of me. She fought half-heartedly. "Whatever I do," I told her when she stopped struggling and lay against me, "I want it to involve you. You're not going to escape me that easily." Bekka laughed, and squirmed her way up to kiss me.

There was a "harrumph" from the doorway, and we both looked over to see Sir Adam and Sticks standing there.

"We're sorry to interrupt," Sir Adam said.

"In that case come back in an hour," I told him.

"I'm not that sorry," he retorted.

Bekka pushed herself off my chest and modestly smoothed down the material of her dress. I caught Sir Adam checking out her legs.

"Do you have any news about Nina Brisbane?" I asked.

"She's been placed in a secured private sanitarium. She'll be taken care of far better there than in any prison or state institution," Sir Adam stated bluntly.

"Plus it keeps the situation out of the newspapers," I said, rustling the papers on the bed. "You also did a nice job covering up Donovan's murderous intentions."

"Thank you," Sir Adam replied, choosing to ignore the slight sarcasm in my voice. "By the way, you were correct about the placement of the explosives in the score cube. Ethan's bomb squad defused the set-up after the Acropolis was cleared last night."

"And Terrance Brisbane?"

"I'm not sure yet," Sir Adam said. "I hate drug smugglers. And I especially hate drug smugglers who are putting their profits into terrorism. Stavoros and Nick Kronos are back in custody again, and this time they're singing their little heads off. We've also rounded up Miles Norton and several of the team's other support staff who were in on the drug running.

"Brisbane has turned all of the Acropolis business affairs and team management over to Caitlin." Sir Adam shook his head at the irony of that situation. "He's also been co-operating by giving us names and contact points connected with running down the IRA-drug network. However, there's no way he's going to get out of doing jail time.''

''What about fancy lawyer antics?''

Sir Adam gave me a cocked eye. ''Brisbane is far bigger than some smalltime punk with a public defender and a cause, but he's a lot smaller than a Richard Nixon or an Oliver North. Nobody is going to give a damn about him. Between Ethan's contacts and mine, he'll go down without a fight.''

I shook my head in wonderment at it all.

''You've done soccer a great service through your actions, Ian,'' Sir Adam continued. ''Don't think for a moment that any of this could have been accomplished without you.''

''I got the best end of the deal,'' I said, and reached out to take Bekka's hand back in mine. She blushed furiously.

''Yes, well . . .'' Sir Adam trailed off. I love it when I can fluster him. ''Actually, I didn't do too badly either,'' he said. ''Caitlin has agreed to sell me the other half of the Ravens, and Sticks has agreed to remain as head coach.''

I looked at Sticks in amusement. ''Switching from coaching goalkeepers to running the whole show, huh? I thought you said you were too old a dog to be learning new tricks?''

''And you said you'd never play in goal again,'' Sticks retorted sharply.

He had me there.

''Tell me, how long will it be before you're going to quit lying around at my expense?'' Sir Adam inquired suddenly.

''The doctor tells me I'll be released from the hospital tomorrow. I should be hobbling around in a week or so. Why?''

''Well, I have a friend who needs to talk with you.''

''A friend?''

''Yes. He's a sports agent. It seems he's lost one of his clients. An American player in the Japanese baseball leagues.''

''He's lost him? How do you lose a baseball player?''

Sir Adam had a smug smile on his face. "I told him I thought you could find him."

"What!" I sat almost upright in the bed.

Bekka laughed at my expression and held my hand to her face.

Suddenly, I could feel the wheels of my fate beginning to turn again.

ABOUT THE AUTHOR

Paul Bishop is the author of several previous novels including *Citadel Run* and *Sand Against the Tide*. He has played both left wing and goalkeeper on soccer teams in England and America. He currently lives in Camarillo, California, with his wife and stepson. He divides his time between writing and his duties as a detective with the Los Angeles Police Department.

THE BEST IN SUSPENSE
FROM TOR

☐ ☐	50451-8	THE BEETHOVEN CONSPIRACY *Thomas Hauser*	$3.50 Canada $4.50
☐ ☐	54106-5	BLOOD OF EAGLES *Dean Ing*	$3.95 Canada $4.95
☐ ☐	58794-4	BLUE HERON *Philip Ross*	$3.50 Canada $4.50
☐ ☐	50549-2	THE CHOICE OF EDDIE FRANKS *Brian Freemantle*	$4.95 Canada $5.95
☐ ☐	50105-5	CITADEL RUN *Paul Bishop*	$4.95 Canada $5.95
☐ ☐	50581-6	DAY SEVEN *Jack M. Bickham*	$3.95 Canada $4.95
☐ ☐	50720-7	A FINE LINE *Ken Gross*	$4.50 Canada $5.50
☐ ☐	50911-0	THE HALFLIFE *Sharon Webb*	$4.95 Canada $5.95
☐ ☐	50642-1	RIDE THE LIGHTNING *John Lutz*	$3.95 Canada $4.95
☐ ☐	50906-4	WHITE FLOWER *Philip Ross*	$4.95 Canada $5.95
☐ ☐	50413-5	WITHOUT HONOR *David Hagberg*	$4.95 Canada $5.95

Buy them at your local bookstore or use this handy coupon:
Clip and mail this page with your order.

Publishers Book and Audio Mailing Service
P.O. Box 120159, Staten Island, NY 10312-0004

Please send me the book(s) I have checked above. I am enclosing $ _____
(please add $1.25 for the first book, and $.25 for each additional book to cover postage and handling.
Send check or money order only—no CODs).

Name _____

Address _____

City _____ State/Zip _____

Please allow six weeks for delivery. Prices subject to change without notice.